ALSO BY EMMIE MEARS

THE STONEBREAKER SERIES

HEARTHFIRE
Book One
TIDEWATER
Book Two

THE AYALA STORME SERIES

STORM IN A TEACUP
ANY PORT IN A STORM
TAKEN BY STORM
EYE OF THE STORM

STANDALONE NOVELS

A HALL OF KEYS AND NO DOORS
LOOK TO THE SUN

EMMIE
MEARS

WINDTAKER
A STONEBREAKER NOVEL

bhc
press™

Livonia, Michigan

WINDTAKER

Published by BHC Press

Library of Congress Control Number: 2022941270

ISBN: 978-1-64397-343-2 (Hardcover)
ISBN: 978-1-64397-344-9 (Softcover)
ISBN: 978-1-64397-345-6 (Ebook)

For information, write:
BHC Press
885 Penniman #5505
Plymouth, MI 48170

Visit the publisher:
www.bhcpress.com

For Sara Megibow,
who believed in this story from day one (harder than I did, at times)
and who has been the best ally I can imagine in this business.

WINDTAKER

PROLOGUE

I THOUGHT I'D know. How to go on. How to make this world make sense.

I thought I'd see into the secret worlds. I thought they'd teach me what I wanted to know. How to fix it.

I thought there would be a quest, a task. Break the stones, free the earth, set it right.

I was wrong.

I know that now.

Nothing is ever so simple that one choice can right lifetimes of wrongs.

It's never about one flaming sword, one halm arrow, one spell broken.

If there is anything I have learned in the cycles since my death, it is that the true quest is work. It's work, and it's work every day.

It's work because it's choices. It's looking into every wrong and knowing that it will take blood and sweat and pain to make it right. It's choosing to make my life harder today, more uncomfortable, more lost, to find something that never should have been lost in the first place.

When I was young, Merin told me that as we age, we reach a point where we are certain, and from that certainty, the only wisdom to be found is to take it apart stone by stone. Only fools rest in their conviction that they have nothing else to learn.

It is ironic that it was her to say it. I wonder if she thinks she lived long enough to reach a point where, having dismantled her certainty for three hundred cycles or more, she rebuilt it in her own image and proclaimed it a god.

I have no answer to that. I have no need of an answer to that.

I do not know much. I know how my body feels on the verge of starvation. I know the tingling numbness of frozen fingers and toes and the fear that blue will blacken and cease being my flesh. I know the kind of friendship that forms when you learn such things with another person at your side. It is perhaps for that I am most grateful.

I also know what it is like to betray, to leave behind the person you have loved the most. Or two of them.

To leave them to an uncertain future, one you are ringing with pain that will haunt them far more than it will haunt you.

But I also know what it is like to set foot on a piece of earth I have never touched and know it for home.

I know that the next new arms around me will be those of an old, old friend, one who has, like I have, surrounded herself with the stones of dismantled certainty.

There is so much more to learn.

K AT COULDN'T help but feel she was racing the wind.
 Suhnsuoc loped tirelessly onward for turns at a time, sometimes seeming as fast as lightning and as light as air despite the kazytya's enormous size, but time had caught up to them in their journey south. She pushed aside the dull ache in her head as she did most days, and through their bond, Suhnsuoc reached out with the tiniest tendril of concern.

I am well, old friend, Kat assured hyr. *I will be easier once we have reached our destination.*

That was as close to a lie as she could come to with her friend, and from the way Suhnsuoc blew out hys cheeks in a sound of whuffing frustration, the large cat knew it. Kat thought hys pace quickened. The headache should lessen once she was where she was meant to be. That was what the elders had said. Kat hoped they were right.

By now, the wolves would have heralded her arrival, Kat thought, if one knew what to look for. It had been cycles upon cycles since the warmlanders so much as heard the howls of wolfsong, but Kat didn't think they had forgotten what it meant.

The old enemy was preparing to move, and this time, they would fail. The land would be freed. Enough biding time, enough waiting, enough sitting in the snow telling stories. The wolves were on the move, and now, so was Kat.

Something like giddiness bubbled up in Kat's chest, making her forget about the headache. For as long as anyone could remember, everything had hung in precarious balance, like a sledge teetering on the edge of a cliff, stable but untenable. This was *her* time now, and she would take it. Every step took her farther to the south than she had ever been.

Over the past turn, the mountains had reared up to the south, growing taller and taller with each handspan the sun crept across the sky. Kat had seen this land through the eyes of the ialtag many times, its sickly barrenness, devoid of nourishment and abundant in death. It was why her people had moved so far to the north; there were challenges living in the tundra where the earth was hard and frozen most of the cycle and the wind bitter, but there was bounty too, for the hardy.

Kat's people were nothing if not that.

But the warmlanders' domain was changing. No longer were the grasses sickly green-grey as they had been, but lush and deep, deep blue, waking even with the waning of Discovery moon, as if so eager to see Revive's rebirth that they could not wait to burst into fragrant, verdant bloom. Even now, the scent of flowers perfumed the air and dotted the rolling hills around her.

Kat had not seen many travelers as she moved, but that was by design. Suhnsuoc had avoided them as much as possible, staying out of sight, stalking around hillocks and moving by night when necessary. It was different here, the terrain far from the tundra or even Taigers to her home's south, but kazytya were like the ialtag in some ways. Suhnsuoc was born with instincts of a thousand-thousand generations of giant cats before hyr, and Kat, as one bonded to a kazytya, got to share in it.

Kat saw the settlement, their destination, sooner than expected. Young trees were leaping skyward around what must be a significant water source, and the waymake had grown accordingly. Even from a distance, Kat counted no fewer than a hundred dwellings spreading out among the trees. The scent of ihstal reached her on the wind, and Kat glanced down at Suhnsuoc apprehensively. The kazytya wouldn't harm an ihstal, but that didn't mean the ihstal knew that.

Suhnsuoc's amusement filtered through their bond. *One can make oneself scarce,* sy said.

"I think not," Kat said aloud, sighing. There were appearances to uphold. A kazytya rider of the distant north couldn't just turn up without her kazytya. "Besides, someone will have seen us coming."

A small spike of anxiety threaded itself through Kat's belly, twisting just enough to make her heart answer with a faster thud, and she put one hand between Suhnsuoc's shoulder blades to calm herself. The kazytya's fur was dense, thick. The undercoat and the longer guard coat on top of it insulated the feline from cold and heat alike, but Kat knew sy was uncomfortable with the level of heat in these warmlands even now. A deep breath to steady herself.

Even as she exhaled, shapes appeared around the walls of the dwellings ahead, and through Suhnsuoc's ears, Kat heard a murmur of nervous alarm. The sun was passing its peak above, and the moon and her sister had already risen, Discovery barely a sliver this close to the birth of Revive. The light in the afternoon cast everything in gold, the color of Suhnsuoc's eyes and her own.

"I guess we're making an entrance," Kat muttered.

As they grew closer, the bustle of the waymake became audible even to Kat's ears, and a crowd began to gather. There were children here, many of them. Her eyes widened at that—from the ialtag, Kat knew that was not normal. Almost all of them were barely a breath over five summers.

But among them, Kat saw who she sought, and she smiled as Suhnsuoc padded cautiously forward to close the distance between herself and the waymake.

Standing with a tall halm staff turned white gold in the sun, the age-changer hyrself. Sy had lost all hys hair and stood with a tall companion who, to Kat's surprise, exuded the same sort of immovable timeless presence as did the person she'd been expecting. Kat had to shake herself before she could speak over the rising exclamations of children and the murmur of apprehensive adults. Her head throbbed.

"A'cu Lystel," Kat said when she was close enough. "It has been a very long time."

Sy exchanged a glance with hys companion, who raised one hand almost imperceptibly in a soothing gesture. Several of the others nearby noticed and relaxed.

"It has been a very long time since someone called me by that name. Here, it is Culy I am known by. You are welcome in Lahivar, friend." Culy's gaze seemed to take in every inch of Kat's surface and as much beneath. It was not an entirely pleasant sensation. Culy continued, "Will you do us the honor of introducing yourself and your partner?"

Kat did not dismount yet, as it would be rude to do so before Suhnsuoc was comfortable. The ache in her head swelled to a dull pound. She did her best to ignore it.

"I am Katrin A'su Alar, ve Irmarhar. This is Suhnsuoc," Kat said. "Bonded at birth, reared with the same milk, sathren and kin. As we are welcomed here, so no harm will come to your home at our doing."

A ripple of surprise, resembling disbelief, went through many of the adults and was quickly stifled. Surely, they knew of these things. Uncertainty wriggled again, and Kat returned her hand to Suhnsuoc's shoulder.

They were not expecting us, the kazytya murmured, *but they will not harm us.*

At that, Kat slid from Suhnsuoc's back to hide her confusion. Her people had told her they would expect her, though the ialtag had been cryptic. But the ialtag were often cryptic.

"I am here to bring a message and to show you the way forward. The wolves move," Kat said. "They prepare."

The unspoken *Why do you not prepare?* hung in the air. Kat could not quite hide her confusion now. This waymake had a look of settling about it, not making ready. Time was short, and the enemy would soon make their move.

Culy opened hys mouth as if to speak, but hys companion spoke before sy could.

"Come. It seems we have much to learn from each other."

When Kat looked up, she met eyes bluer than the heart of a glacial lake, and Suhnsuoc let out an involuntary trill of shock.

Kat regained her senses after a beat, finding her voice. "Yes," she said. "Perhaps you would be kind enough to tell me with whom I am speaking?"

She thought she saw the barest flash of amusement dance across Culy's face, and the stranger gave Kat a wry smile.

"I am Carin Lysiu."

Kat felt shock strike her to her toes. This was no warmlander—this was one of *them.*

Tuanye.

T HE MOMENT they crossed into the Northlands, Clar knew. She felt it shoot up through the soles of her travel-weary feet, through the stout boots that had mercifully held up through the harrowing trek northward through the winter's deepest cold, guided only by Jenin's dreams, or close enough. It was a feeling Clar had never known. *Home.* She was home. The Northlands felt like home. And she was *going* home. A village she had never seen waited, and though relief coursed through her at merely being in the Northlands, her feet yearned for their ultimate goal. Home. It was unshakable, like bedrock.

Clar had never had that kind of faith in anyone or anything, but Jenin had led them with unwavering certainty, night after night, day after day, turn after ever-changing turn. Moon after moon.

The journey that had taken them through the depth of winter became shorter as the days grew longer and Emergent moon gave way to Discovery. They spoke but seldom these days, not needing to double check any of their daily rituals now after so long traveling with only one another's company. Clar had never thought such an intimacy existed as the one she had found with Jenin. She knew the rhythms of hys body, the way hys breathing changed when sy dreamed, and when sy would need a break. She knew to give hyr ample time upon waking to resign hyrself to leaving sleep and the world of dreams behind—truth be told, Clar was far from chatty in the mornings, so this suited her fine—and she knew that now, as they waded through the foothills of the Mad Mountains, with spring blanketing the land in fragrant blooms and the stunted trees in hungry new growth, that Jenin's course was charted directly to the one place Clar felt herself yearning.

Their pace had quickened as Discovery waxed in the sky, hardly more than a crescent. Far to the south, in Haveranth and Cantoranth and Bemin's Fan, for the first cycle in an age, there would be no Journeyers from Haveranth preparing for their own trek northward on Planting Harmonix.

The thought was enough to almost make Clar stumble.

Jenin glanced at her.

"This year's Journeying," Clar said in explanation.

Jenin nodded, hys lips tightening in a firm line. Sy was skinnier than was healthy (Clar had no illusions that she was any better off), and they had been careful to mix their water with Northland water to avoid the horrible sickness Carin and Ryd had warned them about, but in spite of that, Jenin looked peaceful. As at home as Clar felt.

This land was beautiful. The foothills rolled into plains to the north, somewhat like how they did to the south along the banks of the Bemin, but that was where the similarities ended. Clar could see the ghosts of scarcity here even now—maha trees and firs that should be taller, scraggy bushes hiding spindly branches behind spring buds—but everywhere around her, everything seemed to be trying to make up for lost time. The firs had brilliant green reaching out from the tips of their blue-needled branches. Under their feet, the vague path they followed was already in danger of becoming overgrown with eager grasses rippling outward to envelop the hills. They'd passed at least three hives under frantic construction and the buzz of eager bees, and the first wave of flowers had burst into bloom, ice roses of sharp white and sky blue, pink pricklebush, sunny sit-with-me waving in lazy arcs in the breeze. Lupines were pointing skyward, not quite ready to show their colors.

And the birds—even in Haveranth, Clar didn't think she'd seen the sky so full of their comings and goings and chattering conversations and songs. A whit-finch trilled above, almost drowned out by a trio of bluepips on a branch of a near-by bush, their tiny round bodies even rounder with puffed-up, pale-blue downy feathers that broke through the brilliant blue that gave them their name.

Clar lost herself as she walked with Jenin, barely feeling the pack on her back. When they came across a small spring burbling out from the side of a hill, they stopped and drank, wiping perspiration from their foreheads and taking a short moment to eat a handful of smoked meat (she'd lost track of what kind by now). Before long, they were on the move again.

They stopped at dusk, as always, to camp and hunt. Clar had thought game would be elusive here in the Northlands, so clear was her memory of her parents' tales of famine and starvation and want. But there were fat rabbits and even fish in the stream where they set up their camp, and she nearly missed a grouse with her bow when she almost tripped over it. They'd been eating a lot of meat. The plant life was different enough for her to be uncertain about risking much, and it was too early to identify berries by their leaves.

Jenin broke the silence as they each pulled strips of their fresh-killed roasted rabbit from the bone with greasy fingers.

"We'll get there tomorrow," sy said quietly.

Clar's stomach, already almost full, gave a nervous turn at that. "Already?" Her gaze rose unbidden to the east, though she couldn't see past the hillock where they were camped. She swallowed the half-chewed bite in her mouth without tast-ing it.

Jenin nodded.

Clar's emotions warred with each other. It felt an age since they'd left Hav-eranth on the Night of Reflection, trudging northward through the snow as fast as their legs could take them. If Lyari or anyone had sent Silencers after them, she didn't know or care. But in all that time, watching each new moon grow plump and shrivel away into the next, each night of aching joints and muscles, each rush of healing magic to soothe bleeding toes, each morning waking with a near-frozen nose, Clar hadn't prepared herself for actual success.

Something must have shown on her face because Jenin gave her a wry smile, the first she'd seen on hys face in some time.

"If it's too soon, we can camp here an extra day."

Sometimes all it took was hearing the thing you didn't want to realize. The flash of discontent was strong. Sharp. She was shaking her head before she could put it into words.

"Tomorrow, then," Jenin said.

"Tomorrow," Clar echoed.

They spent the rest of the evening under the stars, preparing the remaining meat to bring with them as a gift. They had seeds and a few small items of value that they had hurriedly thrown into their packs, but without speaking of it, both Clar and Jenin wanted to make a good impression when they arrived. Carin and Ryd—even Ras, the former Silencer—had earned their place with the people here. They had forged connections and alliances, lived another life that was as foreign to Clar as the surface of the moon would be.

But this was home. Clar was free.

She would do whatever it took to prove herself.

Just before they went to their bedrolls to sleep, their routine turning together like the wind turning one of Cantoranth's mills, she heard it.

A lonely song rose on the wind itself, echoing through the rippling hills and reaching upward toward the moon.

The skin on Clar's arms prickled, her hair standing on end.

Wolves.

It wasn't the first time they'd heard wolves; the first time had been back in Haveranth. But it was the first time this side of the mountains.

Elusive as always, another feeling pricked at her. Something slippery and just out of reach. It vanished before Clar could pursue it, and its loss left her feeling empty and somehow cheated. She hadn't spoken of it to Jenin—too long traveling, too long with just the two of them. It was little surprise she was becoming prone to fancies and strange hums in her ears.

But even as she drifted off to sleep, she yearned for the feeling to come back.

She dreamed that night of bare feet pounding the grass, the wind carrying her forward on the swell of wolfsong.

• • • • •

They spotted the village of Lahivar not long after the sun peaked in the sky the next day. It was the size of Haveranth, and Clar's face turned involuntarily to stare at Jenin, whose gaze was glued to the village in shock.

"You said it was a bare handful of roundhomes," Clar managed to get out.

Jenin tore hys eyes away from the village in the distance, surrounded by eager trees and what looked like the beginnings of fields ready for planting.

"It was," Jenin said.

Since Jenin had returned to hys body, sy had had no contact with Carin or with the mysterious Culy. No longer able to simply appear where sy wished, Clar knew that Jenin had struggled to adjust to only being able to wander that strange other world in dreams. The people of Lahivar had no idea they were coming.

Clar's feet slowed, shyness nearly overwhelming her.

It will be okay, she told herself, though she was unsure if she believed it.

As they drew near the village of Lahivar, the sound was the next wave to hit her. It had been so long since she had been surrounded by the simple noises of people making a life. There had been plenty of times in the intervening moons where Clar's ears had been full to ringing with the shrieking of the winter wind or the murmur of a stream or the splashing of a waterfall. Birdsong and squirrel chitters. The buzz of insects. That strange, persistent hum.

But people were altogether different.

It was so . . . loud.

Their feet took them toward the north side of the village and the river that bisected it. There was a bridge that arched from one bank to the other, and from the way the ground was disturbed there, it looked like it was newly built, perhaps to replace another.

Jenin was staring at it. "The river is twice as wide as it was before."

Clar's head whipped around to look at hyr in disbelief, but Jenin said no more.

It must have been common for people to approach on foot because no one seemed to take note of them until they passed the first roundhomes, where a gaggle of children were playing a game, hopping over lines etched into the dirt path and tossing stones between each go-round. The children stopped their game and peered at them curiously.

"Hello," Jenin said with a smile. "Can you tell me where to find Carin and Culy?"

The children's eyes widened, their brown foreheads crinkling in consternation.

One of the hysmern poked another and said, "Culy" before a string of words Clar couldn't understand, followed by "Carin," pointing at the newly arrived Jenin and Clar. A pair of hysmern darted off in the direction of the center of the village, almost tripping when they tried to look back over their shoulders and run at the same time.

The rest stared open-mouthed, not hiding their fascination.

"Did you understand them?" Clar asked Jenin.

"Carin said they spoke differently here, but I—" Jenin met Clar's gaze with another wry smile and a sparkle in hys own dark eyes. "No, not really."

The hysmern whispered conspiratorially to one another, a hushed giggle quickly silenced, their eyes looking at Clar and Jenin for long stretches until one of the Hearthlanders met them, after which they looked quickly away with a small squeak. But after a moment, whoever had gone off to fetch Carin and Culy clearly taking too long, one of the hysmern puffed up hys shoulders and took a brave step toward Clar.

"Ina vy Lahivar," sy said proudly, pointing at hys chest. This was followed by a questioning look and a gesture at Clar that seemed to include Jenin.

With a thrill of defiance, Clar understood. She pointed to her own chest and said, "Clar ve Haveranth."

Jenin didn't miss a beat. "Jenin vy Haveranth," sy said, and the hysmern all jumped delightedly, chattering among themselves too fast for Clar to understand.

But movement coming toward them stopped her breath halfway to her lungs.

A sound ripped through the air that Clar didn't realize she could make, and suddenly she was running, her pack hitting the ground behind her.

Clar had never been particularly close to Carin or Ryd, but it didn't matter. She heard people gasp, a collective noise that vanished in the simple sound of Ryd's strangled *"Jenin!"* and suddenly she collided with both Ryd and Carin. Jenin was flung into her side with the force of Carin's strong arms yanking hyr into a tangled embrace of four people all trying to hug each other at once.

Clar was sobbing and didn't know when she'd started. Her knees gave out, but Ryd was supporting her, someone's hand stroking her travel-grimy hair, and someone else's clutched tightly to her side right where her ribs ended, almost enough to trigger a ticklish squirm. Wetness brushed her temple. She wasn't the only one weeping.

"Clar, great bounty, it's you," Carin said, brushing Clar's hair out of her face, her blue eyes enormous in her golden-brown face beneath her mass of black hair. "And Jenin, together. *How?*"

Neither of them could seem to answer. Carin's words sounded deliberate, as if trying to mold her tongue to her former speech felt wrong now, but as Clar slowly managed to extricate herself from the clumsy embrace, she noticed a tall person standing beyond, just out of arm's reach, watching with mingled amusement and curiosity and a touch of concern. Sy leaned on a halm staff taller than sy was. Sy had no hair except eyebrows that were a strange pale brown that made the grey of hys eyes stand out in hys golden-brown skin. Without a single shred of doubt, Clar knew this was Culy. She could feel hys presence, implacable and ageless, and when sy met Clar's eyes, she could only hold that endless gaze for a moment before seeking out one closer to home, closer to familiar.

Ryd had thrown his arms around Jenin, but when Clar looked up at Carin—she was taller than Clar remembered—Clar suddenly felt as if she had turned away from a tiger into the face of a kazytya.

Carin was . . . different.

She *was* taller—Clar was certain of that. But beyond that, Carin held herself with an immovable assurance she'd never had before, and this time when Clar met her eyes, she felt like she was looking into the ancient heart of a glacier.

Clar almost took a step back.

But Carin seemed to sense it, because she closed the distance between them and wrapped her arms around Clar again, pulling her close into a hug so solid, so warm and strong, that it didn't matter that she seemed to have aged a thousand cycles on the inside. Carin wore a light, sleeveless tunic that displayed a sharp tan line where it dipped low at her back to bare her skin as if someone had drawn a paler V across her midsection.

"You are very welcome here, Clar. We are so glad to see you," Carin murmured into her ear. "When Myan came babbling about strangers in the waymake and that they were looking for us, Culy and I never thought to expect the two of you."

Clar reluctantly pulled away, nervous about this new Carin but reassured by her kindness.

Culy hyrself was stepping forward now, nodding even as Ryd and Jenin broke apart with a delighted laugh, hands still grasping each other's shoulders as if to keep that tangible proof one moment longer.

"Indeed," Culy said, hys voice warm like honey and hys syllables as deliberate as Carin's. "I have sensed something for the past few turns, but it seems that Jenin here has undergone some changes since we last spoke."

Jenin's face flushed. "We didn't have time to warn you," sy told the hyrsin. "We saw a chance to leave and took it. We weren't sure we'd ever get another."

"A wise choice," Culy said.

"Clar," Carin began, then frowned. "Or do you have another name we should use?"

"*No*," Clar said, too forcefully. Her cheeks grew hot. "I mean . . . no. My name is Clar."

Something like understanding passed over Carin's face, and she nodded.

"Clar, then," Carin said. "Can you tell us what spurred you to leave? Especially in winter, as you must have left moons ago—that is a terrible risk."

Clar looked to Jenin, then past hys shoulder, where a crowd gathered near the children who were growing bored watching a conversation they clearly didn't understand. Most of the faces of the Northlanders were simply curious, their expressions neutral, but a few looked uncertain. A few others glanced to Culy every few heartbeats as if holding onto the belief the hyrsin would warn them if anything were particularly amiss.

When no one answered, Carin closed her eyes briefly before opening them again, her face a bit self-deprecating. "Forgive me," she said. "You've just arrived, and I'm sure you're exhausted. Come with us, and we'll get you a place to sleep and some food."

"We've brought food," Clar said automatically. "For the village. Rabbit and grouse and some dried fish—and seeds as well. We don't want to burden anyone."

Something in Culy's face softened beyond Carin's shoulder, but then the hyrsin was gesturing to Jenin, and Ryd lifted Jenin's pack, the three of them moving into the center of the village.

Carin reached down and shouldered Clar's pack. The other Northlanders were starting to disperse, deciding there wasn't much left to see here, and Clar felt untethered without Jenin. She'd grown so used to hys presence all this time, and now suddenly sy was out of sight.

They'd made it.

Carin seemed to read her thoughts. "It's okay," she said. "When we first arrived here, it was overwhelming. We didn't understand anyone, and no one knew what to make of us at first."

She grinned, a spark of the Carin that Clar remembered lighting her face. "I think sometimes they still don't quite know what to make of us, really. But we're getting there."

"I've not spoken to another person since before the Night of Reflection, not besides Jenin," Clar said quietly.

At Carin's gesture, Clar followed after her into the village.

"That is a journey that changes you," Carin told her just as quietly, her eyes shrewd and searching. "No one will ever understand that journey but you and Jenin, just as no one will understand ours but Ryd, Ras, and me. And we made most of ours before winter set in, not during. I cannot even imagine."

"We had to," Clar said, more fiercely than she meant to. The breeze rose with her words as if to emphasize them, picking up little swirls of dust between the roundhomes she'd barely glanced at.

"Necessity is the truest motivator," Carin agreed, but a small frown creased her forehead as the breeze died again as quickly as it had begun, and Clar could not read her face. "We will have plenty of time for you to share whatever you wish with us, though who knows what the next surprise will bring."

Carin gave a wry smile that seemed to imply there had been other surprises already, but before Clar could ask what else had happened, Carin simply gestured at Clar to follow as she picked up her pace.

"For now, the important thing is that you're here. I hope that you will one day feel as I do—that this place can be your home," said Carin.

Clar wanted to speak but found she couldn't as she trailed after the taller Hearthlander—well, Northlander, now—and made her way into the village of Lahivar. She both wanted and feared saying what she felt in the deepest core of her: she already did.

D YAVA SAT at his table, the fire cold behind him with the newly warm days of spring, but he fought back a shiver, nonetheless.

Again his parents were here, again begging for word of Jenin and Calyria that Dyava simply did not have. It had been moons since the Night of Reflection, moons in which the land came back to life, more sluggish than any cycle before this one, moons full of new sickness and wolves in the woods, moons full of problems, among which Dyava could no longer count Jenin and Calyria.

His mother and father had aged in those moons, aged more than they ought to have.

"You must tell us," his mother said, her voice managing to both plead and demand all at once.

"I have told you," Dyava said flatly. "But you are so used to your own lies that you forget others sometimes tell the truth."

They did not even have the decency to flinch at that.

"What we do—" his father began.

"Is for the betterment of all," Dyava said, cutting him off, too exhausted to listen to this yet again. "I will not tell you again. I do not know where Jenin and Calyria are. I do know that you have used all of us as your stones on a board for too long, and if they decided they could not even trust *me* with their plans, they have clearly decided they never want to see your faces again."

It still burned, stung like the time Dyava had scraped his arm accidentally on a length of hot metal at Rina's forge and she poured a tincture on it made from bitterberries so it wouldn't scar. But this would scar. Moons were not long enough to heal this wound.

"Dyava," his father said, his words beating like a moth's wing against that burn. "We just want to know they are safe."

"Get out." Dyava was done. He was done, he was done, he was *done*.

"My child." He'd heard that tone in his mother's voice when he was still hysmern and had done any number of small damages or insubordinations. Admonishment with the distinct undertone that said he was being foolish, childish.

"GET OUT." Dyava was grown, and his voice boomed through the roundhome with such force, both of his parents jumped where they sat. "Get out of my home. Never come back unless invited. I may have to share this village with you, but I do not have to put up with you for one more moment if you refuse to believe the truth I have been telling you for *four—rotted—moons*. I don't know where Jenin and Calyria are. They may be dead. They may be alive beyond the mountains. They may be up a tree in Haver's Glen, for all I know. But what I do know is this: they are gone and maybe dead, and that is your fault. Both of you. Your fault for treating your own family like tools to be used until they break. You broke us. All of us. So get out. You are no longer my parents."

Dyava slammed his fist down on the table as hard as he could, and the clay pot of salt in the middle of it jumped with a clatter just as heat flared at his back.

His parents stared past him, wide-eyed, and Dyava turned to see the once-cold fire blazing halfway to the ceiling. He could see the weaves of it, the magic he had so clumsily yanked into being, threads tossed about in the torrent of his anger.

"The Reinvocation—" His mother was silenced by a sharp shake of his father's head.

"Peace, beloved," Dyava's father murmured.

For the first time in moons, when Dyava met his eyes, he was certain his father believed him.

They left without a further word, and Dyava turned around and sat with his back against the table, staring into the fire he did not want to let die.

● ● ● ● ●

When Lyari came by later that night, Dyava had mostly recovered his mood. Something lightened in him at what he had done. His parents had used him abominably his entire life, him and Jenin too. It was all he'd known, so he had thought he didn't have a choice. But he'd made a choice today.

As he always did, he told Lyari everything, and she sat gently holding his hands in the glow of the firelight, both of them straddling the bench at his table and facing each other.

Her frown was small, but present, and she reached up to touch his face when he was finished.

"A weight has left you," she said.

Her fingertips left a tingling trail on his cheekbone. For a moment, Dyava saw himself reflected in the bronze soothsayer cuff on her wrist.

"Yes," he said simply. "Because of them, I lost almost everything I've ever loved."

"Almost everything," Lyari said.

"Almost."

Dyava took her hand in his where it still gently rested against his cheek, turned it over, and pulled it to his lips. He kissed her palm, and her eyes softened.

"I do not believe Jenin and Calyria are dead," she said finally. "The trek north would be dangerous beyond compare, but if anyone could survive it, it is Jenin."

"I have no hope remaining," Dyava said. "They did not trust me to tell me where they went."

"Ah. I believe I am the reason for that." Lyari's eyelashes dipped as she looked down at the bench between them. "And I cannot say I blame them."

Dyava was silent. He dropped his hand to his knee but could not meet her eyes when she looked up to his again.

"Do you wish they had taken you with them?" Lyari's voice was still and quiet, like a pond at dawn, her words like a fish jumping to break its surface.

That was a question Dyava had asked himself countless times in the four moons since they had vanished. Did he? Would he have fled with them into the north, over the mountains in the dead of winter with wolves prowling through the long, cold nights? Could he have left this new love of his behind the way his old love had left him?

Dyava didn't know.

He didn't like being the one left behind, the one made to tell the lies, the one assumed to be the liar, the one who guarded all the secrets but was not trusted with truth.

When he spoke after a long pause, the honesty of his answer surprised even him. "No," he said. "I am where I am meant to be."

"Good," Lyari told him. She leaned forward to lightly brush her lips against his. "Because we have much to do before next summer."

Next summer.

Those two words were colder than the deepest winter snow. Dyava had told her everything, and he had chosen, and he would help her. Neither of them knew what would happen if she tried the Reinvocation with two stones broken—she believed it was safest to assume a second had also been broken—but Lyari was determined she would find some way forward. Some way to save their people from ruin.

Dyava had been left behind again, and he had told his only remaining family to never speak to him again.

He did not know if the people of the Hearthland were indeed his people, but he did know he had no one else now.

TIME WAS slipping away from Carin faster than the Lahivar River's waters raced toward the sea. With every sunrise and sunset, they inched closer and closer to an inevitable reckoning, one Carin seemed to feel echoing through the land under her feet, as if it had already happened or as if the force of it were so powerful, so gargantuan, that the cataclysm could cast its memory back in time.

Almost as soon as the kazytya rider Kat had come, she was gone again, ostensibly to familiarize herself with the warmlands, as she called them. She had hardly been able to look Carin in the eye while she was in the waymake. If Culy had some suspicion of why, sy did not say, but it left Carin feeling uneasy and strangely late, as if something had passed them by and no one could say what it was.

She found herself walking most mornings by the river with Hoyu, the Khardish woman practicing her increasingly fluent Tuan with Carin speaking back in her increasingly fluent Khardish, both of them only using their own tongues to give minor corrections or rephrasings to show a more natural way of speaking. This was their way most mornings, but today, Carin's mind was heavy, and it was Tuan she spoke.

"No ships so far have appeared in sight of shore," Carin said softly.

Hoyu nodded, a sharp, terse movement of her head. "They are waiting for something. Spring, perhaps. It is likely they passed the winter moons in the islets."

"Why would they not simply delay their departure until they were certain to land?" This question had troubled both Carin and Culy since the ialtag had brought them word of a fleet of Khardish ships sailing in their direction with the dawning of Renewal moon. "I do not like their hesitance."

"I do not think it is hesitance," Hoyu told her. "I am certain they will come."

The dark-skinned woman's eyes cast out over the riverbank to the field on the other side, its lush grasses and wildflowers near bursting with the exuberance of spring. The sun would crest the horizon soon. As Carin followed Hoyu's gaze, the first fingers of gold reached from the east across the flatlands, frosting the dew-touched blue of the grass with liquid fire that sparkled outward in a rippling line.

It took a moment for Carin to see what had caught the Khardish woman's eyes. But there was a twitch of a blade of grass and the shape of a rabbit. Beyond, barely visible around the edge of a low hummock, were the tufted ears of a fennec. The small creature was a familiar sight in Lahivar; sy had a den to the north not far from the waymake, and while Carin and Culy managed to keep it away from the cluckers' nests with gentle suggestions of magic, that did not protect the rabbits that were multiplying in alarming numbers in the surrounding fields and warrens.

The fennec's kits were there too, Carin saw. Young and clumsy, they imitated their mother.

It happened almost too fast to see. A blur of motion, the scream of the rabbit, and the fennec trotted back to its young, bushy tail held high and ears twitching.

"If they have not made a move, it is because the conditions are not favorable for them to do so," Hoyu said finally. "That tells me many things."

Carin nodded slowly. "Perhaps they acted rashly in their pursuit."

"Yes. I think this must be true. Your rescue and subsequent escape forced their hand. From what I could learn in our short time in Sahesh, tensions have been high for some time, but most were not prepared for such a schism." With that, Hoyu snorted, plucking at the sleeves of her shirt. Northlander make, a tunic that had been hemmed for her shorter stature and fell over soft leggings she had made herself with no little swearing in both languages from lack of practice. "For the keepers to be split is unheard of. If Rela and Asurashk were made to show their allegiances too early, they will likely be waiting until they are assured they will not simply be tried for treason upon their return. And they will want to know that whatever they seek here will be worth the risks they take."

"I think they already know that," Carin muttered.

She hated waiting for a trap to snap shut, hated knowing that something else was coming when she had work enough before her already. It was like starting construction on a roundhome at Harvest moon's birth with the bite of winter already showing its teeth in the nights.

"Whatever is to come, I am with you," Hoyu said. "They may call me a traitor for it, but if Khardan falls to poison from the west, it will no longer be my home."

"You will always have a home here, my friend," Carin told her. "You risked everything to do what you felt was right and help me. I will not forget it."

As happened more and more often now, Carin heard her voice take on a timbre beyond her usual softness. Where before she had thought of herself somewhat like the fil the Northlanders played around the fire, middle-toned strings stroked by a fyajir-gut bow, now there was something beneath it like the resonance that hovered in the air after someone beat one of the deep, deep drums.

Hoyu noticed too. Expression unreadable, she appeared to listen to something for a moment before responding.

"Thank you," Hoyu said. She appeared to smooth any discomfort by changing the subject. "When do you plan to move upon the next stone?"

"Imminently." Carin glanced back at Lahivar behind them. "Culy said the land should be passable this turn or next, and I admit I am beginning to itch to be done with it. Do you still wish to come with us?"

"Yes," Hoyu said without pause. "If I am ever to return to Khardan, I think my perspective will be valued by our historians."

She didn't have to say that the story seekers among the Khardish were those who counted Rela and Asurashk their peers, but Carin recognized Hoyu's hope that some with integrity would remain.

Carin did not ask much about Khardish politics—it was alien to her, the thought of entire lands negotiating with one another, making compromises, making and breaking promises, sometimes descending into war.

But with the hearthstones breaking and the line of storms gone, this land would need to prepare. Carin knew Culy had had many conversations with Hoyu about Khardan—sy had picked up the language with an ease Carin found distinctly unfair—but she had mostly given the topic of political preparation a wide berth. Perhaps that had been unwise.

"Do you truly think things are so dire that there is a chance you will not return?" Carin asked.

"You left your land behind for less," Hoyu said in reply. "Do you remember what I told you of Maref to the west?"

"Only that they like to dabble in their neighbors' business and look with a greedy eye on Khardan's islands." Carin said this carefully. The sun was above the horizon line now, and the cluckers in Lahivar were rousing with their telltale grumbling to face the day, their singers proclaiming it time to leave their warm nests. "And you have said they do not offer a hand except to reach past yours to grab your wrist and jerk you to the ground."

"That is their way." Hoyu's full lips became a thin line, and she made a disgusted noise. "But I had not thought the Da'sash Dan to be corruptible. Triya should have been a warning."

At Carin's confused look, Hoyu raised an eyebrow.

"Triya is the land Asurashk came from," she reminded Carin. "For some time, they have been mired in civil war, sathren"—Hoyu stumbled over the word—"turning against one another and refugees fleeing to Khardan to escape."

Carin felt a flush of shame for forgetting. She really ought to have been more diligent in listening to Culy and Hoyu's conversations. She nodded to Hoyu to go on.

"Not long ago, Triya was stable and prospering. But it seems Marefi eyes and ears are doubly skilled. It only took them a few moons to upend the power structures there, and you saw what happened in Sahesh." Hoyu gave a rock a kick where it lay half-lodged in the dirt at her feet.

"You are certain they are behind Rela's defection?" Carin asked.

"I have no doubts. He has always desired power, and if they offered it, he would take it. I spent too much time with my feet in the sea to notice the currents in the people," Hoyu said bitterly. "I know I alone could not have stopped the swell of a tide, but that is little help when you are watching your home washed away."

At that, Carin winced, a dual-edged pang of guilt and kinship hitting her in the tender spot beneath her ribs. Hoyu's words of self-recrimination were so close to what she had thought only moments before about failing to pay attention to what was happening around her—and her metaphor was a little too close to the reality of the death wave Carin's breaking of the first stone had inadvertently caused.

Hoyu seemed to realize it a moment later, and her eyes widened even as her hand leaped up to shoulder level in what Carin now recognized as a Khardish gesture of admitting fault or claiming responsibility.

"Da ba'lar," Carin said in Khardish, then repeated it in Tuan, mirroring the gesture herself emphatically. "Don't worry about it. I accept responsibility for the things I have done and for the things I must do before this is finished."

Rather than assuaging Hoyu's consternation, the Khardish woman placed her hand on the back of Carin's neck and looked directly into her eyes.

Carin was uncomfortable with eye contact most of the time; it was too intimate, too exposing. But she did not look away.

"I will be with you to help you bear it," Hoyu said simply before dropping her hand and her gaze back to the rock at her feet, which she gave one more small kick. Then she grinned. "And if it gives me the chance to kick Rela over the mountains, so much the better."

Carin grinned back. "I will save my kicks for Asu, then."

The waymake was beginning to churn with morning sounds behind them, and Carin clapped Hoyu on the shoulder as they made their way back.

Within her, the spirit seemed satisfied with the conversation—for what reason, Carin could not be sure. But she was pleased at least, and thankful besides, that she was not alone. With a jolt, she remembered all over again how not alone she was now. Ryd, Culy, Hoyu, Sart, Ras . . . now joined by Jenin and Clar and the strange kazytya rider from the farther north, Kat. A mystery for another day. The reminder came with gratitude, but as Hoyu peeled off ahead to go find something to break her fast, Carin could not help but glance southward toward the mountains, wondering what would become of those the two newly arrived Hearthlanders had left behind.

BASHA THOUGHT that if he had to listen to Arelashk for even another day belowdecks, he and all the rest of the crew aboard the ship would pick him up by his ears and throw him overboard. Despite his contempt for the man, Basha couldn't bring himself to think of him as Rela—it would not do to risk a breach in propriety. He would, however, happily imagine pitching him into the sea. Asurashk would not be far behind if Basha had his way. For turn after turn and night after night, Basha had listened to their plotting, growing more and more desperate with every passing cloud that wandered across the sky.

Oshu stood beside him at the stern of the ship, no doubt feeling the ungentle rocking as much as Basha did. It wouldn't be a problem, but the sea had been far too restless for Basha's liking since they had been stuck here watching those wandering clouds.

That was the approximate speed of this journey as well. Basha was sour about many things, but the anticipation was the absolute worst. He hated it. The way they had left Sahesh made it seem as though they would be sailing directly to the eastern continent, but then the message had come when they were in the border islets. They had stopped here in Oemua, which made Udum Dhu'e look like Sahesh. Out here on the fringes of Khardan, the people mostly liked to forget they were part of Khardan at all. Not out of malice, really, but those who inhabited the islets here seemed to want to forget they were a part of *people*. Certainly, there was a small village on the island, and certainly people lived here, but they were none too happy about a fleet of Khardish ships moored off their coastline and fishing their waters.

Basha couldn't blame them. He'd resent it too. Especially once they caught a glimpse of the people aboard the ships.

The breeze picked up, and both Basha and Oshu glanced at the mast, where the ropes were easing westward.

"East winds in spring are an ill omen," Oshu muttered.

In the moons Basha had known the Triyan man, he ought to have stopped being startled when bits of Khardish lore fell past his lips, but now he just smiled ruefully.

"Your mother must have been much like my father to teach you that," said Basha.

A moment of surprise, a flash, like someone's foot slipping on an algae-slick plank for the barest instant, quickly righted. Not Oshu's mother, then, though the man was, as promised, so good at keeping to himself that it was a miracle Basha had learned anything about him beyond the name he had uttered once and that first conversation they'd had on the docks of Sahesh. But Basha had a very good memory and an even quicker mind. It was likely the lie would not matter.

"My nursemaid," Oshu said quietly, raising two fingers to shoulder level to admit fault, and this time the flash of surprise was Basha's.

Basha did not want to answer aloud, but he glanced at Oshu to show him his words had not gone misunderstood. He appreciated this moment of trust, and he briefly raised his right fingertips to his heart in a gesture of acceptance, hoping Oshu would understand that.

He did not have time to see.

"Basha-lan," said one of the ship's servants. "Your presence is required by the Asurashk."

Basha nodded without hesitation. "Please inform them that I shall come straight away."

He turned to look at Oshu and caught the barest glimpse of the Triyan man's expression before he turned away without a word, and as Basha moved to go belowdecks, he realized he recognized that look. He didn't think it was directed at him—Oshu was far too contained to show Basha outright contempt.

His mind only half on the meeting with Asurashk, Basha found himself mulling over Oshu's face, over the confidence he had shared, and over how little he really knew about the man. Perhaps he had mistaken that look for something else. Basha couldn't understand, for all the ships in the sea, why a servant would inspire disgust.

All of this was chased out of his mind the moment he entered the cabin where Arelashk and Asurashk waited.

The cabin was at the prow of the ship belowdecks, and unlike the crew quarters that only had portholes, this was a formal meeting room, and it had windows that created a semicircle of magically tempered glass with a full view of the sea beyond. It was all Basha could do not to stare out those windows.

Basha greeted Arelashk and Asurashk as was proper, using every single ounce of training he had to keep his composure as they went through the pleasantries necessitated by protocol, but in his peripheral vision, all he could see was the shapes that had just appeared over the horizon, coming from the southwest. The Ada'sarshk, Arelashk's old friend, seemed unperturbed, standing with his arms folded at the small of his back as he gazed out the window instead of over the table like Arelashk and Asurashk.

". . . As soon as they arrive, we will resupply with their stores and prepare for departure," Arelashk was saying, and Basha wanted to wipe the self-satisfied smirk from the other man's face with his fist. "Your report this morning said that the tides and winds will favor us if we leave today? Welcome news. I feel more than simply tides and winds favor this journey."

Asurashk was quiet, but her own face reflected the smugness on the speaker's.

"Indeed," Basha said. To his own ears, his word came out sounding as if someone else had said it. Distant and wrong, almost drowned out by the litany of thoughts running through his mind. *Treason, treason, this is treason.* "Is this then all we have been waiting for?"

"All?" Asurashk asked mildly. She glanced out the windows. "Ten thousand fighters is hardly negligible."

"The Asurashk is correct, of course," Basha said.

"No less would do." Asurashk now moved to stand at the window. "If we are to recover the prisoners and discover the power they have used to wreak destruction on our lands these twenty-five hundred cycles, we must be prepared that they will not welcome us."

They welcomed you when you first arrived, Basha thought. *And you betrayed them. I helped you betray them.*

"I sense your discomfort, Basha-lan," Arelashk said without looking up from the table, where he stood poring over ancient maps that likely did not come close to truly describing the continent to which they journeyed. "Rest assured that we do not intend to harm innocents."

Who decides who is innocent? Basha nodded instead of speaking. He was clearly not doing as well at controlling his facial expressions as he thought.

But he was first mate aboard this ship, and he was expected to ensure the success of the mission, even if that meant asking difficult questions. He quickly reformulated his plan.

"Are you not concerned that the Da'sash Dan will take the use of Marefi troops as an act of sedition?" Basha asked carefully.

"A worthy question," the Ada'sarshk said.

This Ada'sarshk was the opposite in all respects from the last one he had served. This one had pale brown skin where hers had been dark, golden eyes where hers had been rich, hair cropped close instead of twisted like the waves upon which they sailed. The tarke'e he wore was the same, of course, except for minor embellishments that spoke to nuances of rank and accomplishment. Deep blue and silver. It made him look sickly where his last Ada'sarshk had looked resplendent.

Basha waited for him to go on.

"Some of the Keepers have long desired to treat Maref as a worthy ally rather than a foe to be wary of," said the Ada'sarshk. "They have generously offered to aid us in this expedition, and if what we bring back is as powerful as it seems, it will not be seen as seditious. It will bring glory to all our peoples."

Basha inclined his head. "The Ada'sarshk is wise."

"And what of yourself?" Arelashk asked, dragging his gaze upward finally. "When we find the prisoners, will you be prepared to do as you must to ensure the continued prosperity of our people?"

At this, Basha could speak with all the truth within his heart. "Without question, honored Arelashk. When those at fault have been apprehended, I would personally see them on their knees before the Da'sash Dan for justice."

Arelashk blinked at Basha's sudden zeal, and even Asurashk looked at him from near the windows.

"Strong words," Asurashk murmured.

"The prisoner's escape was shameful," Basha said truthfully. "Khardan stands for justice, and justice must be seen through to its rightful conclusion. With their escape, the prisoner made a mockery of one of our most precious processes. There is far too much at stake to simply stand by and do nothing. I will not stand for division in my homeland, and whatever I must do to restore my honor in the eyes of the Khardish people, I will do."

Arelashk's smile was slow and curving, though Basha felt a lingering disdain beneath it. He thought Basha below his regard, a sailor-bureaucrat with unfortunate connections. No one of real power or consequence. Basha was unbothered; in the eyes of most powerful people, the story keepers and those whose decisions turned the rudder of Khardan's ship itself, Basha *was* unimportant.

The meeting continued into usual logistics, and Basha participated without hesitation, offering his quick mind and all of his zeal to his enemies even as he planned a treasonous act that he could only call an atrocity.

In the distance, the Marefi ships came closer and closer as they spoke, creeping upon the surface of the waves like a portent of doom. Basha had seen them before. They were not quite to the level of Khardish ships, but that was no matter—no ships outside Khardish waters were. But still, they came, the wind and waves drawing them closer, growing them upon the horizon like they were springing forth from the sea itself.

Yes, to most of Khardan, Basha was unimportant.

But that didn't mean he could not do the task he had laid at his own feet.

It only meant they would underestimate him until the moment they no longer could.

CARIN WAS working in one of the gardens when Clar found her. The sight of the land coming to life around her was still a source of awe for Carin. The sounds of her childhood surrounded her. Bees and birdsong, the clang from a forge, spades in soil and water whispering in the river—all these things she had learned not to take for granted.

But it was a melancholy thing to mark. It came with a sense of justice, to be certain, but beneath it was the lingering rage that such a correction was necessary in the first place. Carin had to admit that when Clar quietly cleared her soft voice at the edge of the garden, she needed to take a moment's pause at the reminder that Haveranth was still there, still far to the south, preparing to try and take it all away.

"You were leagues away," Clar said hesitantly. "I'm sorry to disturb you."

Carin rose from her crouch, brushing her hands together to free them of any remaining bits of dirt—a futile hope. "Please, there is no need to apologize."

Carin looked at the young woman. Outwardly, she was all anxiety and nerves and shyness, much as she had ever been in Haveranth. But beneath that was something harder than halm, a core of will that had led her to leave everything behind in the dead of winter and escape.

"I wanted—I wanted to speak with you," Clar said. "We have not had much chance to do so since I arrived."

It was both true and not true. Culy and Carin had spent a lot of time with Clar and Jenin, listening to their descriptions of what had befallen the Hearthland in the moons since the first stones had broken and doing their best to anticipate what might happen with the remaining hearthstones once they followed their friends. But there had been little time in all that to feel like simply two people who had known each other a lifetime.

Carin set down her spade and moved toward the young woman and placed a hand on her shoulder. "Then walk with me if you will."

Carin led her along the river where the ihstal grazed, calling a soft hello to Tahin, who whistled happily in response and made Clar jump.

Tahin, at least, seemed utterly unfazed by the happenings of the world around hyr. Carin envied the animal that.

"It is beautiful here," Clar said suddenly. "I did not expect—"

"It was not always like this." Carin's mood soured again. At Clar's startled glance, she went on. "When we arrived here, there was little fresh water and almost no game. We would hunt for an entire day and be thankful for a squirrel or two. Sickness was rampant; a diseased animal could spoil a bountiful hunt and necessitate ridding an entire waymake of food they had expected to eat for turns."

Clar stopped walking, her mouth hanging open and one hand worrying at the hem of her tunic.

"No crops, no permanent dwellings, only a need to follow where there was water and food and hope that you moved in the right direction to where both could be found. Not out of a desire to live a nomadic life but out of pure, raw need." Carin motioned to Clar to keep walking. "That is the price they paid for our ancestors' pride. It is a miracle they did not see fit to hang us by our toes and leave us to starve. We should be thankful they are content with justice and do not seek vengeance. I would not begrudge them that."

There was a moment of silence as Clar seemed to consider that. "What is it *you* want, Carin?"

At that, Carin couldn't help the sound that escaped her. What a good question that was. She thought of the long days locked in the brig of Hoyu's ship with Asurashk seeking entrance to her mind. She thought of Sahesh with its teeming thousands of people and transport carts that moved with nothing to pull them. She thought of a world that had moved on and forgotten this one, just as Haveranth had moved on and forgotten the Northlands. There was so much to learn, so much to explore, but none of them would get the chance to do that if Lyah— Lyari—succeeded.

"I don't know," Carin said finally. She did not know Clar well enough to confide in her, despite their lifelong acquaintance. Even Jenin—it was Lyari who had been so close to hyr. "What is it you wished to speak about?"

The change in subject seemed to surprise Clar, and she missed a step. "I . . . had hoped simply to talk."

Warmth flooded Carin's face, and she gave the young woman a wry smile. "I apologize. Things have been trying since I left Haveranth, and I am afraid I am not the person you once knew."

"Yes," Clar said so softly Carin wasn't sure she even heard the word. "You are indeed very different."

"It would be more remarkable if I were the same. And foolhardy," Carin said. "Living in times such as these should change us."

"Yes," Clar said again.

She hesitated, stooping for a moment to pick a small, pink flower where it bloomed beside their path. Clar looked wistfully at it for a moment before tucking it into her plaited hair. The gesture was somehow endearing to Carin, and something in her softened.

"You were truly . . . taken?" Clar asked after a long moment.

"Yes." Carin fought the rising tide of anger that always came at the thought. It was like pimia oil meeting fire, a reaction so grounded in the natural order that it *had* to happen. A reflex. A spark. The release of a pulled-taut bowstring that demanded the arrow be loosed. "I did not think I would ever see these shores again."

"I understand that feeling," Clar said distantly, much to Carin's surprise.

"How do you mean?" Curiosity filled Carin, wondering how this person, who she had last known as a child on the cusp of adulthood, could relate to her experience of being kidnapped and taken across a sea on the whims of captors she could not follow or understand without their blessing. The very memory of it felt like shame.

"The moment I was born, I had no choices left to me."

Of all the things Carin had expected to hear, that was not among them. "What?"

"My parents, Jenin and Dyava's parents—they had a plan for us before we drew our first breaths. They cultivated us like crops to be used. They taught us obedience before all else, threatened us with death—ours or theirs or the whole of the Hearthland's—before we could even speak. They put this burden upon us, and we had no choice but to live under it." Clar let out an explosive breath. "The only thing remaining to us was what we did. It has been moons since the Night of Reflection, and I am still not certain I believe we have escaped."

Carin opened her mouth to respond, but Clar was barreling on.

"Do you know how much I envied you and Ryd? We all thought you were dead, of course, but that would have been such a relief to me," Clar said all in a rush. "But you *chose* to leave, and you had not even known the secrets that Merin and the other villagers kept from you. You learned the truth and you acted. You had that power."

The rushing of the Lahivar River was suddenly louder in Carin's ears. The midafternoon sun was golden and warm. In the waymake, people would be preparing dinner, the hunters returning, the gatherers cleaning their finds, the tanners preparing the new hides for treatment—everyone had adapted and was continuing to adapt to something new every day.

Clar's words took a moment to sink in.

"You thought we were dead and you envied us?" Carin said.

She hadn't realized the young woman was crying. Not outright weeping or sobbing, but there were bright, shining tears at the corners of Clar's hazel eyes, and beneath them was something Carin was all too familiar with. Anger.

"Do you know how many times I wanted to die? How much I envied Jenin when I first found hyr? I didn't know then that it was a ruse—my parents made Dyava lie to me. His parents too. They let me find Jenin with hys throat cut and didn't tell me for *an entire cycle* that sy was still alive." Clar scrubbed the tears away from her cheeks with the heels of her hands. "I don't know how we made it through the mountains. Death was our constant companion. Both Jenin and I knew it, but we agreed that if sy came any closer, if sy took us into hys bosom forever, at least we would die free. We would die doing what we believed was right."

Carin was silent for a long stretch of breath. Within her, the spirit felt fathomless, ancient, and weary. The spirit knew this feeling too. It would have welcomed its end had breaking the stone caused such a thing. An entire cycle thinking Jenin was dead. An entire cycle. The *cruelty* of it—that Tarwyn and Silan had done this and Clar's parents as well . . . it was too much to bear.

"How did you survive?" Clar asked then. "When they took you?"

Carin had had many conversations with Hoyu about everything since they had returned, and she chose her words carefully. "For the most part, they treated me with civility. Hoyu—you met her, the short woman with hair like waves—told me that it is custom in Khardan to treat prisoners with dignity. That was mostly true. She regrets, very much I think, that she agreed to them taking me at all. Her home island was hit by the death wave that breaking the stone released. I would not fault her for blaming me for that, even if it may be true that my breaking the stone prevented a more deadly wave with the Reinvocation. We will never know.

"As for surviving, I don't feel I did anything special. It was the spirit that joined me when I broke the stone—that is what saved me and Hoyu too. But I do fear what would have happened had it not." Carin swallowed, thinking of Culy finding her in the world of dreams, helping her come back to herself. She would let no one inside her mind again without her consent. "Hoyu tells me that her homeland is unstable right now, much as ours is here. There are factions causing friction and maneuvering for power. One of them broke with tradition to try and take my memories by force. Had they succeeded, I do not know where I would be today, but I think I would wish for death."

The understanding that passed between them was palpable. Again Carin tamped down the rising rage at Asurashk trying to violate her mind with Rela's blessing and assistance.

Carin could not help the thought that rose in her as the moment stretched out. If given the chance, did she want justice? Or did she want vengeance?

• • • • •

Carin and Clar spoke for some time longer, their conversation turning to less ponderous subjects. For a while, they simply walked together, pointing out flowers and plants that were new to Clar. Carin spent some time coaching the young woman in Northlander speech, going over some of the words and turns of phrase that had shifted in meaning or pronunciation, and though she did not expect Clar to remember all of it at a moment, it could not hurt.

When they returned to Lahivar, Carin busied herself with her usual tasks: mundane things like fetching water for her washbasin for the night and sharpening her belt knife.

She was not surprised to sense Culy's presence as she sat on a stump outside her roundhome, a bowl of spicy rabbit stew on one knee and a heel of fluffy sour bread on the other.

Carin looked up, relief spreading through her as it so often did in hys vicinity.

"Hello," she said with a smile. Warmth quickly followed the relief as Culy bent and planted a gentle kiss on her lips. Carin did not think she would ever get used to the flutter inside her chest at hys touch.

Culy returned her smile fondly. "Hello to you."

Sy pulled up another stump and sat beside her, mirroring her positioning of stew bowl and bread sy had brought with hyr. The waymake was quiet, as most people were eating, though there was the sound of laughter and conversation here and there.

"How are your friends settling in?" Culy asked.

"I have not seen Jenin today, but I had a long talk with Clar," Carin said. She wondered where Jenin was, actually. "I think they are faring… much as I am on my own return." She said this wryly, but she knew Culy would understand.

The hyrsin simply nodded. "Jenin has been spending a lot of time with Ryd, I think, for which I cannot blame hyr. Ryd is a calming presence to most of us."

"That's true, isn't it?" Carin asked, fondness creeping into her voice. "Have you seen Sart at all?"

Culy shook hys head. "She ought to be back any day now. I expect she will have news of Ras and the others to the north in Ryhnas Lu Sesim."

As always, the name Wyt had given her waymake made Culy's lip quirk.

"It feels too quiet," Carin said finally, swallowing a mouthful of stew and enjoying the heat of it warming her. "If, as you say, the Reinvocation is meant to happen at High Lights even a full cycle hence, I would like to be certain that the remaining stones are broken with ample time to spare before then. Even without further urgency from outside forces, I feel we should go soon. One cycle and a season may not be enough time to stop the Reinvocation from succeeding, especially without knowing if the Khardish are coming."

"I think it is likely they will come," Culy said, and Carin followed hys gaze across the hearth-home to where Hoyu was visible eating her evening meal by the fire with some of the fishers. Her confidence had grown, and she looked totally at ease where she sat. Culy went on. "And I feel much as you do. We can leave little to chance here. Perhaps we have already lingered too long."

"Each stone comes with its own warnings," Carin said. She would never be alone again, in a way. She had paid that price for the first stone, and while it seemed Wyt had paid the price for the second at Culy's hands, Carin was not certain there weren't other consequences to yet be seen. "You told me that long ago."

"It was not so very long ago." Culy smiled. "Though enough has changed to make it seem that way, without a doubt."

"Three stones remain. If you are correct"—Carin paused to give Culy a we-both-know-you-are half-smile—"then fertility, sustenance, and the land itself will each have some sort of effect. I do not expect every womb-bearer to suddenly fall pregnant or for apple trees to miraculously sprout from Salters to Taigers overnight, but I wish there was some idea to be had of what this will do. We still are not fully aware of what the spirit in the stone you broke has done."

"I can help with that," a voice said from around the side of Carin's round-home.

Carin leapt to her feet, nearly forgetting about her remaining stew. Her bread did not fare as well, landing on the reed mat at her feet, where Culy reached down and plucked it back up almost before it stopped moving.

"Sart," Carin said. She sat her bowl down on the stump she had just vacated with an unceremonious clunk and threw her arms around the new arrival.

Sart gave her a tight hug, pressing her forehead to Carin's before pulling back and giving her a once-over. "Have you gotten taller? You look taller."

"I don't think so," Carin said, glancing at Culy, who shrugged.

"Hello, Culy," Sart said.

"Hello, Sart." The smile that crossed Culy's face was tinged with sadness that Carin thought she understood.

Culy had kept things from Sart, big things, and Carin understood how that could change the balance between two people.

Sart, however, gave no notice of it. She instead moved to lean against the wall of Carin's roundhome.

"When did you get back? Just now?" Carin picked up her bowl again, but she hesitated before sitting down. She didn't want to have to crane her neck to talk to her friend.

"Just," Sart affirmed. "I ought to have taken Tahin as you suggested. That monster I rode in hys place was so excited to get back to Lahivar I feel like anything I dared eat today still might come back up from all the jostling."

Culy had been about to offer Sart hys own untouched bread, but sy prudently stopped with hys hand half outstretched and took a bite out of it hyrself instead.

"How is Ras?" Carin asked.

"Remarkably well. And remarkably annoying. Valon is about ready to tear her hair out. She's mostly taken over governance of the waymake, which is to say she's organized and distributed everything Wyt was hoarding, and while she is doing an excellent job of it, I think she's itching to be doing anything else. Literally anything else." Sart's smile then was close to what Carin remembered from when she had first met the woman—a bit impudent, just this side of a smirk with an undercurrent of reflected heat that almost made Carin smirk right back, if she was interpreting that look correctly. "Ras, on the other hand, just seems to want to shoot things full of arrows."

"To be fair, he's had a lot of practice," Carin said blandly.

Sart raised an eyebrow, clearly understanding Carin's reference to how she had first encountered the man: on the wrong side of one of his arrows.

"Yes, well. Let's just enjoy the fact that he is on our side now," Sart said. With that, she launched into a more detailed description of the situation in Ryhnas Lu Sesim, and Carin worked on finishing her stew.

Sart was still talking when a flash of movement in the distance caught Carin's eye, beyond the spring that was the source of the Lahivar River.

"... It seems that the spirit is still healing people," Sart was saying. "Only within the waymake itself, but people are still arriving in a trickle to seek it out. Bulber bloat and fleshrot, water-lung and anything else you can think of, it just vanishes, leaving the survivor hale and as hardy as a fyajir in a spring meadow."

Carin barely heard her, watching the ripple in the air. She set her now-empty bowl down on the stump.

"I think I lost her somewhere," Sart muttered to Culy.

"Carin?"

"Ialtag," Carin said suddenly, and then she was off, heading in the direction of the movement she'd seen.

"What?" came Sart's voice from behind her. "*Here?*"

The waymake of Lahivar had spread out quite a bit on either side of the river, but they had made sure to keep one large circle of land clear directly around the spring itself. Clear of animals and clear of people, the river's source was fresh, cold, clean water that belonged to everyone. Slowly, the claysmiths of Lahivar had begun firing tiles and glazing them in myriad colors, and in careful movements just as slow, they had begun to use them to pave the ground around the spring. It wasn't anywhere near done, but Carin loved seeing the deep blues and greens that had been placed first. They rippled outward from the spring like the way the sun backlit a tree when it sank behind it.

It was there she had seen the movement, and her feet carried her there without hesitation. Sart and Culy would be behind her, and while a few others in the waymake glanced up, it was far from odd for anyone to go to the spring at any time of day.

For a moment, Carin wondered if it had simply been a trick of the fading daylight, but then there was a flurry of air that brought with it the scent of warm fur and pine. From one breath to another, colors whispered across the being in front of her, and she was face to face with a giant bat.

The creature was enormous, with wings that stretched as wide as several people laid out head to toe, and like the others Carin had met, this ialtag had white fur that gleamed in the sunlight and bright yellow ears and nose like the buttercups that grew in spring.

Carin could not help the smile that immediately spread across her face. Something in her lightened, and she grew even more buoyant at the way the ialtag's face echoed her excitement.

"Welcome, friend," she said, and at the ialtag's nod, she stepped closer to gently touch its face.

Her suspicion solidified with the contact, recognizing the ialtag as the very creature that had borne her north across the mountains with Ryd and Ras, the first she had met. Joy leapt within her at that knowledge, at the ialtag's reflected and remembered wonder.

You are much changed, the bat said in her mind.

Carin felt the water spirit respond within her, rising playfully like a burbling brook to brush up against the presence of the ialtag in friendship.

What a remarkable thing! We remember you.

This was directed at the spirit and not at Carin. They would, Carin supposed, remember this spirit, since they were familiar with the original spell. The ialtag shared a collective consciousness; all that was known by one was known by all, and so it had ever been. Each of them carried their history with them. A precious gift—and a heavy burden.

Carin became aware of movement at her back and glanced over her shoulder to see Hoyu and Culy and Sart, Hoyu with her face slack in awe and apprehension and Sart wearing very nearly the same look herself.

We come with urgent news, the ialtag said, nudging Carin's hand to draw her attention back. *There are ships moving toward these shores.*

That snapped Carin like a taut bowstring. *Ships? Khardish ships?*

We are not certain, but they come from Khardan. There are many of them, carrying many more within.

Carin sent the image of Hoyu's frigate. *This size?*

Larger.

Fear spiked through her. With what Hoyu had told her of Khardish technology, if it came to fighting, Khardan's explosive powders against bronze weapons would be no contest. Carin felt frozen to the ground beneath her feet.

Please. Tell me all you can. Carin forgot the crowd gathering at her back.

Time had run out.

DYAVA DID not want to go to Cantoranth.

Beyond the fact that Cantoranth's soothsayer had tried to use subjugation magic—Lyari had taught Dyava that term—to control Lyari in front of the entire gathered population of Haveranth *and then* one of his mother's oldest friends had tried to assassinate Lyari only moments later, Cantoranth was also home to one of the last people in the Hearthland Dyava wanted to see: the assassin's child and a newly minted Silencer.

Even so, Dyava found himself a mere day away from the village that lay in the foothills of the Mad Mountains on the eastern side of the Bemin River but near one of its tributaries that came streaming down from the mountains somewhat to the east of Haver's Glen. All because Lyari had asked it of him. He had been there now and again growing up. The villages had always been accustomed to trading goods and gossip. But tension had sprouted in the Hearthland long before the Night of Reflection, and since then, it had only grown more hardy and more invasive.

There would be no Journeyers this year from any village. Not from Haveranth, not from Cantoranth, and not from Bemin's Fan—and that was not even the half of it, with the Reinvocation on the horizon.

Dyava trekked onward on the beaten track that connected the villages. Unlike the Journeying, he was not hugging the banks of the Bemin itself but had peeled off to the east in the foothills. It was a more direct path, and in the lengthening spring days, he would have enjoyed the walk on any other occasion.

The forest was alive with the sounds of spring, and on any other occasion, Dyava would have enjoyed that too. His mind unhelpfully showed him a memory of his younger life, some cycles back when he and Carin had not yet shared emotions beyond friendship but had frequently gone into the foothills to hunt. He could almost see her beside him, skin flushed with exertion and blue eyes bright with youth. How much had the past few cycles aged them both? He was grateful she still lived at least.

There was a flurry of movement in the sun-dappled grasses under a maha tree off to the left, and Dyava stopped as a hare bounded away and then down into a hollow that must have concealed its den. His gaze rose to the sky, where sure enough, a hawk circled.

On reflex, he pulled his bow from his shoulder and an arrow from his belt-quiver. He nocked, drew, and loosed the arrow in one smooth motion. The hawk was lower than a hawk should be to hunt, but Dyava still did not expect to hit it. When the bird screamed and jerked to the side in the sky, he almost dropped his bow. The hawk flailed midair for a moment, then somehow righted itself and beat its wings again, managing to stay in the air despite Dyava having injured it. He squinted, trying to see if the arrow had lodged in the bird's wing, but it was too far away.

But he did see something else.

Dyava was new to magic use, but he was well accustomed to seeing magic done by others. And the hawk, as it winged desperately away, was trailing threads of it.

His parents had taught him to be wary of hawks, and he had never stopped to doubt that. Merin kept a hawk called Lin, and he was certain she used it as her eyes and ears. Jenin and Lyari both had said it followed their path on the Journeying—though Jenin had simply been present for moments, not the entire time—and Jenin had also mentioned that Carin and Ryd had seen a hawk all the way in the Northlands.

The sudden certainty that this hawk was watching *him*, likely due to his proximity to Lyari, stopped Dyava cold.

This could not be Merin's work. Merin was dead. And Lyari was certain that the other soothsayers had minimal magic.

Dyava made his feet start moving again; the pleasant warmth of the day turned bitter around him.

He had barely taken a hundred steps farther down the path when he stopped again.

Merin was dead; that was true. Lyari had burned her alive.

But Jenin was proof that magic could do many, many things.

Dyava wanted to go to Cantoranth even less now.

What had Lyari gotten him into?

• • • • •

Cantoranth was nestled in the foothills of the Mad Mountains, surrounded on three sides by a sharp-edged corrie that housed the quarry deep within where the villagers here extracted stone used all over the Hearthland for roofs and more.

It always had felt claustrophobic to Dyava, and now even more so. In Haveranth, roundhomes were built mostly of wood, except for the roofs, while here in Cantoranth, they were done with dry mortar stone, creating intricate-looking walls that boggled the mind for the way the small bricks of stone fit together despite being all different widths and heights and lengths.

To Dyava's eye, it had always seemed a bit like magic, but at the same time, it also made Cantoranth grey from foundation to gable.

A few villagers looked up when he made his way into the village, but he gave them little notice. Smoke trickled from some of the roundhomes, more than in Haveranth this far into spring, but the air here was cooler, crisper.

It was just his luck that the first person Dyava recognized was Ohrya. Sy saw him coming and stopped, face going as blank as the stone face of the cliff behind hyr. Sy took one step toward him, hys foot stuttering as if it were warring with itself about whether to move.

"Dyava," sy said with no preamble. "What are you doing here?"

Such a good question.

"I've come to speak to Reynah," he said with as little feeling as he could muster.

Ohrya's eyes showed no sign of surprise, but what had Dyava expected? That sy would fall over from shock? Instead, Ohrya simply looked at him. Sy was taller than he remembered, carrying hyrself with the air of someone who knew every muscle in hys body and how to use it to superlative efficacy. Dyava supposed that came with being a Silencer. One had to *be* a weapon, not just wield one.

"Lyari sent you," Ohrya said after a beat.

Dyava gave hyr a tight-lipped smile that said *of course she did.*

Ohrya jerked hys head in the direction of the village hearth-home. "Wait for me to come back. I'll ask if she'll see you."

Dyava's smile turned sardonic. Of course. He simply nodded and started moving. He'd appreciate the chance to sit down, anyway. It had been a long walk. He certainly didn't intend to sleep in the village, but he'd have to camp on the way home too, which hadn't been his favorite thing on the journey to Cantoranth. Not with wolves on the move in the foothills.

As he walked the short distance to the village hearth-home, passing Cantoranth's smithy and two masons' homes opposite each other on the way, Dyava couldn't help but notice that several roundhomes were still standing open to the sky, their roofs having collapsed. The rubble had been cleared, but they'd not gone any further than that. Shocking, almost. It had been moons since the snows had stopped, and he would have thought someone would have reroofed the round-homes to keep the weather out if nothing else. If they didn't, the floors and everything left inside them would be ruined forever.

It would be a shocking waste, but that was the Hearthland way. "Waste" was not part of Hearthlander vocabulary, but it was part of Dyava's. These were a people who burned a home to the ground upon its owner's death. Someone in each must have survived, or these homes would have been consigned to flame.

Take and take and take from the land, never giving anything back.

Dyava's feet found the paved circle that marked the hearth-home and stepped under the pavilion there. Like everything in Cantoranth, it was stone where Haveranth's were beams of wood, but that was not the only difference that struck him.

It had been some time since Dyava visited Cantoranth, but hadn't there been someone tending the fire last time? In Haveranth, Tamat was always there with hys meat roasting or grilling or spitted, ready to share with any weary worker or traveler passing through, but here there was naught but a table with a jug for water and some earthenware cups. Upon closer examination, there was a bowl that looked like it had held berries earlier in the day, but now it was empty of everything except some purple-red juice at the bottom and a few filaments of plant fiber that he couldn't match to any particular berry.

The fire burned, but it guttered.

Dyava couldn't be certain what Lyari had told him—were there *any* remaining hysmern in Cantoranth who would be assigned to tend the fire for the cycle? In Haveranth there were two who would do so for another cycle yet, but it appeared there was no one here. He wondered who was doing it.

He waited for some time, and then he waited some more. The sun passed its zenith and started toward the horizon, which did not make Dyava feel better about the impending night and having to camp without a hot meal. He had enough dried meat and cheese to keep a full belly all the way back to Haveranth, but the night would be chilly here in Cantoranth.

To pass the time, he ate a bit of meat and cheese, wondering belatedly what would happen if Reynah just decided to kill him. He didn't think she would actually do that, but she could. Who knew what she would do if she had tried to have Lyari killed in front of everyone?

Surely Lyari must have thought of the possibility—was sending Dyava here alone some kind of dare? He didn't know, but the thought soured the bite of cheese in his mouth, and he put the rest away, his stomach making an unhappy groan in protest.

It was at that precise moment that Ohrya returned. Sy gave Dyava a perfunctory nod as if to beckon him, and he hopped up from where he was sitting. His muscles protested the action, but Ohrya was already making hys way from the hearth-home with haste, so Dyava quickly followed.

He let himself be led through the village, past the house he thought was Reynah's, which gave him pause. Ohrya did not speak to him as they walked.

The air was quickly growing cold beyond simply chilly, and until that moment, Dyava had not noticed the gathering clouds. The wind carried a distinct dry, dusty scent that was unmistakeable: snow.

That made everything worse.

The second thing he noticed as they passed the penultimate house before the corrie narrowed was the dead wolf hanging by its feet, bleeding out. The next house must have been the tanner's.

Dyava had a healthy fear of wolves, but seeing the creature like that froze something inside him and coated his upset stomach with a sickly, oily layer of unease.

Ohrya still didn't speak, only stopped at the door of the final house in Cantoranth and motioned at it with a jerk of hys elbow.

Dyava gave hyr a sideways glance and said "Thanks," but he didn't wait for an answer.

The door was cracked open, and Dyava didn't bother to knock, either. He had been left waiting all day, and if Reynah wanted to kill him, so be it.

She was seated at a large maha table, one like Lyari's only to the extent that it was made from the same wood. While Lyari's—formerly Carin's, formerly Rina's—was polished and nearly shone red-brown in the firelight, this one was battered, scuffed, and covered in what looked like years of knife marks from chopping things directly on its surface. Dyava would have been embarrassed to invite guests to such a table.

The person with Reynah must have been the tanner, but sy left with one glance at the soothsayer, closing the door firmly at hys back.

"So," said Reynah, looking up at Dyava. A heavy shawl hung around her shoulders, hanging almost to her lap, and clasped at the neck with a bronze brooch in the shape of leaping salmon. "Lyari sends you in her stead."

Her words were pronounced with such a neutral tone that Dyava didn't know what to make of it.

"I would think you could hardly blame her for not coming herself," Dyava said.

"Why? It was not I who ran at her at the Night of Reflection. She is sowing naught but division when we need unity at this most precipitous moment." Reynah's eyes flashed, and this time her tone was not so neutral.

"Unity," Dyava said incredulously. "One of your villagers strikes at the Hearthland's true soothsayer in full view of a throng of people, and you accuse *Lyari* of sowing discord? There is no way you actually believe what you are saying."

"I speak only the truth. She is behaving like a petulant child—threatening to choose her enemies for the Reinvocation, think of it!—and you could do worse than heed me."

Reynah had hardly moved from where she sat, both hands folded primly in her lap. She had offered Dyava no tea, no sustenance, no hospitality, not even a seat at the table.

The tanner's house was, aside from that table, not so horribly put together, though it smelled of chemicals and dead meat. That was hardly worth remarking upon considering the work.

"What exactly is it you want?" Dyava asked bluntly. "You sent people to try and turn me against Lyari, then tried to kill her. You marched to Haveranth and insulted her in front of everyone, and now you make me wait for half a day to speak with you and offer not even the barest grace of hospitality."

"I owe you nothing, you and your double-sided tongue," said Reynah.

Dyava froze where he stood.

"Do you think your family is truly so stealthy as to evade notice? Your parents and their sahthren, saying all the right things and still losing not one but *two* children? If I had my way, it would be them under the knife." Reynah stopped short and looked into Dyava's eyes, her own glimmering a strange gold in the firelight. "I know you know what the Reinvocation will bring. Do not think me a fool. Lyari will go through with it, and you will get to watch how the villagers respond to this duty. You will both understand me before this is over."

"I don't understand you now, that's for sure," Dyava said, finding his tongue again. "That you think you possess some sort of moral high ground is clear, but it is the clarity of a chunk of sea glass a child claims is a diamond. You are nothing but sand and falseness, Reynah ve Cantoranth."

"You know less than nothing, hysmern. We have protected this land for ages beyond your reckoning."

Reynah still had barely moved, only her face, which had taken on a slightly mottled flush. Her pupils were dilated, Dyava noticed belatedly, and she sat rigidly on the bench with her back to the fire, which was the only thing in the tanner's roundhome that seemed to be cheerily carrying on with its day.

Dyava felt a strange sensation take root in his chest. Not magic—he would see any magic Reynah tried to use against him—but something that came only from within. He stuffed both his hands into his pockets and scowled his best, most childish scowl at the older woman. His hands caught one of the pebbles he kept on hand in case he needed his sling, and he worried it against the pad of his thumb.

"Ah, yes. Protected. The way you protected Carin and Ryd?" Let it all show, why not?

The flash of surprise in Reynah's eyes did not escape him. "I know not of whom you speak."

"More lies," Dyava said. "I came only to inform you that Lyari has devised several effective treatments for the heat sickness, but I presume you already know about them, since you were so *generous* to advise Lyari on how to deal with roofs laden with snow and not the other way around. I will refrain from testing your intelligence by telling you what you already know. I'll leave you only with this gift."

Dyava took the pebble from his pocket and tossed it to Reynah, hoping her reflexes would make her jump to catch it. It was a gamble, and the soothsayer simply stared at him balefully as it clunked against the table in front of her instead.

"A diamond for you," he said with aplomb, as if that was precisely what he'd meant to do.

He turned to leave, ready to race down the hill and out of this grey, bounty-less crag of a place.

But he turned at the sound of Reynah's voice.

"You'll learn," she said.

"I hope that pleasure will be yours," he snapped back, and as he turned back to the door, it took everything in his power not to react to what he saw poking out from a stack of kindling.

He threw open the door and did his best to stamp his way out though his legs felt watery, and his face burned as hot as the fire with anger and indignation.

Dyava ignored Ohrya and did exactly as he meant to. He marched straight down the hill, through the hearth-home where someone had finally arrived to tend the fire, and out of Cantoranth as fast as his wobbly legs could take him.

It was only when he was a good distance away from the village, away from the overhanging rock ready to crush him like the giant's fist that had smashed through Haver's Glen, away from Reynah's smugness and intolerable arrogance that he allowed himself to think of what he had seen.

If she hadn't had to have the last word, he would have missed it. It was something that most might have missed even if they didn't mistake it for a simple stick, but Dyava was fastidious about his arrows.

Dyava hadn't been sure, hadn't wanted to so much as think of the possibility, but now, his stride lengthening as he hurried to put distance between himself and the poison of Cantoranth, he was certain.

His own arrow, somewhat cleaned but still touched with blood, broken in half, and thrown in the kindling pile of the tanner's house where Reynah sat practically frozen on a bench as if moving would give something away.

It made sense now, the stretching, interminable time he had been left waiting. Magic was capable of many things, but immediate healing was not usually one of them. Reynah's dilated eyes—she had to have been sedated. She certainly did not *seem* sedate, but there were herbs to take for pain that did not cloud the mind. And she had seemed far less likely to dissemble than Dyava would have expected.

He had only shot one arrow on his journey to Cantoranth.

Somehow, impossibly, it had hit the truest mark when it hit that hawk.

S OMETHING WAS wrong.

That was no mystery—*everything* was wrong in this place, from the earth to the sky to the people and creatures that crawled along the surface and flew above it. Kat's people had been so certain that they would be making ready by now to fight the ancient enemy, to do . . . something at the very least. But while A'cu Lystel—Culy—had informed her that sy planned to see to the breaking of the remaining hearthstones, there was little talk of moving against the Tuanye at all.

Kat made her way across the southern mountains' foothills, Suhnsuoc loping along beneath her, as pensive as she herself was feeling.

The more she saw of these lands, the more she felt as if her skin did not quite fit. Something was very, very wrong.

It was not really as if Kat had expected the warmlanders to greet her like a hero or a savior, not exactly. But her people had raised her as one. She was supposed to lead them to victory against the Tuanye, and instead she found one of *them* among the warmlanders, clearly having usurped the place that was meant to be hers at A'cu Lystel's side.

And Kat was left wondering if somehow everything she had ever been taught was somehow wrong.

"Could someone have made some mistake, Suhnsuoc?" she asked into the wind.

The air was warm upon her face, evidence of the seasons turning, and all around her, the broken land was knitting itself back together again without her help.

No one knows everything, Suhnsuoc replied, though Kat could feel the impression of a frown from the giant cat. *Even the ialtag have limits. Their memory is as shaped by perception as anyone else's.*

That was true, of course. The flaw of a shared mind. Though there was power and context in remembering the experience of everyone who had ever lived, no matter how small, that did not make their memory infallible or less prone to bias than anyone else's.

"Surely the ialtag would have corrected us had we strayed from the course too far," Kat said, more to herself than anything else.

They were nearing where she meant to go. The Tuanye—Carin—had told her about this place, and Kat wanted to see it for herself.

It was the ruin of an old city, and they shortly came into the outskirts of where it had once sprawled.

Kat could see it in her memory, shown to her through the eyes of the ialtag. Once, it had been Alar Marhasan, a fabled city of thousands. Prosperous and built from white stone and sung halm, it had been named for an ancient hero who had laid down hys life to save the then-village from a rampaging giant. Kat didn't know if giants were real or had ever been, but she wasn't sure she wanted to know. Some stories were better without certainty.

The air was cool without being cold, and birdsong filled the breeze coming down from the mountains. Suhnsuoc's ears twitched with both breeze and birdsong, the tufts at the ends almost like an insect's antennae.

Kat didn't like feeling at war with herself. Perhaps Culy and Carin were right and breaking the stones would be enough, but she could not be sure. If her people's stories were to be believed, the Tuanye south of the Mad Mountains would simply try something else. It did not seem as though Carin knew among whom she had grown up, that ancient power lurked in her village, in her own blood.

It wasn't that simple, of course.

Magic didn't care about bloodlines, but the ancient Tuanye had.

Kat tried to concentrate on the swaying motion of Suhnsuoc beneath her as they waded deeper into the ruins of the city. She had a suspicion she wanted to explore here, and if she was being honest with herself, it was that more than the spring and the ruin had pushed her out of Lahivar to travel to Crevasses.

So far, the warmlanders had managed to break two of the hearthstones, and if Kat was right, one of the remaining three should be here. Culy had said nothing of it, and Kat thought surely the hyrsin or Carin would have mentioned seeing it or tried to break it if either had found it here, but even so, Kat had a hunch.

It took the better part of the afternoon to search the ruins, both Kat and the kazytya that carried her seeking the telling tendrils of magic that would give the presence of such an artifact away. They reached the wide plaza she had seen in ialt-ag memories, the river Carin had told her about, and the statues of open-mouthed cats spilling water into it. Kat wasn't certain the cats were meant to be tigers, but time had worn away too much detail to be sure, and even in the ialtag memories, there was a haze about things.

The air was different here.

Everything was different here. A large black bird Kat didn't recognize roosted on the remains of a wall, preening its feathers.

Unnerved, Kat stared at it until Suhnsuoc's feet took them out of its line of sight.

As Suhnsuoc padded across the bridge to the sound of water rushing under it, Kat finally caught wind of something else. Culy and Carin would have noticed this, wouldn't they? There was no need to spur Suhnsuoc onward; the kazytya shared Kat's mind and immediately moved in the direction from which this new pull emanated.

"*Something* is here," Kat muttered.

The sun broke through the clouds briefly, dappling the ruins with gold, but Kat paid it no heed.

As they moved eastward through the ruin along what may once have been a wide boulevard—now overgrown with warmland plants turning their leaves upward—Kat's skin seemed to buzz.

She wasn't the only one. Suhnsuoc's fur bristled beneath her, and the cat stopped briefly to shake.

One is uncomfortable, the kazytya grumped. *Like before the lightning strikes.*

Kat hadn't managed to articulate it yet herself, but Suhnsuoc was right. The air felt . . . charged. There wasn't much lightning and thunder in the far north beyond Taigers, but sometimes a storm would roll in with the tail end of their short summer, bringing the deep, chest-shaking boom of thunder and flashes that lit and forked through the sky.

The sky above Kat's head was not purple-black with heavy clouds, nor did the air smell like rain.

Alar Marhasan stood amid the foothills of the mountains, where once the city had snaked through gullies and clambered over the rises of the hills. It was into one of those gullies the pull led the pair.

They walked for some time, long enough that the sun would soon slip beneath the ridgeline to the west. It cast the gully in yet-deeper golden orange, and Kat dismounted to give Suhnsuoc a break from carrying her. They were slower that way. Kat's mind whispered that she should give serious consideration to the safety of letting night fall in a place like this, but she dismissed the whispers without further thought. There was nothing to be afraid of in the dark, and if anything wanted to test that theory, one scream from Suhnsuoc would have the intruder hightailing it in the other direction.

It was strange here.

The wilderness had mostly reclaimed the hills, but remnants remained visible through the foliage. Boulders too regular to be natural. Trees growing from massive piles of stone that must have once been buildings. There was something here.

The gully deepened and widened into a glen that cut almost due south into the mountains between two hills. Kat had no desire to go deeper into the Mad

Mountains before it was time to bring the fight to the Tuanye, but she found her feet continuing onward in spite of her own better judgement.

There were some recent tracks in the brush and the scent of animals that had moved this way. At least there were until the sun dipped behind the ridge. Kat realized the birdsong had stopped. All that remained was the sound of her booted feet and Suhnsuoc's enormous paws falling lightly on the grass-covered ground. The breeze had died.

Suhnsuoc's tail twitched, making a sharp whip from side to side. It was not as long as a tiger's tail, proportionally, and for the climate of the north, it was covered in much thicker fur, but it still betrayed the large cat's apprehension. Not all kazytya even had tails, but those in Kat's homeland did.

A stream trickled by them to the west, probably fed mostly by runoff from the mountains. One of the things Culy had said was that there had once been some sort of barrier that kept people from venturing farther south. While Kat doubted it was anything physical, as she and her kazytya moved southward with the quieting day, she couldn't help but believe something had been there indeed.

Kat had little magic herself, certainly not enough to feel comfortable calling herself a mage, but she wasn't completely oblivious. It took the better part of a league before she was able to place what she was feeling, the energy in the air that felt like lightning about to strike. Volatile. Wild.

She didn't know what made magic go. There were five branches of it that she knew of. The most basic was abas, energy, from which came the word for magic itself. Perhaps it was raw abas she felt here, or perhaps it was something else. Dyupahsy, potential—that could be it. The sense of possibility, of a bolt from the heavens that could come at any moment.

Magic usually didn't work that way. It was an ever-changing weave of all its branches, like the baskets her people wove from intertwined grasses in the short northern summers.

Even so, when Kat and Suhnsuoc made their way into the cleft of the glen, she still didn't expect what they found.

On a hillock between the walls of a sharp corrie that widened into a ravine, there was an ancient halm that made Kat feel she had shrunk to the size of a bee.

Kat had never seen one so large. Her only point of reference was the hills themselves or the memory of towers and grand palaces. A hundred people joining hands could not reach around its trunk at the base, and had the sun been high enough, it would have shaded the whole of Lahivar beneath its massive branches.

Suhnsuoc had stopped, and Kat had barely noticed she was still walking toward the tree, almost as if in a dream.

She wanted to touch it, to place her skin against its smooth bark as if doing so would allow her to see what this tree had seen. How many ages had it stood guard in front of this jagged fissure into the mountain?

Hardly able to tear her eyes from the halm, Kat forced herself to look beyond it. The walls of the corrie were deceptively green, rounded where balls of moss had grown over time. They almost looked pillowed, and the moss spread around the rock walls to the floor of the glen, interspersed with grasses here and there, but otherwise a dense blanket barely broken.

Kat paused, feeling the ground beneath her feet. It was softer here, a mixture of grass and peat and soil, but the other trees around her gave way to a clearing where a giant ruled alone.

Without further thought, she bent to unlace her boots and removed them. Suhnsuoc still hung back, silently observing with no small amount of unease evident through their bond.

Despite the darkening of the day, soft light emanated from the halm, so soft that Kat first felt she had to be imagining it. Her bare feet sank into the moss, which was still dew-soaked despite the late hour. Surely Culy would have told her if sy knew about such a tree. And surely such a tree could not have escaped the hyrsin's notice. Had sy mentioned a halm grove perhaps? Kat should remember, but a halm grove was not so notable. A tree this gargantuan, however, was.

Surely someone must have known it was here.

Yet as Kat made her way over the spongy floor of the clearing, her skin alight with prickles from head to toe, she felt most sure that no one had. Halm, she knew, had a will. Many did not know that or credit it if they did, but Kat's people were careful archivists of history and lore. They passed this knowledge on from mouth to ear over the ages with the help of the kazytya, like the ialtag themselves in a way, though not so immediately connected.

Kat reached the first visible root, white like bone as it protruded from the moss. Even at this distance, the root was bigger around than she was. The root system of this tree must have stretched deep into the earth. She was already standing on top of it, at least half of the enormous halm hidden away beneath her feet.

There were so few trees in the naked north; few could grow in such short seasons, and those that did were short and scrubby where the harsh winds could not uproot them.

But here in the sheltered cove of rock and waves of moss, this halm had grown to this size.

If halm had a will, could this tree have hidden itself away from the eyes of the warmlanders all this time?

And if it had, Kat found a question igniting in her core as she stretched out one hand to touch the root, which reached waist height beside her.

If this tree could hide itself, it could also choose when to be revealed.

Why?

CARIN WAS not prepared to leave Lahivar. Perhaps it was unease at leaving Clar and Jenin and Hoyu, but that was silly. Ryd and Sart would be here with them, and the people of Lahivar were more than able to fend for themselves. With the Khardish coming, Hoyu had volunteered to stay behind—no one else had any Khardish language yet beyond a few words. Though Carin hated to leave her friend, she could see the look of duty in Hoyu's eyes and her resolve to do what she must.

The morning air was filled with that quiet hush of a day just getting started, and the blue grasses around Lahivar sparkled with dew turned golden in the shining sun. The sky stretched out above them, cloudless and bright, the sun's rays cutting through the tendrils of remaining mist that clung to the river.

Many of the waymake's people were milling about, postponing their chores to see Culy and Carin leave, though there was little ceremony about it, only a hum of nervousness Carin didn't think she was imagining.

If there were a real problem, Jenin could contact Carin and Culy in the unseen world while they slept.

As she mounted Tahin beside Culy on hys own ihstal, Carin couldn't help but wonder when she had become accustomed to the daily marvels of her life. In Haveranth, she never would have dreamed of using magic, let alone being able to speak to someone over vast distances—or being able to travel vast distances in heartbeats that should have taken turns on a ship.

The thought of ships soured her stomach. She glanced involuntarily westward, though she could not see the sea from Lahivar.

Ryd was standing arm in arm with Clar, watching her, and Carin knew that expression of wry exasperation.

"If these Khardish come, we will know in enough time to vanish. Let them find a deserted Lahivar." Ryd dropped Clar's arm and came up to Tahin's flank, stroking the ihstal before reaching up to catch Carin's hand and give it a squeeze. "We will be fine."

Carin squeezed his hand back. "I know."

Just like that, her emotions spilled back over into urgency. Culy glanced at her from where sy had been murmuring to Sart and Hoyu about something, as if sensing that the prolonged leave-taking was causing her distress.

"We will tell you when it is done," Carin said.

Tahin danced beneath her, and without further instruction, the two ihstal were off, turning from the waymake with eager whistles to bear their riders north.

Carin heard people calling out farewells behind her, and she turned back once to wave.

"You are uneasy," Culy said softly, though hys words carried to Carin in that way they shared.

"If the Khardish truly bring war upon us, there will be little we can do to stop them." Carin hated the sick twist of her stomach at that, a conflict of anger and remembered fear. "We will have no need to worry about the Reinvocation if we are all dead."

They were quiet as they rode for a short time, the soft breeze gentle and the morning warming with the sun.

Carin did not yet have the distance from her time as a prisoner to stop herself being transported back to those moments, screaming herself raw aboard their ship, the throbbing of fingertips scraped bloody from clawing against the floor, the heavy helplessness that kept her placid as Rela and Asurashk tried to chisel away the foundation stones of her mind for power.

Even though she knew she was safe—as safe as one could be in this world—her body remembered. Layered upon her own storm of emotions was the spirit's, so intertwined with Carin that she had lost all interest in feeling out the boundaries between them. And still beyond that, Carin felt a spike of bitter worry on Hoyu's behalf. This was not the Khardan her friend had known. Something wasn't right; things had gone so wrong so swiftly.

When she said as much, Culy was quiet for a moment. Carin felt the urge to look back toward Lahivar again, even though it was already out of sight, but she stilled herself.

"I could not speak to the whims of those lands," Culy said carefully. "We have been so thoroughly separate from them for so long that anything I could share would simply be useless. But what I can say is something I do not need to tell you: there are some for whom power is both pride and prize. Once they hold it, they do not easily relinquish it. Their only concern becomes holding onto it, and anyone they perceive as trying to take it from them becomes an enemy."

Carin remembered the Keeper of Keys and the Keeper of Mysteries, the two members of the Da'sash Dan who had aided Rela and Asurashk. Two of the highest rulers in the whole of Khardan.

"Yes," Carin said. "And when that is true, some will use any means they deem necessary against those enemies."

They rode in silence for much of the morning. Carin loved to speak to Culy, especially now since sy had opened up so much of hys life and world to her, but today was different. They both felt the same urgency, despite Culy's calm appearance, and Carin could feel the weight grow heavier with every passing league.

She was not prepared for what they found when they stopped for the midday meal. The sun still shone high above them, warm and bright, and a few clouds now scudded across the sky. But while the land was beginning to change as it did to rolling plains that would give way to Boggers, Carin had not expected to see a stand of trees breaking the plains to the northwest.

"Those were not there before," she said, pointing. "Were they?"

She hadn't been this way many times, only to and from the first stone she had broken—the spirit gave a little burble of remembered gratitude at the passing thought—but there had been no trees, only a few pitiful bushes. She had only been joking when she told Culy she didn't expect apple trees to suddenly spring up everywhere from Salters to Boggers, and while these didn't look like apple trees to Carin's eyes, she had not expected to eat her own words so soon.

Culy's eyes were as glued to the sight as hers. "No, they certainly were not."

"That would imply yet another water source," Carin said slowly. "It has only been a cycle—not even. How have they grown so tall? Where did the seeds come from?"

"Some seeds can lie dormant for a long time," said Culy, but the hyrsin did not sound convinced by hys own words. "Usually, it requires some sort of catalyst to awaken them from such dormancy. A fire, perhaps, or—"

"The crumbling of an ancient spell?" Carin could not keep the wryness from her voice.

"Just so," said Culy, turning away from the trees to look at her with those fathomless grey eyes.

"Every time I find my feet, something new crashes into me," Carin murmured.

Culy came to her side, taking her hands in hys. "I think I know the feeling."

Carin's skin tingled where it met Culy's. As always, something thrilled within her when she met hys gaze. It felt like recognition, perhaps, or the way she had felt soaring above the Mad Mountains, carried by the ialtag.

"We should probably eat so we can get going again." Her voice came out unconvincing, cracking on the last word.

Her lips touched Culy's, and for a moment she forgot about spells, forgot about trees racing skyward across once-barren land, forgot about ships on the sea and forces she could not control. She forgot about the remaining hearthstones. The world narrowed to the points of contact between her body and hys, and when sy dropped her hands, Carin felt like she was falling for the barest moment until sy caught her waist instead, pulling her close to hys chest, hips flush with hers.

The kiss deepened, hungry.

When they finally broke apart, it left her breathless.

Culy's small smirk as sy went to Tahin's side to retrieve provisions didn't help. This wasn't the first time she had been off alone with Culy, but with a start, Carin realized the last time had been in Alar Marhasan, where Wyt's rovers had abducted hyr.

It seemed a lifetime ago. Her lips felt extra sensitive from the kiss, and a thought intruded that Culy was a better kisser than Dyava, which sent a pang of guilt through her. Dyava and Lyari had been the only people Carin had ever kissed before now, and with Lyari it had been little more than childish curiosity, as Lyari and Jenin had been joined at the lips from adolescence onward.

Something else that felt like a lifetime ago.

Alar Marhasan was another thing, though. "Why was Kat so keen to go to Alar Marhasan?" Carin asked, moving to help Culy with the flatbread and dried meat sy had pulled out for their meal.

"I suspect to search for a hearthstone," Culy said.

Carin thought she recognized that tone in Culy's voice, that noncommittal neutrality that had once been directed at her. The spirit made what felt like a mental splash of exasperation—at Culy, Carin thought.

"Will she find one?" Carin couldn't help but feel that bit of exasperation herself.

The woman from the far north and her kazytya were just one of the many oddities this cycle had thrust upon them, and Carin couldn't figure out why Culy would simply send her haring off to hunt for something sy knew wasn't there like a child tricked into looking for the elusive dyungar, a half-rodent, half-bird that didn't exist. (A favorite prank between frustrated parents and capricious older children alike.)

Culy handed Carin some food, looking suddenly at a loss. "You know, I haven't the faintest idea. She seemed determined to go, and I quite frankly wasn't sure what else to do with her in Lahivar. She looks at me as if she expects something of me, and moreover, that she expects me to know precisely what that is. I have had some interactions with her people, but not many, and she was the first to call me by my other name. I suppose I thought letting her go have a look would give me some time to figure out what it is she wants from me."

Carin froze with her hand halfway extended still, then took the proffered flatbread and chunk of dried, smoked rabbit, unsure of what to make of that. She had felt the weight of unclear expectation for moons on end, so she could not begrudge Culy the right to feel unsettled.

"If there was a stone there, shouldn't we have looked for it when we went?" Carin ate without really tasting her food.

They had traveled all the way to the city on rumors of the spring there, and breaking another hearthstone would have saved them a lot of time and worry. It wasn't like Culy to waste journeys. Though Carin couldn't forget that particular one had been cut short for reasons beyond their control.

"Yes," Culy said simply. "Though I have never been able to find it if it is there."

There was a long pause.

The ihstal whistled to one another, grazing not far away and occasionally doing a small prance that the children of Lahivar called their "happy grass dance" with the ihstal's snouts buried in their lunch and only their feet giving little excited hops. For animals that were so hardy in scarcity and looked like they had been hewn from pure light when the sun hit them, they could be delightfully silly beasts.

"Well." Carin thought if she dwelled much longer on the odds of escaping further catastrophe, she would dig herself right into the ground and never come out. "I suppose we should hope she finds it, then."

She looked out over the plains again, toward the stand of trees. For a moment in her mind's eye, she saw the land around them transformed into a deep forest, hearing the wind through branches high above her head instead of the whisper of it running its fingers through grass.

Perhaps what she really hoped was that she and Culy would find the stone they sought. As they quickly finished their short meal and called the ihstal back to continue on, Carin had to wonder what their possible success would leave in its wake.

· · · · ·

The land continued to change around them as Carin and Culy rode northward at a hurried pace. They skirted around Boggers, aiming at Ryhnas Lu Sesim without intending to get close, but where once the enormous wetland had spread out across the inland region, there were yet more changes to be found.

The air was not as heavy with the stink of stagnant water and mud. To the contrary, it felt clean in Carin's lungs, and as they turned their route away from the direction of Ryhnas Lu Sesim to head northeast, they saw why.

No longer was the massive bog a series of waterways and small hillocks exposed between them, but instead a growing lake spread itself out. Carin and Culy could not stop to explore, but twice they passed people traveling toward the coastal waymakes, and all of the travelers looked as bewildered as Carin felt.

For a people who had eked out a living in the wetlands where freshwater was both abundant and undrinkable, people who knew the plant and wildlife as well as their own bodies, such a shift would upturn everything they knew.

Carin and Culy stayed far enough away to escape recognition, but Carin knew Culy itched to stop and talk to people.

"On our way home," she murmured after one group grew smaller in the distance. "With some luck, we will have time to seek answers then."

Culy simply nodded, and the pair rode onward.

All the hyrsin had was memory shrouded by the passing of ages. It wasn't much to try and locate a stone, and the knowledge that Wyt had managed to move the hearthstone in her waymake weighed heavy on both Culy and Carin.

As they left the plains and now-not-so-aptly-named Boggers behind, the air grew cooler again, spring not as entrenched as it was farther south.

Carin could tell as the days and turns passed that Culy was restless. The spirit seemed agitated too, like there was something stuck in a boot that could be felt but not found for removal.

"Are you so worried we won't find it?" Carin asked finally one morning as they hurried to pack up their bedrolls under clouds threatening rain.

Culy glanced at the sky, hands busy securing bags to hys ihstal while Carin did the same with Tahin.

Sy gestured to the halm staff sy carried. "No. My worry is not for whether or not we will find the stone—even if someone has managed to move it, we are equipped to follow it. Between us, we have enough familiarity with the hearthstone spell for my staff to assist us in tracking traces of it."

"Then what worries you?" Carin upended her waterskin over the remains of their small fire to make sure no embers would come back to life with a stout breeze, rain or no rain.

Culy was quiet for a moment, listening to the hiss of steam. "Many things worry me, not least of which being the Khardish invasion. I trust we will hear of that very soon. But I am not certain I can truly say what I am feeling. Urgency without direction—need mired in uncertainty. There are too many variables over which we have little control."

Carin could understand that very clearly. Much as Culy had done for her turns before, she went to hyr, tucking her waterskin away and taking Culy's hands in hers.

"Then let us control what we can, and the rest we will deal with when it reaches us," she said.

It sounded braver than she felt. The many unknowns ate away at her. What would happen if Lyari still tried the Reinvocation, what the Khardish wanted and what they would do, whether more people would come from across the sea, what Kat's people wanted or expected, what would happen when they broke the remaining three stones, whether a little more than a cycle would be enough time for them to dodge fate long enough to even find and break the stones—Carin could go on and on and on. But she believed her own words at the same time.

Culy nodded, clearly thinking through the same branching questions as she was. "That is all anyone can do."

They continued to the northeast, the ihstal sensing their urgency.

The strangest sensation encroached upon Carin as the rain began to drizzle and then dump from the heavy clouds above. The spirit had shown her that it could helpfully keep her and Culy dry, which was both nice and disconcerting. Beyond the oddity of feeling wind but no rain in what was quickly becoming a deluge, Carin could not name the other insistent perception that something else was amiss.

Visibility lost itself in the heavy rainfall as if they had ascended into a cloud, and this far north, it was cold enough that despite being dry, Carin shivered at the bite in the air.

"Should we stop?" she called to Culy over the squelch of ihstal footsteps and the torrent of rain. "I can barely see beyond Tahin's nose!"

"There is a waymake not far from here!" Culy called back. "Only three roofs, but with luck, one will be free."

The rain hadn't slaked by the time they arrived, and Carin was relieved to see that the waymake wasn't even occupied, though it had grown a new dwelling since Culy had last visited.

Without a word, they led the ihstal under one of the roofs to remove their bags and bedrolls, and Carin murmured her thanks to the spirit for keeping them dry when they otherwise would have been soaked through.

The spirit gave a happy sound of approval not unlike the rain hitting the puddles outside. Once the bags and bedrolls were removed, the ihstal pranced outside to go play in the rain and graze. Carin stifled a snort at the sight.

She didn't realize she was staring off into the distance at the wall of mist until Culy said her name, and it hit her that sy had said it more than once to get her attention.

"Sorry," she said, tearing her gaze from her thinking spot.

Culy gave her a wry smile. "I think we agree on where to search for the stone," sy said, then gestured in the direction Carin had been looking. "It seems you feel its presence as keenly as I do."

At that, Carin's head turned sharply to look at hyr. "You think that's what I'm feeling?"

"It is likely," sy said. "I admit my relief. I was afraid it would be fainter."

Carin looked again, wishing her eyes could part the heavy curtain of raindrops that stood between them and their goal. Part of her wanted to leave the ihstal and their things and run now, to get it over with. They were close. A flash of hope and triumph flared briefly in her chest, but she subdued it.

"When the rain stops?" she asked.

Culy nodded, hys own eyes trained on what neither of them could see.
We can do this, Carin thought.

B ASHA THOUGHT nothing could make him feel worse than the sight of
Marefi warships in Khardish waters, but he was wrong.

He should be used to being wrong by now; he'd had a lot of practice. Despite
his long-standing familiarity with the experience, however, he was not prepared
for how he felt when the ships moored off the coast of the eastern continent and
he had to watch Marefi and Khardish soldiers—all mercenaries, but that hardly
assuaged Basha's revulsion—prepare to invade.

There was a settlement here, bigger than Lahivar from what the scouts had
reported, though still crude to Khardish eyes. A few hundred souls.

Arelashk and his pet Ada'sarshk had informed Basha in very reasonable tones
that they had to take the settlement as a base. Basha had nodded along, listened to
their plans, and then returned to his cabin and vomited.

Oshu had come upon him thus indisposed, and Basha hadn't had the strength
to dissemble. Oshu knew, of course, that Basha was a spy. It wasn't something they
discussed, but the understanding was there. Because of that, Basha had frozen in
surprise when the Triyan man quietly fetched a cloth, wet it at the sink with cool
water, and knelt beside Basha next to the toilet, where he proceeded to gently dab
away the remnants of bile from Basha's clammy cheeks, one steady hand on Basha's
shoulder. Out of the corner of his eye, Basha saw the Triyan's paler brown hand
against his own darker skin, which was all over goosebumps—and not just from
the nausea.

"Did you hear?" Basha asked hoarsely, clearing his throat. He *hated* throwing up.

"Only just," Oshu said. "What will be your role in this?"

"Our role," Basha corrected, then swallowed again as his stomach acid
churned. "We will attend Arelashk and Asurashk once the main attack is over, and
we will observe. I have met these people before—not these exact people, most like-

ly—and they wish for me to continue my observations that we may communicate to the Da'sash Dan the necessity for our actions."

His head swam, and his throat burned with bile.

Oshu was quiet for a moment. Basha realized, belatedly, that Oshu's hand was still on his shoulder. A breach of propriety, and Basha couldn't be bothered to care anymore.

"This is a dangerous game we are playing," Oshu said, his voice as soft as his touch. That rage was back in his eyes, and Basha was glad it wasn't directed at him. "What have you gotten me into?"

The last was said with something resembling fondness.

Basha had to suddenly fight the urge to laugh, a panicked laugh that he couldn't let out but thought might choke him if he didn't.

"A mess," Basha said, his honesty surprising even himself. "But I fear if I hadn't, it would have caught up with us sooner or later, somehow."

"I suspect you are correct." Oshu seemed to notice his hand was still resting comfortably on Basha's shoulder and removed it, looking at it with bemused eyes. "Will they expect us, do you think?"

"I hope they do. I hope they are wise enough to run."

• • • • •

The day dawned too quickly.

Basha had recovered himself with Oshu's help, and he couldn't help but notice that something had shifted between them. Before, Oshu had been a practicality, a necessary risk, but at some point in the intervening moons as they waited in the eastern islets and were met by the brazen face of treason, at some point Oshu and Basha had become comrades.

The fleet moored some ways off the coast, to the north of the settlement, where stark cliffs barred them from gaining land for a full league, but beyond was a secluded cove with evidence of travel up to the headland. Basha had not ventured this far north the last time, and he was surprised at how lush the grasslands were. He was used to entirely different ecosystems in the Khardish archipelago, and as they moved on foot toward the settlement at the tail end of a legion of Marefi warriors, he wished he had time to explore this place under literally any other circumstances. Each step felt like he was profaning something sacred. Perhaps he was.

He tried to remind himself as they moved, the scent of sweat and battle anxiety cutting through the sweetness of spring grasses, that Arelashk's purpose was not Basha's purpose. Basha was here to protect what he could of Khardan, yes, but if he could see some way to prevent harm to the people of this land, he would. His Ada'sarshk would want that. He wondered if she had retaken her name. She would, he thought. The title of Ada'sarshk had always weighed heavy on the woman's shoulders. He had appreciated that about her.

Basha felt like a lamb tossed into the waters with sharks, bleeding.

He walked some short distance behind Arelashk and Asurashk. Their Ada'sarshk was still aboard the ship, awaiting orders, and in his place was a Marefi commander whose name Basha hadn't been told. The man was middle-aged, pale skin turned ruddy pink-brown with exposure to the sun over many cycles, and his yellow hair was receding at the temples, though he still wore it long enough to pull into a tail at his back, secured with a leather tie looped around it at intervals to keep it almost clubbed. The Marefi only allowed men in their armies, and Basha didn't think he had ever been in one place where there was only one woman among a thousand men. He wondered briefly how Asurashk felt.

Oshu was not far behind Basha—as an attendant, he would not be seen speaking to Basha unless spoken to first, but Basha took some comfort from the man's presence. He was so lost in his own thoughts that he missed the runner until he was almost upon them.

"Honored Arelashk," the runner said after gulping a breath. "We are in place."

Basha glanced up sharply, then tried to disguise his quick movement.

"Thank you," Arelashk said. The mage glanced at Asurashk, who wore a thin-lipped smile. "Move when you see the flare."

Move?

Basha fought the rising tide of panic that formed in his chest, pressing against his ribs.

Of course. Basha kept his gaze straight ahead on the back of the line of legionnaires in their cured leather and bloodsteel scale. Of course Arelashk would have sent another legion to advance from the south. Which meant—

"Call a halt," Arelashk said to the Marefi commander, a general, Basha thought.

The commander gave a tight nod and, with one gauntleted fist, beat himself against the chest three times in quick succession, one short, one long, one short.

Basha fought the reflex to jump as the line of legionnaires closest repeated it all at once, and it rippled through the column, getting farther away as everyone beat the rhythm on their breastplates and then sharply stopped where they stood. Basha wondered idly how many times they'd had to drill that to get it right. Probably a lot. The Marefi made sure their armies had a lot of combat practice, and most mercenaries in Maref had plenty of ties to the regulars.

The thought soured his stomach again. Basha tried to keep an earnest and open mind toward the countries that shared his world, but Maref was a sticking point, and for good reason. Their people were touchy, convinced of their own superiority, and rigid to a degree that even Basha's strict regard for propriety could not match. He pushed away the thought of just how much water was over his head in this situation and tried to quiet his nerves.

From where he stood on the headland, Basha could not see much from the middle of such a large crowd of people. The others behind him were mostly aides and other nonmilitary attendants, along with carts of supplies and Marefi oxen to pull them. There weren't many oxen in Khardan, but Basha thought he liked the animals more than the people in their land of origin.

One thing he could see, however, was the skull of some beast not far away in the grass. Someone had kicked it slightly, and scavengers had picked it clean. It was a strange skull, huge, indicative of a large and likely ponderous beast. Basha remembered the animals the people here rode—ihsaln? He couldn't recall—and wondered just how different the fauna here really was.

This was Basha's form of escape from unpleasantness. He fixated on small details that could occupy his mind, removing him somewhat from his body, which was full of discomforting sensations and a reality he could not otherwise avoid. It had been a long time since he had needed to escape his body with such regularity.

He found himself wishing he could move back in the column and stand near Oshu. The Triyan man had become such a comfort for him; had he been alone in all this mess, Basha was not sure he would have survived. There was an intimacy that came with being behind enemy lines with someone, whether you wanted it or not. And Basha was finding, more and more often, that he fell into the former category rather than the latter.

So occupied was he with his dissociative thoughts that he saw Arelashk's open hand rise into the air only a heartbeat before the mage released an arcing flare into the sky that exploded in a massive *whoomph*. Basha was not alone in jumping. Even Asurashk almost leapt backward.

For the barest moment, everyone was illuminated from above as if someone had turned on one of the enormous spotlights in Sahesh's famed amphitheater.

Stunned silence followed it, and not a few of the hard-bitten legionnaires shifted uncomfortably before stilling themselves again.

"Well," said Arelashk. "One learns something new every day."

Basha was no mage, but if that had surprised an Arelashk, he thought that was a very bad sign.

The Marefi commander turned to look at him, ruddy face unreadable. "Explain what just happened."

Basha lost a moment in shock at this man speaking to Arelashk in such a tone, but he recovered quickly enough to feel a small spark of satisfaction at the impudence.

"As I suspected, magic here reacts quite differently than we are used to in our own lands." Arelashk was unfazed, of course, and he spoke with the his easy confidence, addressing the Marefi man as an equal, if not a subordinate. "That level of unpredictability is only common in places of extreme arcane confluence."

"Tell me what that means in plain speech."

"Of course, General Ludo." Arelashk flashed a white-toothed smile and folded his brown hands in front of him as Basha had seen him do so many times. "Imagine one morning you woke up and your muscles had exponentially increased in strength. If you were to jump, you might hit your head on a door frame. If you shook someone's hand, you might break bones."

The general simply stared, face impassive.

"What that means," Arelashk said, hunger detectable in the smug words, "is that I woke up this morning with exponentially stronger muscles."

Asurashk did not look at him, but from where he stood, Basha could see the profile of her face at an angle—and the hint of a smile.

"Tell them to advance," said Arelashk.

Basha waited, his breath coming shallow and quick, unable to escape from his body as the marching footsteps of legionnaires blended with shouts of alarm from the settlement just out of sight ahead, and before long, those shouts turned to screams.

· · · · ·

Many had escaped, Basha told himself.

He did not think this was an oversight—it was the Marefi way. If they wanted to slaughter everyone, they would. But frequently, they allowed people to escape. It was a second form of warfare to them, a war that took place in the mind as much as in the flesh.

Basha had seen people fleeing the settlement astride the ihsaln (he was not certain still of the beasts' names), some running on foot with children in tow, and he had also seen a band of fighters unexpectedly cut a swathe through the legionnaires. Basha allowed himself to feel the accompanying surge of glee that the Marefi would pay some blood price at least for their bloodthirstiness. Let them slake it with their own.

Yet as he and the others were told to advance, Basha simply felt sicker and sicker.

This was no fortified bastion—it was barely a village. Its walls were brick and wood and probably no more than a cycle or two old, which was bizarre. The paths, hardly streets, were little more than dirt.

Rela looked as perplexed as Basha felt for once.

Basha wondered if the mage felt a degree of guilt for invading a settlement that was so obviously poor in contrast to what he was used to, but he was immediately disabused of this notion when Rela's nose wrinkled in distaste.

"Whatever wealth of magic they have, they clearly do not know how to wield it," Rela said.

Asurashk sniffed and murmured something in Triyan that Basha didn't catch; he cursed Oshu's distance and wished there was a chance that he had heard her words to translate.

Rela nodded his assent to whatever Asurashk had said, which probably meant that whatever it was, Basha wouldn't like it.

Bodies littered the ground, but the Marefi legionnaires were already beginning to move them. Likely they would burn them outside the settlement to avoid the onset of disease.

Beyond the smaller dwellings that sat squished together was a compound of sorts in the bowl of rock that housed the settlement, and a commotion arose as Basha watched.

"Aha," Rela said.

Basha hated him a little bit more for the amusement in his voice as some of the legionnaires half-dragged someone in their direction, barking something in Marefi that Basha understood as "This one seems to be their leader" but with much less flattering language.

This person was tall and clearly spitting mad.

Rela pulled out a small book that made Basha's anger flare even hotter—he himself had given that book to Carin when she was learning Khardish, and Rela had stolen it. That was considered a war crime in Khardan. Basha added it to the list.

When Rela spoke, it was obvious his pronunciation was abysmal, but their captive froze, clearly understanding something of it anyway.

"Ysim Arelashk," said Rela, which Basha understood as an introduction. "Dysim . . ."

And you are . . .

"Ysim Valon ve Avarsahla," said the woman. "Dysim sahnbasr."

Make that two women and a thousand men. Basha wondered if anyone else was left alive within the waymake proper. He didn't know what the last word she had said meant, but if her tone was any indication, it wasn't a friendly one.

Basha hoped they wouldn't kill her.

"Restrain her," Rela said. "She will stay with us. Having someone who speaks their language will be helpful."

Basha did his best to keep his face impassive, but inwardly, he shied away from wondering how Rela expected to convince this woman to teach him.

Asurashk moved away with the legionnaires and Valon ve Avarsahla, though Basha realized no convincing was necessary if Asurashk simply reached into Valon's mind and took what she wanted.

He could not stop the shiver that shook its way up the length of his spine.

I am sorry, Valon, he thought. *If there is some way to help you, I will.*

The rest of the day passed in a blur. Basha and Oshu were shown to a small hut near the compound and left to their own devices. The walls were so thin, Basha could not so much as open his mouth without someone able to hear him. There was a small pallet in the corner, barely wide enough for two people, and bits and bobs of someone else's life were scattered about the place. A low table held some basic carving tools, reeds, a half-finished woven basket, and a jug of water that was as clean and sweet as Basha had ever tasted.

Oshu picked up the basket with shaking hands, then put it down, then picked it up again. He sat down on the low stool beside the table. His fingers reached out and took hold of a reed, and to Basha's surprise, the Triyan man began to expertly weave it into the basket.

"Not a butcher nor baker, yet a reed basket maker," Basha murmured.

"Something to keep the hands busy when the mind will not stop," Oshu replied quietly.

Oshu met Basha's eyes, and for a moment, Basha saw them as they had been, ringed in kohl the way the Triyan people did, the way Basha himself had asked Oshu to stop when he gave him a new name and bid him follow into the unknown.

"I am sorry," Basha said, the words spilling out of his mouth before he could stop them.

"You have nothing to be sorry about." Oshu continued his weaving, following the pattern the previous weaver had charted.

"Do I not?"

Basha's voice sounded vulnerable to his own ears. He almost did not recognize himself in the words, but they tumbled out much as his apology had. Traitorous. If anyone was listening, their own ears would be perking up to eavesdrop.

Oshu was quiet for a long moment. Finally, he sighed, replacing the basket on the table and rising to his feet.

He came to Basha then, moving closer than was really decorous, but Basha did not move away when he felt Oshu's warmth encroach upon his own, and he did not move away when Oshu took his hands in his own.

"You do not," Oshu said, so softly even Basha could barely hear him.

Something dislodged in Basha's chest that he hadn't realized was stuck there, blocking him, a barrier against . . . something.

Oshu let go of one hand only to raise his fingers to Basha's jaw. "May I?"

In answer, Basha pressed his cheek into the man's hand, feeling the wave of relief and yearning ripple out from that point of light contact.

He did not know what was coming next, in what atrocity they might find themselves complicit, but for the moment, all that mattered was the look of tenderness in Oshu's eyes and the knowledge that, at the very least, they were not alone here.

As CARIN'S absence stretched out, Clar found herself more and more agitated by the day. Her skin felt stretched out too, as though there were something growing inside her but no way to let it out. She thought she might burst if this went on any longer.

Ryd put up with her admirably; he continued to show her around Lahivar, teaching her what he could of Northlander customs and language, generally being a very good friend to both Clar and Jenin.

To her surprise, she also grew close to Hoyu, the Khardish woman who had miraculously arrived with Carin on the Night of Reflection. The woman was serious at first glance, her short stature standing out as much as her dark skin, but the more Clar spent time with her, the more she glimpsed flashes of wry humor, even playfulness.

Revive moon waned into Quicken with no word from Carin or Culy, nor from Ras in Ryhnas Lu Sesim, and Sart had insisted that no news was good news after the ialtag—another miracle!—had warned them of ships approaching.

Clar thought her vocabulary had nearly tripled sometimes since arriving in Lahivar. Words like ships and city, army and ialtag, every one of them a sign of a swiftly changing world.

She was sitting in Lahivar's central plaza when the shouting started.

One of the newly minted farmers came running, and far beyond hyr, Clar could see ihstal approaching at a full lope. Scores of ihstal.

Her heart suddenly trying to leap free of her chest, her brain made sense of the farmer's words a moment too late.

"Get Sart!" sy yelled again, and Clar dropped the sock she was mending and ran.

She hoped Sart was still on this side of the river. Clar dodged other villagers, including a baffled Ryd, calling over her shoulder, "Someone needs help!"

Clar realized dimly that she was leaving a trail of chaos in her wake, much as she had the morning of Jenin's non-murder. She pushed the thought out of her mind so hard that if it were a stone on a lake, it would have skipped upon the surface to the opposite shore and vanished.

She found Sart already moving her way, a look of alarm on the woman's face. She must have heard the yelling.

"Ihstal . . . coming," Clar managed to gasp out around heaving breaths. "Lots of them."

Sart broke into a run, and ignoring her own lungs, Clar turned on her heel and followed.

What had been a serene morning of domestic mundanity had transformed into something—something out of Clar's nightmares. The smell of frightened ihstal melded with the tinny tang of people's own anxious sweat, and layered over that was an unmistakable scent.

Blood.

Sart was barking orders, and villagers of Lahivar scurried this way and that, running to the river for water and into roundhomes for whatever clean cloths could be spared, whatever healing herbs could be grabbed.

Ryd was there, in the midst of everything, as capable as Sart as he helped people get wounded from the backs of ihstal. Some of the animals were wounded too, and they stood quivering or dropped to cushing if they could, feet folded under them.

Clar couldn't move.

Some part of her knew she should help, but all that drew her eye was red. Red against brown skin, red against brown dirt, red against brown leather, red spilling out like life itself to water the earth.

"Easy," said a voice behind her, and Clar felt a hand take hers and pull her away, around the wall of a roundhome, out of sight of the blood.

"Sit," said the voice. Hoyu.

The Khardish woman disappeared and reappeared moments later, or perhaps a lot of time later, pushing a stout wooden cup of water into Clar's hands.

Clar tried to raise it to her mouth, but the water kept sloshing up over the edge. Oh. She was shaking.

Hoyu's dark brown fingers cupped her own, steadying her enough that she managed to sip from the cup, only spilling a little.

"Again," said Hoyu.

Clar obeyed.

She could still hear shouting, groans of pain, and the whistle of an ihstal, so high-pitched it could only be panic.

She jumped, and Hoyu steadied her again.

"What do you feel?" Hoyu asked. "In your hands. In your skin."

Clar's eyes felt unfocused, but she managed to meet Hoyu's, confused.

The Khardish woman looked frustrated, the way she did when she didn't know how to say something in Tuan yet. "Your fingers. What do they feel?"

It was a strange question, but Hoyu seemed intent on an answer, so Clar concentrated on her hands. The carved wooden cup retained its grain, swirls and patterns, even the small nub of a knot the carver had worked into it.

"Smooth and rigid," she got out. "Cool from the water."

"Good." Hoyu looked pleased. "What do you feel in your neck?"

Another strange question. Her neck was taut, or maybe *condensed* was a better word. "Tight."

Why couldn't she make more words? Clar's mouth was suddenly very dry again. She took another sip of water with Hoyu's help.

"Breathe with me," Hoyu said. "In—one, two, three, four. Out—one, two, three, four."

Clar obeyed.

"When you breathe out next time, pretend you are—freeing . . . letting go all of the tight in your neck."

Again she breathed in while Hoyu counted, and again she breathed out, unsure if she was doing it right, but she felt something soften where it had been hard and tense.

"Ba," murmured Hoyu, and Clar recognized the word for good in Khardish.

They sat like that for a while, Clar on a stump and Hoyu cross-legged in front of her after a time, and each time Clar's heart started racing again, they breathed together.

Sometime later, the sounds of chaos ebbed, and Clar came back to herself bit by bit. With the return, she looked guiltily at Hoyu.

"Forgive me," she said to the older woman. "I don't know what happened to me."

"I do," Hoyu said. "There is nothing for forgiving."

Hoyu's face grew somber, and Clar could see that she was thinking about what she wanted to say.

"I do not know how you say it," she said after a long pause. "In my language we say it is a pain-well. It is like a hole you cover up with something but cannot fill. Sometimes you can fall in. It can be hard to get back out. I have seen it in Carin, and I know it in myself."

Oh.

"Grief?" Clar asked tentatively, but Hoyu shook her head.

"It is more than that. Grief is a well that—that fills in over time. It will never be the same as it was, but it can heal. This other is"—Hoyu made an exasperated sound—"sharper. It pulls. Because once you fell in the well, and when you were down there, terrible things happened. You know what is down there, and when you fall in again, it is like the first time again, even if that is not true. It feels true."

There was a word for that. It wasn't one used often in Haveranth, but it was one thing Clar's family had imparted to her, in more than one way.

"Trauma," she said softly. "It is the shock and pain of bad things that happened that one could not escape. It . . . changes you."

"Yes," Hoyu said. "Trauma."

Clar took a shaky breath. "How did you know what to do?"

"I was taught much as you just were," Hoyu said softly. "Back before I was the Ada'sahrsk. I was the only survivor of a fishing boat caught in a terrible storm."

Clar stared at her. "And you became a—ship leader?"

It was her turn to fumble for words.

Hoyu smiled, a grim smile. "I did."

"How?" The question almost fell out of Clar's mouth.

"I made friends with the wind," Hoyu said.

Before Clar could ask anything else, Jenin appeared around the edge of the roundhome where they sat. Ryd's, Clar realized. She'd barely known where she was.

If Jenin was surprised to find them there, sy didn't show it. "Ah," was all sy said. "Sart was looking for the both of you. There is . . . news."

"What happened?" Clar asked. She preferred to hear it from Jenin, here away from curious eyes.

Glancing once at Hoyu, Jenin sighed. "The Khardish attacked Ryhnas Lu Sesim to the north. They attacked from two sides and slaughtered half the people there. Those who made it here were the injured who rode ihstal because they could not walk, but there are others following on foot who had no ihstal."

"The Khardish," Hoyu said.

The woman's fingers worried at the hem of her tunic, the only sign of movement other than the rise and fall of her chest with her breath.

"Ras can tell you more," Jenin said.

Clar's head turned at that. "Ras?"

Ras was the Silencer who had traveled north with Carin and Ryd. Clar had met him once, cycles past in Haveranth. She had not seen him since they had arrived in the Northlands.

Jenin simply nodded, beckoning at her to follow.

Hoyu looked like she would rather be doing anything else besides following the hyrsin back toward the plaza, but she came anyway, sticking close to Clar's side.

Clar spotted Ras in an instant as they drew close enough. He was sitting on a reed mat that was stained red with blood, grimacing as he half-reclined on one elbow, his midsection bare and bandaged at his waist.

He was talking to Sart despite being in obvious pain, and she crouched next to him, saying nothing. She glanced up at Clar and Hoyu when she heard their footsteps.

"Ah," Ras said, looking up at Clar. "I remember you."

He said it without affect—no hesitation or awkwardness. A simple declaration.

Clar nodded once, but it was Hoyu who spoke.

"These Khardish," she said. "Were they like me?"

Ras was already shaking his head. "No. Or mostly not." He winced as he shifted his weight to his other hip and took a shuddering breath. "An army of men, mostly with pale pink skin."

"What did they wear?" Hoyu asked urgently.

Sart was watching the Khardish woman with interest.

Ras glanced once at Sart, then shrugged, which he seemed to immediately regret, as Clar saw his body spasm with pain again.

"Leather tunics with red metal pounded over them. They did not fight with weapons I know, except they all had swords. They used strange bows, but mostly they deflected our arrows with shields, and they used something heavy on their hands. They killed up close." Ras's face was grim at the recollection, and Sart placed one hand gently on his shoulder.

Hoyu was pacing. "Marefi," she muttered, then said something in Khardish that Clar would bet was a curse.

"Marefi," Sart repeated after a moment, understanding dawning on her face. "They were not Khardish?"

Hoyu shook her head, a sharp, jerking motion. She repeated the Khardish curse under her breath, then made a noise of rage.

"Rela has—Asurashk." Hoyu stopped pacing, then glanced wryly at Clar and took a deep breath Clar could count with, so she did, breathing out in tandem with the Khardish woman. Hoyu started over. "Asurashk, who you met. She is working with a man called Arelashk. Rela. A—magic user."

"A mage," Sart supplied.

"A mage," Hoyu agreed. "He must be working with Maref."

"What is Maref?" Ras asked.

"A country beyond the sea," Sart murmured.

Hoyu nodded. "They are known for taking what is not theirs. Did they take people? Alive."

Ras hesitated. "I do not know. Many of us fled, but Valon stayed behind to make sure everyone got out."

Sart grunted at that, anger painting her face along with something Clar thought was fear.

"Rela would want someone alive, a leader," Hoyu said.

"Then we should presume he has one," said Sart. "What are we going to do about it?"

THERE WAS nearly a cycle remaining before the Reinvocation, yet Dyava felt time slipping through his fingers like the current of the Bemin River. He spent his days and nights with Lyari now, tending only to his own affairs insofar as they kept him fed and warm, though with summer coming on, the latter was less of a worry. He set aside his stores as usual, but he did everything in a hurry.

Lyari was teaching him magic.

She seemed amused when he said he'd only ever been able to see magic before; apparently, you couldn't just see the stuff without being able to interact with it, but Dyava's parents had left enough holes in his education that he wasn't surprised they'd concealed this information.

Since Dyava's return from Cantoranth, Lyari had redoubled her efforts in situating herself as the only true leader and soothsayer in the Hearthland, and honestly, Dyava thought that even if she sat on her hands in the hearth-home for the next sixteen or seventeen moons, she wouldn't have trouble succeeding in that effort.

The other villagers were on edge—that much Dyava had expected. What he hadn't expected was the anger. It burbled over like a pot left to boil when too full, hissing and spitting when it touched the fire. Wells were failing, but the villagers dug new ones and organized supplies to make sure everyone had enough water.

Crops were set upon by insects, then some sort of disease, then struck by lightning in a freak spring storm. Villagers gathered what they could, salvaged what was able to be salvaged, counted the turns remaining in the growing season, subtracted a couple out of expectation of an earlier winter, and planted whatever was suitable to remain. Fields that had lain fallow were sown.

Everyone was exhausted, and though Dyava's work was more mental than physical, it seemed to him that the moon of Toil had come far earlier than it ought to have. Revive was waning and would soon give way to Quicken, with Toil still beyond that and Bide to boot.

Dyava lay in bed one morning with Lyari, a stolen moment in the face of yet another day of labor, and he was surprised to feel content.

When he said as much, Lyari raised herself up on one elbow propped on her pillow and gave him a sardonic half smile.

"I'm not sure if I should be flattered or indignant," she said.

Dyava's face grew warm. "It's just"—he returned her smile a bit sheepishly—"here we are, planning to reinvoke a spell that could very well fail because the hearthstones are breaking up north, people are falling ill, everything is falling apart, and I am . . . happier than I've ever been. That's the surprise."

Lyari sobered, the small crease he had grown so fond of appearing between her eyes the way it did when she was feeling particularly pensive.

"The spell will not fail," she said softly. "I swear it to you."

Just one cycle ago, the declaration would have put ice in his spine, but now Dyava hoped simply that she was right.

That soured his mood; was he really hoping she would *succeed*?

"How?" he asked, just as softly.

"Ah," she said, raising a finger to the side of her nose conspiratorially. "That would be telling."

"Yes, that's why I asked," Dyava teased, throwing one arm over her waist and tugging her against him.

"I will find a new anchor," she said after a burst of a giggle. "Tie the spell to a new focus. We will have no need of the hearthstones if I am right."

"And if you are wrong?"

Lyari flung her leg up over his hip, which left certain parts of him demonstrably closer to certain parts of her—something he was not displeased about.

"Dyava," Lyari said, looking at him through her eyelashes, "I am never wrong."

With that, she swiftly turned him onto his back, sliding her leg all the way over him, and Dyava lost himself in the moment and in the heat that built where their bodies joined.

· · · · ·

Sometime later, they managed to pry themselves out of bed and make themselves presentable to the other villagers. Their days had fallen into routine, and Dyava liked that. He and Lyari moved around one another in her roundhome, like wheels turning together, and it was easy to let that flow carry him away on its currents. But every so often, something would sneak up on him.

He had gotten used to thinking of the roundhome as Lyari's, of pushing Carin out of it entirely.

It was small, innocuous things that did it. Today it was the polished maha table when his thumb brushed against one of the intricately carved runes along its edge.

He sat there for a moment, frozen with the pad of his thumb in the groove.

Lyari was in the other room, digging for scrolls again, and when she came out, Dyava was still stuck there.

However, she didn't notice. "It happened again," she said, snapping Dyava out of it.

"What happened?" He jerked his hand away from the rune as if it were a hot ember instead of smooth, cool wood.

"Someone has been in my scrolls. Not the sensitive ones this time, but the other ones."

That made Dyava freeze again, but this time not because of Carin.

A cycle ago, a lifetime ago, Lyari had suspected Calyria of coming into her roundhome during the times Lyari was out, and Dyava had tried to keep his cousin occupied to rule her out as a possible culprit. But then Calyria and Jenin had vanished on the longest night, and it seemed nothing had happened since.

At least until now.

"I had truly thought it was Calyria," Lyari said, sounding utterly dumbfounded. At Dyava's look, she hurried to add, "I did not *wish* it to be her, but since it did not continue after she disappeared—"

"It's okay," Dyava said, interrupting her and giving her a reassuring smile. "I honestly don't know what I thought. You had a right to be suspicious, I think. She and Jenin most certainly had secrets."

Lyari seemed to relax, her shoulders lowering a bit as if she had just noticed them creeping up around her ears.

"If it wasn't her, though . . ." Dyava trailed off. "Do you have any other ideas?"

"Not a one." Lyari came and sat opposite Dyava at the table, placing her fingertips on top of its smooth surface to make tents with her thumbs. She drummed them against the wood for a moment. "It had to be since yesterday, though."

They had spent much of the day in the village hearth-home, so it would be difficult to narrow down a time beyond midday to dusk. Just about everyone in the village was out of their sight at some point during that time.

Dyava thought of the ward his parents had placed on the secret tunnel that connected their home to his, where they had hidden Jenin. He hadn't helped make it, but he'd had to be familiar with the strands of magic woven to create it.

"You have an idea," Lyari said with a small smile.

"I don't know if it will work." Dyava got up and went into the pantry, taking a jar at random from among the many pots and containers of jams and spices Lyari kept there.

He concentrated on what he wanted. Magic came easier to him now, but still a sheen of perspiration broke out on his forehead at the complexity of what he was attempting. The simplest things concealed the most intricate workings. Life and potential, a mirror into a moment in time—if his parents' ward had worked by reflecting back a time before the tunnel existed, maybe his could reflect the moment someone touched the ward.

He also knew how to conceal the weaves, invert them back upon themselves, hiding them from magic users. *That* had startled Lyari, and she had yet to be able to replicate it.

Convinced it was an admirable attempt, Dyava emerged from the pantry with the jar. Lyari watched him, amusement warring with curiosity.

"If you think dusting it with flour would work to see if anyone leaves marks in it, I think our sneak may be a bit beyond that," she said.

Dyava set the jar on the table in front of her. "Open it."

She raised an eyebrow, but reached out to do exactly that. Dyava felt the tug of his magic unraveling, but Lyari didn't seem to notice. An image of her face from the perspective of the jar in her hands came unbidden to his mind, giving him a momentary surge of vertigo as he saw her from two different directions at once.

"Was it giving you trouble?" she asked dubiously, handing the jar back to him. "Or did you just want some redberry jam?"

"Neither," he said. "You didn't feel anything when you opened it?"

"No," she said. Curiosity lit her eyes. "Did you do something to it?"

Triumph lit inside him like fire touching pimia oil. "I did indeed."

"Did it work?"

Dyava grinned. "Yes."

It didn't take long for Dyava to repeat his process on the more sensitive items Lyari wanted to keep an eye on. He tried not to get his hopes up; it had been moons since this person had tried to sneak into the roundhome, so it would be silly to expect their plan to bear fruit quickly. Even so, as he and Lyari left the roundhome to go about their days, Dyava couldn't help but be proud of himself.

It was a warm day, a day so lovely he could almost forget the tribulations of the previous few cycles. There was much to do at this stage in the season, so Dyava spent the afternoon in his one small field, pulling out weeds that were taking root around his vegetables and tilling his compost pile with the remains of the turn's food. Tomorrow would be a feast day, as it always was the fifth day of the turn, and while things were not so bountiful as they had been, the Hearthlanders were still very lucky to have more than they needed. Feast days had slowly become less exuberant, but they were still pleasant for the company and offered a bit of levity. If nothing else, it was a chance to see the village's only baby. Good luck getting more than a glimpse, though. That baby was by far the most precious person in the entire Hearthland for now.

Dyava was stopped with his spade lodged in the dirt, mopping his sweating brow with a towel and trying not to turn the sweat into mud with his soil-covered hands, when an image flashed into his mind. The same awkward angle as he had seen Lyari's face from the jar, but it was not Lyari's face this time.

He frantically looked toward Lyari's roundhome, but it was just out of sight from his field. Not wanting to be seen running, he stopped to wash his hands at the pump outside his own roundhome, and then he turned tail and walked briskly in the direction of the village hearth-home, which would take him past the place he really wanted to see.

It couldn't have taken more than twenty heartbeats for him to scrub his hands in the cold water, but by the time he got within view of Lyari's door, there was no one visible. Suppressing the urge to look back as he passed it, he carried on to the fire where Tamat would be tending hys grill as usual.

Dyava made small talk with the hyrsin, accepting some curried mutton in flatbread and making the correct noises at the correct intervals to appear engaged, but he kept his peripheral vision glued tightly to the roundhome at the edge of his line of sight.

When he was done eating—he hadn't even tasted it—he bid Tamat farewell, deciding that if he couldn't catch the culprit coming out of the roundhome, he would do the next best thing.

His feet took him there without even trying. The route was so familiar, he could have sleepwalked it on his hands. He had walked this way countless times in his youth, though it had come to an abrupt halt at High Lights two cycles past.

When he heard the clang of hammer on metal, his feet stuttered to a stop. His heart seemed to beat in rhythm with the strokes. Dyava made himself continue on, mind whirring through the possible explanations.

Sure enough, Rina was there, hammering diligently at something he couldn't identify on sight. Her back was to him, and she was close enough to the roar of the forge that there was little chance she had heard him approach. Dyava turned away, thoughts racing like wildfire in last cycle's dried grass.

Rina hadn't seen him, but he had seen her.

Of all the people Dyava expected to be tinkering with Lyari's things, Rina was last on the list. Yet he could still see her face, a nervous eye turned away from what she held, burned into his memory.

Carin's mother was the one Lyari sought.

The old fear crept back upon him like an enemy so familiar it may as well be a friend.

He didn't know if he could tell Lyari.

THE MOON and her sister would not be seen tonight, Carin knew. Revive had faded, and tomorrow Quicken would be born, but as she and Culy made their way toward the growing pull on their consciousness, Carin thought grimly to herself that the moon's rebirth this time brought with it some extra layer of omens. Her heart quickened, her footsteps quickened, her breath quickened. Time quickened around them.

Culy felt it too—Carin could tell without asking. They had left the ihstal behind at the small waymake, and Carin was certain the animals would follow the gentle urging to flee if anyone tried to take them.

The news from Lahivar and Ryhnas Lu Sesim had reached them as they traveled northeast, and Carin had felt a grip of fear almost overcome her knowing that Rela and Asurashk were within a pair of turns' ride away. Had they been just a day or two later, they might have seen the advancing Marefi forces.

Culy had been trying to contact Valon ever since, but sy had been unsuccessful. Though Jenin said Hoyu thought she had to still be alive, Carin remembered too well the heaviness in her body, the drugged and dream-locked sleep Rela and Asurashk had induced in her. Valon was likely beyond their reach for now, maybe forever.

So they hurried.

The spirit sensed the urgency. They were so close, so close. Carin could feel the presence of the stone in a way she hadn't expected. Culy described it as a thread tugging hyr toward it, but Carin could almost hear it, like a once-familiar song sung in a quiet voice carried on the wind.

The land here spread out, barely rippling as it turned into taiga that would turn into tundra and then pure ice in the farthest north. Kat's people lived beyond the taiga. Carin shivered at the thought of it.

There was little to no break in the grasses, still squirming toward the sun after the long winter. What would this land look like in a cycle's time? At the next High Harvest?

The questions died in her mind, and Carin stared ahead at a lump in the ground. It was barely even that; nothing distinguished it from the surrounding land, but Carin could feel the hearthstone there, calling to her.

The water spirit sloshed to and fro in Carin's consciousness, like a bottle tossed from hand to hand. Fretful, she thought.

Culy felt it too and turned to give Carin a tight smile. "Are you ready, my heart?"

Carin nearly teetered on her feet at those words—the effect Culy had on her was still difficult for her to believe—but even as she swayed, hys presence steadied her too. A strange duality.

"Yes," she said simply. "It's long past time."

Something felt different here than it had at the first stone, and despite her readiness, she hesitated.

"Was it like this with the other stone?" she asked. "With Wyt."

"What do you mean?"

"Do you not feel it?" Perhaps her teetering was not simply lovesickness after all. She tried to put words to it. "Like a potter's wheel when the pot goes off balance on one side."

Culy looked at the lump before them with consternation. "I believe you're right." Sy looked sharply at Carin. "Very astute."

She gave hyr a rueful chuckle. "I almost blamed it on you making me swoon."

Culy's burst of sudden laughter pealed through the air like a struck bell. "I hope I don't make you feel like you're about to spin out of balance."

"Only in the best way," she murmured, then grew solemn again. "We should be cautious here."

"That would be true regardless," Culy agreed. "The forces here are primeval and have been disrupted. Though of all of us, you and I are best equipped to handle any eventuality."

"And if we die, at least it'll be someone else's problem," Carin said brightly.

"That's the spirit." Culy winked—actually winked—to punctuate hys own pun, and this time the sudden laughter was Carin's.

Some of the tension faded as they approached the stone. Carin couldn't even see it. The sun was behind a cloud, but there was enough haze that there were no sharp shadows, only that strange unlight of a day that can't quite make up its mind what it wants to be.

Culy pulled hys staff from hys back and held it out to Carin. They had talked about this on their journey north. The staff could help protect them if something went wrong, though Carin still didn't fully understand how.

They used their combined magic to slice through the sod and layer of peat. The stone was surprisingly close to the surface; it didn't take much to expose it to the air. Who knew how long it had remained covered there, how many cycles or ages it had simply lain under its blanket of earth and growing things.

With the sod pulled back, the stone's surface revealed the rune *pey*, like a scale filled to weigh its contents. If Culy was right, this was the fertility stone. Carin wasn't sure what the rune of applied force had to do with fertility, but she also hadn't been sure what the rune of will had to do with illness and health, so she supposed it was open to interpretation.

She and Culy knelt side by side in front of the stone. The scale was upright for them, its stylized bowl containing what she knew was meant to be a measure of pimia oil represented by a vertical line crossed perpendicularly at intervals to form a pear shape—or it would if one connected the open ends. It was symbolic as well as literal. Pimia oil weighed relatively little in a bottle, but it was one of the most precious commodities Carin knew. An accelerant for flame and a ward against water alike, something deceptively small could have weight far beyond how hard it was to heft in one hand. Or, of course, what seemed to just be a rock could be the focus of an ancient spell draining the life from the land and dooming an entire people to starvation and misery.

Perhaps the most appropriate symbol after all, this one.

Carin's hand slid down the shaft of the staff, meeting Culy's in the middle. Already she could feel the magic in the halm rising to meet their will. With a nod to her lover, Carin opened her mind and laid her free hand upon the stone just as sy did.

If touching the spirit inside the water stone had felt like plunging down and down and down and down into the deepest oceanic abyss, touching the fertility spirit felt like getting torn apart at a level so infinitesimal Carin could not conceive of it.

Culy's hand tensed against hers, and her own arm went rigid against the stone, her elbow locking in place. The spirit—the one that was a part of her—exploded like a water spout in panic, and it was all Carin could do to maintain contact with the stone.

"It's okay," she managed to say aloud, not knowing why she chose those particular words. "We're not here to hurt you. We're here to set you free."

The water spirit jumped guiltily at that, and immediately the water spout splashed into stillness like it had never been. Instead, it swelled within her, reaching out tentatively for the chaos that roared around them.

Absurdly—unhelpfully—the image that sprang to mind for Carin was of a clucker about to lay an egg, its frequent and increasingly alarmed squawks that were such a familiar sound for everyone, made all the stranger by the fact that the bird would not be darting every which way while making them. No, like this stone that had lain buried for so long, the clucker would simply be sitting somewhere, kicking up a racket that could be heard all the way on the other side of the village or waymake.

"I'm going to break it," Carin said. She hadn't realized her jaw was clenched so tightly, and it almost hurt to release it.

The tiniest movement of acquiescence from Culy was all she needed.

Her heart gave a stuttering stop for one impossible, too-quiet moment in the midst of the stone's gibbering cacophony. It went on long enough that Carin was afraid they had failed, that this stone would not be broken.

But then her heart gave a hiccupping leap she *felt* inside her ribcage, and the stone jumped beneath her palm, and it cracked down the middle.

With the water stone, the force had thrown them all backward and knocked them out cold. The illness stone had somehow burned away all of Culy's *hair*. But Carin was not prepared for the way the ground leapt beneath them as the sharp report of the stone breaking somehow reached her ears after Carin thought it should have.

She and Culy were pitched to the ground, thrown against each other in a tangle of limbs and halm staff, and the earth rippled the way the waves had underneath Hoyu's ship.

Dimly, she remembered Culy telling her about earthquakes. She hadn't fully appreciated at the time what a horrible feeling it would be to have the ground lurch under oneself.

An enormous gust of wind blasted outward from the stone, throwing Carin's hair into her face and Culy's alike.

The water spirit had obviously bonded with her when she broke its prison, but the spirit trapped in Wyt's fortress had not done so with Culy or anyone else present. Carin didn't know what she expected from this one, but every time she tried to scramble back to a sitting position, she found it impossible with the gale whipping around the grassland. She'd be lucky if she had skin left.

And then, suddenly, it was passed. Carin's head spun as she lay sprawled with Culy, still half-entangled and more than half-dazed. The water spirit gave a helpful burble that Carin thought was meant to be encouraging, and she tried to sit up, focusing on her hand as the world spun around her like she had been spinning circles until dizzy.

Or like she'd had far too much to drink.

"Oh, no," she said and half-crawled, half-sprang away from Culy before she lost her last meal to the wind-whipped grasses.

Carin hung her head, miserable, distantly aware that poor Culy was in a similar state. Her stomach heaved a few more times, and she spit upon the grass, hating the way her saliva flooded into her mouth. They hadn't even brought the waterskins, which she now regretted.

She collapsed back to the earth a moment later, barely managing to aim herself away from the mess she'd made, and it took all her strength to roll farther away so the smell wouldn't give her stomach any further ideas.

On her back, staring up at the sky, the light had changed. Carin didn't have the faintest idea how long she and Culy had been here, but it had been long enough that the haze had burned off. Now the sky was dotted with fluffy clouds that were far too cheerful. The sun was far too bright. Carin groaned and pushed herself to a sitting position.

Culy had beaten her there, but not by much. Sy held hys staff like it was the only thing keeping hyr from landing on hys face in the grass all over again, and when sy looked up at Carin, Carin barely managed a wan smile.

"Let's . . . not do that again." Talking was a bad idea. Carin swallowed again and regretted that too.

As her vision slowly cleared, she took in their surroundings.

"Culy—" she breathed.

The land around them had *changed*.

• • • • •

Her nausea forgotten, Carin managed to push herself to her feet and stand. The water spirit gave another happy burble as if to say *See? It's fine.*

Where shortly before there had been empty grassland, still groggy from winter, now there was a lush meadow spreading out around them. What had only been grass was now visibly *moving*, and the sight was so strange Carin felt a flash of fear as she watched the plants around her encircling the fractured stone, reaching toward the sun, leaves unfurling, drinking in water from somewhere below, buds forming and opening before her eyes.

She heard Culy's shocked intake of air as sy saw it too, and Carin managed a pair of lurching steps back to hyr before dropping back down to sit beside hyr in awe.

"I have never seen anything—I mean—" Carin gave up.

Culy reached out and took her hand, twining hys fingers with hers. "Yes."

Together they sat like that as the sun slowly dipped toward the western horizon. There was little she could say about it. When she thought about fertility, she had erroneously assumed it meant only the baby-making type, but that had been folly. Of course there were other types of fertility—or the same type, just affecting things far beyond people alone.

She had watched the simple difference the water had made for the land, and if it had created such changes and bounty before this stone's breaking, Carin could not imagine what would happen next.

"Hello," Culy said, and for a moment, Carin thought sy was speaking to her, but almost before her head stopped turning in hys direction, she felt a new presence.

It was calmer now, this spirit. If Carin had to give the feeling she got from it a name, she would say it was almost bashful.

Like with her own companion, she felt gratitude rolling off of it, and at her acknowledgement, the buds immediately around the stone burst into bloom.

Carin could not help the gasp that escaped her at the sight of hundreds of tiny wildflowers—minuscule lavender starflowers and bright yellow mustard flowers, shy pink baby's blush and speckles of white breath-of-spring, sunny sit-with-me and breathless daisies, all against the vibrant blue of the grass.

She felt the presence of the spirit swell like the rising of the breeze around them, and it brought with it the scent of flowers and sun-warmed meadow grass.

But just as suddenly, the spirit's gratitude and warmth grew quiet and wary. Not of Carin and Culy, but of something else. It pressed against her, against the water spirit within her, and with a surge of hope and countless cycles of lost time, it plunged into the earth and was gone.

Or not gone. Both Carin and Culy turned as the spirit's presence moved away from them toward the southeast, and it left the ripples of changing grass in its wake.

"What did we just see?" Carin murmured.

Culy was quiet for a long time before sy responded. "This place was once the site of a temple, a holy place, built to mark where the gods were said to have created the world."

"The Tuanye?" she asked, dubious.

"No, long before then. It was that legend that brought the Tuanye here, to some degree. But I did not know what was true when I was born, and I do not know what is true now." Culy took a deep breath in and exhaled. "The temple was beautiful, though. A place of quiet reflection where choirs came to sing, and their voices would blend together and fill the chamber with sound so pure and resonant you could feel it in your skin."

Carin stared. She didn't know what a temple was or even what a choir was, but the thought of such a thing felt like magic all over again.

"Perhaps someday something like that shall exist again," she said quietly, fighting in vain against the yearning that filled her all of the sudden before giving into it and letting herself want.

There was a sense of possibility with Culy that Carin had never before experienced. She had somehow seen more of the world than sy had in some ways, but in other ways, Culy remembered wonders she could hardly comprehend. But sitting there, new grass and moss already draping the edges of the newly broken stone, filling in the crack down the center, Carin felt part of something new. Something ancient, something shaping the world. It felt right to have borne witness to life springing up around this stone, to share that memory with someone so dear to her. When she turned to Culy, sy was already watching her, and without a word, sy reached for her and enfolded her in hys arms, and together they lay on a carpet of lush new life and celebrated their own.

AT THE edge of the west, in that hollowed out corner of a cove, Basha was hiding in his hut.

It was a ridiculous thing, really, but he was not about to go roaming around. Though he had no magic himself, Basha knew a curse when he saw one.

Nearly everyone in this settlement—which they had learned was called Ryhnas Lu Sesim, a name Valon ve Avarsahla stubbornly refused to translate for her captors—had fallen ill. Valon remained hale and hardy, and Basha could not but admire her for it. While she did not laugh at Arelashk as he demanded in his broken Tuan to know what was affecting the Marefi and Khardish people, she may as well have, and try as Asurashk might, Valon's will was every bit as strong within her hard head as without.

Basha had been asked to speak with her once, and he had tried. She looked at him keenly when he spoke his few words of Tuan and mentioned Carin. That was the extent of his success. If he were her, he wouldn't trust him either.

By some miracle, Basha and Oshu had not fallen ill, but by their own agreement, they pretended to.

They spent their days with Oshu teaching Basha Triyan and their nights in exquisite torture, the heat of their bodies side by side but not daring to be half as close as they wanted to be. It wasn't just the proximity of two Marefi legions but the place itself. It felt wrong to want to make love in a place where people had been murdered. Basha did not make a distinction between war and murder, especially when one side so vastly outnumbered the other it was like stomping on a rodent that was only going about their business.

He hated that analogy as soon as he thought it. People weren't vermin. And frankly, neither were rodents. Everyone deserved to live in peace.

He wasn't even sure Oshu was feeling the same thing he was, that beautiful heat, that belly-deep desire. Basha was very confused.

But on the fourth day of the second turn since their arrival, a heavy-handed knock came at the door.

Both Oshu and Basha leapt to their feet, though they were clothed and seated next to each other on stools at the table, and Basha called out, "Enter."

He did not expect Arelashk himself to walk through the door. The mage looked . . . in poor health.

"Honored Arelashk. One's presence is unexpected." Basha adjusted his stance to show proper deference and saw Oshu doing the same to an even greater degree.

"I gather that." Arelashk coughed into his elbow, a horrible, wet sound.

Basha suddenly wished he had a shower.

He waited to be spoken to, and once Arelashk finished coughing, the man straightened in the doorway. "We will be moving on shortly. Make ready."

"Yes, honored Arelashk." Basha nodded his acceptance of the change in plans, but inside, his mind was racing.

Surely, Arelashk had not come here himself just to say something so small. That was a servant's job.

"You will speak to Valon again before we depart. She will come with us, but this must happen before we leave." Arelashk looked about ready to fall over as he stood.

"If the Arelashk pleases, when will we be departing?" Basha asked, his eyes downcast.

"Before the sun sets. This is a dismal place. Do what you must."

With that, Arelashk turned and left. Basha stared after him.

He waited until the mage was well and truly gone before turning back to Oshu. He couldn't relax, not now. Arelashk would not tell him more than that in front of Oshu, but clearly the mage was ill and suspected it had something to do with where they were.

"We have little to prepare, but—" Basha began, but Oshu cut him off.

"Go. I will make ready."

With that, Oshu turned his back as if to tell Basha to go away, and Basha stifled his fond smile as he opened the door Arelashk had just closed.

They were not far from the compound, a larger building with a quaint garden that seemed to have supplied the settlement with some food. It was just as well they would soon leave, because Basha could still hear the screams of its people. He did not know how many had escaped, but he hoped a good number had. Much as he tried not to think of it, he also knew that he should not distance himself. There would be time later for him to process, time for his own self-recriminations. For now, he needed to go see a prisoner yet again.

Valon was being held in a small room off what seemed to be a dining hall, from the fireplaces and cookware that looked well-organized and cared for. When the Marefi guards saw Basha coming, they gave him a curt nod in unison and opened the door.

If Basha had any illusions about who was in charge here, his first look at Valon ve Avarsahla disabused him. He immediately barked at the guards to fetch him water and clean clothes as well as food.

Since he had last seen her, Valon had been badly beaten. She stared at him with absolute hatred in her blackened eyes, then shook her head and started to laugh.

Basha chose his words very carefully. He had not learned much Tuan, but he had learned a few phrases. Enough to say this. "Dynah ysim."

He tried to pour as much truth into those two words as he possibly could. Basha didn't know the literal translation of them, but it was as close to a Khardish *I'm sorry* as he could get under the circumstances.

Valon's laughter ceased, and she peered at him. One of the guards came in with a bowl of water and some clean clothes and cloths, and Basha dismissed him again with a reminder about the food and drinking water.

He dampened one of the cloths in the bowl and wrung it out again, shaking off the excess. Placing the bowl on the floor, he moved toward Valon carefully, kneeling an arm's length away from her and making no move to go closer without her permission. She had dried blood on one cheek from what looked like a broken nose. If Basha had to guess, he would say they beat her until she passed out, and the blood had dripped down the side of her face with gravity.

He wished he could say something that would communicate his fury, but such a wish was pointless.

"Valon. May I?" he asked instead, holding up the cloth and miming wiping his own face.

After a long pause, Valon finally nodded, though she still flinched when the cloth touched her face.

"Dynah ysim," he said again, and then again. "Dynah ysim."

He wanted to tell her that it was wrong what the Marefi had done. By his presence here, Basha was complicit. He had come with an invading army his country had sanctioned for their war crimes against others, and it was at Arelashk's bidding the Marefi had entered Khardish waters at all, let alone this continent.

At some point, as he carefully wiped the dried blood from Valon's face, he realized she was crying. She said something he could not make out, her eyes pleading with him. She had lovely eyes, brown and bright like his mother's. Her hair was cropped short, also like his mother's, but where his mother's was tight, springy curls, Valon's was tousled waves. Besides, Valon was young enough to be his child, and he didn't know why he was even comparing the two of them.

He wiped away her tears as gently as he could, and she repeated what she had said, glancing at the door as if waiting for it to open again.

"I don't understand," he said softly, making what he hoped was a universal gesture of confusion.

Valon moved her head as if trying to scratch an itch on her collarbone with her chin, then repeated the sentence again, urgent. Then again, moving her head more insistently, her chin meeting the fabric of her tunic.

And Basha saw what she wanted.

There was an outline of something beneath her shirt, like a pendant. Not, he thought with some irony, unlike the necklace he had given to Oshu. Khardish mages generally did not bother with such things, particularly mages of Arelashk's stature, but at this point, Basha was not one to question why Arelashk did anything.

He held his hands up to Valon, dropping the bloody cloth in the bowl. She leaned forward, hope lighting her eyes, though again she flinched when he touched her as if afraid he was going to reveal his kindness as a trick. He found the leather cord that held the pendant concealed under her tunic where it would rest against her skin. That, more than anything, told him it was arcane in origin. When there was such a thing as an amulet with magical properties, it had to be touching the user's skin to do anything. Oshu's strangely twisted metal cord was the same. The moment Basha lifted it away from Valon's skin, she sighed, a sound of pure relief like he had never heard before.

The thing had no clasp; the ends of the leather appeared to have been clamped into the pendant itself so it couldn't be removed, especially when one was tied up.

Basha dropped it on the outside of her tunic for a moment to reach for his belt knife, but after a moment's consideration, he decided against the blade. If it were cut, Rela would see it and know.

Valon was watching him, the urgency returning to her eyes. Outside, Basha could hear footsteps coming toward them.

"Dynah ysim," he said, and he grabbed the leather in both hands and yanked as hard as he could.

Valon jolted backward with shock, and Basha dropped the pendant onto the dirt floor just as the footsteps stopped outside of the door. In one fluid motion, he stood, his booted heel coming down hard on the pendant. He heard something crunch, and he turned his foot just enough to conceal the leather thong along with it.

The door opened, and the Marefi guard looked surly at being sent to run errands for a prisoner, but Basha put on his best fed-up bureaucrat face and simply held out his hand.

"In Khardan, we have standards for how our prisoners are treated. If I hear that anyone has harmed so much as a toenail on this woman again, I will have both of your heads for it." Basha took the proffered jug and plate of plain flatbread with distaste. "Get her a meal you yourselves would willingly eat or I will see to it you only eat what you have given to this one until you are back in Marefi waters."

He thrust the plate of bread back at the guard.

"We are not in Khardan," the other guard said, a warning in his voice that Basha did not like.

"Perhaps you have not noticed that we are also not in Maref, and we sailed here under a Khardish banner, so unless you want your head to decorate a pike outside of this settlement you massacred, showing you the same care you showed its residents, you will do as I say." It was too much. Basha had gone too far in voicing his displeasure at how they had taken the settlement, and at the sound of the next voice to speak, he almost lost what remained of his countenance.

"Yes, quite," said Arelashk. "The honorable Basha makes a very good point. It would not do for the Da'sash Dan to hear that Marefi allies committed war crimes under a Khardish banner. Do as this one says."

The lump under Basha's boot suddenly felt like a mountain. If Arelashk came any closer, if he decided to walk into this small closet of a room with Basha and Valon, he would not be so sanguine.

Both of the guards snapped to rigid attention before almost scurrying away, and Basha braced himself.

"Strong words," Arelashk said. "I knew you for a man of honor. You do Khardan proud."

"This one has been beaten, honored Arelashk," Basha said. He was truly pushing his luck now, but if he was honest, he really just wanted to see what the mage would do.

Arelashk's hesitation was only an instant too long. "Beaten, you say?"

This was it. The mage closed the distance between them, but he stopped at the threshold as if coming any closer would be beneath him.

He glanced once at Valon and sniffed. "So it seems. I will ensure this does not happen again."

With that, Arelashk stifled a cough and strode from the room. The moment he was gone, Basha kicked the door shut and heaved a breath out, grinding the amulet into the dirt a bit more before kicking that too across the room and nudging more dirt over it.

His chest was heaving, and his skin felt like lightning had struck it.

But when he looked down at Valon, something in him relaxed.

She swallowed hard. She likely did not have to understand what he had said to have some idea of what had happened.

"Bry a'tua dysim," she said, and that was one other phrase Basha knew in Tuan from Carin.

Thank you.

· · · · ·

They moved out shortly after Basha left Valon, having made sure the woman got proper food, and Basha was both surprised and not surprised to get a message from Arelashk putting him in charge of overseeing the prisoner's care. As he left Ryhnas Lu Sesim behind, an empty husk that had once been a bustling village, Basha could not help but feel as if the Marefi army were the equivalent of locusts. As a student of history, he had seen their conquests and attempts at expansion across the continent on the western side of the sea. As seneschal to an Ada'sarshk, he had seen firsthand the refugees pouring into Khardan from Triya's civil war—widely understood to have been enabled by the Marefi rulers—and was aware of

Khardan's quiet moves to protect what remained of the Bohoyu tree people from Marefi incursion.

And now they were here, seeking power.

Basha would have to be very careful in his movements, but if he applied his fastidious nature correctly, he could help Valon while also strengthening Rela's trust in him.

The column moved to the southeast, following who knew what. Rela had not communicated where they were going, and while Basha was certain Rela knew of Lahivar, he couldn't be sure Rela would want to go there next.

It was slow going for the first few days of marching south—the legionnaires' health improved the farther away from Ryhnas Lu Sesim their feet took them, which boosted morale and reinforced Basha's certainty that the place had been cursed.

They stayed within view of the sea, and in the distance, Basha could see the fleet tracking their progress to the south. Dispatches arrived daily and were sent back accordingly, and if nothing else, Basha had to admire Marefi organization.

One turn into their march to the south, they came across another settlement. Or it had been. It was a peculiarity that mystified Basha, and when he was beckoned to attend Arelashk and Asurashk, Basha arrived to find them arguing.

"I tell you, Lahivar is where there will be information we need," Asurashk was saying. "Whether Carin is there or not is inconsequential. There are others who can give us what we need, and it is the only other permanent settlement in these lands."

The threat in her words was plain to Basha's ears: destroy Lahivar and destroy the people's blooming shift in their way of life.

Basha stayed quiet.

"Carin is the key," Arelashk said, his gaze aimed to the northeast. "I am not convinced Lahivar will have anything useful for us when we lack their language, and from what you have said, they have little in the way of written traditions. To learn from oral traditions, one must have deep understanding of the native tongue."

Asurashk's eyes fell on Basha. "This one learned some little of Tuan," she said. "And you say the prisoner Valon is easier with this one than with others. Perhaps—"

"It is a start, but hardly enough." Arelashk cut the Asurashk off mid-sentence. His gaze drifted to Basha, appraising. "It will, however, need to suffice until we find Carin."

He coughed again, though to Basha, he sounded much better than he had. Basha could not ask about the curse or Arelashk's interpretation of it, and in truth, he was only happy to have somehow escaped it himself. It had not affected everyone equally, and Basha had not seen any patterns himself except that he and Oshu had remained hale.

Asurashk was quiet, almost sullen. Basha felt a flare of anger at that. She had been pushed into a role she still did not fully understand, and while she was eager—overexuberant, to be honest—to use the power that came with her station, she cared little for the duties and responsibility that came along with it. An Asurashk was rare; the last Basha had heard of had seen a hundred rainy seasons. Then again, it wasn't as if Arelashk was a paragon of the title Arelashk himself.

For ancient institutions meant to be incorruptible, Basha was finding they were painfully rife with poison. Or perhaps it was simply that an institution was only as incorruptible as the people who made it up.

Lost in his thoughts, he had missed the last thing Arelashk had said, though it was not directed at him, at least. Basha straightened not a moment too soon.

"Basha," he said. "What can you tell me of this place?"

Asurashk stiffened, her eyes seeking Basha's face as if she wished the force of her stare could send him sailing into the surf.

Basha ignored her as best he could, taking in the settlement—if such a word was appropriate for a place left unsettled—with interest.

It was situated between two large dunes that were covered in scrubby grass that gave way to sand closer to the sea. There was evidence of fire pits under the open air, as well as what Basha could identify as a kiln of sorts, or some sort of forge meant to heat things to a high temperature. For glasswork, perhaps?

There were seven structures of a rather large size, poles dug into the earth off the sand and capped with tiled roofs. The clay for such roofs would have to have come from elsewhere—Basha doubted any would be found this close to the ocean with the sandy soil, though he could be wrong.

Among those structures, there were another eight smaller structures, built similarly with five poles and a roof, each dug into the dirt to what equated to hip height. Basha ducked into the nearest one. There was no hole for smoke, no chimney, so it was likely smoke would gather, which seemed impractical. He peered up at the roof, finding it difficult to see in shadow. Ah. He smiled to himself.

At the highest point, there were gaps for smoke to escape, but the design of the roof created overlap between the tiles that would keep water out, which meant these dwellings were meant to guard against the weather. Yet they had no walls.

"Fascinating," he said aloud. "Honored Arelashk, I believe this is a temporary settlement, but it is maintained to a high degree of functionality."

He stepped up the single in-built stair to get back out, then pointed at the roof.

"Those tiles would have to be made elsewhere, but you can see some variation in them where some have broken and been replaced. The poles are also in good shape, which is impressive with this much exposure to the sea and no trees in sight." Basha gestured at the open walls. "I would expect they bring their walls with them. Some sort of tent fabric, likely, something that does not weigh too much to be carried but is effective to keep out the weather."

"The houses in Lahivar were similar pole structures, but they had walls," Asurashk said, her curiosity piqued in spite of herself, Basha thought. "And I have already told the Arelashk that these are a nomadic people, following resources. Scarce resources."

"Fresh water would be the immediate concern here," Basha agreed, though that had not been an issue in Ryhnas Lu Sesim, nor in Lahivar. "I do not think it is coincidence that the settlements with the highest level of permanence were found where there is abundant drinking water."

"Thank you for stating the obvious," Arelashk said.

Basha summoned his many cycles of experience with such barbs to keep his face serene, though inside he wished he could glare at Arelashk the way Asurashk had glared at him.

"I believe someone was here recently," Basha said. He pointed into the dwelling he had just vacated. "It has not been very windy, but this close to the sea, it is reasonable to assume that there would be more sand drifting inside the structures than there seems to be now."

"Indeed," said Arelashk.

It would be foolish to think that word of what had happened in Ryhnas Lu Sesim hadn't traveled. Who could blame these people for wanting to be far away from the strangers who had murdered their fellows?

The Arelashk was staring off to the northeast again, and if Basha had to guess, he would say the man looked conflicted.

"Lahivar is the most reasonable choice," Asurashk urged. "We need not repeat our actions at Ryhnas Lu Sesim. The threat will be enough."

Basha hated her a little more in that moment, but outwardly, he nodded his assent. Though it would be foolish to think she did not mean to use violence.

After a long silence, Arelashk sighed, tearing his gaze away from the dunes to the north.

"Very well," the mage said. Then he smiled. "I can find that one wherever the path leads."

His hand rested for just a moment on the hip pocket of his trousers, and Basha was certain of what lay within: the little book Basha had given Carin. Somehow Arelashk was using it to track her.

Some time later, Basha went to Valon for his now-daily visit. He didn't know if Arelashk had discovered the amulet missing yet; for all he knew, the mage had been pointedly ignoring the captive as they marched and he recovered from his illness. But Basha had no way to ask her yet, so instead he settled for bringing her evening meal and exchanging words with her. The guards could hear and see them, so he had to be careful.

"Bowl," he said, tapping the bowl he held.

"Garat," said Valon. She mimed eating, a somewhat ironic glint in her eyes, as he was about to feed her. "Gan."

They went back and forth for some time, and to Basha's relief, Valon repeated back the Khardish words and phrases with alacrity, even remembering some from the day before without prompting.

When he was sure the guards were bored of listening to this game, Basha held Valon's eyes and said casually, "Lahivar."

He said it only once, and Valon's eyes widened. She glanced at the guards, then made a frustrated sound only a little too dramatically. "Lahi'alar," she said insistently. "Lahi'alar."

"Lahi'alar," Basha said, playing along as if she had just corrected him.

But before he left, she again repeated: "Bry a'tua dysim. Bry a'tua dysim."

C LAR HATED feeling useless.

After that horrible day when the survivors of Ryhnas Lu Sesim appeared in Lahivar, she poured herself into caring for them as best she could, distracting herself from her trauma—it was not a word she had ever truly considered applying to herself. She kept her hands busy and her mind busier, doing tasks slightly outside her comfort zone that she needed concentration to complete correctly, like fashioning pegs for the carpenters and fishing lures for the fishers. She was capable enough, but they required a high degree of attention to detail, and though her fingertips grew red and sore from holding tightly to small objects, her plan worked.

It worked so well that when Jenin came running breathlessly into the round-home they were sharing one night, Clar was so startled she pricked her finger on the bone fishhook and yelped, dropping the clucker feathers in her lap and the fine-spun waxed thread she used to bind them.

"Sorry," said Jenin, chagrin flickering across hys face in the golden lamplight. "It's just—I've heard from Carin. They did it. She and Culy broke one of the stones."

Clar stared, then glanced out the open door, where the sun had set, but the sky was more dusky than dark still.

"I fell asleep by the river," Jenin said sheepishly. "But it's good I did. They must have been exhausted from the stone to be asleep too."

A surge of hope rose in Clar's chest, quickly smothered by her all-too-pessimistic wariness.

"So only two remain," she said.

She was doing her best to imitate Northlander speech, even with Jenin, hoping that keeping herself submerged in it would help increase her facility with the language, but it was hard not to slip back into old patterns with her cousin.

"Only two remain," Jenin said. "And the kazytya rider is back."

This was spoken with a glow of wonder, and even Clar had to agree it was warranted. In all the stories about kazytya, she'd never heard of anyone riding them like an ihstal—imagine!

Jenin came over and knelt beside Clar, helping her pick up the scattered feathers and bone hooks, deftly respooling the loose thread around a clucker leg bone she'd saved for that very purpose, and sy put one hand on her knee.

"Clar," Jenin said softly. "It is okay to hope."

It rankled that Jenin always seemed able to hear her thoughts, and she opened her mouth to retort that she was just being realistic, but Jenin shook hys head at her.

"It is okay to hope," Jenin repeated insistently.

Clar had been practicing breathing—a ridiculous concept, but one she grudgingly had to admit was more useful than she wanted it to be—and she put it into practice now, if only so she wouldn't snap at her friend.

"It is also okay to be cautious," she said finally. "But you are correct. This is good news. What will we do now? Did you tell them about—about the other way-make?"

"There wasn't time. Carin kept the contact short—all she said was 'it is broken' before she was gone again. Some of the others are going to discuss what to do shortly. I think most of the Northlanders are content to leave it with Sart, but who knows? If I can help, I will."

Clar admired Jenin's ability to throw hyrself into a task, like the way sy used to do a boulder plunge off the bridge in Haveranth in summer, leaping into the air and curling up into a ball only to smash into the water and send a splash wave out in every direction. Usually this was part of trying to hit Dyava and Carin, with Lyari's help. Clar had seldom been truly part of their little group, but she'd liked those days.

But the thought of Carin and Culy not knowing what had happened in Ryhnas Lu Sesim bothered her. Surely that should be a priority. Carin would not have been so short without reason, though. Clar had heard what had happened to Carin in Khardan, about the mages trying to use her dreams to get to her memories. Perhaps there were dangers in the unseen world Clar was not aware of. The idea of someone spying on her dreams made the hair stand up on her arms.

As soon as Jenin finished helping her reorganize her things, sy was off, and Clar's concentration lay in pieces that couldn't be picked up again so easily.

With a frustrated sniff and a quick smack of her lips sucked against her teeth, she decided to go for a walk.

The air outside was lovely. It was early enough in the season not to have too many of the tiny biting flies or white-socks, and the air was fragrant with the smells of roasting meat and vegetables. Clar's feet took her out of Lahivar to the east, around the edge of the spring and toward the road where sometimes she could see people traveling past the waymake on their way to the sea or sometimes to Lahivar.

But tonight in the fading light, there was only a very large shape coupled with a smaller one, facing east.

It was strange to see a kazytya at all, let alone sitting primly with hys back to her, a person cross-legged on the ground at the cat's side in easy companionship.

The kazytya—Suhnsuoc, Clar remembered someone calling hyr—turned hys head at the same time Kat did, which made Clar stop in her tracks.

"Forgive me," she said, about to turn on her heel and choose another direction.

But the kazytya rider simply got to her feet and shook her head, looking at Clar appraisingly. "There is nothing to forgive."

Kat spoke carefully, aware that Clar was not fully comfortable in her understanding yet, and Clar appreciated the gesture.

"I just needed a walk," Clar said after a beat, and when Kat gestured at her to come join her, she did, hesitating only a moment.

This close, she could smell Suhnsuoc, a surprisingly warm scent like suntouched fur. A little musk, but nothing unbearable.

Clar sat in the grass, near the depression where Kat had been a moment before, which the other woman quickly reoccupied.

"Have you heard?" Clar asked. "About the stone?"

Kat nodded once, though she looked perplexed, looking to Suhnsuoc yet again as something seemed to pass between them.

When she didn't say anything after that, Clar awkwardly picked at a blade of grass that was almost black in the falling dark. Quicken moon and her sister would be rising soon, barely bigger than a crescent, and Clar felt that press of time as she knew everyone in Lahivar was feeling it.

"Did you find anything in the city?" Clar hoped it wasn't obvious how much she tripped over the strange word.

"Yes," Kat said. "And no."

For a moment, Clar didn't think she was going to expand on that, but Suhnsuoc made a chuffing sound, and when Clar looked up in surprise, Kat went on.

"I did not find a stone there. But I did find something unexpected," she said slowly. Then in a rush, "Is A'cu—Culy the sort who hides things?"

Clar almost dropped the blade of grass she held between her fingers. "I could not say, but knowing Carin, I think if there were something significant, neither of them would keep it hidden."

"So you do not know," said Kat. "You are—your people are south of the mountains."

Clar thought Kat had been about to say something else, and she couldn't stop the bristling prickle of her own hackles going up. "My people are here."

Kat held up a hand. "I meant no disrespect," she said, though the words sounded bitter in her mouth. She sighed, uncrossing her legs and raising her knees in front of her to lean forward and brace her arms on them. "Or perhaps I did. There has been much damage done. But you are here now, and you chose to leave of your own volition. That cannot have been easy."

There was silence then, broken only by the sound of Suhnsuoc's breathing. The large cat didn't appear to be paying attention to the conversation, though Clar thought it would be folly to assume sy wasn't.

"Nothing is ever as it seems," Clar said finally. "Leaving was the easiest thing I've ever done, in the end. The most natural thing to do, the logical outcome of a lifetime of lacking choices in everything."

Kat looked sharply at her, then laughed. Suhnsuoc shifted hys weight, standing only to raise hys hindquarters in the air to stretch hys forepaws and settle down into a loaf-like position. Like with the ihstal's cushing. Clar felt a smile forming on her face despite the feeling that this conversation was like walking barefoot on jagged rock.

"I never expected a kazytya to do something so cute," she blurted out.

Kat looked at the animal and laughed harder. "Suhnsuoc, she says you're cute. Are you going to stand for that?"

Clar half-expected a warning growl, but to her surprise, the enormous cat started to make a sound that she had only heard about, never expected to hear in real life. After all, most large cats wouldn't let someone this close to them, let alone relax enough to make such a sound. She wasn't even sure tigers *could* purr. Some of the cats around Haveranth had purred for her, but her family never had the animals in their own home.

"You're purring?" Kat asked Suhnsuoc accusingly. "Traitor."

Clar grinned, even if it was a bit lopsided.

"You said nothing is ever as it seems," Kat said a moment later. "What do you mean?"

That was a good question. Clar wasn't entirely sure what she had meant. She hesitated before replying, listening to Suhnsuoc purr. She would never dare, but she wanted to lean up against the kazytya and see if she could feel the animal's rumble.

"I think," she began, then stopped. "I think we all make assumptions based on the information we have, which may be correct or may not be. We can only ever do our best with what we know, but also, we always have a choice. It may not be a good choice, but there is always a choice. For a long time, I believed I had no choices. I let them take my name from me. I lost myself. But I was wrong. It wasn't too late."

Kat looked her over as if reassessing her all over again. Maybe she was. Clar found she didn't mind the scrutiny.

"Yes," Kat said. "The true failure is not to adapt when we expand our knowledge, to only keep on as we ever have. You are correct."

The way she said it made Clar think Kat had been warring with something. Even as she watched the strange other woman, Clar thought she could see that something breaking off and floating away. When Kat took a deep breath—like Clar had so many times recently, deliberately—and let it out again, she seemed lighter.

"Yes," Kat said again. "Just because something turns out to be other than it seemed does not mean there is no hope."

It was so close to what Jenin had said to her that Clar did a double take.

She smiled. "Whatever brought you here, I am glad you came, Kat."

Suhnsuoc's purr grew louder.

If Clar hadn't known any better, she would have thought Kat was blushing at her words. The woman was about her age, maybe a little older, and her cheeks were perpetually rosy like she'd been out in the sun without shading her face for a long time. It was hard to know if she was actually blushing, but when she didn't say anything, Clar decided to change the subject.

"What was so unexpected that you found in your travels?" she asked.

Kat looked up, mouth open as if trying to decide whether she regretted mentioning it at all. "An ancient halm," she said finally. "So large that if it were in the center of Lahivar, it would engulf the plaza and more. The whole of the waymake could rest easily under its branches."

Clar was already reeling. "Surely Culy would know of such a thing."

"Exactly."

"We need to tell Sart and the others." Clar scrambled to her feet.

Her fingertips tingled, and one of her feet had somehow already fallen asleep. When she put weight on it, she winced, flexing it.

Kat looked up at her, alarmed. "Do you truly think they do not know?"

What she meant was *Can you truly trust Culy?* and Clar knew it, but if Carin trusted Culy, that was good enough for Clar.

"There have been many strange things, stranger things. I am certain they do not know." Clar put out a hand without thinking to help Kat up, and the woman took it. Her grasp was firm and warm, and the slight pressure against Clar's over-worked, still-tender fingers lit up her skin.

In an instant, Kat was on her feet. As they hurried back toward the waymake together with Suhnsuoc bringing up the rear, Clar felt, rather than simply believing, that perhaps Jenin and Kat were right. Perhaps there was hope.

K AT WAS not sure when the woman called Clar had stopped being one of *them* and started just being a person, but she'd be lying if she said Suhnsuoc hadn't had something to do with it. Suhnsuoc was an excellent judge of character, and Kat couldn't remember the last time the kazytya had let anyone but her hear hyr purr.

She and Clar had found Sart and the others in the plaza, the other southerners and local warmlanders having a heated discussion on what to do next, but as soon as Kat and Suhnsuoc arrived, everyone stopped talking like something had sucked all the air out of the world.

Uncomfortable with everyone's eyes on her, she got it over with and told them exactly what she and Suhnsuoc had found in that glen. From their reactions, Kat had to grudgingly admit that Clar had been correct. Their shock was genuine, and Suhnsuoc nudged hys agreement at Kat's elbow to confirm.

"Naturally Culy goes haring off to the other side of the continent just when we need hyr. Again. Sometimes I feel like all I've done my whole life is trail along after hyr to get hys attention," Sart muttered, then looked up when she realized everyone was staring at her, nonplussed. "Never mind. It's nothing. I'll just . . . ugh. They even have Tahin."

Sart looked so defeated at the last sentence, but Kat had no idea who Tahin was or why that was significant.

"Suhnsuoc and I will be faster," Kat said before she could stop herself.

Sart's crestfallen face grew smooth. "You think you could find Culy?"

"I may be able to reach hyr," Jenin started, but Sart shook her head hard.

Jenin looked ready to protest.

It was Clar, though, who spoke next, her soft voice carrying.

"It may be too risky, Jenin," Clar said slowly. "With what Carin told us about the Khardish mage and what he did to her, we must assume they have access to the unseen world. They may already know we are breaking the stones, but the last thing we should do is lead them to an ancient, sacred tree."

Shrewd. Kat gave her a nod of approbation, surprised to see Sart doing the same.

The Khardish woman, Hoyu, who hovered at the edge of the conversation—likely in part due to it still taking effort to follow the conversation, especially with the addition of new accents and dialects, much like Clar and Jenin—also nodded.

"I agree," Hoyu said hesitantly, her careful pronunciation precise and confident. "And we cannot know what the Marefi people have brought to this . . . problem."

One of the warmlanders, Mari, nodded as well. She was an older woman with a sleek cap of black hair with a sharp band of silver-white at her temple, tucked behind her ear. "It is better to send someone." But a moment later, Mari added, "One alone is also a risk, however."

"Clar can come with me," Kat blurted out, then barreled on before anyone could stop her. "Suhnsuoc can easily bear the two of us, and sy is faster than any ihstal over longer distances. Hys sense of smell is a benefit as well, and we communicate directly. It is the most rational choice."

Clar was staring, her mouth open in a small circle of surprise, and she wasn't the only one.

"If you wish to, of course," Kat added hastily. "I am happy to go alone."

"I'll go," said Clar, though she looked to Sart as if to ask permission.

"Interesting," Sart said, drumming her fingers on her knees. "Well, saves me from having to ride that disaster of an ihstal again and also saves me from chasing

Culy from Crevasses to Taigers, so it's a win-win as far as I'm concerned. You're sure you can find them?"

"I have no doubt," said Kat.

• • • • •

It wasn't long before Suhnsuoc was lying down so they could climb on hys back, supplies secured to hys leather harnesses in a way that sy could bear while running.

"Don't forget," Sart said. "You must tell them of Ryhnas Lu Sesim if they do not already know."

"Be on your guard here," Kat said in answer.

Sart bared her teeth. "We are no easy meat."

With that, Kat slid one leg over Suhnsuoc's back, looking to Clar, who was embracing Jenin and Ryd at the same time. The man Ras stood some distance away, near Mari and some others whose names Kat did not know. He had said little since she had met him, or at least to her, though part of his subdued demeanor could likely be attributed to the nearly mortal wound he had sustained fleeing the way-make to the north.

"Clar," Kat said. "We must go."

Clar pulled away from Jenin and Ryd, who each clasped her on the shoulder once more.

As far as Kat knew, this was the first time Clar would be on her own away from people she knew, so perhaps Kat should not be trying to rush her. But after a few heartbeats, Clar turned away from her friends and came to Suhnsuoc's side.

The kazytya looked over hys shoulder expectantly.

One is afraid, Suhnsuoc said, amusement tickling across the bond.

Wouldn't you be? Kat answered. Aloud, she said, "Suhnsuoc would like you to know that you do not need to be afraid."

That is not what I said.

"Stop being so literal," Kat muttered, and the large cat made a frustrated chirrup of a whine.

For whatever reason, that ridiculous noise seemed to settle Clar's nerves enough to swing her leg over the kazytya's back, settling herself in behind Kat.

It had been some time since anyone else rode Suhnsuoc with her, but Clar was smaller than her and still too skinny from the long trek across the mountains she had made with Jenin.

"Hold onto me if you need to," Kat said, and immediately she felt Clar's arms slip around her waist. Her hands clasped at Kat's belly, and Kat tried not to squirm from the sudden ticklish sensation.

"Be careful," was all Sart said in farewell.

Suhnsuoc chuffed and rose to hys feet, and Kat and Clar swayed with the movement.

The kazytya was mindful enough of a new rider that sy took careful steps at a walk through the waymake, and gaggles of children came running to watch, waving goodbye and calling out hellos to the cat, who seemed far too delighted with the attention for Kat's taste.

Attention hog, Kat said. *You're worse than a seal in a fish bucket.*

Suhnsuoc added a bit of lift to hys step, almost a small pounce, and Clar made a startled sound.

"Don't mind Suhnsuoc," Kat said dryly. "Sy's just showing off for the kids."

"Showing off?" Clar asked.

They were nearing open land now, passing by the last roundhomes and villagers of Lahivar.

"Sy loves to be the center of attention," said Kat.

Always, always, when she was out with Suhnsuoc on the threshold of uninhabited land, Kat felt the pull of excitement in her core to be able to *run*. She felt it now, itching to tell Suhnsuoc to go, to fly across the lush blue grass as if soaring through the sky itself, but she was afraid Clar would panic.

So instead she turned her head to look over her shoulder, barely able to see the other woman. "Do you think you can manage if we go a bit faster?"

"What? Oh! I will . . . try." Clar sounded determined, if a bit faint at the prospect.

Suhnsuoc was clearly as antsy as Kat was, but to the kazytya's credit, sy held back, gradually increasing hys pace to a lope, then pushing faster and faster as Clar clung to Kat's midsection.

When Clar let out a *whoop*, Suhnsuoc slowed suddenly to a stop, only for Clar's head to collide with the back of Kat's.

"Ow," Kat said reproachfully.

"Oh, I'm sorry!" Clar gasped behind her.

"Not you, Suhnsuoc. That was clumsy of hyr. Did sy go too fast?" Kat massaged the back of her head where Clar's forehead had hit it, thankful the other woman was a little shorter than her so it hadn't been her nose. That would have stung and been unfortunate for the nose.

"Oh! Erm, no." Clar fell silent, her grip loosening and then tightening again. "I—great bounty, that was phenomenal."

Now Kat really did crane her head around to try and see Clar's face.

A decidedly smug warmth emanated from the kazytya through the bond as if the cat were saying *I told you so*.

"You really mean that," Kat said dubiously. "Well. Good."

"Yes," Clar said. "Let's go."

For the first time that Kat could recall, Suhnsuoc moved at someone else's urging, almost springing into motion.

Oh, Kat had missed this in even the short day or so since she'd been back in Lahivar. The wind in her face, the smells of the land all around her, Suhnsuoc's glee, all of it.

She'd never thought someone else would share it with her.

They traveled like that for days, rising early, hunting together, and sleeping under the stars. The spring air was giving way to the warmth of summer, and Kat wasn't sure she had ever experienced anything more freeing than having her days to run with Suhnsuoc and her nights to lounge with Clar in thick, verdant grasses and listen to the chirps of birds and insects and watch bats swooping through the air.

Kat could almost forget the purpose of their journey.

Before they slept each night, on bedrolls side by side, they took turns pointing out constellations to one another, checking their traditions against the other's traditions, seeking similarities and differences in a sky that showed different faces depending on where one was on the land. Clar showed her the Great Halm and the Hearthstar; Kat showed Clar the barest edge of the Standing Snow Bear, only its right hip showing above the horizon. As the days went on and Quicken moon came to fullness in the sky, dimming the stars around her and her sister's insistent glow, they began to make up their own.

Kat wasn't sure who started it. Perhaps it was Clar insisting that a cluster of stars looked like a fil and telling Kat seriously that there was once a musician who always traveled alone through the hills of some far-distant land, playing for anyone sy encountered. But the musician always vanished before sunup until some in the audience tied hyr down one night out of jealousy for the long, lonely nights without music that had come before. When the dawn came, the musician was gone, having vanished with the first rays to touch the earth. But when night came again, they saw the musician's fil spelled out in stars across the sky, always visible but making no music for them. They wept with their folly because still the fil would vanish with the new day.

Kat had listened raptly to the tale, and when Clar finished, she had wanted to weep. She asked if it was a tale the southlanders told, and Clar said shyly that she had made it up.

Or perhaps it was Kat, some night before or after that—they blended together in the best way, a dreamlike mix of soft breath and happy sighs and Suhnsuoc purring beside them—telling Clar her own yarn about the salmon that went so far upstream it encountered her people in the frozen tundra to the north. The salmon had left everything it knew behind and had no idea how to get back. A seal came to it and promised it could take the salmon back to its people, but the salmon knew a seal for an eater of salmon and swam away. And then an orca came to it and promised it knew just where the salmon's people were too, but the salmon knew the orca for a killer and swam away. And finally, a baleen whale had come to the salmon and promised it could return the salmon to its people, and the salmon knew the baleen whale for an eater of krill, and so it swam inside the baleen whale's open mouth, where the baleen whale promptly swallowed it along with the krill, and well, that was the end of that.

When Kat finished, there had been a moment of horrified silence, and Clar had burst out laughing so loudly, Suhnsuoc jumped, and hys tail puffed up, which made her laugh harder, and that made Kat laugh, and soon the two of them were dripping tears down their cheeks with sore stomachs and cheeks.

"That's *horrible*," Clar managed to get out around belly laughs that doubled her over.

Suhnsuoc got up and turned around in a huff, lying back down with hys back to the two ridiculous people sy was forced to travel with, and Kat sobered long enough to say, "Yes, well. The point is, don't get in a beast's mouth to get somewhere." And then she'd started giggling all over again.

I'll put you both in my mouth if it will make you shut up, said Suhnsuoc through the bond, which helped matters about as well as could be expected.

Their good cheer kept them in light spirits for more than a turn northward, when Suhnsuoc spotted a group of people traveling in their direction.

"What do we do?" Clar asked from her perch behind Kat. Her breath tickled Kat's ear.

"They are warmlanders," Kat murmured, then stopped herself. "People from here. We should approach with caution, for they may not know of my people."

They kept some distance from the travelers, a family from the look of it, but they waved with as friendly an air as they could to show they meant no harm. The family gave them a wide berth but waved back, and one of the children exclaimed in fear that may have been colored with wonder.

"Where do you come from?" Kat called out.

"We were bound for Silirtahn," one of the strangers answered, "but you should not go anywhere near there!"

"Why not?" Kat asked, and Clar's arms tightened around her waist.

"There are many strangers with armored tunics and many weapons moving south along the coast. We are going inland—the only other waymake south of Silirtahn on the coast is Lahivar." The stranger plucked one of the children from the ground and held hyr on one hip. "We had heard Lahivar was safe, but the strangers are too many."

"Thank you for the warning," Kat called.

"Don't know why the cat people have come this far south, but you should be on your guard. The strangers also have boats—ships. Enormous boats. They send smaller boats back and forth every day. I watched them for half a turn. If I can, I will send word to Culy." The child in the stranger's arms squirmed, pointing at Suhnsuoc.

"Kazyt!" the child cried. "Big!"

Despite the stranger's news, Kat smiled. "Sy is indeed big." She had the sudden urge to cover Clar's hands with her own—the southlander was clinging to her so tightly it was a little hard to breathe, but the pressure seemed to root Kat where she was. "We are seeking Culy ourselves. If you manage to send word to Lahivar, I am certain they would be grateful."

"We will do what we can," the stranger promised. "May you find what you seek."

"And you," Kat said.

The child was still craning hys neck to point at Suhnsuoc when Kat murmured to the kazytya to hurry.

"I wish Jenin were here," Clar said that night as they tried to settle into sleep.

Kat's stomach had been churning all day since that meeting, and not even the lemonleaf plant she chewed was helping to settle it.

"Why?" Kat asked carefully.

"Sy can travel the world of dreams. Surely now the need outweighs the risk." Clar was weaving several blades of grass together, but they sprang apart, and she let them scatter with a small gust of wind.

"You are right," Kat said, feeling a small measure of relief she couldn't quite account for.

It took them both ages to fall asleep that night, and Kat would have worried her tossing and turning was keeping the other woman awake had Clar not been doing the same thing. Suhnsuoc was fast asleep. Cats.

"Kat?" Clar whispered sometime after the moon had set.

"Yes?"

"Are you frightened?" Her voice was so small in the night, like the tiniest stars farthest away, pinpricks of light in her words.

Kat had to think for a moment—not about the answer to the question, but whether she wanted to tell the truth.

After listening to her own traitorous breath go shakily in and out several times, she sighed.

"Yes," she said.

"Me too." Even though Kat couldn't see her in the dark of night lit only by the stars, she got the feeling Clar was wrestling with something. After another moment, Clar went on. "I just found home. I am afraid for them and for all of us."

Her words sent a pang through Kat that she couldn't suppress. Home. She used to know where that was. Sometimes she felt a longing for a place she wasn't even certain existed—perhaps it existed outside time, outside this world, even.

But before that chance encounter today with the strangers, she realized she had found such a place. Wind whipping and carefree, pictures drawn in the sky and the warmth of someone beside her who spun stories from starlight.

"When I was a child," Kat said, surprising herself, "I used to imagine I could step outside my body. I would see myself bundled in my blankets from above in the glow of the oil lamps. I would see my home from above, all our dwellings rounded against the northern cold, the sky brighter and clearer even than here on a good night, and nights that stretched out far enough to devour the days in winter.

"And then I would see the tundra, and then the maps I used to pore over with the elders, learning the land to the south and what lay beyond. I would see the whole of our world, suspended in nothingness like a giant ball, and I would see our moon and her sister and the sun that gives us warmth. And I would see that some of the lights we see in that sky are other worlds, like our stories say, and some share our sun and others have their own, and all the lights in the sky at night were innumerable possibilities of worlds we will never reach, and for a moment I would be suspended among all of them, the tiniest speck among tiny specks."

For a heartbeat or two, her words hung in the air, and Kat felt it again, that infinite expanse.

Clar's breath gusted from her in a loud *whoosh*.

Kat went on. "And then, just as quickly as I expanded, I was back in my blankets and furs, bundled warm in a small pocket of space. I could feel my fingers and toes, and if I poked my nail into the pad of my finger, it hurt a little."

Kat wasn't entirely sure what her point was. She'd never told anyone that story.

But she heard movement that sounded like Clar was nodding her head against her bedroll.

"We can only control what is here," Clar said softly. "We can only do what we can."

Yes. "Yes."

Kat lay there in silence again, her hands stretched out on either side of her, and she jumped when Clar's hand crept into hers.

"Is this okay?" Clar whispered.

"Yes," Kat said and swallowed.

Somehow, impossibly, they fell asleep.

When Kat woke, Suhnsuoc was looking more smug than usual, if such a thing could happen, and Kat's hand was still holding Clar's.

Her head felt fuzzy; they hadn't slept much, and today would be long without the rest.

Suhnsuoc's paw came down beside her head, and hys whiskers tickled the side of her face. Kat found herself staring at the upside-down face of a very large kazytya, puffs of morning cat breath humid against her cheeks.

"Fine, I'm up," Kat grumbled.

Clar stirred beside her and woke with a yelp at Suhnsuoc's proximity, which sent a wave of amusement through the bond.

Kat supposed she'd have to let go of Clar's hand sometime, and it may as well be now. She gave it one last squeeze before letting it fall and pushed herself to her feet.

And blinked.

"What—" she breathed, disbelieving.

Clar stumbled to her feet beside her, wide-eyed. "How is that possible?"

"It's . . . not," said Kat, which was an absurd thing to say, since it obviously had happened.

They had gone to sleep in lush spring grass.

They had awoken in the middle of a halm grove, five bone-white trees surrounding them, somehow already as tall as if they had been growing for cycles.

It is happening, said Suhnsuoc. *We wake.*

WHEN CULY jerked awake beside her, Carin jolted out of sleep, her heart leaping with her as she tried to orient herself.

"What happened?" she asked, kicking off the furs she had slept under.

Her skin was sweaty in the warmth of the morning sun—they had overslept—and it was as if spring had ceded its territory to summer already in the past few days.

"Valon," Culy said. "She said the Marefi forces are moving on Lahivar. She was blocked from entering the unseen world. Somehow that mage Rela has learned a way to stop captives from dreaming at all."

Carin's pulse fluttered in her throat, like there was a terrified bird just under the fragile skin at the cleft of her collarbone, beating its wings against the hollow there.

She didn't fully understand how Culy was able to communicate with Valon when Valon had little magic and couldn't enter the unseen world consciously by herself, but if Culy was right—

Just like that, she was back in that hut in the park in Sahesh, unmoving, trapped in her own body. Rage bubbled up in her stomach, and when Culy reached out and took her hands, she realized she had clenched both of them at chest level like claws, every joint in every finger rigid.

Culy's touch drew her back to herself bit by bit, but it was several cycles of breath before she could form words.

"Is Valon okay?" she asked.

Her voice came out rough from sleep and the sudden rush of anxiety and fear. She cleared her throat, working her bare toes into the dew-wet grass at her feet off the side of her bedroll.

"She has been mistreated, but she said there is one among the Marefi and Khardish who has shown her kindness—it was he who removed the talisman or amulet keeping her from dreaming. But she does not know how much longer that will remain undiscovered." Culy smiled, mirthless and dangerous. "It seems they invaded Ryhnas Lu Sesim and killed . . . many. But the spirit seems to have had feelings about that."

Carin felt something sharp and bright inside her chest, something that matched Culy's danger.

"What do we do?" she asked.

Was Ras alive? She felt certain that he would have helped get people to safety as best as possible, but if Valon had been captured, who knew what had become of anyone? Grimly, she thought of Valon again within an enemy camp, again a captive, again alone. If they lived through this, if they were somehow successful, Carin would personally make sure Valon ve Avarsahla was given whatever she needed for the rest of her life.

"As I see it, we have two choices," Culy said. "We can continue on to the fourth stone or we can return to Lahivar. Valon said the army is moving on foot. For all the Khardish advancements you saw, it seems those do not extend to Maref, which is a boon to us. An army can only move as fast as its slowest soldiers and its supply chains. While we are farther away, we are faster, and we know our land where they do not."

"What could we do in Lahivar? Our magic will make little difference against an army." Such a horrible word, one Carin should not have had need for. "All we would be able to hope for is evacuating our people. Surely someone in Lahivar will be aware of what happened . . ."

She trailed off. Could they assume someone from Ryhnas Lu Sesim had made it to Lahivar alive? She had spoken to Jenin, but she had only said three words to hyr out of fear.

Culy seemed to follow her thoughts. "You were right to be cautious with Jenin. I have far more practice than you in remaining hidden in the unseen world."

That was abundantly true.

"I do not know what is best," Carin said after a long pause. "I hate feeling helpless."

"You are anything but helpless, my love."

That should have made her feel better, but it didn't, really.

"If we make for the next stone and cast our bet for Lahivar being able to take care of itself—a fair bet, as they are very capable—we could lose the waymake. Homes can be rebuilt and crops resown, but people cannot be brought back from among the dead," Carin said. "The stone has been there all this time and is unlikely to move."

Culy nodded. Hys bald head had grown tan in their travels in the sun, and there was a smattering of freckles starting to appear, slightly darker against hys brown skin, though sometimes, like now, Carin caught hyr reaching out of habit for the ends of hair that sy no longer had.

Hys hand dropped when sy realized it, and sy sighed. "I agree. Much as I want to pursue the stone, I would not leave Lahivar in danger."

Something loosened in Carin's chest, and the muscles of her neck relaxed. "Then let us go."

• • • • •

Tahin and Siuhn, Culy's ihstal, practically flew over the plains. Carin was sore and tired from many turns of hard riding already, and the rhythm of ihstal feet seemed to meld with her heartbeat over the days as they pounded southwest, leaving burgeoning life growing behind them.

The strangeness was inescapable. Though they had traveled this way only days before, the changes in the land made it look alien to Carin's eyes. Frequently, she and Culy would look at each other from the backs of their ihstal with awe, bordering on alarm, at a landscape so swiftly becoming something new before their eyes. The northern edge of what had been Boggers was dotted with new trees, trees that grew taller as they stopped for a meal, trees that would likely become a forest before they next passed this way.

With the water stone, the changes had been stark, and Carin had watched them unfurl over moons and moons. It seemed with each hearthstone they broke, the changes picked up their pace. Carin did not think they could keep up.

"You said we know this land and the invaders do not," she said one day when they allowed the ihstal a rest at a walk, Quicken moon showing a waning half in the daylight sky. They were in a meadow bursting with flowers and bushes Carin thought would be heavy with berries by Harvest moon. "But already everything I know about this land has changed."

"I perhaps spoke too soon," Culy said wryly. Sy looked unnerved to Carin's eyes. "Time has faded even the brightest of my memories of what came before, and I would not be foolish enough to think that breaking the hearthstone spell will mean everything reverts to what it was before. It is more likely that it will become something altogether new."

"Something altogether new," Carin repeated.

They were soon on their way again, the ihstal ready to run once more.

Something yet stranger grew in the edges of Carin's awareness. It reminded her of the earliest days of her magic, when her leaving Haveranth had triggered her abilities. It felt wild and new, raw and unshaped.

Now, when she reached for her magic, it sprang to her use almost as if it had a will of its own. The spirit exulted in it, drew strength from it, and that alone was enough to make Carin cautious. The water spirit that had become part of her was already immensely powerful—it had transported her and Hoyu across an ocean in moments. It had rerouted rivers and watersheds for the turning of ages.

Now, when she rode, she could feel Tahin beneath her, feel Siuhn running not far away. She could feel Culy in a way that was new as well. Beyond that, it was as if she could sense the nearness of every creature above the earth and burrowing through it.

So when she felt the movement of something large converging upon her path, she drew Tahin to a halt immediately, calling out for Culy to do the same.

"What is it?" Culy asked, alarmed.

"Do you not feel that?" she said. "Something is coming."

"Some*thing*?"

They had reached the rolling hills that bordered Salters and Boggers, and they could not see so far in the distance now, especially with the changes in the land and the growing trees.

The spirit surged in triumph just as a kazytya bounded into view from the south, bearing the woman from the far north—and someone else.

"Clar?" Carin stared, putting one hand on Tahin's neck to calm hyr.

Culy looked sharply at Carin as the riders grew closer. It wasn't long before Kat halted Suhnsuoc not far away, murmuring something Carin could not make out.

"What are you doing here?" Culy asked.

"Looking for you, A'cu Lystel," Kat said.

Suhnsuoc lowered hyrself to the ground, and both Kat and Clar dismounted, looking practiced and at ease.

Carin was still stuck at the sight of Clar astride a kazytya—and making it look natural!—and it took a moment for her to find her words.

"What news from Lahivar?" Carin asked. It had to be urgent. "Have the Marefi come already?"

Clar and Kat exchanged an alarmed glance.

"What?" Clar asked. "How do you know about the army?"

"Survivors from Ryhnas Lu Sesim arrived three turns back," Kat said. "Your fellow Ras was badly injured, but he is recovering. And we encountered others just a few days ago who were bound for Silirtahn but found the Marefi headed south."

Culy nodded grimly. "There is one held captive by the Marefi I was able to contact. She said they are moving in the direction of Lahivar."

Color drained from Clar's face, and she leaned closer to Kat. "I feared that would happen."

"If that is not why you are here, why have you come to find us? How did you even find us?" Carin asked.

Kat indicated the kazytya. "Suhnsuoc can track better than even the wolves. We came with information I found in Alar Marhasan. We did not think it safe for Jenin to contact you, but if you have heard from a prisoner, perhaps we were wrong."

"You were not wrong," Culy said, hys voice smooth. "Jenin has many talents, but I have experience sy does not. You were right to come yourselves. Tell me what you have come to say."

· · · · ·

When Kat was done describing what she had found south of Alar Marhasan, Carin again sat in stunned silence.

She had already been overwhelmed by the number of things moving across the land like stones on a board, things shifting with every passing day that were completely outside her control. But a halm that old and large would have the power to uproot mountains.

Halm had always been the rarest of trees, sacred and known for its hardiness, but it also lay at the heart of magic, Culy had taught her. Halmers could only work the wood with magic. Halm trees grew in groves of five, and they grew in response to magic, whether funneled through their jet-black seeds or—if the legends were to be believed—in response to great need.

One halm alone was something Carin had never heard of.

When she said as much, Culy shook hys head. "They do not grow alone."

"But I saw it," Kat protested.

"I believe you," Culy assured her. "I do not believe it was just one tree, however."

Sy held out hys staff to Kat, at the wood that twisted together so tightly that it had molded itself into one solid piece at the base where it swirled into a flame-like globe at the top. It was exquisite and powerful; working with halm meant working with the will of the wood itself, for the trees were alive like people were alive. They had a will of their own.

"This staff was born of five different trees," Culy said. "Not carved from one branch."

"You are saying that what I saw was five halms that had . . . grown together?" Kat asked dubiously.

"Just so," said Culy.

"How long would it take a halm grove to reach such a massive size?" Carin said.

"I could not say. Seeing the changes that have occurred since we broke the last stone, I think any guess I could make would be wrong." Culy gestured around them at the saplings, the flowers, the bushes.

The very air smelled different than it had only a short time before.

Carin could tell Culy was itching to see this tree, and some of the thousand questions that immediately arose had to be in the hyrsin's mind as well. If the tree was there, was there still a hearthstone near Alar Marhasan? Would they even be able to track it the way they had tracked the last one? But even as she thought it, she felt with a jolt that she would. The closer the spell got to crumbling, the more the remaining stones seemed to sing.

Clar and Kat exchanged a long look, and Carin watched them curiously. Clar had not seemed to form a friendship with anyone in Lahivar before now, but somehow she had ended up here with Kat.

"Did something happen?" Carin asked suddenly.

"Yes," said Clar. "We went to sleep last night in a meadow and woke surrounded by five halms that grew overnight."

"Less than overnight," Kat amended. "We were awake far into the darkest hours."

At that, Clar blushed and said hurriedly, "We couldn't sleep."

Carin would have to be amused about that later. "You are saying that five halms grew without being planted, in a circle around your bedrolls."

It sounded ridiculous. All of this sounded ridiculous; forests springing up overnight, flowers blooming in front of their eyes, and *feeling* the presence of people and animals were all impossible things.

But Carin could no longer doubt even the most far-fetched of all possibilities.

She was about to say something else when she looked at Clar, who had suddenly gone still, looking puzzled.

"What is it?" Carin asked the young woman.

"When Jenin and I—when we crossed the mountains," she said, then stopped, clearing her throat. "In the Hidden Vale, we stopped to rest. It was warm there in the dead of winter. We rested in a halm grove. I thought it was just a fancy that I could feel something there, but I think I feel it still. Or again. I'm not sure. It's probably nothing."

Culy looked at her sharply, hys grey eyes as always seeming to pierce through layers of hidden things.

"Can you describe what you felt?" Culy asked. For the intensity of hys gaze, hys words were gentle, and Carin loved hyr a little bit more for it.

"It felt like . . ." Clar trailed off almost as soon as she'd begun. She scuffed one foot on a clump of grass. "It sounds very silly."

"Clar," Carin said, "you're speaking to two people who talk to ancient rocks to break them and a third with a cat in her head. I think it's safe to say there is little you could say that would seem silly to us. Everything is changing around us. The earth beneath our feet is changing as we live and breathe."

Carin pointed at a maha tree that had been up to her waist when they stopped and now was inching toward her shoulder.

"At this rate, if we tarry here, we will be lost in the woods without ever having entered them," Carin said. "Do not be afraid."

It was easy to say that, and the nervous laughter that rippled through all four of them belied the fact that none of them were fully comfortable, but Clar straightened her shoulders and nodded.

"It still sounds silly to me," she muttered. "I could . . . feel the wind."

"I take it you don't just mean in the usual way," Carin said dryly.

Clar blinked. "What? Oh." Her mouth fell open like she hadn't even *considered* that bit sounding silly. "Well, now that's even worse. No, not in the usual way." She frowned, chewing on the corner of her bottom lip, but after a moment, her eyes lit up. "But that helps. Usually the wind is tangible but not something you can touch on purpose. It brushes against you and flows through your fingers, but you cannot reach out and grab it." Clar glanced at Kat again, who returned her look with an unreadable expression on her face. "But sometimes I feel like I could. Like it's . . . mine."

Her lips curled in a sheepish smile as if to say *I told you so*, but Culy was already shaking hys head.

"That is the opposite of silly," Culy said. "Your magic is waking."

Kat twitched, her eyes going to Suhnsuoc. The kazytya returned the look impassively, then looked away and began licking one enormous paw.

Clar's eyes widened, and her sheepish smile went slack. For a moment she looked like she was going to object, but then she simply shook her head.

"Ryd too," Carin said. "Has magic always been this common?"

"It was once," Culy said. "To lesser or greater measure."

"What do we do now?" Kat asked gruffly. "Return to Lahivar?"

Carin's mind ran at full speed. "I think Culy and I need to see that tree." She looked over Kat's shoulder at the kazytya who was still grooming hyrself and seeming to pay little attention to the conversation happening nearby. "Can Suhnsuoc stay unnoticed?"

"What are you thinking, Carin?" Culy asked as Suhnsuoc sat up with a baleful look that suggested the cat had heard and understood Carin's question—and found it insulting.

"Kat and Clar covered the distance to get here very quickly. If they could scout the movements of the Marefi forces—"

"They could give Lahivar sufficient warning to evacuate," Culy finished. "And also ensure the people's flanks are guarded when they leave."

"Yes," Carin said.

"But where will they go?" Kat asked. "You warmlanders have no other permanent waymakes, and despite the many changes making food and water more abundant, people will need shelter."

"Ryhnas Lu Sesim," said Clar. When everyone looked at her, she shrugged. "If the Marefi have abandoned it already, it would make sense."

Culy seemed to ponder that. "It's not a bad idea, though it will not be easy to guide all of Lahivar's people around an army."

"The people of Lahivar are not helpless," Carin murmured. "And if those who survived the attack to the north are healed, there will be fighters among them."

"Suhnsuoc could easily make sure Marefi scouts don't make it back to report," said Kat, her teeth glinting with a smile that said this idea would not be unpleasant to the kazytya.

"And as you said, Culy, our people know the land," Carin said. "It could work. They will not want a wasted march back to the north—however many supplies they brought with them, it cannot be infinite."

"We must break the remaining stones to ensure the Reinvocation fails," Culy said softly. "If we do not do that, it may not matter what the Marefi do or do not do. But until then, we must also keep our people safe."

Nods of agreement moved through the small group. When they departed, the maha tree had passed Carin's height, and though they all left in directions familiar to them, each step took the four travelers farther into the unknown.

BASHA HAD a headache. A splitting headache. For days he had attended Arelashk and Asurashk, listening to them bicker as Arelashk's temper grew more and more brittle, Basha struggling to keep his countenance mild in the face of Asurashk's growing insistence on capturing the village of Lahivar by any means necessary.

It seemed the Marefi general, Ludo, was also pushing for this, as he wanted a viable base of operations and a staging point for further incursion into the interior of the continent. With Ryhnas Lu Sesim far from suitable, Lahivar was the obvious choice.

Basha had stopped eating except what little bits Oshu could force him to choke down when they happened to be in the same place for mealtime. His stomach constantly felt as though he had drunk a bottle of vinegar. He was fairly certain he was developing an ulcer.

The thought of Lahivar under siege was a repugnant one. It was bad enough remembering how Asurashk had abused their hospitality at their last encounter, let alone imagining her coming back with an army to use it as the bow that would launch arrows straight to the heart of this place's people.

Several times, the scouts had reported traces of people's movements. The locals never ventured close enough to be seen, but sometimes they left something behind that the scouts could find, mundane things like scraps of leather or the remnants of a fire pit dug into the earth.

They had been marching for what felt like an entire cycle, but it had really only been about one moon in total. While Basha was glad the Marefi had not the technology to supply their armies with autocars or worse, his feet were not used to walking so much.

Each night in the tent they shared, Basha and Oshu worked soothing balm into each other's feet for the inevitable blisters.

In truth, he had almost forgotten about the amulet.

When he walked toward Valon's tent one day after the day's march south though, he was still some distance away when he heard the sound of Arelashk's shouting.

An Arelashk shouting—it was such a breach in decorum that Basha froze in his tracks before hurrying onward. The mage sounded positively *frothing*.

The two guards outside the tent were unfamiliar yet again. Basha had heard that the Marefi rotated prisoner guards frequently to lower the risk of them forming any sympathy for their charges, but he didn't know if that was true. As it was, Arelashk didn't seem to understand why no one could tell him what had happened.

"What do you mean you don't know? Do you not have a guard roster to refer to? Someone needs to tell me immediately when that amulet disappeared, or I will start flaying guards one by one until I get an answer." Arelashk looked as if he might do just that. Spittle clung to the corners of his mouth, and his threat was made only slightly less effective by the cough that wracked his shoulders when he tried to continue.

One of the guards had apparently had enough. "You've got no right to speak to us that way. We take our orders from the guard captain. Talk to that one if you've got a problem."

Basha had to give the Marefi man his due—his tone was almost bored, and his Khardish was flawless. Arelashk, on the other hand, looked like he was going to burst into flame at any moment.

Unfortunately, Arelashk took that moment to notice Basha's arrival. "You," he said, "tell me immediately. Has the prisoner ever been wearing a necklace since you have been coming?"

Basha had tried to prepare himself for such a question. "A necklace, honored Arelashk? I have seen no baubles upon that one's person."

"It is not a bauble, you fool," said Arelashk. "It is a priceless artifact with a purpose beyond the reckoning of a seneschal."

"If it's that special, why'd you put it on a prisoner?" the same smart-mouthed guard said. "A mage as smart as you ought to know better."

It happened so fast, Basha stumbled backward as a flash of orange light lit the guard's face.

A cord of crackling energy appeared around the guard's torso, pinning his arms to his sides, and before the guard could so much as make a sound, there was a sickening crunch as the cord contracted, cutting through the guard at the ribcage. Both halves hit the ground one after the other. The quieter, more prudent guard scrambled back several steps before regaining his senses and standing at sharp attention, though Basha could see him quivering.

Basha smelled bile and voided bowels.

"Now," Arelashk said to the remaining guard. "You will fetch your guard captain directly with a complete list of the guard rotation since we arrived on these shores."

"Yes, honored Arelashk," the guard said.

He turned on his heel and ran, leaving Basha alone with the mage and the man he had just cut in half with his mind.

Basha thought he might be sick. Again.

But when he looked at Arelashk standing over the body, he thought he saw the man tremble.

"You say you saw nothing on the prisoner's person," Arelashk said as if he had not just killed someone for impudence alone.

Basha could not answer, but it didn't seem to matter.

"It is of no consequence." The mage folded his hands in front of his stomach. "There are other means to achieve our ends."

There were other soldiers around, but they all kept their eyes diligently trained on their tasks, managing by some miracle to need to move away from the gruesome scene in front of the prisoner's tent.

"When the guard captain arrives, give instructions to come directly to me," Arelashk commanded. "And come to me yourself once you are finished with the prisoner."

"Yes, honored Arelashk," Basha said.

"And have one of those useless ones clean up the mess."

With that, he was gone, leaving Basha with the spike of a shiver that had struck him with a person's death being reduced to the word *mess*.

To distract himself from the smell and what had just happened, he focused his attention on what he had seen of Arelashk's reaction. He had not imagined the mage trembling. And despite the abilities of magic, he had never heard of such a thing being possible. Basha shuddered at the thought of an army with the ability to simply kill with a thought.

Arelashk and Asurashk had come here for power; that much, Basha knew. Power could mean different things to different people. It was a gargantuan risk to consort with the closest thing Khardan had to an enemy to pursue it, though, and the more he considered it, the more he thought he could be right. The Arelashk had risked everything to get his hands on Carin with Asurashk, and their failure had exposed something Basha did not think they had been ready to expose: the fractures in the Da'sash Dan.

As Marefi soldiers eddied around him, their murmurs barely audible to Basha's distracted ears, Basha's mind worked through the tangle he had caught himself in.

Both the Asurashk and the Marefi General Ludo wanted Lahivar, albeit for different reasons. Arelashk wanted Carin. But that was not enough. The mage had to know that eventually he would have to return to Khardan. He could not simply stay in this unfamiliar land forever, and the manner of his return could decide the fate of Khardan as a whole. Not only Arelashk's life hung in the balance here, but also whatever goals he had that had brought him to this point. That made him desperate. And desperate men were dangerous.

Basha could not be certain how close they were to Lahivar now. They could not be more than a turn away. Five short days of marching between an army and a village the size of Udum Dhu'e. Five short days before the tangle tightened around Basha's chest.

By the time the guard captain arrived with new guards, stoically ignoring the bisected corpse of one of his men and its entrails spilled out on a carpet of fresh spring grass, Basha had formulated the beginning of a plan. Or at least something he needed to do before he could make an actual plan.

"The Arelashk wishes to see the guard captain immediately," Basha said. "And wishes for the area to be cleaned."

The guard captain was a stout man about Basha's height, which wasn't very tall. He had the type of Marefi skin that went from white to red and back again with nothing in between, and his red-brown hair was streaked with grey and tucked behind his ears.

"The general will hear about this," the guard captain said.

"I expect you are correct," said Basha.

The guard captain nodded curtly to a pair of guards standing beside him, and they set about their work cleaning up the corpse, which Basha pointedly did not watch.

With that, Basha entered the tent, where Valon waited, clearly aware that something had happened, but she did not know what.

There was little to nothing Basha could do for her, but at least he could attempt to answer that question.

When he pantomimed the guard's death, she looked confounded at first, but Basha remembered a word he had heard Carin repeat several times in Lahivar.

"Abasla," he said, then mimed dying.

Valon looked at him blankly. After a moment, understanding lit her eyes. "Abaslas."

Ah. He had been close. "Abaslas," he repeated, then, "Lahi'alar?"

He was hoping she would remember her own correction and what he meant.

She was as quick as he gave her credit for. She said nothing, only nodded. Then there were mages in Lahivar.

That was something, at least. Though unless those mages could do what Arelashk had to a hundred legionnaires at once, it would make little difference.

Still, perhaps there was some chance. He could only guess that the amulet he had destroyed had something to do with limiting Valon's magic abilities.

Slowly, he pointed to her and asked, "Abaslas?"

Her hands were still bound, but in front of her, they rose to stay a short distance apart. A little.

She raised her hands to her face and mimed sleeping, then gestured with her chin the way she had indicated the amulet to him, then shook her head vigorously while repeating the word. It took Basha a moment to comprehend what she meant, and she had to do it several times before it made sense.

The amulet interfered with sleeping magic? This tickled at the edges of something he knew, something he had been told when last he saw Carin and his Ada'sarshk in Sahesh. Arelashk and Asurashk had kept Carin asleep, to subdue her for Asurashk's magic.

There were stories of dream-stealers, fables mostly. But Arelashk had elevated the idea to acts of desperation. When the Ada'sarshk had found Carin captive in Sahesh with a member of the Da'sash Dan, Basha thought that had been the moment that drove Arelashk to that desperation.

He mimed sleeping and said "Abaslas?" and pointed to her.

Valon frowned, her eyes narrowing briefly in uncertainty, but then she nodded. Sleep magic.

Perhaps *dream* magic. Valon had had many nights now with which to do something Arelashk had tried to keep her from doing.

Or perhaps it was not Valon he was afraid of.

The moment the thought struck him, he was certain he was right. "Carin," he said softly, almost a whisper.

Valon's head snapped up, and the whites of her eyes showed bright with fear.

Immediately Basha realized his mistake, and he held both hands up, trying to communicate safety, but he wasn't sure he succeeded.

Valon relaxed a little, but she shook her head as if to say Carin wasn't involved.

The language barrier was a problem. Basha wished he could simply say something, anything useful.

He felt he was teetering on the edge of something he could use.

Asurashk and the general wanted Lahivar. Arelashk wanted Carin. But if Valon thought Carin was not the only one who had whatever power Arelashk was trying to keep at bay, perhaps Basha could work with that.

Basha's opinion didn't particularly matter—he was a bureaucrat, not a decision-maker. He kept the records of other people's decisions.

After a bit more attempting their clumsy conversation, he left Valon, hoping that to a desperate man, a bureaucrat might be just the ally he would need.

• • • • •

When Basha made his way to Arelashk's tent, he heard raised voices before he even entered.

No one bothered to acknowledge his presence, but that was not a surprise.

The general was there along with the guard captain, both of them fully red in the face; Basha thought he should be able to feel the heat of their anger pouring off of them.

Asurashk was there as well, standing to the side without saying anything.

"You murdered one of my men," the guard captain said. His Khardish was good, though heavily accented, and he looked as though there were many other words he would prefer to use, all of them progressively less diplomatic.

"Your men managed to not only violate the express agreements of our cooperation in mishandling the prisoner, but one also lost an item of arcane significance that was integral to our presence here," Arelashk said. Any traces that he had been shaken by his murder of the guard were gone, replaced by seeming serenity.

"If such a thing was placed on a prisoner, one would expect its significance would be explained to those guarding the prisoner. Particularly if it could have an impact on our campaign in an unknown land." The general's voice was every bit as cool as Arelashk's, though his face betrayed his true feelings on the matter. A vein pulsed at his temple. "It is now even more important for us to establish a workable base if the loss of this 'item of arcane significance' could jeopardize our goal. You promised coming here would result in access to what you called consequential advantages, but so far we have only experienced blisters and a mysterious illness that seemed to fall upon two entire legions overnight."

Basha stood by the entrance to the tent as close to one corner as he could without his head brushing the canvas, hands clasped in front of himself.

The general was going on.

"I will not allow you to further put my men at risk without very good reason to believe we will leave this blasted land with something to show for the effort. Until then, we will march to this village, occupy it, and send for reinforcements." The general seemed to think that settled the matter.

Asurashk did exactly what Basha expected her to do. "Honored Arelashk, we ought to listen to the general. If this one believes it is best for the legions to gain a firmer foothold here before moving into the interior, it may be the right thing to do, especially since we otherwise have little to go on."

This was it. Basha's moment to gamble. "Honored ones, if you will forgive me—the Arelashk has asked that I share anything I learn from the prisoner."

All eyes in the tent turned immediately to the bureaucrat in the corner.

"By all means," said Arelashk.

Basha forced himself not to swallow. "With respect to the honored general and to the Asurashk, the prisoner has not reacted to mention of Lahivar except to go silent. But when I mentioned a particular name to the prisoner, that one showed surprise—and fear."

It *was* a gamble, and it was one Basha hoped would not return to bite him.

"From the prisoner's unguarded response, I think the name is an important one, and we ought to pursue this with all possible haste." Basha did not look at Asurashk when he said it, but out of the corner of his eye, he could see her face go stony. "She reacted very strongly to the name Carin."

Arelashk's eyes lit up—a flash that was gone in an instant.

"This is the name of the prisoner who escaped you," the general said flatly.

"The one I am able to track—and the one I have been telling you we ought to pursue. The rest of the people here are inconsequential. They are villagers, and even their mages have no formal training. Hedge mages at best, but for this one." Arelashk knew he had won now, and though he did not meet Basha's eyes, Basha knew his gamble had succeeded. "This one released a wave that devastated Udum Dhu'e. This one knows the secrets of walking dreams."

"Stories," the general scoffed.

"Truth," said Asurashk, who did look Basha's way, reassessing him, recalculating her own goals, knowing now she could not side with the general. "If you do not believe me, take my hand. I will tell you your deepest fears in front of your guard captain."

The general muttered something in Marefi Basha barely caught, but he didn't have to guess what the tone meant.

"And if I refuse to follow you chasing wild hares?" the general asked.

Arelashk looked at the guard captain and lifted one shoulder in the manner of Khardan's elite at their most dismissive. "I will do to you and your guard captain what I did to that other one, and your second in command will do my bidding without knowing what we seek, and we will gain this power for Khardan and use it to wipe Maref off the map."

The guard captain began to splutter, but one sharp movement of the general's hand silenced him.

"You could not—" the general began.

"Imagine what would happen if your emperor woke up one morning and ordered his personal guard to execute every traitor in his house and those traitors happened to be every member off the imperial family," Arelashk said conversationally. "Now imagine the same happened in every ruling house of consequence across the length and breadth of Maref."

The general's face, having begun this conversation fully pink, was now whiter than the sands of the Beach of Bones.

"Do not pretend you would not do the same. This alliance is like floss glass," Arelashk said. "But ultimately it is you who has the most to lose. You are in an unfamiliar land with an ocean between you and reinforcements. I can have a message in Sahesh tomorrow, and the entire might of the Khardish navy will bar your passage home."

To Basha's shock, the general managed to find his tongue. "And what does Maref gain from helping you, then?"

"One would think," Basha said, playing his final tile, "that having such power as an ally would be far preferable than an enemy."

"As the esteemed seneschal says." Arelashk unfolded his hands.

"I will prepare the legions," the general said. "In which direction do we march tomorrow?"

Arelashk smiled, one hand slipping into the pocket of his trousers where Basha knew he kept Carin's book. Instead of answering, he simply stared pointedly at the general until the man could not maintain eye contact.

"You are all dismissed," the mage said.

As the lowest-ranking person present, Basha left first, for which he was grateful. He immediately made sure that the turns he took around soldiers' tents pushed him out of sight, lost in a sea of strangers.

By the time he made it back to the tent he shared with Oshu, he was trembling from head to toe, and it took all of his self-control not to hyperventilate. His head swam with the effort of holding in all of his emotions and reactions, and he hoped to every possible god—alive or dead—that he had made the right choice.

Oshu sat up straight when Basha came in, the Triyan's face immediately full of alarm.

"Are you—" he began, but Basha cut him off with an urgent hand.

Basha sat down on his bedroll, almost a fall, and he put his head between his knees, taking long, even breaths.

Not thirty of those breaths passed his lips before orders started rippling through the camp in Marefi—orders Basha hoped his dangerous work had helped to change. He would not know before dawn whether his ploy had been successful, but he clung to hope.

Oshu went still, listening—most Triyans knew the Marefi language as a means of surviving their aggressive neighbor's proximity—and then he too let out a long exhale.

"I do not know how, but I know you had something to do with this," Oshu said.

Basha began to laugh, weakly. "I am a fool."

"No," Oshu said. "You are a man they will overlook and underestimate to their peril."

And with that, Oshu came to sit beside Basha, putting his arms around the Khardish man's still-shaking shoulders, and Basha knew he would go through the entire terrifying evening all over again just to feel Oshu's warmth at the end.

DYAVA HAD taken to walking in the forest.

If Lyari had noticed his distance, she had not remarked on it.

Dyava was lying again.

He couldn't bring himself to tell her that it was Rina who had been in her roundhome, Rina who had been rummaging in her scrolls, Rina who had cast the blame on Calyria for all those moons.

Perhaps there was some sort of explanation. Rina had lost a child. While usually the elders remembered the Nameless, it was seen as an act of compassion to allow them to forget if the Nameless shared with them an intimate connection. Or so his parents had told him, anyway, and Dyava suspected at least on that they were right.

Perhaps Rina was simply looking for an explanation for feelings of loss she couldn't explain, for stretch marks on her belly, for any number of things that suddenly erasing a child could spark.

The simplest thing would be to ask her. To confront the blacksmith and tell her he knew she had been in Lyari's things. At least once more she had done it, a different part of the house the second time. Whatever she was looking for, it was clear she hadn't found it.

Perhaps asking would be best.

But if Dyava asked, that meant he would have to tell Lyari or risk her finding out another way.

So he was lying again.

The woods were a dangerous place to be near sundown these days. Haveranth had lost several other goats to the wolves despite taking precautions, and their voices were heard frequently in the foothills, day and night.

With the sun still flickering golden through the leaves of the trees, not quite obscured by the hills, Dyava figured if he got eaten by wolves, at least this would be a pretty place to die.

But when he stepped back onto the old woodcutter's path that led back down to Haveranth by way of his parents' conu orchard, the two faces he saw made him wish he were surrounded by hungry wolves instead.

"What do you want?" he said flatly to his mother and father.

"Please listen to us," said Tarwyn, her voice pleading. "You must listen, Dyava."

"I was very clear when we last spoke. I told you to never come near me again." Dyava was proud of himself for keeping his tone level. Though after the last time they had made him angry, he was a bit fearful for the welfare of the surrounding trees. Unlike his hearth, they were not made to be set on fire.

"Son, please just do one thing for us. You have magic now. Do something small." His father Silan dug in his belt pouch and pulled out a stub of candle with lint stuck to the wax. "Light this candle."

This had to be some sort of trap. There was no way his parents had followed him out into the woods—where he came to be alone!—just to make him light a rotting candle.

"If I do this, will you go away and leave me alone?" he asked.

"If you still want us to, yes," his mother promised.

That made Dyava wary. His mother had the same shrewdness as Jenin, though she didn't usually apply it to get Dyava blamed for breaking a favored jug.

Dyava took the candle from his father and held it in one hand, gingerly like it might cause him to fall asleep for a hundred cycles or some nonsense from a children's story.

"Just light it," he said, dubious.

"That's all," his mother said.

Dyava was more confident with his magic now, but for several turns he had done nothing with it. There had been too many other things to do, the labor of keeping plants growing and making sure villagers had water.

He reached for threads of magic to spark into fire, and no sooner had he opened himself to it than there was a torrent of threads that converged on the wick and ignited it. Dyava yelped and dropped the candle onto the ground, where it broke in half and was engulfed in an instant.

Without thinking, he tried to smother the flames with the dirt, but he also used magic for that. Instead of simply covering the broken candle with soil, there was a muffled thud, and the candle was punched a foot into the earth with a puff of smoke and dust.

"What did you do?" he demanded.

His mother laughed, a disbelieving and exasperated sound. "You think we did this? This was you from root to crown. You would have seen if anything came from us."

Dyava was a fool—this was how they got him. She was right, of course. He would have. Which meant whatever had just happened was indeed his magic alone.

"Explain yourselves now, or I will walk away," he said. "No lies and no half-truths. No games, and none of your rotted insinuations that I know where Jenin and Calyria are. The moment you mention either of them is the moment I leave and never look back."

Dyava's father relaxed at that, his taut neck visibly softening. "Magic has become volatile," Silan said. "We do not know whether the original spell somehow . . ." The older man appeared to grasp for words.

"We don't know if our ancestors somehow staunched the flow of it," his mother said, and his father nodded in relief. "It seems strange that they would have done something that would have also limited their own power so much, but it seems difficult to deny."

"Did magic become volatile like this before the last Reinvocation?" Dyava asked, intrigued despite himself.

He could have been injured by that candle if he hadn't dropped it as quickly as he did.

"No," said his father, exchanging a long glance with his mother. "But last time, all of the stones were intact."

Oh.

Oh. Shit.

"You think they broke another stone," Dyava said. "It would have had to have been recently—sometime since the birth of Quicken."

"Yes." His mother now seemed to unfold with relief, her shoulders drooping away from her neck where they hovered when she was anxious, which was often.

"There has to be more," Dyava said. "What is it that made you come find me? It cannot only be what happened with my magic."

"We think if Lyari attempts to perform the Reinvocation, the backlash will be enormous," said his father quietly.

"Do you remember what happened when Jenin decided to hit the chipped glass vase with my maul?" his mother asked.

Dyava winced because he did. It had been a small blown glass vase from Bemin's Fan that Jenin had been given as a gift. When it chipped, sy had decided to see what would happen if sy hit it with the butt of the maul on the chopping block out back of their roundhome. Dyava had gone with hyr out of curiosity.

The first swing, Jenin had missed by a finger width. It was usually Dyava that did the wood chopping, and for good reason. He had better aim.

But the second swing, Jenin hit home, and the force of the heavy metal axe butt hitting the delicate glass had caused an explosion; shards of glass went flying everywhere. Even with Dyava standing at what he had thought was a prudent distance, he took one of them to the cheek and another to the side of his neck. He was lucky they were small.

Jenin was similarly lucky. Sy had a shard the length of hys little finger lodged just above hys eyebrow. Any lower would have cost hyr the eye.

"You think we're going to be plucking glass shards out of our eyebrows," Dyava muttered.

"Dyava," Tarwyn said in the tone she had used when he was being particularly obtuse. "Imagine if everyone in Haveranth were crowded around that bottle when it exploded. And imagine that bottle was the size of the village hearth-home."

If that candle had erupted in fire, her words sent tendrils of frost snaking up and down his spine.

"If you punch a wall, the wall punches back," said his father. "Force that has nowhere to go will turn back on itself. And a force as massive as the Reinvocation—"

"Would obliterate everything around it," Dyava said. "But the Reinvocation doesn't even take place in Haveranth. It happens in the meadow to the south, far out of the village where no one lives."

"Dyava," his mother began.

"Stop saying my name like that. If you have something to say, say it and stop making me guess only to make me feel like a fool!" With effort, Dyava managed to let go of the rage that threatened to take over him.

"Do you remember the story of Haver's Glen, about the giant?" asked his father.

Dyava just stared at him.

"The first invocation of the spell broke the earth, Dyava," said his father. "It tore apart mountains. And that was spread out over five stones so the impact would be lessened somewhat."

"*What.*" Dyava had to close his eyes. He couldn't look at his parents for ten breaths. Ten long breaths. When he opened them, the rage came bubbling back. "You are choosing to tell me this now. Now, barely a cycle before the Reinvocation. You waited until Jenin and Calyria—you—" He spluttered out the last words, too angry to be coherent.

"Neither of us were alive last time," his mother said flatly. "And the stones have never been broken before. We had hoped that despite being broken, the stones might hold some power to maintain balance of sorts. Forgive us for not being able to predict the future."

The sun had dipped behind the maha trees now, and only a few slanted rays made it through to the ground where they stood.

"What do you want me to do?" he asked, defeated.

"Help us stop the Reinvocation. By any means necessary." His mother's eyes pleaded with him.

Dyava wondered if this was simply to save her own skin. After all, if the world broke down the middle of Haveranth, it wasn't like anyone in the village could avoid falling into whatever abyss opened up.

"If I help you," he said, "that's it. The day after High Lights one cycle hence, I will be gone. I will go north and find the others if they live. I will go live in the rotting mountains by myself for the rest of my life. I don't even care. But I will be done with you, done with this place and its parasitic drain on everything good. I do this, and I am free to never see or speak to either of you again."

He knew it hurt them; they were flesh and blood as much as he was. Dyava knew they loved him as best they could. He also knew love wasn't enough. It wasn't enough.

"If that is what you wish," his mother said. "We will not stop you or try to find you."

"I will send word to you when we can next speak," Dyava said. "Lyari mustn't know."

His own words felt like poison dripping down the inside of his ribs. Poison of his own making this time.

"There is yet time," said Silan. "But there will be much to discuss."

"No more secrets," Dyava said. He felt like he had aged enough to remember the last Reinvocation.

"No more secrets." Tarwyn lifted a hand as if she wanted to reach out to him but thought better of it and instead took Silan's hand.

His parents walked away the way they had come, and Dyava was left in the falling dusk.

What could he do? Who could he believe?

If his parents were wrong, the Reinvocation would still kill people. Those people would just be handpicked by his lover. If they somehow managed to stop the Reinvocation, what would success even look like? Dead crops and babies that didn't live to breathe their first breath? Wells full of mud? Wolves roaming the village?

For all his talk of freedom, Dyava didn't think there would be anything left of him when all this was done.

THE JOURNEY southward toward Lahivar felt very different than the journey north.

While Clar still clung to Kat's waist as they rode Suhnsuoc over the ever-changing landscape, the urgency that claimed them also stole their voices over the long days as the light lengthened, creeping toward High Lights and the birth of Bide moon. Bide. Never had the names of the mooncycle felt as appropriate as they did this time. Bide until the stones are broken. Bide until the time comes to move. Bide until the scouts pass by.

They had started seeing Marefi scouts only a day after they had parted with Culy and Carin. The people were strange, all men to Clar's best guess, with ruddy skin and colors of hair she had never seen, including hair as red-orange as the sugar tree leaves at harvest time. Facial hair was thicker, far different than any Clar had ever seen.

Suhnsuoc alerted them whenever there were scouts nearby, and though the kazytya was enormous, sy was an expert hunter, far better than any person on two legs. Sy prowled the rolling hills, leading Kat and Clar around the scouts and once close enough to see the entire Marefi force's camp, though they immediately fled at the sight of so many campfires.

When they finally overtook the pace of the army, they hung back rather than running ahead to Lahivar.

"Suhnsuoc can make the run in a day if pressed," Kat said. "It would do no good to evacuate the waymake only to have the force split and come at us from both north and east. They could pin the people against the mountains that way."

Clar agreed. It would not be an easy needle to thread, giving Lahivar enough notice to pack up and leave but not too early or too late.

The next day, they spotted another group of travelers, this time coming from the north. As with the last family they had encountered, they hung back and waved, though this time with more urgency.

"If you are making for Silirtahn or Ryhnas Lu Sesim, you should choose a different destination!" Clar called out.

The travelers, only three adults this time and all with ihstal laden with packs, exchanged a wary glance.

"Why is that? And what would a kazytya rider from the north know?" one answered, and the tallest of the three elbowed hyr in the shoulder.

"Only what one can see with one's own eyes, much as yourself," Kat replied. "And what we have seen is an army of strangers that attacked Ryhnas Lu Sesim before the birth of Quicken moon, and they stand between you and Silirtahn."

The travelers murmured to one another low enough that there was no way Clar could hear them, but Kat snorted after a moment.

"What?" Clar asked.

"Suhnsuoc said they had heard of the army but didn't believe it. It seems people have been fleeing to the east and spreading the news." Kat turned to look over her shoulder, giving Clar a sardonic glance.

"Where do you go, then?" the taller stranger called.

"Where Suhnsuoc says it's safe for us but not for the strangers' scouts!" Kat answered, and a ripple of laughter went through the travelers.

"We should all be so fortunate as to have a kazytya looking out for us," came the reply.

"Suhnsuoc mostly just looks out for hyrself," Kat fired back, and Suhnsuoc tossed hys head and looked back over hys shoulder reproachfully.

That brought more laughter from the strangers.

"Truly, though," the shorter one said, tucking a long black lock of hair back from hys face. "Where should we go? We're Boggers folk mostly, but there's a lake where the bog used to be, and when we went south to Crevasses, we were told to go north where there was fresh water."

"East would be safest, friends," Kat said. "Though I imagine you're fed up hearing a different direction everywhere you go. I can tell you that the hyrsin Culy was eastbound last we saw hyr, which was only a few days ago."

The travelers spoke in low voices among themselves again, though this time Clar saw a few nods.

"You're sending them after Culy and Carin?" Clar whispered. "Is that a good idea?"

"Better than any alternative I could think of," Kat replied.

After a few more moments, the travelers nodded. "We'll go east," they said.

"Watch for haze on the western horizon," Clar called out suddenly, and Kat again looked over her shoulder. "The force of strangers is large, and they build many fires at sundown. If you can see the smoke from their fires, do not stop for the night if you can travel safely onward."

The travelers stared, then gave a nod and turned their ihstal eastward.

Their path soon took them over the rise of the next hill, and Kat patted Clar's hands around her waist.

"That was quick thinking," Kat said.

"We have had winds from the west since we left Lahivar." Clar was afraid to move, because Kat hadn't moved her hand away again, and Clar was afraid if she twitched, the other woman would. "I thought it would bring the smoke inland, and hopefully that would give them enough warning to stay out of the path of the scouts."

"It is better to be cautious and cranky tomorrow than reckless and riddled with regret today," Kat said.

It sounded like a proverb Clar had never heard, but she liked it.

Kat tensed then, and her hand dropped from Clar's, leaving a void of warmth in the sudden breeze against Clar's bare skin.

"Speaking of scouts," Kat said, "Suhnsuoc has scented a pair of them, which means we need to move."

The kazytya was already moving, dropping to a crouch to slink behind a hillock that was now crested with bushes and gangly saplings. Clar's heart beat faster, and she tried to focus on the now-familiar scent of Kat's hair, which she usually wore in one long plait woven together from three smaller ones that pulled her hair back from her forehead and out of the wind.

Clar had gotten used to riding Suhnsuoc, but when the kazytya moved in a crouch like this, it was difficult to keep her balance. Even though she knew her feet were in no danger of dragging on the ground, her boots hit bushes and other foliage, which for some reason was just as disconcerting.

"Rot," Kat muttered.

"What?"

"They've crossed our path, and Suhnsuoc thinks sy left tracks they could easily find." Kat paused thoughtfully. "Though who is to say there are kazytya across the ocean? Perhaps it would do this army some good to find the tracks of an obvious predator."

"An obvious large predator," Clar added, liking the idea of this army imagining a huge, stalking monster in the hills that could eat wayward scouts. Which was still possible anyway, considering their promise to Culy and Carin not to let the scouts get to Lahivar and report back.

"Suhnsuoc does need to hunt tonight. I reckon I can convince hyr to leave whatever's left of hys kill in a place these scouts won't miss it." Amusement colored Kat's voice. "And you've yet to hear the other sound a kazytya can make. Sy might frighten someone else with it, but it would be worth it to give those invaders something to be scared about."

Clar was intrigued and a little afraid to ask.

When they made camp that night, Suhnsuoc left them alone to hunt, ranging off to the north to make sure sy could still keep track of any Marefi scouts who wandered in their direction.

"Can you still hear hyr from where we are?" Clar asked curiously, sitting in the grass with her legs splayed out to stretch her muscles so they didn't tense up from riding all day.

"Yes," Kat said without hesitation. She crouched just on the other side of Clar's left foot, looking into the fire. "The bond is unbreakable, even by distance."

"That is . . ." Clar trailed off. "Intense."

Kat laughed. "I suppose it is. It is just normal for me." Then she tensed. "You may want to prepare yourself."

"For what?"

A piercing scream ripped through the air like a serrated knife through meat. It echoed across the low hills, seeming to come from everywhere and nowhere. Clar's skin prickled, and her entire body burst into gooseflesh. Even her scalp felt like every hair on her head lifted with the sound.

She stared at Kat. "That was Suhnsuoc?"

Kat gave her a fierce grin. "Yes."

Clar had heard rabbits scream, and she had heard deer scream. But while tigers roared, she had never so much as seen a kazytya before Suhnsuoc, and she certainly had not been familiar with the sounds they made. There were some smaller cats in the mountains near Haveranth, lynx and some the size of a goat's kid, but they were elusive beyond the few that had seemingly decided it was nicer to have a warm bed and scraps from a villager's table than sit up in trees waiting to pounce on rabbits. Those were the only cats Clar had seen up close before now, and Suhnsuoc was a bit beyond that. The pet pouncers of Haveranth were a far cry from this.

The scream filled the air again, this time even longer and more drawn out. Clar's body reacted much in the same way it had the first time, like it remembered a time when that scream could come for her people.

And then, farther away, a mournful howl joined the tail end of the scream, followed by another. And another. And another. Soon there was a chorus of eerie music drifting across the land on the breeze, and Suhnsuoc added hys voice again.

"Wolves," Clar said in a half gasp. "This far north?"

"I think you mean this far south," Kat said, a bit wistfully. "The wolves here have been the companions of my people for a very long time. When they began to move southward, that was when I knew it was time for me to do the same."

Clar couldn't quite wrap her mind around a people living in comfortable proximity to not just one but *two* species that were nearly mythical to her. She forgot her stretches and simply sat with both hands hanging onto the grass as if she were afraid the world would shift beneath her, so she had to hold on.

"Will the wolves come closer?" she blurted out.

Kat chuckled. "If we're lucky. They may even have recognized Suhnsuoc's voice, but it's more likely they are just saying hello."

"How—how big are they?" Clar asked.

"Big," said Kat.

"Suhnsuoc big?" Clar tried to imagine a wolf and failed. She thought they were like foxes or corsacs but larger.

"Not quite as big as Suhnsuoc, no. But close." Kat stared in the direction the wolves had called from. "I'd wondered if we'd see or hear them. Like Suhnsuoc, they can stay out of view if they want to, but they do like to sing."

"I've heard them before," Clar said slowly. "But in the mountains to the south, when I still lived there."

Kat swiveled her head to look at Clar again, one eyebrow raised. "Wolves? Are you sure?"

"That's a sound I'm not likely to forget," Clar said wryly. "We started hearing them in autumn of the last cycle. They killed some goats in the village, which had people worried."

"They must not be very fond of the village," said Kat. "They're usually considerate about where they hunt."

"I don't blame them," said Clar.

She couldn't keep the darkness from her voice. She wondered what Dyava was doing, if he hated her and Jenin for abandoning him. She wouldn't blame him, either, but he would not have fled with her. Clar was not certain she would ever forgive him for letting her believe she had found Jenin dead. At least if he would not forgive her leaving, they would be even, in some sick way. But she still believed what he had done was worse.

Harming others purely because someone told you to was something Clar could not understand.

Kat was watching her. "You have a lot of anger," she said after a moment.

Clar met her gaze, freezing midreach to her toes. There didn't seem to be any judgement in Kat's expression, and the words sounded neutral to Clar's ears.

"Yes," Clar said finally. She flexed both feet one more time, enjoying the pull of her calf muscles, then tucked her feet in to sit cross-legged. "I suppose I do."

"Why?"

"My family forced me to lie my entire life. Because we knew the truth of the Hearthland's bounty, it isolated us from everyone in the village. The only people I could 'trust' were my parents and my cousins." Weariness crept over Clar's being again, that familiar, age-old exhaustion that came from having to wear a mask everywhere you went.

"You say trust like a lie," said Kat.

"Because it was," Clar replied simply. "How do you trust people who abuse you for their own ends? Who make you a pawn in their game and tell you it will be your fault if you slip and someone dies? They tell you they are the only people you have, and they're right, but you are never anything but a tool to them. You are only useful if you do what they want."

Her words seemed to strike the other woman deeply. Kat rocked back on her heels where she had crouched so comfortably until now, her arms wrapped around her knees.

Kat frowned, only a little crease between her eyebrows, and for a moment it looked like she wanted to say something, but some thought made her close her mouth again almost as soon as she had opened it.

They both jumped when another blood-chilling scream erupted in the air, closer this time.

Kat glanced in the direction of the sound, getting to her feet. "Suhnsuoc is coming back. Sy says sy left a halka corpse where the scouts will find it on their way back to their camp."

"Sy got between the scouts and the army?" Clar asked, impressed but a little alarmed. "Is that safe?"

"They had no idea sy was there," Kat said with a grin. "Sy also said the wolves left a contribution."

Clar wanted to ask how the kazytya could communicate with the wolves, but she figured the answer would be beyond her. Instead, she stood as well, walking closer to the fire. Her backside was damp from sitting in the grass, and the evening cool was crisp enough to threaten a chill.

To her surprise, Kat joined her, standing in companionable closeness.

"I think you and I have more in common than I had first expected," Kat said suddenly, all in a rush. "Which is not so remarkable, as I did not expect to have anything in common with one of the Tuanye. But I know—to some degree—what it is like to have the weight of others' expectations upon your shoulders."

Clar turned to look at her, unsure what to make of that. Kat's face glowed in the firelight, touched with gold. Her brown eyes reflected the sparks that spit up, and for a moment Kat looked as if she had been thrown out to sea without boat or sight of land to be seen.

"I have wondered why you came here alone," Clar said. "You don't have to tell me. At first I thought there must have been more of you, that perhaps you had simply split up to cover more ground. But you are alone, aren't you? You and Suhnsuoc?"

Kat's laugh cracked when it left her lips. "Yes, we are alone. I thought I knew why, but everything I was told has been wrong."

Clar went still at that. She knew that feeling. "Why—why did you come?"

Her question slipped out, hesitant but curious, unsure whether she really wanted to know the answer.

"To lead the warmlanders against the Tuanye," Kat said mirthlessly. "To strike as their spell failed, to ensure it would never be reinvoked again."

"Do you . . . still plan to do that?" Clar's chest felt hard and tight in the middle. She glanced in the direction of the Marefi army without meaning to, imagining a force descending upon Haveranth, Cantoranth, Bemin's Fan.

"There appears to be no need," Kat said. "No one told me what to do if someone had broken the hearthstones. I don't think even the elders would know what to do with that."

"They don't know?"

Kat laughed again. "No, but I think the ialtag tried to tell them."

When the other woman turned to look at Clar again, it felt like the fire burned in her eyes. Clar took an unconscious step toward her, feeling the heat of Kat's body even warmer than the flames beside them. The memory of waking with her hand in Kat's surfaced. She couldn't look away.

Kat seemed to come closer too, though Clar didn't see her move. Or maybe they were both moving, as if some unseen force pulled them toward one another.

Kat's hand rose, hovering just to the side of Clar's face. If Clar leaned a finger's width to the left, her cheek would come in contact with Kat's palm.

She leaned.

Her lips met Kat's almost at the same time. For a moment, they hung suspended in their combined surprise, but then Clar's hand found Kat's waist, the firm muscles of her torso, and Kat's other arm mirrored hers and pulled her tight up against her body.

Clar had never been kissed before, and she wasn't sure if she was doing it right. Kat's lips were warm and soft, gentle. Hungry but coaxing more than capturing. Something woke in Clar's belly, hot like the fire and every bit as ready to send sparks into the night sky.

A scream rent the air, almost on top of them.

The two women jumped apart, and immediately, Clar's heart started pounding all the harder, she and Kat staring at each other as if they had forgotten the rest of the world existed.

Suhnsuoc came trotting up to the camp, tail high, looking enormously pleased with hyrself.

"You're an absolute menace," Kat said to the feline, darting a glance at Clar that seemed both exasperated and resigned.

Clar laughed helplessly as Suhnsuoc started to purr, a little afraid the kazytya had screamed on purpose out of disapproval, but then the giant cat padded over and affectionately butted hys forehead against her shoulder.

Something in Clar melted, and Kat's face softened from frustration to something more tender.

Clar had seen the kazytya do this to Kat but never to her.

She thought of Kat's confession, and as the other woman went about unrolling her bedroll, Clar couldn't help but feel like she would follow her anywhere.

RYD FELT, as the days went on with no word, that everything in his world had been moved ever so slightly to the left. Not much, not enough to make it a stranger to him, but just enough to make him feel like he was tripping over things he didn't think were in his path, barking his shin on a stool he thought he would clear, and losing his balance when he stood up too quickly.

For a time, he worried that the bulber bloat had come back. He poked at his side enough that his skin became pink on the paler surface of his abdomen where it didn't often see the sun. Where before that would have sent pain spiking through him enough to make his vision swim, now it just irritated the surface and left it feeling vaguely bruised.

Life in Lahivar was tense. The children were quieter, and the adults assigned them chores that were just different enough to indicate the possible need to pick up and leave. There was a prolific number of baskets turning up throughout the waymake, densely woven enough that people could fill them with living plants— this was the work of older children and younger adults who guided them. The number of carts tripled in the turns after Kat and Clar left, and the leatherworkers all had blisters from making extra harnesses for the ihstal that would pull them.

Scouts ranged to the north every day, Ras among them, though Sart and the others kept trying to get him to stay and rest.

Ryd lent his hands where they would be most useful, setting aside his carving of mundanities to instead advise on plants that would most likely survive being moved, adding an extra bit of strength to someone moving a heavy item, spending hours smoking meat that they could pack with them.

Had the land remained as it was when he and Carin and Ras had first arrived, there would have been little hope of preparing for an entire waymake full of people to flee these invaders.

Yet still Ryd felt a bit helpless, a bit like a fil string *almost* in tune.

Hoyu helped with the preparations as much as he did, and Ryd thought that the Khardish woman perhaps felt the same persistent itch of futility as he did.

"Will it be enough?" she asked him as they stood tending the smokers for the fourth day in a row.

Ryd wasn't sure he'd ever get the smell out of his hair. He already felt a headache coming on. The smokers were set up on the south side of the river almost on top of the spring that fed it, mostly so the winds blowing in from the sea would take the smoke away from the waymake instead of toward it, which mostly worked as hoped.

"I don't know," he said honestly. "If what Ras guessed about the size of their army is true, they could surround us without much trouble."

Hoyu was quiet for a moment. "The scouts have said their ships follow them down the coast. If the ships outpace the army, that would be a sign they planned to send in more from the sea. It is good they have not yet."

"Do you think they will come here?" Ryd asked. "What do they want?"

"It will depend," she said. "I cannot say what the Marefi want with any certainty, but if I had to guess, I would say they were promised some sort of power. Their country is warlike, aggressive. If they thought there was something they could use here, they would want to take it."

"From what Carin has told me, I cannot imagine there is anything here that would be of interest to them. We live so simply compared to your cities and your ships." Ryd could not imagine such a thing, and he wasn't sure he wanted to.

"Magic," Hoyu said. "Arelashk is a mage of no small power. He has trained with the finest in Khardan, and his specialty is the arcane ancients. His title means 'story collector,' just as Asurashk's means 'story seeker.' If there is anything this land has, it is stories and arcane secrets."

Ryd could not argue with that.

The wind blew smoke into his eyes, and they started to water, stinging.

"You know," he said irritably, "if I indeed have magic, it would sure be nice if I could use it to keep the smoke out of my eyes."

Hoyu chuckled. "If we could all use magic to escape life's incon—troubles, we would never get anything done."

Ryd thought she had stumbled over the word *inconveniences*, and he again felt the flash of pleased surprise that she had come so far in their language. Then again, surrounded as she was, she didn't have much choice. It wasn't as if she could escape it.

"I just want to feel like I can help," Ryd muttered, batting at his eyes with the heel of his hand. "At least in Ryhnas Lu Sesim last time, I had some sort of direction to point in. I hate waiting."

"As do I," Hoyu admitted. She glanced westward in the direction of the sea. "If your skills seem unhelpful right now, simply imagine how I feel."

A commotion arose in the waymake, and both Ryd and Hoyu tensed.

"Go," Hoyu said. "I will watch the smokers."

Ryd turned and ran. The bulk of the waymake was on the north side of the river, so he hurried around the spring where a well-trodden path had taken root since they still had no bridge. The bridge had been a plan for summer, but as the old saying went, even the best-laid plans could break with the dawn of a new day.

He saw Mari hurrying upstream, and when her eyes fell on him, she beckoned urgently. "Come," she said. "Your friend Jenin."

Fear spiked through Ryd's chest, immediately taking him back to that horrible day of his Journeying, waiting with Lyari and Carin at the village hearth-home in Haveranth for Jenin, who would never arrive. Hearing the screams. Clar's hands covered in blood.

Jenin and Ryd were sharing a roundhome these days, and Mari made a beeline toward it.

"Is sy okay?" Ryd asked.

"Sart is with hyr. Sy won't wake. I went in to find hyr, and hys body was shaking and jerking in hys furs."

Ryd almost flew through the door.

Sart sat behind Jenin's head, a hand on either side of hys cheeks. Jenin's entire body was rigid but shaking, and hys eyes were partly open, rolled back to expose the whites.

"What is happening?" Ryd asked.

"Seizure," Sart said through gritted teeth. "But not a normal one."

Ryd shot a panicked glance at Mari. He didn't know what a seizure was, but he didn't think this was normal at all.

"Not normal?" Mari said, and Sart shook her head once, sharply.

"Magic," Sart said. "This can happen if someone overreaches."

"What was Jenin trying to do?" Ryd asked, confounded.

Again there seemed to be nothing he could do to help, and he stood there in the doorway with his hands worrying at one another as if doing so could make it stop.

"I don't know," Sart said. "I'm trying to give hyr some energy to break hyr out of it, but sy's fighting me."

"Why would sy be fighting you?" Ryd couldn't keep the disbelief from his voice.

"Stubborn fool," Sart muttered, ignoring Ryd's question. "You're not Culy."

"What can I do?" Ryd asked. "Give me something to do."

Sart had a sheen of sweat forming on her upper lip, and when she looked up at him, she looked like any energy she wasn't expending for Jenin was focused on not throttling Ryd.

"Get out of here," she said. "I need to concentrate."

Ryd and Mari hastily obeyed, almost stumbling over each other as they went out the door. A small crowd had gathered, and Ryd wondered what it seemed like to the Northlanders to have so many strangers arriving and doing strange things, bringing strange problems.

No one looked anything but concerned though, and Ryd figured they'd heard Sart well enough.

Ryd stalked back toward the spring. His feet felt wooden. Everything felt out of control. The one thing he was good at was useless right now. What good were bone needles in the face of an army? Even a hundred halm bows wouldn't be enough. Ryd couldn't fight, and he didn't think he could stomach stabbing anyone anyway.

His ear gave a twinge where—what felt like a lifetime ago—a Silencer's arrow had lobbed off a bit of his earlobe. And again when the rovers came to Lahivar, he had narrowly escaped death. It was Sart who had come to his rescue that time. She must have been tired of putting out fires.

The sense of strangeness that had been pushing at the edges of Ryd's consciousness surged again, and he hit his foot on a small lump of earth that shouldn't have caused him any trouble. He felt hysterical laughter bubbling up in his chest. Maybe he was going mad.

It wasn't wrongness that he was sensing, more like *otherness*. Maybe it was him. Maybe he was off somehow, out of step with everything else, the one discordant note from an otherwise perfect harmony.

Hoyu could manage a bit longer.

Ryd's feet had taken him to the eastern edge of the spring, a small pool that had grown deeper and deeper as the force of the water from below had hollowed out a place for itself. Moss was already growing around it, and the rocks left behind where the soil had washed away were pale grey, the water a clear blue-green. It seemed to have stopped expanding, which was a small relief.

He sat on a rock at the edge of the water, staring into it. It had gotten substantially deeper since he had last bothered to look at it, the bottom far enough down now that peering into it gave him vertigo. Though the water's strength was enough to make a river, it looked deceptively serene, ripples the only clue that there was movement in the deep.

So many changes in such a short time. Everyone was just trying to swim with the current, trying to keep their heads above water so they wouldn't drown in the deluge.

Yearning almost overtook him. His crafts were good for him. He liked to make things with his hands because he could see the progression of his work throughout the day, point to it if anyone asked what he'd been up to, and it brought with it a sense of satisfaction. The same with gardening, with watching seedlings break through the earth to reach out for the sun. You could watch them change with the passage of time, new signs of growing life appearing with each new day.

But right now everything was simply waiting and preparing, like the bunched muscles of someone about to run a race. Gathered energy needed somewhere to *go*. It needed out.

Something built in his chest, like a howl or a scream. He couldn't be sure. He couldn't just stand by the spring and yell into the watery abyss or people would think he really had lost himself somewhere.

He pushed himself off the rock and sat right on the ground where other feet had worn it bare of grass, though some clung near the expanding carpet of moss. It felt good to touch the earth.

Ryd wanted to *do* something, but if he couldn't, he would at least take comfort in feeling the world beneath his hands, proof that maybe it hadn't moved after all.

He didn't expect the *thrum* that pulsed through his palms.

Staring down at his hands, Ryd held his breath, wondering if he'd imagined it.

But there it was again, a hum almost, not like the movement of water, but like something stirring.

Alarmed, he scrambled backward, and his back bumped into an edge of the rock, sending a small shock of pain through his shoulder blade.

The hum continued, and he felt a presence at his back that was not a rock.

When he turned to look, he almost sprang backward into the water.

Directly behind the rock he had vacated, fanning out in a circle that formed almost a crown upon the Lahivar River's head, were five bone-white halm saplings.

· · · · ·

When Mari came running toward him only to skid to a baffled halt, Ryd was still staring at the trees.

"What did you do?" Mari asked, breathless.

"I . . . didn't do anything," Ryd said. "That's the whole problem. I was sitting here feeling upset about not being able to do anything, and the trees just *happened*."

"Halms do not just happen," Mari said. "Did you plant seeds?"

Ryd shook his head mutely.

Mari let out a low whistle, scrubbing a hand through her short black hair.

"Sart wanted me to tell you that she got Jenin out of the seizure," she said. "Sy's waking up but a little groggy."

"I'll go right away," Ryd said.

"Ryd," Mari said as he passed her to head into the waymake. She tucked her silver streak of hair behind her ear.

"What?"

"Remind me to tell you the halmer's tale," she said.

Ryd didn't know what that was supposed to mean, so he nodded and hurried ahead to the roundhome, where the crowd of people had dispersed, and only a few of the smaller children were nearby. They were playing a game of tig or some intricate combination of other games Ryd didn't know from the way they were waving sticks around as they ran.

Sart was still sitting behind Jenin, looking like she had a whole apple stuck in her throat, but Jenin wasn't thrashing anymore, only propped up on one elbow, swallowing every other second. The room smelled faintly of vomit.

"What happened?" Ryd asked.

"Rot if I know," Sart said irritably. "I am waiting for sy to explain why sy decided to risk this kind of magic at a time we are all about to burst like a belly balloon full of too much air."

"I was trying to find the last two stones." Jenin's voice came out hoarse, and sy cleared hys throat. "I couldn't just sit around with that army approaching."

"That does not help my mood," Sart said. "You could have died."

Jenin looked at her as if sy half-wished sy would have. Ryd fetched a wooden cup and poured water in it from the jug on the table.

Jenin took it gratefully and sipped, grimacing.

"I don't know how you snapped me out of it, but I'm glad you did," Jenin said. "Thank you. Things have been different—wilder—since Carin and Culy broke the last stone."

"You think?" Sart said. "But I didn't do anything to snap you out of it. Something else must have. I didn't have enough energy left to give you."

A suspicion began to dawn on Ryd, and as he placed the jug back on the table, he stared at the bits of dirt that still clung to his palms where he'd laid them against the earth.

"What's the halmer's tale?" he asked suddenly.

Sart snorted. "You want story time?"

"Please," he said, and she frowned at his earnestness.

Jenin sipped hys water, looking sideways at Ryd's swift change in subject.

"There's an old story of someone who said he was a halmer, but everyone who asked him to make something always got a no. He traveled from place to place, wearing the halmer's brand, but he left a trail of angry people behind him because he'd never give them what they wanted." Sart got to her feet, apparently satisfied that Jenin wasn't going to drop dead anymore.

"Is that it?" Ryd asked, perplexed.

"Of course that's not it," Sart said. "One day, in the far east of Sands, a waymake decided they wouldn't let him leave until he made something of halm for them. Five days turned into five turns, and still the halmer refused to halm."

Her lip quirked at her own twist of language, and Ryd remembered that she had once pretended to be a halmer herself. The rover who'd almost taken Ryd's life had once made such a demand of Sart.

"What happened after five turns?" Ryd asked.

Sart gave him a smile that carried a hint of the trickster in her, of the woman who had jumped from beast to beast on the edge of a cliff while hunting, spinning tales that spread through Ryhnas Lu Sesim.

"The waymake woke on First Seed of the sixth turn to find the halmer gone . . . and five young halms were growing in a circle around their huts." Sart stretched her shoulders and twisted her head from one side to the other, cracking her neck. "They demanded something of halm, and the halmer delivered—five new trees that none of them could use themselves."

"The halmer had planted the seeds without them knowing?" Jenin asked.

Some color was returning to hys face, which sent a wave of relief washing over Ryd that did not quite dull the dawning sensation of anxiety that the tale had planted in him.

Sart shook her head. "The halmer had no seeds. No one did. But the will of the halmer is the will of the halm—the truest of them are never alone."

Ryd felt as if he'd dumped the jug of water down the back of his tunic.

"So tell me, Ryd, our resident halmer—why do you ask?" Sart straightened her back, her eyes boring into him.

He cast a desperate look at Jenin, who was watching him with every bit as much interest as Sart.

"Halms are a potent source of magic," said Jenin thoughtfully, taking another sip of water.

Sart turned sharply to look at hyr, then back to Ryd inch by inch.

"I guess I have something to show you," Ryd said.

DYAVA HAD never seen anything like it.

He supposed that was what life was supposed to be—a series of surprises until the final surprise of death—but even though he was barely an adult in the eyes of the village, he was beginning to feel like an old man.

The field before him, Lyris's field, should have been knee high with abundant and eager squash plants by now, but instead nearly every plant was withered and dead where only a few days before, they had been hale and thriving.

"I don't think I can take much more of this," he muttered.

He crouched in the field, picking up a wilted leaf.

Dyava couldn't see anything wrong with it when he turned it over in his hands, but that didn't mean anything. You couldn't really see the illnesses people got either, only their effects. It could have been some sort of plant disease. If the people of the Hearthland knew little about their own diseases, they knew even less about any that might affect their crops.

Lyris was standing at the far edge of the field, the baby on his hip, and he looked as worried as a still-new father might, staring out over the wreckage of moons of hard work now lying flopped in the dirt.

Dyava made his way back over to Lyris, shaking his head as he did. "I don't know what happened. I'm sorry."

"People are talking," Lyris said. The baby tugged on hys father's hair, which hung a little past his collarbone, and Lyris winced. "They say this is punishment."

That made Dyava forget what he'd been about to say. "Punishment?" he asked as mildly as he could.

"You've been on the Journeying," Lyris said softly.

"Yes," Dyava said. "And that means I know which direction the punishment flows—how could this be punishment for us?"

Lyris shrugged. "There's talk that old magic is waking up and doesn't like what the ancestors did."

That was a little too close to the truth for Dyava's liking. He eyed Lyris warily.

"Whatever it is, Lyari is working on a way to fix it," Dyava said, trying as hard as he could to sound reassuring.

The baby did not look convinced. Dyava smiled a crooked smile at the child waving, and the wee thing burst into a grin, showing a few new teeth breaking through hys gums.

"We believe in the soothsayer," said Lyris, giving the baby a bounce with a fond smile despite the heavy topic of conversation. "But at this rate, people will go hungry."

"I know," Dyava said.

The weight of those two little words pressed upon him. Hunger, thirst, illness—barren fields and barren bodies. His parents had been right. Something else had shifted, and things were tilting out of balance faster than he thought they should.

Of course, none of them really knew what *should* be at all. How could they?

He talked a bit more to Lyris before heading back toward the village. Something was bothering him. Well, what *wasn't* bothering him lately?

He walked down one of the rows of dead squash plants, squinting up at the scudding clouds that blanketed the sky. Rain wouldn't do much for them.

Looking back down at the carpet of wilted leaves, he stopped.

What he'd thought were just drifting strands of broken spiderwebs caught his eye.

It was subtle, barely visible. He crouched, then knelt, bending over and leaning on one hand so he could see. In the diffuse light of an overcast day, it was almost impossible to make it out against the dirt.

He reached out one finger and tried to catch one of the strands. It didn't stick to him like it should. His finger passed right through it as if it weren't there at all.

He froze where he was, staring at the field as if it were indeed an enormous spiderweb, and he was caught right in it, trapped as an unfortunate fly.

It wasn't disease that had done this to the field, and it wasn't even the breaking of the hearthstones.

This was deliberate, and it was done with magic.

· · · · ·

Dyava had to go to Lyari with it. He would tell his parents, too, but this was a step beyond their plan.

As he hurried to her home, thankful Lyris had turned and gone inside before he saw Dyava with his face almost in the dirt, Dyava felt whatever little bit of hope he'd had crumbling like ash in the wind.

If it wasn't enough that the spell was falling to pieces, that disaster after disaster were striking the village, now someone had turned to purposeful sabotage.

He was passing the plot of land where Old Wend's roundhome had sat when he was struck with something else. They had never figured out who killed Old Wend.

Haveranth was not very large, nor were the other villages in the Hearthland. While it wasn't true that everyone knew one another, it was true that there were few people one had not interacted with at some point if they were from the same village. There were a few scattered roundhomes outside of the village proper, people who liked to keep to themselves, but the soothsayers always kept an eye on them. Few could survive completely alone—people needed each other. If nothing else, one accident could prove fatal, and no one was a master of all trades, however proficient they were at some.

Dyava wasn't sure why his mind had taken that particular route, but when it dawned on him, he stopped walking.

No one was alone. Everyone was connected to someone else somehow, and someone would have had to see something. He wasn't sure if he was still thinking about Old Wend or about the strange magic residue on the field of dead squash.

And, of course, there was the matter of the hawk and Reynah's injury.

Very few people openly used magic in the Hearthland for more than trifles, and whatever had been done to that field was far from a trifle.

Lyari had said that the other soothsayers had very little magic of their own. This increase in magic and volatility would not give anyone the finesse required to do something so complex, no matter the strength of brute force.

Dyava started walking again as the afternoon sun broke through the clouds, sending fingers of light down to touch the earth with gold. A few droplets of rain spritzed his face, but he ignored the wetness on his skin.

Considering what his family had done with Jenin, there was very little outside the realm of possibility for those with the ability to manipulate magic with skill.

He could barely allow himself to think it, let alone consider voicing it to anyone, but he could no longer ignore so many oddities stitched together.

That hawk, Merin's hawk, was her spy. It was bound with a particular type of magic, one Dyava's parents abhorred. Subjugation, Lyari had called it. Forcing another creature to do one's will.

If Reynah—and Harag in Bemin's Fan—had only simple magic, there was no way such a thing could be done by their hand, but Merin had been capable of it.

Few people knew the extent of the bond. Dyava wasn't certain that the price for such magic was as high as sharing injuries—but what if there was something else involved? Jenin had been able to leave hys body and appear at will anywhere in Haveranth and even beyond, with difficulty.

What if—someone's body was killed when they were not in it?

Or what if they somehow escaped while they were being killed?

Dyava had reached Lyari's roundhome, but he couldn't make himself go in.

The idea sounded preposterous. So absurd he should not even be entertaining it.

The spell that sustained the Hearthland's bounty was fading, and magic was wilder, stronger.

From what little he had studied of magic, and what he had seen of Jenin and how taxing it had been to make contact with Carin, Dyava thought it was a reasonable assumption that if someone managed to escape hys body at the moment of a murder, it would take that person time to recover enough strength to act upon the world again.

And a sudden rush of wilder, stronger magic could be just what sy needed to do it.

The door opened before him, and Lyari peered at him. "What are you doing just staring at the door?"

"Something's wrong," he said, and she immediately moved aside so he could come in, shutting the door behind them.

"What is it?" she asked when the door closed.

Dyava had seen his parents cast wards countless times, but he hadn't tried it himself, especially not with magic the way it was now. He tried, gingerly, feeling it leap where before it had flowed, and the concentration it took him to do something relatively simple left him winded. He wasn't sure what would happen with a ward spinning out of control, but for all he knew, trying to make the two of them safe from prying ears could make the whole village go deaf accidentally.

Lyari watched him, confusion turning to wariness.

"Have you been using your magic regularly?" he asked her quietly.

She shook her head and barked a short laugh. "No. I've been exhausting myself with other labors."

"You should try something very small. *Very* small, and probably nothing involving fire," he added when she reached for an oil lamp that was sitting on the end of the table closest to the door.

Her hand stopped halfway to the lamp, and she frowned.

Dyava kicked off his shoes and went to sit at the table, looking around for anything that would be useful without inadvertently exploding or punching a hole in a wall—or a person.

The salt cellar was in the middle of the table, and he decided that was least likely to cause serious injury. He took a pinch and dropped it on the table. Lyari came to stand at the head of the table, leaning forward on her hands and looking at him like he had licked the slab of polished maha instead.

"Just try to—move the salt or something. Nothing big." He was going to feel very foolish if nothing happened.

He didn't have to worry long. Lyari's gaze turned to the salt crystals, and then they went flying. He heard the faint patter of them hitting wood—and from the ping, something metal as well—but he couldn't have told anyone where they went.

Lyari stared. "What just happened?"

His parents were going to kill him for talking to her about this, but he figured it was for the best anyway. The last thing anyone needed was the village soothsayer accidentally murdering someone because she didn't realize her magic had gotten more powerful overnight.

"Something has changed with magic itself," Dyava said. "And it gets worse."

Her face grew grim as he told her about the field, and if she didn't immediately jump to the same conclusion he had about who had done it, she did understand in an instant the implications.

"I know that spell," she said. "It's complicated and very finicky. It was meant to be used on animals that would not calm, but it was also used on certain weeds that resisted other means of control."

"It looked like it drained the life out of the squash," Dyava said, trying and failing to imagine what that spell would look like used on an animal.

"That is precisely what it does," she said. She grimaced. "It's . . . a much milder version of the spell I'm meant to reinvoke one cycle hence."

Dyava sat back on the bench, stunned.

"What does this mean?" he asked.

"Beyond someone very powerful obviously working to sow chaos in fields that should only be growing squash?" Lyari took a shaky breath. "It means many things, but mostly that time is running shorter than it should be."

Dyava grasped the edge of the bench with both hands, unsure of what that meant but not liking the unease that slithered up his spine.

Lyari looked at him and smiled. "Do not fear," she said. "This is a complication, but it is not so dire."

"What do you mean?" Dyava asked carefully.

He could hear his heartbeat pounding in his ears.

"I have been trying to figure out whether the Reinvocation could be done sooner," she said after a beat. "I didn't tell you because I thought it was moot. Ultimately, the answer was no. The amount of magic necessary is extraordinary, and next summer there will be help that wouldn't exist this cycle."

The pounding in his ears had stopped with the words *whether the Reinvocation could be done sooner*, but it started up again with a stutter of relief.

Except Lyari was going on. "Until now," she said. Relief painted her face as hope blossomed in her eyes. "If magic has become that much more powerful due to the first two stones breaking, I could do it sooner, secure the safety of the Hearthland for another five hundred cycles. We could be done with this."

Dyava only stared at her. She didn't even seem to see him for once, only looking at the table, now completely clear of salt.

"We could be done," she said softly. "Forever."

PART OF Carin wanted to go straight to the fourth stone, the one she and Culy were nearly certain they could track. But time pressed upon her. Though there was supposed to be one cycle remaining before the Reinvocation, Carin did not want to leave anything to chance. If they could break all five stones now, a cycle early, they could rest somewhat assured that the Reinvocation would fail.

But Kat's report of a halm that ancient appearing out of thin air in Crevasses was too much to discount, and so as Bide waxed on the heels of Quicken moon's waning, Carin and Culy rode into Alar Marhasan after pressing hard for turns.

Carin was tired, her joints and bones feeling the stretch of time spent traveling without cease, but even though she had been to Alar Marhasan once not so very long ago, already it had changed.

When they approached the plaza where she and Culy had once stood, looking out over the ruins, the fifteen stone tigers now poured water from their mouths into that wide bowl that became a river.

There was evidence of animals moving through—Carin could see new growth all around. Tracks crisscrossed the ground, and in trees and in the cleft of ruins, she counted at least seven bird nests visible just from where they sat atop the ihstal.

"Everything changes," she murmured.

"Just so," Culy said.

It felt different than it had. Carin could feel the hum of the stone that had been their goal; it yet hovered at the edge of her awareness. But here there was something else.

"I think there is a stone here," she said, but her face tensed with a frown.

Kat had told them roughly where to find the tree, but as they moved toward the gully, Carin didn't need her directions. She and Culy spoke little, the ihstal moving toward the pull with only a nudge of knees to guide them.

Soon, however, Tahin started to resemble hys name, padded hooves dancing across the mossy ground and whistles trilling through the air.

"They are nervous," Culy said.

Carin nodded her assent and dismounted. "We can let them stay where they are more comfortable."

She wished she'd asked Kat how Suhnsuoc had felt, but she hadn't thought to. Kat had said the air felt different, alive almost.

That was a good description to Carin.

With a gentle whisper to the ihstal, Culy and Carin made their way deeper into the glen.

When the tree became visible in the distance, Carin stopped in her tracks.

"How could such a halm remain hidden?" she said, breathless at the sight of it.

Kat's account had not done the tree justice. It was immense, its trunk a veritable cliff of white wood. Its leaves had not yet burst their buds, but they dotted it with red in the daylight, the sun touching the new growth like garnets spilled over bone.

Against the green of the moss and the blue of the scattered grass that grew in bursts throughout the glen's floor, it was an otherworldly sight.

"Only by its own will," Culy said softly after a pause long enough that Carin had forgotten she'd asked a question aloud.

"There is a stone here, but . . . isn't here?" she said. "Do you feel that?"

Culy nodded.

Together, they ventured closer to the tree, though the word closer meant very little when something so vast reached for visitors with root and branches long before one could lay a hand on its trunk.

"I do not hear any birds," Carin said suddenly. "Why not?"

For the first time in Carin's memory, Culy looked utterly perplexed.

"I could not say," sy said. "Everything here feels strange. Both charged and sluggish, like if lightning could strike underwater."

Carin had to agree.

They made a slow circuit of the tree, very slow. The roots were so large near the trunk that they were twice as tall as both visitors. While occasionally they could duck *under* a root that had grown up to bow away from the earth, mostly they had to walk out far enough from the trunk to step over.

They were close to the southernmost side of the tree when Carin tripped stepping over a root and threw out a hand to catch herself.

When her palm touched the halm, every nerve in her body seemed to light up like the torchbugs on a summer night. The tree was *warm* to the touch, and its warmth suffused her, welcomed her like an old friend.

"Carin?" Culy was calling out her name—sy was some distance ahead of her, and she didn't remember hyr being that far away.

Carin didn't know how many times sy had said her name. She pulled her hand back from the tree and immediately missed it.

Culy closed the distance between them, concern upon hys face.

"I felt something," she said, looking at her palm as if expecting to see some sort of mark. "Have you touched it?"

"No," Culy said.

After a moment's hesitation, sy reached out and laid a hand on the root.

Hys grey eyes lit like something had put a glow behind hys irises, and Carin took a startled step backward. Had she looked like that?

The tree itself seemed to give off light. Light was the revealer of things, cutting and bright and sharp, something to be wary of. But darkness birthed all things, including halm. Halm seeds were the deepest black like the void of myth from which had sprung everything above and below the earth.

"Culy," Carin said.

The hyrsin hadn't moved, and Carin could see why sy had called her name when she herself had touched the halm.

Instead of trying again to get Culy's attention, she put her own hand back on the white wood.

Again she felt that sense of welcome, of warmth. This tree had stood guard over this glen for ages gone by, hidden from everyone. Why?

The stone should be here. Carin could feel it, here and not here, a force both magnetic and repellent at once.

It was one thing to know on some level that halm had a will. It was something else altogether to place one's hand on a tree and feel it respond. Carin had touched halm many times her whole life—she had a halm bow, a halm knife. She had seen halm groves and touched their trees in passing. As hysmern, she had played in their shadows, marveling over their smoothness where other trees had rough bark. It was as if halm were carved from light itself.

But now, here, in the shadow of a tree so ancient time ceased to have meaning under its boughs, Carin felt that every other halm she had encountered had failed to prepare her for the immensity of this one. Not just its size or the fact that this root came up to her thigh and from here it would take a hefty throw to toss a pebble far enough to hit the trunk.

This tree spanned . . . everything.

When she finally pulled her hand away—somehow at the exact moment Culy did—she met her lover's eyes with certainty that her own reflected back the shock she felt.

"Have you ever—" She stopped as Culy shook hys head.

"I want to get closer," Culy said, and it was such a simple sentence in its strangeness that Carin simply nodded.

Together they closed the distance to the trunk, almost a hundred paces from where they had stood. Here, Carin could see the way the roots branched from the trunk, the twists of white wood, shadow in the clefts where the roots twisted. Far above them, branches wider than a person was tall spread out from the tree's center. This close, she may well have been staring at an uneven wall.

Could the stone be *inside* the tree somehow? Could the ancestors have placed it inside a grove of five halms knowing they would one day grow around it and keep it immobile and unreachable?

When she said it aloud, Culy shook hys head.

"I don't think so," sy said. "I think I would have heard about it. I don't think the stone is here."

"What would we even do if it was inside such a tree?" Carin murmured. "Halm cannot be cut."

That wasn't entirely true, but she knew Culy would understand. Halmers could work the wood, but while they had created processes, Culy insisted those processes were instead more of a ritual that allowed halmers to do their work with magic while making sense of it in their own minds. Carin wondered if, once a halmer was aware of hys magic, if sy could work halm without the ritual, like Culy had made hys staff for all Culy said sy wasn't a true halmer. That would be a question for Ryd in the future, perhaps, if they all managed to survive this mess.

"I am not certain the stone is inside the tree," Culy said, frowning. "If it is, the tree does not want it found."

As if in answer, the white bark of the halm suddenly began to glow, first like a shimmer, then more intensely, like the full moon.

"Which begs the question of what the tree does want," said Carin, tearing her eyes away from the light of the tree to meet Culy's startled gaze. "Any ideas what this means?"

Culy held out a hand, eyes on hys palm for a moment before looking back to Carin. "Perhaps we could find out."

Gingerly, following Culy's example, Carin placed her hand back on the trunk of the tree.

This time the change was instantaneous. She may have gasped; Carin didn't know. From one blink to the next, the glen was gone.

• • • • •

It was as if the stone had pulled them both into the unseen world, the world of dreams, the world of spirits. But unlike when Carin and Culy dreamt together, they were not in control.

"Where is this place?" Carin asked, trying to make sense of the world around her and trying harder to suppress the rising tide of panic.

They were in what Carin recognized as the hills southeast of Sands, a strange between-place where before there had been little life and a lot of sun.

Her surroundings answered her question a moment later.

Carin felt the pull of the stone a moment before she saw it. It lay exposed atop a hill, and like in her dreams, thinking of it was enough to transport her there, though unlike her dreams, she did not think it was her doing.

Culy was beside her, looking rattled, a rarity since they had been acquainted.

"Has this ever happened to you?" Carin asked, and the hyrsin shook hys head.

"I have . . . communed with halm before, but it has never been so insistent." Culy's lip quirked before sy seemed to address the air around them. "There is no need to be so forceful. We are listening."

Hys words hung in the air for a moment, and then the ground vanished beneath their feet, blurring into scrubby, spiked bushes that seemed to inhale water from the earth below and burst into bloom all at once.

They had moved westward, Carin thought. She was not familiar with this part of the Northlands, but she felt the change as if the halm were guiding them toward a particular destination and wanted them to be aware.

The ground blurred again. West again, now in the midst of Boggers where the bog had been transformed into a lake bigger than the Jewel far to the south and a forest had encircled it almost overnight, the trees thirstily draining the former wetland of its muck, life sprouting from every hummock, every fold of the land.

And that was not all that had changed overnight.

This time Carin felt her sharp intake of breath even as Culy saw what she did. The army.

The Khardish and Marefi forces were moving inland—away from Lahivar and away from the sea. Already they were camped on the eastern shore of the new lake, likely thankful for the abundant fresh water.

"They changed course," Culy said. "They are moving due east."

Carin turned to look back to the east where they had come from. "They are making straight for the stone," she said urgently. "And they are moving quickly. They must have turned away from Lahivar almost when we did. Culy, if they reach the stone before we do—"

"There will be thousands of soldiers between us and our goal," Culy finished for her.

As soon as sy said the words, they were back in the glen, blinking away the sudden shift in location.

The enormous halm still glowed beneath their hands, and Carin felt wariness wash over her.

"How can we be sure this is true?" she asked.

"Can we risk doubt?" came Culy's answer.

Carin shook her head, not sure if she meant it in answer to Culy's reply or merely as a helpless gesture in the face of everything changing around her faster than she could keep up with. The spirit, which had been quiet all this time, chose that moment to swell and crest like a breaking wave, washing away her uncertainty.

"We need to go. We must beat them there," she murmured. "You said Wyt managed to move her stone away from the shore. We cannot risk these invaders doing the same. They could take it away from here, and who knows what effects that could have?"

Even as she said the words, Carin felt a flash of fear.

"If Lyari reinvokes the spell with that stone aboard a ship or in Sahesh or somewhere in Maref, it could be disastrous," she said. "Not only for us, but for anyone around it. It would look like a weapon. If Maref is half so inclined to aggression as Hoyu has said—"

"They would take such a thing as an act of war," Culy said. "Yes. You are quite correct. We cannot allow for even the possibility of one of the hearthstones leaving this land when we know so little of the possible consequences."

"If there is a stone here with this tree and we can't find it, it is unlikely any of the Khardish or Marefi seekers could discover it," Carin went on. "But the other stone is out in the open."

"Yes. We are in agreement," Culy said, placing one hand back on the halm. "Thank you."

There was risk in being shown some sort of vision by a force they could not explain. Carin had experienced such magic on her Journeying, in the cave where they were to learn their true names. She was all too aware it could be used to lie.

But what choice did they have?

As one, she and Culy hurried back out of the glen, their feet moving swiftly across the ground.

"We should travel as long as we have daylight," Culy said, putting two fingers in hys mouth to whistle for the ihstal.

Carin heard Tahin's answering whistle and Siuhn's a moment later.

"I will forego sleep if I must for us to succeed at this," Carin said. "I will not let the stone fall into the hands of Rela or Asu. All they seek is power."

A horrible thought intruded into her mind as Tahin trotted up to her, tossing hys head and looking eager to be far, far away from that glen and from Alar Marhasan as a whole.

She climbed onto Tahin's back. "There are too many ways the stone could be used against our people," she said softly as Culy mounted Siuhn beside her. "Even if they used it to strike Maref, it would likely fall on our heads. We could not stand against even one nation seeking dominion over these lands—with both Khardan and Maref, we would be slaughtered."

Culy stroked Siuhn's neck, looking pensive. "All we can do is what we can do," sy said finally. "That and no more. And you and I, my love—we can do much."

With that, Culy gave her a sharp smile, a dangerous smile. The kind of smile between gods about to rain down vengeance from the heavens.

Culy was right. If devastation was coming to these lands, well, every action deserved a reaction.

As they murmured their instructions to the ihstal, padded feet eagerly bursting into a swift run northward, Carin let herself smile back.

"SUHNSUOC SAID what?" Sart was staring at Kat like she had heard her wrong, and Kat was getting tired of repeating herself.

"The army has turned eastward," Kat said. "Some days ago, it appears. Our own scouts have not returned, but sy is searching for their trail."

Sart had been sitting on a stump near the central plaza of Lahivar, sharpening one of her knives, but at Kat's words she had jumped to her feet, and now she paced, her feet making almost no noise on the ground.

"Where could they be going?" Sart muttered. Then she looked up sharply. "Could they somehow be heading for one of the remaining hearthstones?"

Kat had already thought of this possibility, but hearing it out loud didn't make her feel any better about it. "It may be best to assume they are. Carin and Culy said they can feel the stones—we must assume that of other mages."

"But it could just be because they have broken stones themselves," Sart said. "It could be that they simply have an affinity for them now."

"How would we know?" Kat asked, irritated. "Unless we have some way of testing it, we are just guessing. It is safer to presume the worst and prepare for it rather than hope for the best and regret it."

"And Culy and Carin have gone to Crevasses to look at a tree. Rotting shit," Sart said. "The army could simply be seeking Carin."

Sart struck Kat as the type of person who needed to *do* something, and since she was stuck in Lahivar with little to do, she was getting more and more irritable by the day.

"The army still has ships off the coast, yes?" Kat asked.

"Yes," Sart said. "Don't remind me."

"Could we not, I don't know, try and intercept anyone they send ashore?" Kat thought the scouts had reported seeing boats going to and fro between the army and their ships, likely bringing messages and supplies.

Sart seemed to consider that.

"When they were camped out closer to the sea, it would have been too risky to chance losing people," Sart said thoughtfully. "But the farther away the army gets, the longer any messages have to travel."

The warmlander woman grinned.

"It may not yield much, but we do have someone here who can read their languages," Kat said, thinking of the Khardish woman Hoyu. "Perhaps we will get lucky."

Sart looked around the waymake, where people were busy under the cloud of tension that had persisted since they heard the army had destroyed Ryhnas Lu Sesim and was marching on Lahivar.

Luck.

There was a lot to be said for luck, Kat thought.

She didn't know if the army turning away from Lahivar was good or bad luck.

She hadn't seen Clar in some time today—off with the halmer, she thought, likely admiring the new halm grove that had sprung up around the spring at his bidding.

Kat and Clar had both carefully avoided talking about their own experience with such a thing. Kat didn't think she could really manage the implications. Neither of them had worked with halm in their lives, but they had woken in a grove of the trees themselves only a few turns back.

If Sart was someone who needed to act rather than plan—the other woman took off in the direction of the ihstal with a hurried farewell—so was Kat. Since she and Clar had arrived back to Lahivar, they had spent their days trying to prepare the waymake to flee, but now that didn't seem to be necessary, though everyone would still go about their days as if it could be.

Kat was meant to be acting here, acting upon events rather than reacting to them.

She didn't know if her idea would work, but it was worth a try when she was sick of sitting around waiting to run for her life.

Kat set off to the north, in the general direction of Suhnsuoc, who was still scouting.

One thing about the ialtag was that they tended to watch certain people they deemed of interest. Kat hoped she still fell into that category.

She walked as the sun crept its way across the sky, clouds obscuring it only to reveal it again, golden rays breaking through the bigger ones to fall upon a summer land that was by now almost teeming with life.

She didn't have to go far.

Just to the north, in a small glade of newborn saplings, a telltale ripple in the air told her she had found who she sought.

The ialtag showed hyrself as Kat closed the distance between them, and when she drew close enough to make contact, she caught a distinct whiff of amusement along with the touch of soft, white fur.

The giant bat rested on the ground as if sy was as comfortable there as hanging from a perch or flapping through the air. There was a splash of red on the ialtag's left foot.

Just noticing it prompted an answer.

One of the strangers shot an arrow at me. It is of little consequence.

Alarmed, Kat almost withdrew her hand. *They saw you?*

Heard, it seems. A touch of wryness colored the ialtag's thought, though from the small wave of unease that followed after it, the rest of the ialtag didn't share hys assessment.

Why have you sought us? The ialtag's mental voice was not one that was familiar to Kat, but the feeling behind it was.

I was raised to lead the warmlanders against the Tuanye as their spell weakens. Time grows short. We have only a cycle remaining before the Reinvocation, and if we do not prepare now, there will be no one to lead.

The silence that came on the heels of her words had weight to it, almost like a heavy cloak suddenly thrown over her head.

Is that what you were raised to do? The ialtag sounded, if possible, even more noncommittal.

Kat did withdraw her hand for a moment then, staring in shock at the creature before her. After a heartbeat or so of hesitation, she raised her hand to the ialtag's cheek once more and nodded.

The ialtag sent pictures instead of words this time. Kat as a baby, almost the same size as a newborn Suhnsuoc, as the two of them shared their first meal amid their growing bond. Kat's baby cheeks were almost painfully round—it had taken her most of her life to grow into them, and no one at home let her forget it—and Suhnsuoc's eyes were still yet to open.

Suhnsuoc's mews melded with Kat's cries, as they so often had. The others of Suhnsuoc's litter were nearby with their own babies. There was nothing remarkable about this among Kat's people.

Then came Kat as an older child, this time apart from her fellows. Where they learned to hunt and build, Kat learned that and more. History and magic, stories the others took for simple fables but to Kat were truer than anything else she knew. She saw the elders teaching her about the hearthstone spell, about what was coming, how close they were to a chance to strike back.

That is what they taught me, she insisted to the ialtag.

A spear will skewer a salmon as readily as a trout, came the answer.

Confused, Kat didn't answer for a moment. *Are you saying they prepared me to spear other prey?*

A spear has many uses. That is all.

Kat felt frustration tighten her jaw. *Perhaps if they had intended to plant me in the ground and use me to catch throwing rings, they could have better prepared.*

All people use what they know as best they can, said the ialtag. *Your people are no different. But no one knows all things, and some things are simply believed long enough that they feel like knowledge. All anyone can do is what they feel is right according to all of these things they believe and know.*

What is it you want from me, then? Kat asked, her frustration turning to exasperation. *I am not to return home until after the time of the Reinvocation passes. But here I am simply waiting. These people are not prepared to face an army, let alone be one.*

Is leading an army truly what you believe you are meant to do? The question was said without judgement or malice, but Kat felt affronted anyway.

Kat had been made to believe exactly that. Hadn't she? She was meant to lead the warmlanders against the Tuanye, to strike them down before they could renew their evil for another five ages.

"Are you saying they're wrong?" she said out loud, knowing the ialtag would catch her meaning.

When people are set on a course, little can dissuade them, sy answered. *But you need not fight the shark under the sea if you wish to win. You must simply use the tools best suited to the endeavor.*

With that, the ialtag pulled away, breaking the contact hyrself. Before Kat could protest, the enormous bat sprang into the air. The wind from hys wings blew Kat's hair into her mouth, and she irritably spat it back out, wanting to yell after the creature but knowing it was pointless.

She could feel Suhnsuoc in the distance, but the kazytya was coming closer, likely spurred on by the irritable waves pouring off hys bonded rider.

Kat kicked a clump of grass and sat down with her back to one of the saplings. Everything was so *alive* here all of a sudden. She swore the grove had grown in the short time she spent conversing with the giant bat.

The trees here were unknown to her experience, but she could remember from her studies. Maha, for carving and building. Sugar trees, for their sweet sap that could make syrup and more. Doubloon trees, which were good for neither. Kat wasn't sure what a doubloon even was.

She had hoped that the ialtag would give her some sort of direction, but instead they had done the exact opposite. Sharks and spears and salmon. She snorted, hand brushing across the blades of grass. It tickled.

The ialtag were frequently cryptic. It wasn't that Kat was particularly attached to the idea of leading. If she were honest, it didn't sound enjoyable. She had no desire to go to the southern villages, especially not to fight, whatever their sins.

If Clar was to be believed, which Kat thought she was, those villagers weren't fighters. Most of them, anyway. They were much as people in Lahivar or her own waymake far to the north. Crafters and fishers and smiths.

Okay, she found herself thinking, *if the south is the sea, is it full of sharks?*

It felt absurd to be asking the question, but she grudgingly had to admit that the ialtag was right. If the goal was to hunt the sharks, the strategy wasn't to drown on the way to get to them. Or to kill a bunch of seals and salmon in the meantime.

Suhnsuoc came into view in the distance, cresting a small hill before vanishing behind another rise between them.

Kat welcomed the kazytya's return, but as she turned her attention to her lifelong friend and companion, she realized it wasn't for her sake Suhnsuoc had returned.

Suhnsuoc's mind was grim, and hys gait was urgent.

What happened? Kat asked, scrambling to her feet.

The kazytya chuffed in greeting, which faded into an impatient, chirping whine that almost became a growl.

Alarmed, Kat hurried to hyr as sy lowered hyrself to allow her to climb on hys back.

I am not certain. I will show you.

· · · · ·

They ran for the better part of the afternoon—Kat hadn't quite realized how much ground Suhnsuoc had covered in the time sy had been scouting—and though Suhnsuoc assured her that the army was far out of the range of being an immediate danger, Kat was not convinced.

Her stomach sank when she saw what Suhnsuoc had led her to.

It was a waymake on the edge of what had been Boggers, on the southern edge of the newborn lake. The rising water had claimed a few of the huts, but the others had been occupied recently.

The sinking feeling in her belly became nausea.

Tracks, said Suhnsuoc.

Kat didn't need the direction. There were tracks everywhere, which said the army had passed through. They must have been going due east from where they had been aiming at Lahivar, taking them along the southern edge of the lake and directly past this waymake. Kat couldn't see the waypost that would give her its name, and she couldn't remember off the top of her head what it had been or if it had even been written on the maps her people had used to teach her.

She slid off Suhnsuoc's back, leaving one hand on the kazytya's shoulder, more to reassure herself than the cat.

With a glance at Suhnsuoc, she moved toward the huts.

They were still covered in canvas. That was the biggest clue that set Kat's body buzzing. No warmlander would simply pick up and leave without their canvas. Kat pulled back the overlapping flap where it was secured under the roof. There were still things within the huts, too but in disarray, as if someone had simply grabbed whatever was close to hand in a hurry. A waterskin sat on the floor by the fire pit, something else that would not be carelessly left behind even with water returning to the land in force.

"Could they have run?" Kat asked uncertainly.

She didn't need to wait for Suhnsuoc's answer. She could see what Suhnsuoc saw, smell what Suhnsuoc's powerful nose could smell. The people who had been living in these dwellings moved due east from the waymake.

"They were unharmed, at least," she murmured. There was no scent of blood she could distinguish, nothing having been spilled, anyway.

Kat could not guess why they had taken prisoners. Even if they still had the woman from Ryhnas Lu Sesim, Valon, surely more people were simply more mouths to feed.

She was inside the third hut when it hit her, and she had to reach out to brace herself on one of the hut's poles, the treated wood carved with careful vine designs that would have made her smile fondly under other circumstances.

There had been children in this hut, but that wasn't what made Kat want to sick up. While it was probably how they had avoided bloodshed—what faster way to gain a parent's cooperation than threatening hys child?—it was the thought of Carin that suddenly made Kat certain of why the invaders had taken prisoners.

She stumbled out of the hut, and Suhnsuoc met her there, nudging her with hys head in concern.

Without needing to speak of it, Kat set about gathering what things she could and undoing the canvas from the three formerly occupied huts. Small, useful things went in bags. Food in another bag, which she attached to Suhnsuoc's harness. The waterskins she emptied and left hanging from hooks in the huts where someone could use them but they wouldn't mold.

Anything less portable or immediately useful, she put up under the eaves of the huts where there was a small built-in ledge to keep things out of the way if one didn't mind them getting smoky. The canvas could not really be helped; it was dry now, but it would get wet and could rot easily. Suhnsuoc wouldn't be comfortable carrying three heavy rolls of canvas all the way back to Lahivar, and they were going to need to move quickly. But Kat couldn't bear to waste them, so she took them all into one hut toward the middle of the waymake where she thought they had a better chance of staying out of the rain with the easterly winds. She propped them against each other in the center on end, leaning them against the beam in the center of the roof that held the hook for pots.

Kat hoped it would be enough. On her way out, she remembered something her people had taught her. At home, it would be pointless to do it, because the rocks would simply vanish against the snow that covered the ground and everything else for most of the cycle. But here, against the red-brown maha and the deep-blue grasses, white stones would be visible.

She kept a handful of them in her belt pouch, as she had been taught.

She took out five small pebbles about the size of her thumbnail, and she found the waymake's waypost. Lahbas. Where the water stops.

Kat supposed this had once been the edge of Boggers, but now Boggers had become a lake. She wondered how the names of things would change.

But for now, she put the five white stones on the waypost as a sign to anyone who ventured this way to beware.

As she and Suhnsuoc made their way back south toward Lahivar with the sun dipping toward the horizon to their right, Kat dreaded telling Sart and Hoyu what she thought must be true.

If that other, that Asurashk, had tried to delve into Carin's mind to get information, what would stop her from doing the same to anyone else?

"Faster, Suhnsuoc," Kat murmured.

BASHA THOUGHT if he had to be near Arelashk much longer, he would actually explode.

They had been traveling east for three turns now, long enough for the midsummer moon to be nearly upon them, and many times over long enough for Basha to count a thousand reasons to blame himself for his own predicament.

As far as Arelashk and the army were concerned, things were going splendidly. Not only were they making good time, but also the weather had been perfect. Warm without being too hot, sunny without being too bright, a gentle breeze most days, and stars in the sky most nights. They had had a little rain, but nothing like the monsoons in the archipelago or the socked-in, wet-wool feeling of Triyan winters that Basha had experienced one too many times, which was exactly once.

Arelashk was leading them. How, Basha was not certain. Though Basha attended Arelashk and Asurashk most days, they were careful not to speak too freely in his presence, which left Basha stuck wondering and more anxious with every passing day. It was a bit like watching a swarm of fire ants crawl up your legs and having no way to stop them. They were going to bite eventually, and until then, you would feel their thousands of tiny feet against your skin, knowing at any moment you could be injected with burning venom at a thousand different points of contact with your flesh.

Which is to say Basha was not doing well.

In the turns they had been marching eastward, the only comforts Basha found were his nights alone in his tent with Oshu and in his increasingly fluent— but increasingly guarded—conversations with Valon ve Avarsahla.

Basha had little magic, and he certainly hadn't enough to protect his conversations from unwanted listeners.

When he met with Valon one night under a waning moon, Basha wished he indeed had magic. Perhaps he would be able to understand how they kept waking in the mornings to find new trees all around them that hadn't been there the night before.

The tent where Valon was kept was small and serviceable, and Basha was glad at least that she had not been further mistreated. He studiously avoided the other prisoners, but he could not escape hearing about them or about Asurashk visiting them each day.

"You are well?" Basha asked Valon in Tuan.

She seemed pleased by his advances in her language. But now she simply nodded. Her tent was lit only by a small bulb, a half sphere of glass that absorbed the light of the sun during the day and shone at night. They were cheap enough in Khardan, but the Marefi soldiers seemed to find them a novelty, as did Valon.

As he did every night, Basha waited until the guards resumed their conversation outside the tent. Some of them weren't as chatty as others, but they had learned swiftly that guarding Valon was boring, so it wasn't uncommon for Basha to find them playing a game of recall or bones when he left.

"Do you know where we go?" he asked.

She glanced over his shoulder at the tent flap. "Where we are going," she corrected.

"Do you know where we are going?" he repeated.

"No," she said.

"Do you have—do you expect?" Basha didn't know the word for guess yet. He tried to mime thinking and shrugged.

A smirk played about Valon's lips—laughing at him, probably. He didn't blame her. Building conversations from scratch when you were both starting with nothing of each other's languages was not easy.

"There is nothing east. Silan." She said the last word so dismissively that it took a moment for Basha to process that he didn't know what silan was.

"Silan?" he asked.

Valon made a frustrated noise. "Silan. Silirtahn."

He recognized the name of the village on the coast. A place name or a noun? He frowned.

Valon tapped the floor with her foot. "Irtahn," she said. Then she made a wavelike motion with both hands, pretending to stop at an imaginary line at her toes. "Water. Lahlar."

Basha watched her blankly. His memory jogged. "Lahlar," he said, lighting up. "Asa."

Valon returned his look just as blankly. "Asa."

"Sea," he said. "Lahlar, in Tuan."

He made the same wavelike motion with his hands, and Valon cracked a smile.

"Asa," she repeated. She made the motion again and switched back to Tuan. "Lahlar . . . artus irtahn."

She paused at *artus* at the invisible line.

"Ah," said Basha. Shore or earth, then. "Silan?"

Valon indicated the invisible line and scuffed her foot on the tent floor with some frustration, then mimed brushing her hands off. "Irtahn at the lahlar."

Basha frowned, not sure he was understanding. There was nothing east but . . . sand?

"Sand?" he asked.

She shrugged. Of course there was little way for them to check his understanding. For all he knew, she was talking about the tide.

He left not long after, still feeling frustrated, though he doubted Valon was any less so.

Basha ducked out of the tent and nodded to the Marefi guards on duty—a game of recall tonight, as they barely acknowledged him, fixed on the overturned tiles on their low table—and headed for Arelashk's tent.

When he got there, he could hear voices inside.

"You are saying you think what I am sensing is a stone?" Arelashk's voice sounded far more excited than Basha thought a rock merited.

Asurashk's voice piped up after a moment. "Yes. They are as shocked as we are about the changes in the land—they could not hide their surprise from me. They know of other stones, one to the north—"

The mage made a dismissive sound.

"And one on our current course. If you feel nothing to the north as you have said, it is possible it is already beyond our reach," Asurashk finished, sounding tired.

Basha was not sure if he should go in now, but he figured he may as well. Waiting would just make it worse if this was a conversation he was not supposed to hear. Besides, Arelashk was expecting him.

He cleared his throat and pulled the small bellstring on the outside of the tent to alert them to his presence. "Honored Arelashk, honored Asurashk, I have come to report."

"Enter," said Arelashk.

Rela's tent was almost as sparse as Valon's, but where Valon had only a small bedroll and a chamber pot, Arelashk had a low table made of lightweight bamboo, and it was strewn with papers, though it was dark in the tent, and he had only one bulb lit. Arelashk sat on a cushion at the table, eyes scanning everything upon it as if by doing so he could spot some pattern that had heretofore eluded him.

At Basha's arrival, though, the mage gestured absently, and three more bulbs flared into brightness. Asurashk's face glowed in the sudden light, emerging from the shadows at the far end of the table. She did not acknowledge Basha except to nod.

"Tell me," said Arelashk. "Did Carin ever speak to you of the stones of power?"

Basha shook his head truthfully. "No, honored Arelashk."

The man seemed to ignore his answer, turning to Asurashk. "If what you have seen is true, there may only be two of them left. Objects used to anchor a spell like you have described would be immensely powerful, no matter how close to a spell's end they are recovered."

Asurashk nodded her assent. "The people here have little idea of what lies hidden in their land, apart from knowing it exists. There are legends about the location of this one, however. That it sits at the site where a great beast was slain in ages past, the last of its kind. They differ in whether the beast gave its life or had it taken, but the people agree that its body fed a village on the brink of starvation and allowed them to survive."

The Arelashk nodded thoughtfully. "Magic so complex as the spell your Carin described would be rooted in places of significance. Places can absorb power, potential, whatever you like to call it. It is the weight given to them that makes them important, so it does not matter whether this beast was a willing or unwilling sacrifice—the point is the memory that the beast died, and through its death, others lived."

The air in the tent seemed go grow tight around Basha's throat. He did not pretend to know the significance of arcane geography, but he did know he wanted Arelashk far away from any item of such power.

He wanted to ask how such a power could even be used, but he did not dare.

"Despite their ways of life being so different than ours, we could learn much from the study of such an object," Arelashk mused. "Imagine a spell that allowed for control of nature itself."

Basha did not trust himself to move. The very thought froze him to the tent's floor. He thought of Udum Dhu'e and the death wave that had almost wiped out the island—that likely would have, had it come when it was supposed to. The death waves that had come every five hundred cycles as an *accidental* effect of this spell would have scoured Udum Dhu'e of everything but vegetation. The implications of such a thing being purposeful—weaponized—were staggering.

"Indeed," said Asurashk, her eyes only on the table in front of her.

"Such a thing would be enough to bring order out of the chaos none of us want," Arelashk said quietly.

He seemed to realize he had said more than he meant to in front of Basha, so Basha bowed and said, "All suffer in times of chaos," which he hoped was enough to satisfy the other man.

"How far away are we from this stone?" Asurashk asked.

"Perhaps three turns, if we maintain this pace," said Arelashk.

By the birth of the midsummer moon, then.

Arelashk dismissed Basha with orders to try and glean information about the stone from Valon, to which he readily agreed.

Basha had joined this expedition for Khardan, but until now, he had not fully considered what that meant.

Every day until now, he had gone about his life as best he could, ignoring the inevitable truth that was ready to fall.

He had come for Khardan—for his Ada'sarshk, who had risked all to do what was right—and he had forgotten to ask himself a most important question.

Just how far was he willing to go to stop someone who wanted to wield the power of a god?

• • • • •

The next day was another long march. The army was used to such things, but Basha was not. He was a seafaring man. His feet had blisters where he didn't think blisters could exist.

He brought Oshu with him to his audience with Arelashk and Asurashk that night, and unlike the night before, they did not speak of the stone or anything that could be considered sensitive. Basha was used to logistics and correspondences; as first mate and seneschal, that was his due and his duty. It bored many people, but Basha found satisfaction in it.

He had hired Oshu as a spy, due to Arelashk and Asurashk frequently reverting to Asurashk's native Triyan when they had been traveling from Udum Dhu'e to Sahesh, but that had been in vain. Oshu had not been near the two of them enough to hear anything of consequence, and now in the midst of a Marefi army where many would have at least passing knowledge of Triyan, it would be foolish of Arelashk and Asurashk to think someone wouldn't understand them. Neither of them were fools.

Despite the futility of his desperate attempt to have an ally behind enemy lines, it wasn't as though Basha had been unsuccessful. Oshu had become dear to him.

So as they sat in Arelashk's tent, off to the side with Basha's lap desk and Oshu attending on Arelashk and Asurashk as well as a trio of the Marefi officers, Basha was shocked to catch a glimpse of something he had seen once before.

Oshu was refilling the water cups for those working—not including Basha, who was a subordinate—and for the barest moment as Oshu turned away from Asurashk, his eyes lit with something Basha could only call revulsion.

Perhaps hatred.

Basha was so startled that he missed something Arelashk had said, trying to piece together from the continuing conversation whether that something ought to have been written down.

The meeting was nowhere near over, and Basha could not be certain of what he had seen. He would have dismissed it had he not noted something similar once before, when they were still aboard the ships and awaiting the Marefi fleet. Basha had assumed it was nothing, but perhaps that was not the truth.

Basha did his best to concentrate on the task at hand, redoubling his efforts to keep his reports and notes as meticulous as could be, but his mind tried to wander every time Oshu ventured near Asurashk to bring refreshments or remove an empty cup.

By the time they finished, Basha was all too aware he had missed dinner, and a headache took root in his left shoulder. He would need to rest his eyes or be useless tomorrow when the headache crept to its destination at the base of his skull.

He was quiet as he made his way back to their tent. Thankfully, the mess tent was directly in their path, and Basha took a soldier's rations for himself and for Oshu without thinking.

"Thank you," Oshu said as they walked away.

Basha looked up from his hands, startled that he had broken propriety even in such a small way. The Marefi soldiers would never notice, but Basha felt a flush of ingrained shame with a pinch of anger at himself not far behind.

They reached their tent quickly, and as always of late, Basha felt a weight recede from his shoulders. He removed his shoes at the tent flap, also as always, and he handed Oshu his rations, sitting down on his bedroll to eat.

Marefi rations were nothing to complain about. They had perfected packets of dried protein and carbohydrates with enough calories to sustain an army without having to worry about dishes. Even the packet was edible, and most people Basha had seen did eat it, though it was a bit starchy for his tastes. Basha was no scientist or mage, but he appreciated efficiency, even when used by people he would prefer did certain things with less of it.

"You are quiet tonight," Oshu said about halfway through his ration of meat.

Basha hesitated. "I would like to ask you something, but it may be sensitive, and if you do not wish to answer, I will trust your judgement."

Oshu sat back, his next bite forgotten.

"I will be truthful with you, Basha," he said softly.

"I know." Basha was somewhat bewildered by his own confidence.

"Ask." Oshu set his food down on the packet beside him.

"I have noticed that sometimes you have a look of"—Basha tried to find the word he wanted—"intensity. A look of intensity about Asurashk, I think. At first I thought it had to do with something else, but she is the commonality."

It was as if total calm came over Oshu in that instant. As if superimposed upon him, Basha saw instead the surface of a lake before the wind has woken for the day. Unblemished serenity, no hint of what could be found beneath.

Transfixed, Basha watched him, wondering how such a change could happen so quickly. He had heard of mages and scholars who sometimes dedicated themselves to the practice of separating themselves from all emotion, but Basha thought surely even they could not do it so cleanly as Oshu.

When he spoke, it was like a fish breaking the surface at dawn. Basha jumped.

"I knew her by another name," Oshu said, his voice still quiet as the sunrise. "She was my love once."

Stunned, Basha could not find his words. Had anyone else been in their tent at that moment, had he been in company of someone to whom he was meant to show deference, Basha would have been undone. As it was, he was safe enough to simply stare.

Telmoryn Sih. That was Oshu's name before Basha had so thoughtlessly given him another one.

When Basha did not speak, Oshu continued. "We fled the war in Triya. We were bound for Sahesh when her magic manifested, and I was the only one she told about it before the wave."

The wave.

Once, Basha had been taken to see the biggest clock in Sahesh. It stood in an out-of-the-way rotunda, unremarkable if one did not know what one was looking for, and the most remarkable thing about it was that one could go *inside* it. He had been a child, awestruck by turning gears and how many tiny things had to fit just so in order to make something larger than his house perform its duties.

Basha felt like that again, feeling gears tick into place, turning against one another with the musicality of time.

"I thought her dead," Oshu said.

His voice sounded very far away, and Basha understood that too. Sometimes it was necessary to leave one's body when remembering something that had left oneself irrevocably changed.

"Until I brought you to the ship," Basha said, his voice hoarse. "Until you saw her again."

"That is not my love," said Oshu, and the vehemence in his words matched the flashes of rage Basha had seen before, the sparks that had made him ask. "The woman I knew was not vengeful or cruel. She would not chase a prisoner to the ends of the earth or cooperate with a man like that."

Basha understood why Oshu did not want to say Arelashk's name.

"Sometimes I have thought I died in that wave," Oshu murmured. "That I died and was taken to the place of punishment, and that for my sins I was meant to watch my love become unrecognizable to me. I might have lost myself in hatred were it not for you."

For the second time, Basha was not sure he had heard correctly. "Me?"

"You wanted me to work for you." The word *spy* went unsaid, but Oshu's meaning was clear. "You impressed upon me the danger of this position, and I had nothing left to lose. But when I saw what you were doing, when I saw who you were, Basha, you allowed me to see that I was not simply being tormented."

They were both quiet for a moment, and Basha realized a tent was likely not the best place to be talking about this. Not that anywhere in a camp of enemy soldiers would be.

"She has made her own choices," Oshu said. "And I have made mine. We were going to Khardan to build a better life. Not to bring with us everything that made us leave our home."

Basha moved almost before he was aware of it, leaving his mostly uneaten dinner on his bedroll and going to sit beside Oshu on his own.

"It is improprietous for me to say what I would like to say," Basha said. "But I would like to tell you that you are free of any obligations you had to me, though I understand that saying this in the middle of a foreign continent and in the midst of an invading army is less than helpful."

Oshu's face broke into a smile then. "I have not stayed thus far out of obligation, Basha."

"Was it because you need transportation home?" Basha asked wryly.

Oshu chuckled. "No. It was because you made me want to find home." He sobered. "I do not know what will happen to this place. I do not know what will happen if this mission is a success by its leaders' standards. But whatever comes, I am with you."

Basha hadn't known his heart could make that noise, loud enough for him to hear it, a *thub* he felt throughout his chest.

He fought the sudden urge to laugh at the situation in which they were now mired. It wasn't as if anything had changed in the past short stretch of time.

But everything had changed.

Basha had been willing to risk himself, but now, as Oshu reached for his hand and Basha's fingers interlaced with his, he would have to find some way to get them both out alive.

RYD STILL wasn't sure he believed that the halms had grown at his bidding. He had spent nearly every moment since among them, Hoyu and Jenin at his side, which is how he was there when Kat appeared in the distance upon a Suhn-suoc running at full tilt toward Lahivar.

He realized he hadn't seen her in at least half a day, and he had thought Suhn-suoc was out scouting alone.

Hoyu and Jenin stopped mid-conversation, both getting to their feet when they saw where Ryd was looking.

Suhnsuoc came to a halt outside of the circle of halms, laden with bags Ryd was certain had not been there earlier. Kat slid from hys back almost before sy had stopped moving.

"The army is taking people," she said without preamble. "Suhnsuoc found a waymake that was abandoned—huts still covered, people's things simply left where they were."

"You're certain?" Ryd asked.

Kat nodded. "I brought what could be salvaged. I do not know if there will be a chance of getting them back alive, but I thought . . ."

"Why would they take people?" Jenin asked, getting to hys feet.

Sy still looked a bit tired after hys misadventure in the unseen world, but it was Hoyu Ryd couldn't look away from.

Her face had gone bleak and closed off.

"Asurashk" was all she said.

That was enough. Ryd was running toward Lahivar.

By the time he had found Sart and told her what Kat had found, the others had caught up, though Kat hung back with Suhnsuoc, relieving the kazytya of hys burden.

"I didn't want to simply leave everything to be wasted by the weather," Kat said.

Sart gave her a sharp nod. "Put anything personal in Ryd's roundhome. Any foodstuffs will be used."

Before, in his frustration and helplessness, Ryd had been overwhelmed with the need to do something. Anything. Now was almost worse.

"Think," Sart muttered. She looked up at the others, glancing at a few other Lahivarans who were milling about in confusion. "We have a charming variety of problems."

That was one way of putting it.

"First, we have a spell breaking down that a bunch of rot-for-brains turds want to reinvoke that will return this land to a state of decay for another five hundred cycles. But since that is not supposed to happen until next summer, we suddenly have a more pressing issue." Sart didn't seem to care that people were listening, and Ryd couldn't blame her. "We have a fleet of ships off the coast with who knows how many more soldiers, and we have an army moving eastward across our land, taking our people to dig around in their brains for information about how to what, exploit the myriad failings of our ancestors? Is that a useful summary of what they want?"

"Rela and Asurashk said Carin was a dangerous mage," Hoyu said slowly. "That her power needed to be contained."

"Contained is just a way of saying available for the 'correct' person to wield it against their enemies," Sart said.

Ryd didn't think she was wrong.

"Carin told us that the death waves have come every five hundred cycles with the Reinvocation," Ryd said. "If someone knew how to cause such a thing on purpose—"

"It would make that person the most powerful force in the world," Hoyu said.

"But the spell requires blood," Jenin said.

"Do you think someone willing to invade another's mind would have trouble deeming people as expendable enough to murder?" Ryd asked quietly. Then, to Hoyu, "You have said that your homeland is unstable. Would they want such power?"

"That is the wrong question to ask," Hoyu answered. "The question is whether whoever is in power will see it as a necessary risk or not. I wish I could tell you who is now in power, but I suspect the Arelashk and Asurashk's plan is to use whatever they find here to assure their favored faction wins whatever struggle exists in Khardan."

"What do we do?" Jenin asked.

Sart pinched the bridge of her nose, looking like a headache had suddenly taken up residence. "What can we do against an army?"

"If Culy and Carin are successful in breaking the remaining stones, the Reinvocation will fail," Jenin said confidently. "We will at least not have to worry about that, and there is an entire cycle remaining before that."

"That would be more comforting were it not for the army," Sart said. "Especially since that army is heading in what seems like a direct path toward the penultimate stone, and we haven't the faintest idea where to find the last one."

"The most logical thing would be to find the last stone," Ryd said slowly. "That is something within our control. We cannot alter the course of the army, and we cannot know whether Carin and Culy will get there first or not. But if we can find the fifth hearthstone—"

"We could break it ourselves," Sart said. "Well. It's definitely not a plan, but it's an idea."

"You thought it was in Crevasses," Ryd said to Kat. "But you only found a halm?"

"No stone, unless it was somehow inside the tree," Kat replied. She didn't look convinced either way.

"I could seek it in the unseen realm," Jenin said, and when Sart immediately began shaking her head, Jenin pushed onward. "We have something we didn't have before now—a halm grove."

"Would that work?" Kat asked. "They are tremendously powerful, but I am not sure how they would help you locate the stone."

"I would need Ryd's help," said Jenin, giving Ryd an encouraging smile.

"Me?" All eyes immediately turned his way. "I don't know how I would be of use."

"You are a halmer, and not only that, you also grew those halms. You will be my connection here so I can find my way back." Jenin started as a new person entered their small circle, then gave her a rueful smile. "Clar has done this for me before in smaller ways."

Clar herself did not look excited at the prospect. "It's dangerous," she said, looking confused. "Someone will have to explain to me what's going on."

When everyone fell silent, Jenin took Clar and Sart aside, and from the way Sart was nodding, Ryd thought it had already been decided.

To his surprise, Kat was watching Clar with an expression he couldn't quite name. They had been much together in the past turns, beyond even traveling to seek Culy and Carin, but now Kat's face was guarded, yet tenderness hovered in her eyes too. When she glanced at him, Ryd hurriedly looked away.

"Ryd," said Jenin, beckoning to him. "You will need to prepare."

• • • • •

Ryd didn't think his palms had been this sweaty since his days in Haveranth. He had no idea what he was doing, but Jenin seemed confident enough for the two of them. That, he realized ruefully, was something else that was familiar from Haveranth.

The news Kat had brought had rippled through Lahivar as dusk turned to night, and conversations around the fire in the hearth-home were quiet, muted, like a world seen through smoke.

Ryd wiped his hands on his trousers.

He was the first one to the halm grove. To his eyes, the trees seemed to glow in the darkness, an eerie sensation he wasn't sure was real. They were so white that it could just be reflected moonlight from the waning face of Bide and her sister.

Bide. How appropriate.

The others approached in a trickle, Hoyu and Clar arriving together with Kat not far behind, Sart and Jenin bringing up the rear along with Mari. Ryd was glad to see Mari. She was sensible enough that he trusted she would talk sense into anyone who got too absurd. Even Ras, of whom there was no sign.

"I didn't expect an audience," Ryd muttered, and Clar gave him what he thought was supposed to be an encouraging smile.

Jenin had told him that he would essentially do what Sart had done for hyr, but on purpose this time. Safer, Jenin said, and it would also allow for more freedom in the unseen world.

Ryd had no idea what the rules of this unseen world were or how any of it worked, but Jenin insisted his job was to feel the halm grove. That and that alone.

Sy also had said that doing it this way meant he would see whatever Jenin saw, and Ryd wasn't entirely looking forward to that.

"It's okay," Jenin said.

"Shouldn't we worry that Khardish mage might see what we're doing?" Ryd asked.

"We are not contacting anyone," Jenin said. "Because of that, it will be much, much harder to even know we're there."

Ryd would have to take hys word for it.

He sat with his back up against the easternmost tree, which grew directly across from the spring, the other four halms perfectly equidistant and symmetrical on either side of him to form a circle.

Since Culy had informed him what halmers truly did, Ryd had learned to listen to the trees, to the wood. He did that now, relaxing his back against the trunk of the tree. There was almost a hum to it, almost a song he could sing if he could just hear it a tiny bit better. It moved between the trees and their branches, more present here in the grove, but Ryd found he could feel it even from his roundhome if he concentrated.

Here with his back touching the tree trunk, it was as easy as breathing.

Jenin sat down in front of him, the hyrsin's back turned toward Ryd. Sy scooted forward enough that sy could lay hys head in Ryd's lap, handing him a folded blanket to make it more comfortable. Ryd was certain his feet would fall asleep if they were here too long.

Ryd placed his hands on either side of Jenin's face as he had been instructed, reaching out to the halms even as his skin made contact with Jenin's cheeks.

"I don't know if I'm doing this right," he mumbled. "I—"

His words cut off as his perspective suddenly shifted.

"Jenin?" Alarmed, Ryd heard his own voice as if it were coming from outside his body.

"It's okay," Jenin's voice said, and it sounded like it was coming from *him*. "You're just seeing through my eyes. If you speak, I think the others will hear you, but they won't hear me."

Ryd tried to stem the panic that wanted to bubble up at the discomfiting strangeness of being outside his body but not.

"You think this is bad, you should have been me when I was dead," said Jenin dryly.

"What now?" Ryd whispered, not liking the sensation of hearing his own voice coming from outside his head.

"Now you let me concentrate. The unseen world is like dreams—if you think about something hard enough, you will find it or create it. We don't want to create anything, just find the stone." Jenin's voice was soothing, but while Ryd understood the words, he had no idea what any of this meant. "Maybe you can help with that, too. Concentrate on the spell and the stones. You were present when one of them broke. That could help link us to what we want."

That made a vague sort of sense, so Ryd tried to obey, thinking of Ryhnas Lu Sesim and the stone in Wyt's garden. That stone had been . . . loud. Angry. Bubbling over with sickness it had been forced to eat for five hundred cycles.

Ryd tried to think of the spell itself, about the water stone Carin had broken, the other stone to the north which had recently followed. He thought of the fourth to which he hoped she would reach before the army did. And he thought of the final stone, wondering where it could be if not in Crevasses where Kat had sought it.

The world shifted.

Dismay pooled in Ryd's stomach—or Jenin's. Maybe both. He couldn't be sure.

They were in Haveranth.

It was the last place Ryd wanted to see right now, the village of his birth. Some things were different—Merin's roundhome was no longer visible where it used to be, just on the edge of the village. It felt different. Tense. He couldn't have explained it to anyone.

"That's not right," Jenin mumbled. "Try again."

Ryd tried again to concentrate on the fifth stone, seeing in his mind's eye what he imagined it to look like.

The world shifted again.

This time he thought something was closer. They were in a meadow that stretched as far as his eyes could see, and there was a stone there, waiting.

"No," said Jenin. "That cannot be right."

"What?" Ryd asked. "Why not?"

Jenin turned, and Ryd's vision swam with the sensation of his eyes moving without him doing it.

And he saw what Jenin meant. Jenin had turned northward, and in the distance, barely a smudge on the horizon from here, were the Mad Mountains.

Which meant the stone lay south of Haveranth, well beyond any of their reach.

"How can that be?" Ryd asked. "That should be impossible."

"I don't know," Jenin said.

Sy sounded every bit as lost as Ryd felt.

Then another sound pierced the air, and Ryd was flung back into his own body so hard, his head cracked against the trunk of the halm behind him.

Everyone was sitting on the ground around them, looking ready to spring to their feet at the sudden movement, and Jenin flailed in Ryd's lap, scrambling to a sitting position and looking up at the sky as if sy expected something to fall out of it.

Ryd's head throbbed where he had hit it.

"What happened?" Sart demanded. "Ryd said something should be impossible."

Slowly, Ryd's mind processed the sound that had made Jenin panic.

The screech of a hawk.

Jenin met his eyes, hys own wild and showing white all around the dark, dark brown of hys irises.

"Then it's true," Ryd said. "How?"

"How am I here?" Jenin asked. "I didn't want to believe it, but I think it must really be her. I can't think of anyone else in the Hearthland who would have that type of power. You have seen the hawk in the waking world."

Dread sickened Ryd's stomach. They had done this to try and find answers, to find something they could do, but all they had found were more questions and a solution so far out of reach, a mountain range lay between them and any chance at useful action.

And worse.

"What hawk?" Kat asked curiously.

Sart was shaking her head. "No. Nope. Because that would go from creepy to terrifying, and we have enough terrifying to try and manage right now, you rotted—"

She seemed to shake herself and take a breath. Ryd thought she had been about to fling an insult at him and the others who had come from Haveranth, and she was well within her rights if that was true.

But Sart closed her eyes, and he watched her chest and stomach rise with a deep breath.

"What hawk?" Kat asked again, irritation creeping into her voice.

"Not a hawk," Ryd said, looking at Clar. "Merin."

Clar shook her head vehemently. "No. That's not possible."

"Clar—" Jenin began.

"Lyari killed her, Jenin!" Clar shouted. "Really killed her! You saw it!"

Ryd's head hurt. He looked around at the confused faces surrounding them. Kat, Sart, Mari, Hoyu. This had brought all of them together from the farthest reaches of this land and others.

He couldn't help it. He started to laugh.

Every eye turned to Ryd.

"I'm sorry, Ryd, what's funny?" Sart asked, her voice acerbic.

"Who needs two impossible problems when you could have three?" Ryd slowly got to his feet, wincing at the sting at the back of his head. "Ancient evil spell, got that. Literal invasion? Got that too. Three-hundred-cycle-old soothsayer back from the dead and flying around as a hawk? Why not?"

"What?" Kat said, shaking herself. "A hawk?"

The way she said it made Ryd think she didn't just mean the surprise of an animal.

"Yes," he said slowly. "Merin used a hawk to spy on people in the Hearthland, and we've seen that exact hawk here. And Jenin and I saw it in the unseen world."

Kat shook her head, either in disbelief or denial—Ryd wasn't sure.

"You say someone killed this person? But the hawk remained? You're certain it's the same hawk?" Kat's voice was quiet, but the urgency in it was unmistakeable.

"Yes. The woman who is going to perform the Reinvocation killed her. It was to be Merin who performed the Reinvocation before that. Lyari murdered her when she found out what—what the Hearthland does to the Nameless." Clar spoke up, and something ineffable passed between her and the kazytya rider. "The Nameless are those who refuse to stay after learning about the spell."

"This soothsayer. Is she a mage?" Kat asked.

Jenin nodded. "Yes, a very powerful one, though she is . . . subtle about it. She lived simply in Haveranth. Few of us ever saw her use magic, but my family knew of her power. And about the hawk she bound to herself."

Ryd did not know enough about magic to comment, but one thing was clear to him. "Jenin, someone that powerful could have done what you did. Used death to—inhabit the unseen world."

Jenin's face was ashen, but sy didn't disagree.

"Okay," Sart said bluntly. "Merin is old and powerful. Whatever. What does this mean for us?"

"I don't know," said Ryd. "Maybe Culy or Carin would know, but I don't."

"What would you do if the person who murdered you was aiming to complete the Reinvocation spell hyrself and had taken over your place in your village and home?" Clar said wryly. "Merin has been alive a long time. Do you truly think she will be content to simply wash her hands of this and let Lyari continue on in her place? If she is still alive, why would she constrain herself to simply watch her people go on?"

Jenin opened hys mouth to answer, then shut it again.

"Did you at least find the stone?" Sart asked, sounding as if she didn't dare to hope.

Mari looked completely lost, but she turned to look at Jenin and Ryd expectantly.

"No," Ryd said at the same time Jenin said, "I don't know."

"Which is it?" said Sart.

"We found *a* stone," Jenin said. "But I don't know if it's what we were looking for. I hope it wasn't."

"Why?" Clar turned her head to the side, her upper teeth worrying at her bottom lip.

"Because it's in the Hearthland," Ryd said.

Kat's head snapped up at that, but she said nothing.

T HE DAY dawned overcast, and it suited Carin's mood.

The closer she and Culy came to the stone, the more the air felt alive, and the ground beneath their feet felt like a dry stick bent almost to breaking point. One more bit of pressure and it would snap, sending splinters flying out everywhere.

They had entered the part of the Northlands called Sands, a desert that stretched to the uninhabited hills to the east that Culy said eventually turned to forest and then cliffs at the eastern sea, which Carin had never seen.

But they were, as always lately, on unfamiliar ground.

The changes coming to the land had not bypassed Sands. What had been desert was now something else. Carin had not thought much could grow in sand, but all around them, things grew.

Carin could name little of what grew. Bushes with spiky leaves and bright red flowers, strange, squat plants with smooth arms and spines sticking out of them, crawling vines that looked like they were made entirely of small green berries. Carin wondered if they would pop if she pinched one of the berry-like things between her fingers.

"Where we are going," she said to Culy, "you say it is the site of a beast's death?"

Culy nodded atop Siuhn, reaching out to stroke the back of the ihstal's neck. "An ahrclys. An enormous creature, the size of perhaps twenty fyajir together, if not bigger. Bigger than a kazytya by far but a gentle animal. In the cycles before the spell, there was a war, and food was scarce. The ahrclys was hunted into extinction. There were not many to begin with."

That struck at Carin's heart. She could not imagine killing the last surviving beast of an entire species, even to eat.

"Some say the beast knew sy was the last of hys kind and wished to join the rest, lying down to die and feed the people," Culy said. "I could not tell you what is true. I saw one only once, from afar."

Carin started, remembering that Culy had grown to adulthood in another age, only to be thrown into sleep for many ages more.

"Pey," she murmured. One of the five branches of magic. Force. The power to move, to push, to reach, to climb.

Culy nodded. "Everything the ahrclys brought with sustenance, channeled into creating a different future for others."

Carin was starting to understand. Each of the hearthstones had purpose, tied into some greater meaning. And each of them deepened her revulsion for the Tuanye who had created something so monstrous for their own personal gain.

"Let us release whatever poor spirit has been bound to such an act," she said, and she nudged Tahin to go faster.

The stone was close. This time Siuhn and Tahin did not balk at the proximity, which made Carin think back over the glen and the enormous halm. She had never seen animals react strangely to halm, but it only solidified her instinct that something was very strange in that glen.

"Any sign of the army?" Carin asked.

She could see the stone now, on a bare hillock that even since the vision two turns ago had altered with the newness of the landscape. Plants were poking up through the sandy soil around it, and some of the spiky bushes stabbed through the surface of the earth.

She dismounted, still wary despite no evidence of anyone having come this way in some time.

Culy shook hys head, but hys brow furrowed. "They are not within easy distance, but I suspect they are not far."

Carin's finger fluttered against her thumb, an anxious flurry of movement and one she was not prone to doing. Consciously, she shifted her shoulders, allowing them to relax instead of tensing and creeping up toward her ears. She didn't know how long they had been so tight.

"This feels different," she said after a moment of cataloging the feelings and sensations in her body.

Culy watched her thoughtfully for a moment, then seemed to shake hyrself as well.

"It feels like something nearing breaking point," Carin said. "It seems obvious that it would be the spell about to break, but I do not think it is that. Breaking the stones doesn't seem to break the spell itself, only chip away at it bit by bit like a mason at a quarry."

"You are correct." Culy looked past Carin at the stone, finally sliding down from Siuhn's back. The ihstal whistled and trotted away to investigate grass. "It is with the Reinvocation that the spell will either be strengthened or left to die."

"Then why does it feel like pressure about to explode?" Carin asked.

"I do not know," said Culy.

They ventured closer to the stone, and though the sensation was stronger there, it did not seem to be changing, which Carin found to be a relief—at least to an extent.

She knelt by the stone without touching it, reaching for the water spirit within her with a question.

The spirit responded like a shaken jug, sloshing in surprise that calmed after a moment to a curious trickle.

The spirit did not know the details about the spell—while it had a breathtaking range of experience and knowledge about the land itself, a spirit was neither a mage nor an expert in the arcane. Carin could also claim to be none of those things.

"The spirit does not know," she said to Culy.

"Spirits are often quite single-minded," Culy replied. "It is both a strength and a weakness. As with the one in Ryhnas Lu Sesim, if perverted from their purpose, they will retaliate given a chance. Perhaps that is what we are sensing here."

"Perhaps," Carin said.

She was not entirely convinced.

Breaking the previous stone had taken some time, and it had left both of them in a state for some time more. Without knowing how close the army was to reaching them, Carin knew they needed to do this now, but still she hesitated.

"Consequences," she murmured.

Saying the word out loud seemed to strengthen her resolve.

She repeated the word, this time turning to look at her lover. "Consequences. We will face what comes."

"We will," said Culy.

Together, they placed their hands upon the stone.

Somewhere above them, a bird let out a raucous caw.

• • • • •

If the previous spirits Carin had encountered were strange, it was nothing compared to the force that rose to meet her here.

Almost like with the halm, the world around her vanished, leaving her in a sea of rolling hills and trees that could have once been Sands before it was a desert.

The beast that stood before her was unlike anything she had ever seen. Where the other spirits had no form, clearly this one did. It had maintained itself as the ahrclys, as Culy had called it, but beyond that Carin could give it no name.

Culy's estimation of its size was also dwarfed by the reality. Perhaps time had dulled hys perception—Carin did not know. But the creature towered over both Carin and Culy. Even had she been on her feet, she would have hardly reached the beast's knee.

It was somewhat like an ihstal, she thought. Like an ihstal, the ahrclys was sleek, short-furred, and elegant. The fur itself was pale, almost silvery. But where the ihstal had cloven, padded hooves, the ahrclys had paws. Its legs were slender, strong. Carin imagined it could spring into the air and crash back down with enough force to shake the ground.

The ahrclys's face was long and gentle, with eyes to either side like an ihstal and ears shaped like raindrops that came to a tufted point and swiveled to listen as Carin watched it. The eyes were inky-black, limpid pools that were somehow fathomless. Carin did not know if the ahrclys truly had had eyes so unnerving or if that was simply the spirit bound to this stone.

But beyond the strange eyes or the enormous, graceful stature of the beast, it was crowned by a pair of antlers each the size of doubloon trees. Upon the antlers, moss grew, and tiny flowers Carin could not name, all the same kind but ranging from white to blue like the summer sky.

Carin could not imagine anyone hunting such a beast.

Though the air still felt brittle around her, from the ahrclys, all Carin sensed was relief. A whisper of *finally*, a sliver of hope.

Carin wanted to go closer. Some part of her wept to know she would never see this creature in the flesh, never watch a herd of them move through the hills like giants, never marvel at one of their fawns.

Culy was beside her, an expression of loss upon hys face. How much had Culy sacrificed in all of this? Everyone sy had ever known in childhood, every memory of things no one else alive could share.

Sy seemed to sense Carin's thoughts and shook hys head. "It is not worth dwelling on what has been lost," sy said. "Only what we can build from what we have."

The ahrclys simply watched them, saying nothing.

Unlike the other stones, there was no final push, no remaining burst of energy to tip it over the edge and break.

Carin felt rather than saw it happen, the ahrclys relaxing, looking off into the distance to the south.

She was present still in her own body, kneeling next to Culy in front of the now-broken hearthstone, but she was also standing in a memory of the ancient past, watching a spirit of the last of a species of titans. Carin did not know if the spirit simply had cloven to the symbol or if this truly was the spirit of the last ahrclys to walk these lands. She supposed it didn't matter.

The ahrclys seemed to want something. Without looking at Culy, Carin reached out to the animal.

Like the water spirit, it did not speak to her in words. Instead, it met her with a feeling like the brittle tension of before but amplified.

It was as if time stopped all around her only to speed up in the small sphere she occupied, the moon rising, setting, waxing, waning, and the sun dipping back and forth across the sky in its strange wave pattern. Carin didn't have to count to fifteen to know she was watching the passing of one cycle. The one cycle remaining before the Reinvocation.

As if assured she understood, the scene changed, and she hovered far above the earth, looking down at a land she did not recognize. She felt it below her, the verdant forests and rich rivers that crisscrossed the landscape. The mountains, she knew. The Mad Mountains rose to the south, snowcapped and every bit as stark and forbidding as they remained today. Just as she grew eager to take in the beauty of it, a puff of white exploded upward in the midst of the mountains to the south, and a moment later, a concussive boom sounded in the distance.

What Carin did not expect was the sound that followed. A wave of *something* spread out on either side of the initial white plume, and a cacophony of animal sounds reached her as clouds of birds launched themselves into the air, winging frantically northward.

Not far behind them, but far below her, she saw the moving spots of herds of fyajir, saiga, halka, wild goats and sheep, a pack of wolves, even a pair of kazytya and what she thought was a baszyt all running toward the north away from . . . whatever had happened.

Carin lost her breath as a new wave began, followed by a crackling that at first she could not place until she realized what she was hearing was the trees breaking by the hundreds as the lush forest below was struck by some invisible force that was like a scythe cutting across a field of barley.

And she knew what she was seeing.

Her eyes sought something in the distance, in what would one day be called Crevasses.

Even as she saw it, she saw it fall. Hardly visible amid the trees and sheltered from the initial wave only by the grace of being in the shadow of the mountains, Carin saw the city of Alar Marhasan shiver as the ground beneath it moved.

Why would the spirit show her this moment? Why would this ahrclys share such a moment of complete destruction? If she thought Udum Dhu'e was bad, watching the annihilation of cities and habitats and animals and the cracking of the land was unbearable.

Distantly, she could hear herself screaming. At least she thought it was her. It could have been the people of Alar Marhasan or the animals who were too close to the cataclysm to escape.

This was what the Tuanye had done in their spite.

This was their vengeance upon people who refused to bow to them.

This was the wrong that demanded to be righted.

Yet as the images faded and Carin was returned to her knees by a broken rock in a desert coaxed back to life, what stayed was a warning.

If Lyari tried to reinvoke the spell before Carin and Culy could locate and break the final stone, *that* was the force that would be funneled into the remaining hearthstone.

That was the future they would face again.

• • • • •

Carin came back to herself some time later. She could still see the ahrclys in her mind, its silhouette magnificent against the light into which it vanished. She did not think it was truly gone any more than the water spirit with her was truly gone or the spirit in Ryhnas Lu Sesim was truly gone. But what would it do? Had it so little hope?

It took Carin a while to realize she and Culy were not alone.

It was the feeling of being watched that first alerted her: a tingle, a prickle. One of the oldest sensations of life, to be in the sights of a hunter.

She raised her head slowly, seeing Culy still kneeling with closed eyes beside her.

"Culy," she murmured, and hys eyes snapped open.

Carin reached out one hand to Culy, who took it.

She was staring into the face of a wolf.

Carin had never seen a wolf. She only knew what it was from drawings in Merin's scrolls, just as she had seen a kazytya thus before ever encountering Suhnsuoc.

The wolves were almost as large as the giant cat, though after the ahrclys, they seemed smaller.

A wolf lay on the ground on the other side of the stone she and Culy had broken. The rune pey had cracked down the middle of its stylized basin, ever-so-slightly askew.

An animal at rest was not about to attack. Carin was certain enough about that to relax, at least a little. If the wolves intended violence, they could have begun when she and Culy were occupied with the stone. Again, the light had changed enough that Carin thought they had been occupied for quite some time.

The one wolf was far from alone. Out of the corner of her eye, Carin could see at least four more on either side of them. She wondered where the ihstal were and hoped that Siuhn and Tahin hadn't spooked too much at the presence of such large and obvious predators.

Unlike Kat's bond with Suhnsuoc, Carin didn't think she had a way to simply ask the wolves what they wanted. She and Culy were quite surrounded, she thought, and if the wolves wanted something, she hoped they would figure out some way to communicate it.

"What do we do?" she asked Culy.

Culy gave her an enigmatic half smile and got to hys feet, holding out a hand to help Carin to hers.

Her knee popped when she stood, and her feet were asleep, sending familiar shooting pains up through her soles as feeling slowly returned.

Culy said nothing, only extended one long-fingered hand toward the wolf that still reclined before them.

Tendrils of magic curled from hys palm, so thin they were barely visible to Carin's eye, and they reached out for the wolf.

The wolf got to hys feet, nose twitching as sy scented the air, and then sy threw back hys head and howled.

Gooseflesh rippled over Carin's skin, spreading out from the crown of her head and down her arms and legs like a wave cresting in her body. More voices joined the first, surrounding them from all sides.

Carin could have no way of knowing what the wolves meant by it—she had no reason to understand them—but the way they sang sounded triumphant.

From somewhere to the west, another howl arose, begun with a series of yips before swelling into a ululating cry that made a discordant counterpoint to the howls around the broken stone.

Almost as one, the wolves surrounding them broke and ran toward the west as other voices rose and fell to the northwest, then to the southwest.

Culy had turned to look in the direction the wolves had run, and though Carin knew rationally her sudden urge to flee was ungrounded, she couldn't shake it.

"Culy," she said in a low, urgent voice.

"Yes," Culy answered. "The army is coming. We must leave."

Sy whistled, and the answering whistles from Siuhn and Tahin pierced the air.

"We will be faster than they will," Carin said, her eyes straining to search the horizon to the west for signs of movement.

"Yes," Culy said again, "but they are many, and we are but two. We will ride southeast."

The ihstal reached them, their padded hooves prancing eagerly on the sandy ground. If they were distressed by the wolves, they did not show it.

Carin flung herself over Tahin's back, hearing Culy do the same with Siuhn.

Again, her mind whirled with too many new things. Changing land, animals, everything. Magic that filled the air so much she could taste it on her skin.

This stone had come with a warning. Carin thought she understood. What she had seen, what the ahrclys had shown them—she thought if they couldn't break the final stone before the Reinvocation, it could break the world.

They could not allow that to happen. Not if there was any hope of stopping it. Who knew if Lyari would persist in the Reinvocation with stones broken, if she even knew they were broken. Carin thought she did, but Jenin and Clar believed she still planned to go through with it. Perhaps Lyari's act was as desperate as her own. Did Lyari believe she was doing the right thing? She must.

Grimly, Carin settled into position for the long path ahead. Lyari was wrong. The spell could not go forward. Too many had suffered.

"Where did the wolves go?" she asked Culy as they urged the ihstal into a run. They rode in the direction of now-darkening clouds that filled the eastern evening sky.

"They will intercept the army's scouts to buy us time," Culy said.

"How do you know?" Carin couldn't help but ask.

Culy flashed her that enigmatic grin again. "They are old, old friends."

Again the wolves' howls rose in the distance, spread out this time.

The ihstal's feet pounded into the sand, kicking it up behind them. Carin was tired of running, tired of moving, tired of being barely one step ahead from something that wanted her dead or worse.

But beside her was Culy, who had borne this burden far longer than she had. If sy could do it, so could Carin.

They would persist. They had to.

IF DYAVA had thought Lyari's pronouncement a simple wish, a fleeting fancy, he was disabused of the notion immediately. No sooner had he woken the next morning then he discovered that she had already left her bed, a note on her pillow beside Dyava's head to say that she had many preparations to see to.

For the turns that followed, he tried to learn whatever he could of her plan. His parents thought there was no way the Reinvocation could take place an entire cycle early, but they had been wrong about so many things before.

As Bide waned in the sky, only a bare five turns before High Lights and the Reinvocation, Dyava didn't think he could keep food down.

He met his parents in the tunnel where Jenin's body used to lie. His mother couldn't seem to look at the pallet where Jenin had been, keeping her back to it at all times.

"You said you would have some sort of plan," Dyava said. "Our time is short. I need to know anything you know that could help us assess the danger of Lyari going ahead with this, and you cannot deny the possibility that she could succeed."

Tarwyn and Silan exchanged a glance.

"You are right," Silan said.

Dyava didn't think he had ever heard his father say those words. "I know," he said. "I have been trying to tell you—we all have been trying to tell you—"

He knew that continuing would just make him start to splutter. How much time had they lost because his parents and Calyria's were so stuck in the rut of their own certainty? He gathered himself before starting again.

"What will she need? How does the spell work?" If Dyava thought about how little he truly knew about magic and the Reinvocation he had been raised to stop, he would leave his body like Jenin had and simply float into the sun.

"She will need the sacrifices. Five families and at least one person from each living generation," Tarwyn said after a moment's pause. She closed her eyes as if she couldn't believe she was saying this out loud. Maybe she couldn't. "Traditionally, they take one family from each village and draw lots on which village the remaining two come from."

"Draw lots," Dyava said. His head swam, and he blinked a few times to gain his bearing. He tried to take deeper breaths. "They draw *lots*."

"If you are having trouble with that, you are not prepared for this work," said Tarwyn flatly. "Did you expect a blood sacrifice to be pretty?"

"No," said Dyava. "I expected you to prepare me appropriately, not hide information from me until the last possible moment when we now have little chance of success."

Tarwyn opened her mouth as if to protest, but to Dyava's surprise, she then closed it again and nodded.

"At least drawing lots is more fair than the soothsayers simply choosing people they don't like," Dyava muttered. "If fairness exists in such a thing."

"There will be fifteen people in total," said Silan. "It always works out that way. Fifteen people, fifteen moons, to represent the cycle. Five families' potential, five hundred cycles."

"She will need to perform the sacrifices herself. Usually, all three soothsayers work together to do this, but with tensions as they are"—Tarwyn looked at her bondmate—"she may or may not use their help."

"Will that have a material impact on the spell?" Dyava asked.

Tarwyn shook her head. "The Reinvocation usually draws from the magic inherent in the mooncycle. Every five hundred cycles, there is a confluence of the moon and her sister and their pull on the tides as we draw closer to another celestial body. It is present already—you will be able to see the tip of the tiger's tail in the night sky glowing brighter—but it peaks one cycle from now."

"Is the difference between this cycle and the next so vast?" Dyava had never considered magic pulling on the moon or her sister, on the stars in the sky. He knew so little. "Or is it enough for her to succeed this summer with all of the changes?"

"You must remember that until now, our knowledge has been theoretical, my son," said Tarwyn. "We were not alive for the last Reinvocation, and our family members who were did not have enough arcane knowledge to describe it in detail. I cannot tell you how it works."

Dyava didn't know what made him angrier, that his parents had acted like they had all the answers his whole life or that they actually didn't.

"Then as I said, we have to assume it's possible," Dyava said. "We cannot afford not to."

In the dim light of the secret room, Dyava longed for the comfort of darkness and ignorance. He wished he knew nothing of any of this. He wished he had forgotten Carin and Ryd with the rest of the village. He felt like his knowledge and understanding was like this rotted room. Light revealed all, but there wasn't enough of it to help him. Just a strange, fragmented unlight that made the muddy shadows of what he didn't know all the more unbearable.

He had missed what his mother had said in response. "What?"

"I asked if you know who the sacrifices will be," she said.

Bile sloshed in Dyava's empty stomach. "No. I don't."

But he had told Lyari everything. He couldn't pretend there wasn't a chance she would choose his parents—though that would mean she also had to choose him. His grandparents were dead, but Dyava was the only remaining person from his generation.

"What else will she need for the spell?" he asked, trying to push that abhorrent thought out of his mind. "Aside from immense amounts of magical energy and the blood of fifteen living souls."

"The hearthstone," said Silan, clearing his throat. "Magic isn't like some of those children's tales, Dyava, like the farmer and the wolf. She needs no ingredients, no hairs from anyone's head."

Tarwyn, however, was frowning. "She is missing something she needs, which is where much of the danger comes," she said. "The Reinvocation previously depended on the five hearthstones being whole and unbroken. Without that . . ."

"Right," Dyava muttered. "If she pours that much power into one stone, we get Jenin's glass vase."

"It would be shared with any other stones that remain connected," Tarwyn said. "The danger would not be limited to Haveranth."

"Well, since with Jenin gone, we have no way of warning anyone north of the mountains to stay away from the remaining stones, I will restrict my worry to problems within my power to solve." Brave words, but Dyava felt even sicker.

If Carin was still trying to break the remaining stones, if she was doing it now, which he was certain she was, there would be a chance she would be close to them at the wrong moment. Lyari could kill her after all, without even meaning to.

"The final one is here," said Silan. "It is the stone she needs to use for the Reinvocation."

"I don't know if that makes it better or worse," Dyava said. "There could be one or two still remaining unbroken in the Northlands, but we have no way of knowing for certain."

And Carin had no hope of breaking the final stone before the Reinvocation. But maybe Dyava did.

• • • • •

When Dyava finally left the secret room, he felt like he had aged five hundred cycles in one handspan of the sun moving across the sky.

He had no idea if he could actually do it—he thought the remaining hearthstone was in place to the south, in a meadow where Lyari would perform the Reinvocation. He could get to it, without a doubt. But he didn't know how to break it. How had Carin done it?

Not for the first time, Dyava was almost overcome with respect for the first person he'd ever fallen in love with. Again and again, she had surprised him. She had survived, chosen something he never could have hoped to choose for himself, and unlike Dyava, who had spent his entire life being taught it was his duty to stop the Reinvocation, she had gone off and gotten far closer to succeeding than anyone ever had.

He didn't know if the Reinvocation would work. For all he knew, it only needed one stone to take hold. Perhaps all five had been necessary for the initial casting, but one could be enough to maintain it. Or maybe it would have some other sort of effect that they could not predict. Surely Lyari would be taking the broken stones into account. Dyava had told her everything, and if she was so certain she could perform the Reinvocation at *this* cycle's High Lights, she would not have failed to consider the possibilities. Unlike his parents, Lyari was methodical. Meticulous.

No one who had grown up with the half-wild, disheveled girl could have predicted that she would become so calculating, so contained.

Dyava went about his chores without really seeing what he was doing. He washed his dishes and the sink, tightened a bolt on his water pump, swept the floors, went out to the garden and checked his plants, all like he wasn't even present, like his body was simply going about tasks without him needing to give it direction.

He was so lost in his work that he didn't register someone walking down the road from the foothills until she had passed his roundhome. One woman, walking alone. She was dressed in robe of purple vysa, belted at the waist with bronze and with the bronze cuffs of the soothsayer on her wrists.

Reynah.

Dyava's heart nearly stopped, and he was so abruptly back in his body that the sensation of fledgling panic threatened to overwhelm him.

At the Night of Reflection, Lyari had told Reynah in front of the entire village—as well as contingents from both Cantoranth and Bemin's Fan—that neither Reynah nor Harag were welcome in Haveranth again without express invitation.

There was no way in this bountiful earth that Lyari had sent such an invitation, and Reynah was dressed very clearly to mark that she did not need permission.

Any trace of her injury was gone; she walked with both hands swinging freely and naturally at her sides. Striding with purpose toward the village hearth-home, Reynah did not appear to be going to Lyari's house, and Dyava did not know what to do.

If he ran to Lyari, it would look like panic, and Lyari would not thank him for it. If he did nothing, that would also look suspicious, since Dyava had been present at the Night of Reflection and had taken a direct role in protecting Lyari in front of everyone. There was no way Reynah had not seen him outside his roundhome.

All of this passed through his mind before she was out of sight, and Dyava hurried back inside. He quickly washed his hands and stripped out of his work clothes, grabbing a wet towel to wipe off dirt and bits of plant matter from his bare arms and face and neck, and then he carefully dressed in something that would not be out of place on a feast day but also would not look strange on a normal afternoon.

He walked to the village hearth-home unsure of what to expect. He had not forgotten the squash field, but he did not think Reynah had enough magic to have done such a complex spell herself. Which left his previous fear rearing its head in his mind.

Lyari had killed Merin. Dyava had seen her body. But he knew that didn't mean she was really dead. Someone as powerful as Merin could have done what Jenin did more skillfully than Jenin had.

If Reynah couldn't perform such magic upon the squash, perhaps she could have with help.

The village was quiet as was always the case at this time of day, with everyone working in their fields or at their crafts, though Tamat stood as always at hys spit, ready to feed anyone if there was need. Dyava was unsurprised to see that was where Reynah had stopped, and Tamat was speaking to her, though a bit apprehensively.

Reynah had her back to him.

Dyava had to make a choice. Either he could turn and run to Lyari's now when she wasn't looking or he could go speak to her himself.

What would Lyari want him to do? He had absolutely no idea.

After only one more breath, though, he turned toward Lyari's roundhome. He knew he didn't *need* to be the one to tell her, but someone would have to, and it may as well be him.

He only hoped she was there and not off doing something away from the village. She had been gone more often than usual of late, and it would not do at all for her to arrive back to find Reynah watching her with that smug smile.

This was yet another moving piece Dyava did not need.

He hurried to Lyari's roundhome, his mind whirling through a thousand things he could barely articulate to himself. He let himself in without knocking, as he usually did, and Lyari looked up at him from where she sat at the long maha table, which was covered in scrolls. The one in her hand drooped toward the table with the weight of five small circles of white wax.

"Dyava," she said, her voice surprised. "What are you—"

"Reynah is here," he said.

"What?" Her voice was so flat, so unemotional, that it immediately struck terror into Dyava's heart.

From one breath to the next, Lyari went from surprise to radiating danger, and Dyava was very grateful it was not directed at him.

"I saw her coming from my garden. She is dressed all in purple, and last I saw her, she was speaking with Tamat in the hearth-home."

"Purple." Lyari's upper lip curled a fraction of an inch. "So she means to make a scene."

Dyava nodded. "I think she must."

Lyari considered that, looking out over the scrolls. "I did not want to show my tiles this early," she murmured. "But I cannot let this stand."

"Lyari?" Dyava asked.

It wasn't that she'd been secretive lately, but she had been mired in her scrolls and preparations, of which Dyava was not part. He had very carefully given her space in that regard, making sure she knew he was there if she needed him, but also making clear that he would not push. Dyava played a dangerous game, but he had made his choices now. There was no going back.

"I will need you to put these away," she said, rising to her feet like she had decided on her course of action. "In the secret place. Make sure no one can touch them."

Dyava immediately set about gathering the scrolls without looking at them. "What are you going to do?"

"First I am going to change," she said. "Then I will meet you in the hearth-home. And then I'm going to reveal to the village that their troubles are about to end."

It felt as if a rotten peach pit had burst in Dyava's gut. Lyari turned away to go into her room almost immediately, and he tried to focus his mind on the scrolls. He would have to tell his parents not to touch them if they came into the tunnel, though he knew they would want the chance to look at them.

He didn't know if there would be time or if there was anything in these scrolls that would even be of use in such a situation as they had found themselves.

He heard Lyari moving about in her room as he carefully rolled and stacked the scrolls to place in the wooden crate beside the table.

The scrolls were tidy and ready before Lyari came out, and Dyava did not waste any time. He left her roundhome out the back door that was not visible from the village hearth-home and hurried home as fast as he could without seeming like he was rushing.

His home was just as he'd left it, of course, and he dipped down the stairs into the cellar without a second thought. He only hesitated when he got to the secret room. Lyari knew he could hide his wards, disguise his magic, and invert it so no one could see what he had done. Which meant if she made it down here before he could come back, she wouldn't know he had left them untouched. His parents could look over them, see if they could figure out what Rina had been searching for or simply if they could discover anything that could help them avert catastrophe.

But Dyava wasn't certain it was worth the risk.

He pulled out one of the scrolls, skimming over it. It looked like a discussion on relative force—theory he had become passingly familiar with, but nothing inherently useful.

Replacing it, Dyava pulled out the next one. He didn't know how long he had before Lyari would wonder what was keeping him. He couldn't make immediate sense of any of the scrolls he pulled out. The words were understandable enough, but he had no basis of reference for their application to the matter at hand. But there had to be *something* in there Lyari didn't want Reynah to have.

With a noise of frustration, he set about creating wards, knowing it wouldn't do to only reveal who disturbed them this time. If it was Reynah, they didn't want her to simply grab them and escape somehow.

He carefully wove together a spell that would both reveal and incapacitate someone bent on handling the scrolls. He didn't think it could kill a person, but it would hopefully render the intruder unconscious.

As soon as he was done and satisfied the wards would hold, he ran down the passageway to his parents' house, hoping they were home.

He was not so fortunate. The moment he emerged from their cellar, it was obvious they were out. The fire was banked, and he knew from the tidiness of the table that they had left for outdoor work. As a child, they had used an old slate and a chalk stick for messages, but Dyava couldn't exactly write "stay away from the box in the secret passageway" on something that any visitor could stumble upon.

There wasn't time for him to dither about it. He grabbed the slate and the chalk, hoping his parents were observant enough to notice its absence from the wall by the shelf of crockery in the kitchen, and he ran back down the stairs. He scribbled what he hoped was a clear warning without being suspicious on the off chance someone else saw it. He hung the slate just inside the passage on a hook where they had once kept some of Jenin's clothes for when they would bath hyr so as not to leave hyr to become grimy in the long moons sy lay sleeping beneath the earth.

With that, Dyava scurried the rest of the way back to his own roundhome and tried to gather himself before leaving.

Each step he took toward the village hearth-home made his heart sink just a bit lower into his stomach. What could Reynah want? There was no way he could think to prove that Merin had somehow survived, but he thought it was likely Reynah was helping her.

When he reached the hearth-home, already a small crowd was gathering, and Lyari sat comfortably at a table with a plate of grilled mutton and yams, and Reynah sat across from her just as comfortably.

Dyava hadn't expected to arrive to a shouting match, but he hadn't expected to see civility on display either.

Reynah looked up when he arrived, giving no indication that their last meeting had been a good deal less than cordial. It wasn't until he was within a table-length of the pair of seated soothsayers that Dyava saw the struggle being waged beneath the surface.

Most magic users didn't have his ability to see magic in use. Some developed it over time, but to Dyava, it came naturally. It had been his first talent with magic, before he realized he had to be using magic to see it in the first place.

So he doubted any of the bemused bystanders milling about the village hearth-home could see the strands of magic weaving through the air between Lyari and Reynah. Nor did he think they were aware that, despite their pleasant and insipid conversation, there was a bitter tension locked in a contest of wills right out in the open.

Lyari would know he could see the tendrils of magic reaching across that table, each woman seeking a weakness to exploit and finding none yet. Reynah would not know what he could do, even though he had warned Lyari on the Night of Reflection. There were far simpler explanations for that incident.

Which meant that Reynah wouldn't know Dyava could see the rest of the threads of magic she wore over every inch of her purple robe. It blended with her skin, her hair, coated the bronze at her wrists with a sheen that seemed like it ought to glimmer in the light of day.

He hadn't seen it in Cantoranth. It hadn't been there.

Dyava glanced across the hearth-home, where conversations were starting up again now that people seemed to think the danger of violence had passed, and he saw his mother staring back at him.

The intensity of her look almost made him lose face. He could hear Lyari asking about Cantoranth's crops.

He thought he could not possibly be right, but something, some spell was woven so closely to Reynah's skin she may as well have been dipped in it.

Dyava didn't think Merin was back anymore. He knew it. Because she was here.

B ASHA KNEW something had happened from the plume of black smoke that suddenly rose from the direction of Rela's tent. They had just stopped for the evening, and the tents had barely been pitched when there was a muffled *whoomph*, and when Basha turned to look, smoke. And fire, of course, for the closer he got to the smoke, the more obvious the flames.

Immediately the air was full of yelling as soldiers sprang into action to keep the blaze from spreading.

"What has happened?" he demanded of a captain who stood issuing orders to a company of the Marefi men.

"Do I look like I know?" the captain snapped. "That mage probably decided he didn't like the shape of someone's eyebrows and burned them off."

Normally, Basha would have said something about the officer's tone and choice of words—he was speaking of an Arelashk!—but Basha was not about to argue today. He moved in a trot in the direction of the fire. Running would be improprietous despite the obvious emergency; the soldiers' job was to contain the fire. His was to unravel its cause and effects.

It wasn't Arelashk's tent that had been incinerated, he saw as he approached, but a nearby soldier's. Likely a simple case of the tent having been in the wrong place at the wrong time. Arelashk and Asurashk were outside, pointedly ignoring the conflagration while soldiers scurried about with waterskins and formed a line to the nearby stream, already dousing the fire, a pulse of hisses rising with each new container of water thrown upon it.

Basha blinked smoke out of his eyes and slowed his pace, approaching Arelashk and Asurashk with what he thought was prudent wariness. He didn't really think the Arelashk would move from immolating tents to immolating people, but some care would hardly be amiss.

"Basha," said the mage as if a cloud of smoke was not billowing into his face with the breeze. "You are timely, as always."

"Thank you, honored Arelashk," Basha said. "How may I be of service?"

"You may find a commanding officer and tell him to send the scouts east as fast as they can go. They are to return as soon as they find a stone. It will be"—he looked at Asurashk—"on a small hill, likely with a rune carved into it. I expect they will find it has broken."

He said the last word with the force of a punctuating crack not unlike a stone breaking itself.

"Yes, honored Arelashk," Basha said.

He turned on his heel and strode in the other direction, back whence he had come. It did not take long for him to find the Marefi officers in charge of the scouts—he had been sent on similar errands before—and he noted the look they exchanged at the change in orders. Arelashk would want to know.

By the time he returned, Arelashk and Asurashk were inside the mage's tent, and when Arelashk bid him enter, Basha did so and immediately made himself unobtrusive. Arelashk was standing against the back wall of the tent, looking like he still wanted to set things on fire.

Asurashk sat calmly on a cushion, and though Basha did not think she was afraid of her mentor, she had a veneer of calm that seemed a little too serene for someone in her position.

"They have taken it right out from under us," Arelashk was saying. "We cannot allow them to get to the remaining ones."

"If we had marched on Lahivar, we could have discovered where the remaining stones are," Asurashk said.

"Do not be stupid. They would have had to be moving already to have reached this one ahead of us. We will turn south immediately, and as soon as the general is here, I will have him send his fastest ahead of us." Arelashk glanced once at Basha, who nodded simply to convey he had completed his part of the request. "You do not feel it, but I do. There is something yet to the south. We will reach it before Carin, and we will keep it from her and whoever dares venture close to it."

Basha did not like the sound of that. Beyond the idea of marching southward for some undisclosed amount of time, Arelashk seemed far too confident that his goal was still achievable, and his anger at Carin would only grow if she impeded his plans any further.

Asurashk nodded her assent, though her facade slipped ever so slightly. Basha pretended to be focused on the notebook he carried.

"The mountains are not farther than two turns from here," Asurashk said. "At a forced march, they should be reachable before midsummer."

Rela paced back and forth, not acknowledging Asurashk's words.

"We are limited by the Marefi army's lack of technology and their insistence that infantry is preferable when speed is sometimes a necessity," Arelashk muttered.

"It has served them well so far," Asurashk said smoothly. "We do not have the mounts that people here seem to. And the Khardish have refused to share the secrets of autocars to Maref."

"For good reason. Khardan does not want every advance of our technology to feed the Marefi war machine," Arelashk said irritably, though to Basha's eyes, it seemed the mage thought such a policy shortsighted.

Basha, however, was relieved. Not that Khardish autocars could simply drive across unpaved terrain in a strange land where there would be no means of charging their power sources. No, such technology would be nearly useless in any case, at least here.

The rest of the meeting fell into arguing and negotiating with the Marefi general and his underlings, who arrived shortly thereafter, to which Basha listened with as rapt attention as he could spare from his note taking. There was some small comfort in thinking that this entire situation would be resolved to some degree by midsummer, but not knowing what sort of resolution that would be left Basha still mired in dread.

Best case scenario, in Basha's mind, was that Carin and her people were able to neutralize or otherwise render useless whatever it was Arelashk said he could sense to the south. Basha had no idea what it was, whether another stone or something else, but he would have to hope for Carin's success. He had no idea how she had returned home—even if autocars could drive on water, it did not account for Arelashk's assertion that she had seemed to jump hundreds of leagues across the sea in the space of an hour—but it seemed undeniable that she was indeed here.

The other scenarios were much worse. As the Arelashk had so helpfully articulated, the Marefi war machine was a hungry beast, and anything the army found, they would expect to use for their own purposes. That the Arelashk was supremely outnumbered two thousand to one didn't seem to cross the mage's mind.

Which left Basha wondering if whatever it was they sought was something he thought powerful enough to mitigate such a starkly forbidding factor as pitting himself against an army. That was indeed a horrible thought, and it was one Basha could not reconcile with any reality he knew.

As the meeting dragged on, his stomach turned to lead. Runners came and went from the tent with alarming frequency, sending out scouts in several different directions, all of them with different orders. Those sent to the south were to seek and apprehend Carin and whoever was with her. Those sent to the west were to keep the army apprised and to have their reserve prepared to march. That Lahivar stood between the sea and Arelashk's destination did not escape Basha's worry.

Still others were sent out to capture more of the locals. It was watching Asurashk's face that made Basha begin to understand how Oshu could have come to hate her. She was prepared to abuse any number of people if it meant she would get what she wanted. Basha had known plenty of malicious people over his life's cycles, but he did not think he had ever met someone so bent on vengeance as the story seeker from Triya.

If he and Oshu were to survive this, Basha was going to need a plan—and soon.

· · · · ·

Despite his general dislike of the Marefi nation's politics and proclivities, Basha had to admit they were good at what they did. Before first light the next day, they began a forced march to the south.

Basha and Oshu were to march with Arelashk and Asurashk, which meant they both got to hear the mage's observations of the landscape—something that was changing almost before their very eyes.

Basha had thought they were about to head into a desert as they moved eastward, but since they had turned south, he wasn't so sure. While the ground was still sandy, the foliage that was sprouting almost by the hour was lush and green, the grasses a deeper blue than Basha had ever seen even in the bits of Khardan inland enough to have grasslands, which were admittedly sparse. When he was not too tired, he had taken to sketching some of the plant life in his notebook, hoping he could ask Valon what things were called. Though considering how quickly they were observing changes, it wasn't outside the realm of possibility that even Valon might not know the names of some of this flora.

Their route was taking them through rolling hills, and Basha was thankful for the occasional chance to move downward rather than up a slope, though his blisters did not entirely agree. The sun slanting into his eyes threatened to give him another headache.

"More saplings," murmured Arelashk, and Basha looked down the hill and off to the west where indeed there was yet another grove of young trees.

"It must be the effects of their spell breaking down," Asurashk said with confidence, raising one hand to dab away a sheen of perspiration. The spring had quickly given way to summer with the new moon, and being from Triya, Asurashk was unused to heat. "Though I cannot imagine how it is possible for such things to be so abundant and swift."

"We have barely begun to explore the frontiers of what is possible with magic," said Arelashk. "Much has been lost that we must rediscover, and a place that has been in isolation for two and a half thousand cycles will hold many secrets."

From what little Basha knew of it, there was much that had been lost for good reason. Dangerous magics, used to control and dominate, which frequently rebounded back on the one wielding it in unpredictable ways. At least that was what Basha had heard in the stories, and he knew that, myth or not, most stories were grounded in some level of truth, some lesson someone had learned the hard way.

Khardish mages beyond even the Arelashk's ken and status, the Eduashae, kept some knowledge locked away and guarded by their most trusted minds. Not even the Da'sash Dan could gain access to it. As Basha watched the back of the Arelashk's head, he saw another facet of the man's motivation that he had not yet considered—lacking the ability to get such secrets legally the traditional way, Arelashk had decided to circumvent the barriers entirely.

And would possibly start a war between Khardan and Maref in the process, but Basha could only worry about one catastrophe at a time, and he needed that to be the one that was currently chafing his blisters.

He didn't dare look at Oshu too often, but he knew the man was as nervous as he was himself. It was disquieting to be in a land where there were no forests they had seen, yet everywhere they looked there were young trees that looked barely a cycle old. Worse was that the trees were growing far faster than they ought to be. Soldiers had had to move their tents in the middle of the night on occasion when they were woken by something pressing upward out of the ground that, instead of being squashed, seemed determined to grow.

Yelling began to the eastern flank of the column, and Basha squinted into the sun, which was still on its climb upward from the horizon.

It was difficult to make out the Marefi shouts from where he stood with the other bureaucrats at the center of the column, but before too long, he heard the word *medic.*

Arelashk raised one hand. "Find out what it is."

Understanding this was an order for him, Oshu immediately moved toward their left, in the direction of the eastern flank.

The yelling grew louder and more urgent as the column halted.

An eerie song rose into the morning sky, covering Basha's skin in prickles.

"I suppose that is an answer," Arelashk said smoothly. "An army of two thousand and they cannot deal with a wolf or two?"

Basha had never seen a wolf, and he wouldn't have recognized the sound had they not been hearing it periodically in their march from the coast inland. When they had been marching on Lahivar, the sound of howling had been a frequent occurrence, along with the remains of animals that had been savagely mauled. There had been strange screams in the night as well, enough that Basha had been thoroughly uneasy until one night they weren't heard from again. He remembered that night had come after they turned to the east, and part of him wondered what would have happened if they had continued onward to Lahivar.

Oshu returned after a short time, and he bowed to Arelashk and Asurashk, eyes downcast.

"Wolves have killed three scouts, honored ones," he said. "A fourth and fifth are injured badly."

"How many scouts remain unaccounted for?" Asurashk asked.

"Twenty," Oshu answered. "But many of those were traveling westward, not east or south."

"Is the general increasing patrols?" Arelashk asked.

"Yes, honored Arelashk."

But the mage was staring over Oshu's shoulder. It took a moment for Basha to make out what he was looking at.

In the distance, at the bottom of the next hill, Basha could see the eastern edge of the column. Beyond them was a hulking shape he could barely make out, except that it dwarfed the soldiers closest to it. After a moment, something moved near it, and Basha realized it wasn't alone. Dark grey and massive, the creatures stalked the edge of the column, and a ripple of unease cascaded through the assembled soldiers.

"What are they waiting for?" Arelashk muttered. "Must I give the orders to shoot them?"

He had barely finished speaking when the twang of bowstrings reached Basha's ears, but the shapes moved faster than he would have thought such enormous creatures capable. With a growl audible even over the hum of the soldiers' talking, both shapes bounded off to the east, apparently unharmed.

"Wolves are usually not so bold," Asurashk said quietly. "They attack only when they sense a vulnerability or out of desperation. The scouts I can understand—the wolves would see them as separate from their pack, but coming so close to the army itself is unusual."

"You seem to have some experience with the creatures," Arelashk said, his voice dry.

"My family were shepherds in Triya," Asurashk said. "Wolves are fond of sheep."

Basha kept himself from glancing at Oshu, trying to reconcile a shepherd's life with the woman ready to raze a continent.

"Ah, yes. You have said this before." The Arelashk shifted his weight as marching orders cut through the air. "I think these wolves will find that we are not sheep."

Basha wanted to ask if it was normal for wolves to leave their mangled prey around the perimeter of their territory. He did not think it was. What predator would be so wasteful?

He kept looking off to the left, almost hoping for another glimpse of the animals. Whatever they were doing, Basha did not think the wolves were simply scouting prey.

OF ALL the things to be fretting about, Clar did not think romantic troubles were high on the list of acceptable priorities at a time like this. Despite that, however, Clar was fretting about it.

It wasn't exactly trouble. Kat had not been ignoring her since they returned from their journey to find Carin and Culy, but something was clearly weighing on the kazytya rider, and Clar couldn't bring herself to try and force a confidence if Kat wouldn't tell her voluntarily.

Clar had taken to riding westward on an ihstal called Saba, whom Hoyu had named. The animal was quick and spirited, young enough that sy hadn't been named sooner, but old enough to ride. Clar found that Saba was more than willing to cart both herself and Hoyu around the countryside whenever either of them needed a moment away. Which was often. They didn't go together—the whole point was being alone—but sometimes it felt like just as Clar could take no more worry, no more staring off into the south across the mountains, she would flee to the ihstal and find Hoyu just returning, calm-faced and resolute. Or the other way around. No matter what, Saba liked to run, and if left to hys own devices, the ihstal would drive the older members of the herd to angry whistles and stomping feet for all hys prancing in circles.

Clar had a wry appreciation for the sense that her need to escape provided an additional benefit for everyone involved. The older ihstal got some peace, Saba got to run for leagues upon leagues, and Clar and Hoyu got to feel the wind in their faces for a while. It was a chance to forget—what had Ryd called it?—their litany of impossible problems.

On a day like today, with the summer sun beating down on her back and a cool breeze rolling in from the sea and north from the mountains, Clar almost really could forget.

She was always careful to remain alert to anything amiss. Sometimes she had the strangest feeling that if she could just go fast enough, something would happen. Saba loved to go fast, but sy still wasn't as fast as Suhnsuoc, and Clar hardly thought Kat would let her go haring off with the kazytya alone. It would be too strange without Kat, anyway.

That day, on the First Bud of Toil, Clar didn't think she could outrun the knowledge that one cycle from now, this would all be over, for good or ill.

It was little comfort when she could not know what was to come of it. She imagined an army of Marefi soldiers descending on Haveranth in the flush of the Reinvocation and shuddered. If that happened, Clar was sure she would already be dead.

The breeze picked up as she and Saba ran, and for a moment, Clar lost herself in ecstasy of what felt like flight.

She had listened to Ras and Ryd as they talked about the ialtag flying them over the passes of the Mad Mountains, but she couldn't imagine it. It was almost too frightening to picture being dependent on wings, but with Saba's feet devouring span after span of grass beneath them, Clar thought this was close enough for her.

A trickle of sweat worked its way down her back between her shoulder blades, and she let out a small whoop, to which Saba responded with a whistle of hys own, muscles bunching and stretching all the more.

She couldn't explain the sudden sensation that spilled over her. It was almost like catching a whiff of something foul, rot or decay or a chamber pot left out in the sun.

Before she could think about it, she was nudging Saba in the direction from which she sensed it. It wasn't a smell, not exactly, though as they ran, quieter now as if the ihstal could sense Clar's urgency, she did pick up a scent that struck her with alarm.

Surely they hadn't run all the way to the sea, had they?

Yet as they cleared a small rise, Clar caught a glimpse of it in the distance, a smudge of blue-green on the horizon.

And that was not all she saw.

The Marefi fleet must have sailed out of sight of shore to disguise their movements, because they had reappeared now, here.

Clar slowed the ihstal, who gave a low whistle of protest before Clar's hand on hys neck stilled all movement.

Her eyesight had always been good. Now that she wasn't moving, she could see the ships hovering far closer to shore than she would have liked. Why hadn't their scouts reported it?

There were two explanations Clar could think of. One was that the scouts were dead. The other was that she was the first to see, which meant whatever was about to happen had only just sprung into motion.

She counted the ships, not that she knew how to make sense of the number's relevance. There were smaller boats on the edges of the ships, barely visible. The ships must have been truly huge to be able to also carry boats. Hoyu had said the boats were used to bring people ashore, as the ships had to stay in deeper water.

If they had ventured this close to shore, that had to mean more people were coming.

"*Ahsh*," she said to Saba to quiet hyr, and she slid off the ihstal's back, motioning to the animal to venture away from the sea.

Clar knew they had ways of seeing at a distance. It was likely she had already been spotted. She listened, hearing only the whisper of the waves meeting the beach and the wind in the grass. That sense of rot returned, north of her.

She skirted the rise that gave way to the beach, trying to stay low so that anyone at sea level wouldn't be able to see her even if they had one of the instruments Hoyu had described.

Her legs began to burn after a while, but Clar kept on, increasingly certain that she needed to see what was coming.

The sun had sunk about a handspan when the sensation grew stronger, and Clar stopped, unsure of what to do. Once in the Hearthland, when she had been hunting, she had almost come between a tiger and its prey, a young saiga likely not long after weaning. She had felt a tremor, an instinct, and she felt it again now. The feeling that there was something more dangerous than her about.

Her breath coming in slow, shallow waves, Clar made her way around a headland that overlooked a beach that had a wide crescent of sand at all but the highest tide.

She stopped.

It was low tide, and the beach was as exposed as it could possibly get.

It was full of soldiers.

They were barely a day walking from Lahivar.

• • • • •

Clar wished the ialtag would show up as she ran to meet Saba and almost vaulted onto the ihstal's back. She didn't think the soldiers had seen her, but she veered to the north just in case, murmuring to the ihstal to go, to run faster, to chase the wind as it rolled eastward on its journey in from the sea.

If the journey to the sea had passed in barely a blink of an eye, the journey back to Lahivar seemed to take an entire cycle. Somewhere on the way, she had started to sweat, and Clar could smell the fear on herself. Saba could smell it too, and the ihstal let out anxious whistles as sy ran.

The sun was full in her face as they reached Lahivar, and in a moment of irony, there was Hoyu walking toward the western edge of the waymake, doubtless to take Saba out for a run herself.

The Khardish woman blanched when she saw Clar, however, her dark brown hand leaping as if to help Clar down from Saba's back despite Clar still being much too far away.

"Hoyu," Clar gasped. "Soldiers."

Hoyu closed the distance between them so fast, Clar half wondered if she had simply leapt through the air, and then she *was* helping Clar down from Saba's back. Clar's legs were trembling, as were Saba's. The ihstal immediately trotted to the river and sank to hys elbows to drink from the cold, flowing water.

"Where?" Hoyu asked, looking past Clar to the west.

"Gathered on the beach." Clar took another gulping breath, feeling as if she had swallowed air in a bubble that tightened her chest. "So many of them. I counted twelve ships. I don't know if there were more out of sight."

"They sailed west to stay out of sight," Hoyu murmured, confirming Clar's guess. "They must have some way of communicating with Rela's people."

"There is no path inland that does not put Lahivar in their way," Clar said. "It's time. We can wait no longer."

"I will go to Sart," Hoyu said. "Catch your breath. You will need it."

Hoyu squeezed her shoulder tightly, just once, then strode a few paces away before stopping again.

"Catch," she said, pulling her waterskin from where it lay harnessed at her belt, and she tossed the skin to Clar.

Clar caught it, though barely. Her hands shook.

She opened it and drank gratefully, wanting to call out a thank you to Hoyu, but Hoyu was running. Great bounty, the woman was fast.

Where could they go if the army was coming here? Clar had no idea, no way of knowing where could possibly be safe for a waymake of several hundred souls. Out of the cauldron, into the burning hearth. That was the saying her mother had used, was it not?

Clar walked on teetering legs over to a stump that sat just at the edge of the waymake. She didn't know whose roundhome the stump belonged to; it was one of the newer ones that had sprung up even since she had first come to Lahivar. Clar wondered if it would still be here when they returned. If they ever returned.

Like with the soldiers, a strange sensation tickled at her again, this time like the scent of her own fear, and she did not have to follow it to know it was the waves of anxiety pouring off the waymake as news undoubtedly spread. As if in agreement, a drum began to beat, a signal they had worked out when Rela's portion of the army had been bearing down upon them.

Clar put her elbows on her knees and leaned forward, her head in her hands as she tried to collect herself enough to be useful. The waterskin sloshed with the movement, its surface cool where it rested against her cheek.

She barely had time to register the footsteps before she heard her name.

"Clar," said Kat.

Clar pried her face off her palm and the waterskin and sat up. A wave of exhaustion threatened to put her face on the ground if she wasn't careful.

"I just heard," Kat said softly. "You saw them?"

Clar managed a nod.

"I've sent Suhnsuoc to make sure any scouts of ours return," Kat said. "Sy hasn't found any yet, but sy's on their trail. If sy has to carry them back, sy will."

"Thank you." Clar tried to get to her feet, but Kat gave her a gentle push back onto the stump.

"You're about to drop. Your things are packed, yes?" Kat stared at her until she nodded again.

They had all been ready to go for turns now. Until that moment, Clar hadn't realized just how much she had been hoping they wouldn't need to.

"I'll be back," said Kat.

The sounds of bustling buzzed around Clar as she sat, her heart beating out a report out of step with the drum but too fast for her sitting to be considered restful.

For turns they had been trying to decide what to do, but they didn't know enough of the movements of the army to truly decide. If the bulk of Rela's forces were still moving due east, the Lahivarans could go north, but Ryhnas Lu Sesim was too close to the sea to be safe. According to Ras and Sart and the countless others in Lahivar, there were plenty of waymakes to be found throughout the Northlands, but none of them were large enough to sustain, well, a village. Lahivar had grown to the point that Clar wasn't sure she could call it a waymake, and she doubted it was big enough to be called a city. Perhaps if all of the Marefi soldiers stayed, there would be enough people to fill a city. Maybe enough people to build one.

Clar did not want the Marefi soldiers to stay.

She just wanted to stay here, in Lahivar.

A current of despair threatened to pull her under, and she pushed herself to her feet. Sitting here was not helping.

She must have been lost in thought longer than she had supposed, because Kat was making her way back to Clar, looking alarmed.

"What's wrong?" Clar asked, and Kat simply took her by the shoulders and shook her head.

"Why are you not resting?" Kat frowned.

"I can't just sit there while there are things to be done. I can rest later."

"When? When you've been—" Kat broke off with a sudden cry of anguish, her hand falling from Clar's shoulder. "Suhnsuoc."

Clar's breath shuddered mid-inhale. "Is sy okay?"

Kat's eyes showed white all around. "Sy's frightened. Running. One of the scouts was dead when sy found hyr, but sy's carrying two others—three others, rot."

The kazytya was strong, but carrying three riders would be a lot, especially if they were about to be fleeing and in need of speed.

Gaze distant, Kat shook herself.

"The scouts didn't encounter the army, only a group of Marefi scouts. Those will report back to their leaders, but Suhnsuoc had to decide between killing them and rescuing our people." Kat swallowed, and Clar instinctively took her hand.

"Sy made the right choice," Clar said.

The flurry of movement engulfed them as Lahivarans hurried around the two women, and Clar hated feeling helpless. When she said as much, Kat stared at her in disbelief.

"You warned us," she said. "I can think of nothing more helpful than that. Our scouts could have died. The army could have been at our feet before we knew they were coming. You have literally saved Lahivar, Clar."

Clar didn't feel like she'd saved anything yet. "We'll see."

Someone pressed a rolled-up flatbread into her hands and was gone before Clar could thank hyr. She knew she needed the energy, and though she didn't expect to so much as taste it, when she bit into it, her tastebuds flooded with spice and juicy venison. Saiga, probably. It was still hot, and Clar tried to savor it. There would be little chance of many hot meals on the road ahead.

Before much longer, a steady flow of people streamed out of Lahivar to the north.

Clar and Kat hung back with Sart and some of the others, though Ryd and Jenin and Ras had gone to keep watch over the people. The most vulnerable were sent ahead, in carts pulled by ihstal or riding if they were able, and Clar hated knowing that they could be going into danger.

Kat's eyes scanned the western edge of the village constantly, searching for the first view of Suhnsuoc. When the kazytya appeared, Clar saw the tension recede from Kat's shoulders. Despite their bond, Clar could imagine needing the reassurance of having her companion back in easy distance.

The kazytya did not seem too tired, even though there were three riders on hys back, clinging to each other as if the ride had exhausted them; maybe it had.

One of them had a gash over his eyebrow that had crusted over with dried blood that made a smear from his left eye out over his cheek where he had clearly tried to scrub the blood away.

"They do not seem to be moving tonight," one of the other scouts said wearily. "Though if they march at dawn, they will be here well before sundown. We must be out of their path by then."

"Is Lahivar their goal, then? What do you think?" Kat asked this aloud, but Clar thought she was mostly speaking to Suhnsuoc.

"I couldn't say," said the woman who had spoken. Ira? Clar couldn't remember her name.

"Suhnsuoc says it is likely they plan to intercept the rest of the army or wish to use Lahivar as shelter." Kat made a derisive sound. "They are bringing supplies from the ships."

Clar did not like the sound of that.

Sart was looking out over Lahivar with an unreadable expression. "If I could make the river rise up and swallow them, I would."

The anger in her voice was unmistakeable. Clar couldn't blame her.

"Then we will have to teach them a lesson some other way," Clar said softly. "Until then, we must keep your people safe."

Sart met Clar's eyes, startled, but after a moment, she nodded. "Our people," she said. "And we will."

And then they were moving, the scouts given ihstal and sent on ahead, and Suhnsuoc lowered hyrself to allow Kat and Clar to climb on hys back. Kat did just that, but after a moment, she sniffed, and Clar could almost hear an *Are you sure?*

"Suhnsuoc says you should ride with us," Kat said to Sart. "Sy insists sy isn't too tired, and even with three people, sy is faster than an ihstal, though it will be difficult to get used to."

Sart did not look convinced, but after a moment, she nodded.

Just before Clar slid her leg over Suhnsuoc's back behind Kat, she thought she saw a glimmer of tears in Sart's eye. She did not yet know the older woman well enough to comment on it, but when Sart settled herself at Clar's back and wrapped her arms around Clar's waist, it seemed like she held on tighter than she needed to.

To Clar's great surprise, a bark of laughter erupted behind her, a puff of breath in Clar's still-sweat-dampened hair sending a small shiver up her neck. Sart was laughing?

"I used to think convincing a kazytya to carry me was the most ridiculous thing I could imagine," Sart muttered in explanation. "I guess I need a better imagination."

Clar didn't know what to say to that, but she removed one of her hands from Kat's waist and gave Sart's hand a squeeze.

Clar wanted to look back at Lahivar, at least once more to fix it in her mind as it had been. For the first time in her life, in spite of the ongoing fear and in spite of everything they faced, she had never been happier in all her days.

We'll come home, she told herself, a promise she cast out on the wind. *We will come home.*

KAT HAD never been so tired.

     She never would have suggested they continue through the night, but as Suhnsuoc made hys way along the trail of Lahivarans fleeing their waymake, Kat knew even the most tired of all of them wanted to continue.

The summer nights were short. Not as short as they were in her home village, but short nonetheless. It felt as if the sun barely dipped beneath the horizon before it popped back up a short distance away from where it had set.

They had decided to go straight north and then to aim eastward, but everyone was wary of possibly encountering the other half of the Marefi force. No one knew where they had gone after they had changed course and headed away from Lahivar.

It was almost a full night and day before they finally did stop on the Lahi'alar where two branching roads met. They were barely visible in the new growth that had unfurled over the land, and Kat thought that by summer's end, the well-traveled byways of the warmlands would be fully overgrown.

It had rained briefly during the day, but everyone was so tired that it was welcome; it felt refreshing in the summer heat to have some respite—and to have water that wasn't sweat to evaporate from their skin.

When they stopped, Kat half expected everyone to drop where they stood. Even the ihstal were clearly tired, and the one Clar and Hoyu had taken to riding, Saba, actually fell asleep where sy stood between one bite of grazing and the next.

Suhnsuoc loped off the moment Kat and Clar and Sart dismounted, and Kat didn't blame hyr. After carrying people for so long, sy would need to hunt and replenish hys energy.

Needing to stretch her legs after such a long time astride the kazytya, Kat found herself wandering near Hoyu. The Khardish woman looked ill at ease, her fingers toying with the hem of her tunic while she stared into the west as if she could burn the ships at sea if she wished hard enough.

But she looked over at Kat when she heard footsteps in the grass, and Hoyu gave her a warm smile, if wan.

"At least no one can say it's been a boring summer," Hoyu said softly.

Her language had improved to near-flawless fluency, which Kat admired. She had been curious about the other woman's Khardish, but she didn't know her well enough to ask if Hoyu would teach her. Perhaps someday, if they survived.

"No," Kat agreed. "Boring is the last word I would use to describe this summer so far."

Despite the lighthearted words, Hoyu's small frame seemed weighed down, like an iceberg hiding most of its bulk below the surface of the sea.

"You are troubled," Kat said after a moment. "There is ample reason to be, of course, but though this is not your homeland, you worry for us."

"Yes," Hoyu said. "What Rela is doing is wrong. It is against everything my homeland stands for. That he has brought a Marefi army to this place is . . . monstrous."

The last word had the air of something very deliberate, like Hoyu had taken great care to learn the vocabulary for what she was feeling, and she used it with exquisite precision.

"There are many monstrous things," Kat said softly.

"True enough, but it hurts when they are done in your name. Or near enough." Hoyu's voice came out bitter. "Though if I live to have the chance, I will pin this crime on Maref and on the Keeper of Mysteries if it is the last thing I do on this voyage."

Kat didn't know what a Keeper of Mysteries was, but the title sounded important.

They were only a short distance away from the bulk of the camp, and already Kat could hear some snores that said some of the Lahivarans had indeed dropped when and where they stopped. Kat hoped she herself would be able to sleep.

"Will you go home after this?" Kat asked suddenly. "Is there a home to go to?"

Hoyu gave her a fierce smile. "The sea is my home. If I am able when this is done, I will return to my ship. If not, well. May it one day bring me back to its depths, however that may be."

Hoyu was quiet for a moment, still looking westward.

Kat was about to move away when the Khardish woman spoke again.

"What of your own plans?" she asked. "You are also not from this land, at least not the way they are."

Hoyu's chin indicated the rest of the warmlanders, and Kat nodded.

"I cannot say," Kat said. "I haven't thought far enough ahead to consider it. My whole life, my people prepared me to come south alone, for their own reasons. I am finding out those reasons may or may not be grounded in truth or sense, but in a way, it doesn't matter. When you spend your whole life preparing for one thing, what do you do when that's done?"

"An excellent question," said Hoyu.

Her gaze traveled across the collapsed group of refugees and fell upon Clar, who sat in the grass with her knees pulled up, her arms wrapped around them and her head lolling forward as if she was trying to keep it from flopping and failing. Clar was exhausted.

"You and Clar have grown close," Hoyu remarked after a moment. "She cares for you."

"Yes," Kat said, because she didn't know what else to say to that. "She is special to me."

"We all likely owe her our lives." Hoyu's simple statement was spoken with the confidence of a simple truth, so softly Kat doubted anyone but she herself could have heard it.

"I think you are right," said Kat, almost as softly.

"Sometimes I think of everything that had to happen for me to be here right now. Had I not been Ada'sarshk of a Khardish frigate, had I not brought with me the one person who could have seen into another's mind, had I not listened to that person." Hoyu glanced eastward then, perhaps thinking of Carin. "Sometimes we forget that a small change in course, no matter how slight, can put you so far away from your goal that you cannot find the way back. A lesson all seafarers learn the hard way at one point or another."

The last sentence came with a small, self-deprecating smile. Hoyu had never shared a confidence with Kat before—not that they'd had many opportunities to speak. Kat thought the woman must be very lonely here, among a new people and with the only others of her land collaborating with an enemy for its destruction.

Kat thought about that for a moment, then said slowly, "Perhaps it would be worth also considering that no matter how far away from our current course a destination feels, any small steps we take toward it can have monumental effect later."

Hoyu's head turned sharply to look at Kat, and she nodded. "Yes. This is a good way of thinking about it."

With that, the Khardish woman gave Kat one more small smile and picked her way back toward the group, where she found a patch of grass and curled up around her bag of possessions, leaving Kat wondering about her own course.

• • • • •

Suhnsuoc returned some time later, the large cat practically oozing self-satisfaction Kat didn't think entirely stemmed from having eaten most of a fyajir somewhere off to the south.

One has discovered the path the army took, Suhnsuoc said, settling down in the grass to groom hyrself.

That got Kat's attention. She waited for Suhnsuoc to go on.

The trail is just north and goes east. It is some turns old, but that many on foot leaves marks even the new growth cannot swallow so quickly.

Kat itched to follow it, to see where it ended up, but she knew if she didn't sleep soon, she would be useless as anything but a warm body.

Instead, she found Sart about to drop off herself and told her what Suhnsuoc had discovered, finally curling up against the kazytya's side and dozing off.

She woke some time later in darkness that was already beginning to lighten to the east.

Clar was not far away, already sitting up. From the soft rise and fall of Suhnsuoc's breathing, the cat was still asleep. When Clar glanced her way, Kat smiled and patted the grass next to her.

After a moment of hesitation, Clar got to her feet and came over, sitting beside Kat almost close enough to touch.

"Did you sleep?" Clar asked in a near whisper.

"Yes," said Kat.

The makeshift camp was already stirring, a few people wincing as they realized falling asleep in the sun had left one side of their faces markedly pinker than the other, and a few of them dug around in knapsacks and belt pouches for salves.

"Did you?" Kat asked.

Clar nodded. She still looked tired, her hazel eyes dark in the predawn dimness.

"Suhnsuoc found the route the army took," Kat said. "It seems they were headed due east."

"Are you going to follow the trail?" Clar looked over at Kat, an unidentifiable note in her voice that could have been anxiety.

"I don't know." Kat leaned back against Suhnsuoc's stomach, hearing a gurgle of the large cat's digestion. One big paw twitched in her peripheral vision.

"I wish there was some way to warn Carin. After what Jenin and Ryd saw, though . . ." Clar trailed off. "They were right to be wary of the unseen world. If Merin is truly still alive, there is more danger than we thought."

"We will have to trust that she and Culy are able to do what is necessary and that they can keep their distance from the army. We are fortunate the army does not have ihstal. They will be forced to move only as quickly as their slowest, though from what we have seen, their slowest are not as slow as ours."

Kat supposed the army only took people who could march long distances with relative speed, but it did put the Lahivarans at a disadvantage. While they had many ihstal, they did not have as many ihstal as people, and even the most hale of the animals couldn't carry someone forever.

Looking around, it was clear that though the warmlanders had settled in Lahivar, none of them had quickly forgotten the way they had lived their whole lives. Knapsacks dotted the field where they had gathered, and every adult had the tools and items adapted to making life from place to place. Kat saw rolls of canvas folded and strapped where they could easily be carried, and she knew if they were forced to scatter, the warmlanders would find waymakes and adapt. But some of the children would have almost forgotten what it was like to live along the Lahi'alar, the pathways that traversed this land. Those who did remember would remember a land alien to the one they now walked.

It was in that moment that Kat felt hope kindle. Like a small flame sheltered in the palm of her hand against the bitterest winter wind, she felt its guttering warmth against the dawning of a new day.

She didn't know what her people would expect her to do if they knew what the warmlanders faced.

Without thinking, she took Clar's hand and kissed it without turning her head.

"What was that for?" asked Clar quietly.

"For the first time in twenty-five ages, in twenty-five thousand cycles of the moon and her sister across these skies, we have a chance to choose what we will be," said Kat. "Not what we were forced to by necessity, not the choices of the very powerful over the weak—but we can thrive."

It sounded strange to say it in the midst of a few hundred people displaced by a literal army. Just one cycle ago, the idea of an army was some fantastical construction, a concept Kat could not fully appreciate. She had thought of leading some faceless crowd against the Tuanye before she had any inkling of what such a thing even meant.

In the early morning quiet, it took Kat a moment to register that she was hearing heated voices over the enthusiastic birdsong around them.

"What now?" she said, trying to peer around Suhnsuoc's shoulder in the direction of the voices.

Clar got to her feet to look and sighed. "I think Sart and Ras are arguing."

"We should go see what's happening," Kat said, though it was the last thing she wanted to do.

Lahivarans were stirring, but no one seemed to want to venture any closer to Ras and Sart, and Kat couldn't fault them for it.

She and Clar approached cautiously, not wanting to get in the middle of anything. Hoyu and Jenin were off to the side, but Ryd was nowhere to be found. Knowing him, he was probably looking after Lahivarans who needed extra help with something. Ryd always seemed to turn up when someone needed something.

"You weren't at Ryhnas Lu Sesim," Ras was saying. "They had no intention of trying to speak to us, only to massacre whoever was there."

"Do you really think they will go back there?" Sart asked. "It's the only place big enough to accommodate more than a few families at once."

"If they have enough of a force to send in more legions now, they could have easily left people behind to hold the waymake," Hoyu said. "What they have done is a war crime even by Marefi standards, which tells me these legions are not official Marefi military. They are likely . . . I don't know the word. Paid to fight."

"Mercenaries," Kat said softly.

"Mercenaries," Hoyu said, her voice uncertain as she pronounced the unfamiliar word.

"What is the difference?" asked Ras.

He still held himself to favor his right leg, which told Kat the muscles of his core had not yet knit together to heal as much as she would have hoped, if even standing upright was still a source of discomfort.

"A military is the arm of a nation. They do the bidding of the nation's rulers and—in theory—abide by its laws," Kat said. No armies had existed on this continent in thousands of cycles, but her people had taught her history, as well as they could. "Mercenaries are blades for hire. They may all work under one leader or be contracted as a group, but they are paid to fight."

"Marefi mercenaries are almost always former military," said Hoyu. "They have a reputation for doing work that the official military cannot or will not. But there is an understanding that sometimes that is by design."

Kat didn't like the implications of that. She had assumed Maref was involved openly, but it could be more complex if Hoyu was right.

"Either way, it is not safe to return to the coast, Sart," said Ras. "No one who escaped Ryhnas Lu Sesim will go back there while there are still these mercenaries on our soil. But people are accustomed to making their way across the land. It will be best to—"

"What, split up into small groups that stand no chance against even a small scouting party of trained fighters? *Rovers* were always a danger, and they were only opportunists who seldom killed when they could turn people loose to rob another day," Sart said. "These Marefi people don't hesitate to spill blood."

"Sart is right," Clar said. "We need to find the best possible chance to keep people safe."

Jenin was frowning where sy stood over at Hoyu's side. "I have to agree with Ras too, though. Returning to another waymake that close to the coast would put people in unnecessary danger. Some of the families were talking of it in the night. If I could scout in the unseen world, we could simply avoid the army."

"That's not safe either," Sart said. "As you and Ryd proved last time. And the time before that when you almost *died*. Magic always has limitations, even if that is simply the possibility of encountering people who won't hesitate to use it as a weapon."

Jenin nodded hys assent after a moment, but sy didn't look happy about it.

"We can't scout in the unseen world, but Suhnsuoc and I can scout in this one." Kat pondered that for a moment. "We know the army went east. If we perhaps stay on their trail—well, my mamo had a saying. 'The safest place for the seal is in the orca's wake.'"

Sart gave her an appraising look, scrubbing a hand through her shaggy black hair. "I've been known to use that philosophy myself." She muttered something under her breath that Kat couldn't quite make out other than the word *halm*. "Okay."

Ras went quiet, one hand going to his side unconsciously.

"There aren't any good choices here," said Sart. "I don't know how I ended up the default person people turn to when they don't know what to do, but despite their collective lapse in judgement, I don't exactly want to let them down, either."

She blew out a breath, looking over the nearest family of Lahivarans, who were very studiously pretending not to have heard what she said as they passed out something to their children to break their fast.

Sart turned her gaze to Hoyu. "These mercenaries—should we expect even more of them?"

"I do not know," said Hoyu. "But until we do, I think perhaps following Kat's mother's advice would be best. I do not think safe is an option for us right now, but perhaps we will be safer."

Sart nodded. "Can you live with that, Ras?"

"Yes," he said. "I think the others from Ryhnas Lu Sesim will agree."

As they started discussing strategy, Kat turned back to Suhnsuoc, hoping the kazytya had rested enough. Part of her wanted to ask Clar to accompany them, but Suhnsuoc would be less likely to overburden hyrself with only Kat to carry. She was surprised by the pang of regret that came along with that thought.

It was going to be a very, very long summer.

THERE HAD been no time to speak to his parents since Dyava had discovered—or thought he had discovered—Merin somehow having taken over Reynah's body. He saw little of her over the days that followed, to the point that he wondered for a time if he had simply imagined it. Reynah had moved into a roundhome that had sat empty for a time—the roundhome Lyari had built and intended to move into after her Journeying, before she had taken Carin's. Dyava wondered if anyone remembered that it had been Lyari's. If they forgot Carin because of magic, whose home did they think Lyari had moved into? Jenin's? Jenin hadn't built one. Such questions were too much, though, and as time crawled onward toward High Lights, Toil moon lived up to its name, keeping Dyava occupied. He almost preferred it that way. Sometimes, when he lost himself in an everyday task, he could forget what was coming.

Those times, he thought the remembering demanded a higher price than constant awareness. Each time he caught a rare glimpse of Reynah, usually walking with Lyari through Haveranth, though, he would feel as if someone had put a snowball down the back of his tunic. If it truly was Merin, she would have to be immensely more powerful than his parents had ever expected.

He didn't know what spell could do such a thing, though if he had to guess, he would think it similar to whatever had allowed Merin to control the hawk.

Dyava just hadn't considered the possibility of such a spell being used on people.

His parents had always said that controlling another being was an abomination, but Dyava had always likewise wondered what the difference was between their use of threats and warnings of death and violence and someone taking a more direct route. He supposed it didn't matter in the end. In just a few short turns, it would be High Lights, and Lyari would attempt to perform the Reinvocation early.

Dyava still had no idea if she could succeed.

On the First Stem of Toil, he encountered Reynah alone for the first time in the village hearth-home, and any hope he'd had of being mistaken vanished with the sight of the webs of magic, thin as spider silk, draped over every inch of her just like the first time.

She watched him blandly from the table where she sat drinking from a large mug of icemint he could smell from where he stood.

"Hello, Reynah," he said, deciding it was best to proceed as they had last ended. "I see you have decided to force your 'help' upon Lyari despite her wishes to the contrary."

"Lyari understands—as you do not—that she needs my help if this plan of hers is to have any hope of success," Reynah said smoothly. "While she may be the one *true* soothsayer in the Hearthland, as she so kindly reminded myself and Harag, she lacks the knowledge and the discipline to do what she must. Quite frankly, without my help and Harag's, she will fail. The only reason I am here is because our people cannot survive her failure. Harag and I must make certain that she succeeds."

"You know you cannot stop her," Dyava said. "That's really it, isn't it? You know she will go ahead without you, and you're afraid that she *will* succeed more than you fear her failure."

Reynah looked Dyava over like he was a compost pile in need of a good turning with a pitchfork.

"The only thing I fear is this land falling into ruin because of the impulsiveness of an impetuous child," said Reynah. "Or even two, since we are likewise blessed with your presence at Lyari's side."

Her eyes were as hard as agate, and remembering what she had said in Cantoranth about his family, Dyava held his tongue.

Tamat, as always at her grill stationed at the edge of the village hearth, pretended to be out of earshot; Dyava could tell and was grateful for that. He couldn't imagine she wasn't shocked to her marrow at the way he was speaking to a soothsayer.

Dyava decided not to dignify Reynah with a response and turned on his heel, headed to the smithy.

He hadn't spoken to Rina since finding out it was she who had been snooping in Lyari's roundhome, but that was just one more thing on the list of frustrations and points of anxiety Dyava didn't know how to manage.

He needed to pick up a new pan Rina had crafted for him. Such a mundane thing at a time when he was preparing himself to stop three powerful soothsayers from reinvoking a spell that would alter the fate of countless people on both sides of the mountains. A pan. If Dyava was both alive and had something to cook when Toil waned and gave birth to Gather, he would count that a victory.

The sounds of the village seemed somehow distant around him. He could hear Stil, the carpenter, banging away on something, and there was the sound of someone pumping water behind the nearest roundhome to his left. Dyava already felt separate from it all. For a short while after he had told Lyari the truth, he had felt whole. Like perhaps he could go on, be part of something. That there could be a place for him after all.

But Reynah's appearance had changed that. Or perhaps it had been his parents drawing his attention to the arcane shift that had set him back on this path.

Dyava wasn't sure he would survive this.

He wasn't sure if he wanted to.

The smithy was oddly quiet for afternoon, but in the summer moons, Rina did sometimes limit her time with the forge in full heat. When working in front of blazing hot fire day in and day out, it didn't do to have nowhere to escape the sweltering warmth.

He found her in the smithy nonetheless, seated at a workbench on a high stool with her attention fully focused on something small. She looked up and bundled it away before he could see what it was when she heard his approaching footsteps.

"Dyava," Rina said with a smile, reaching her hands forward to stretch her shoulders and sitting up straighter. "It's been a while. Your pan is hanging on the hook just there."

On the wall closest to him, there were a number of items Rina had either made or repaired for villagers, and while pots and pans were a common one, his was immediately recognizable by the rune she had edged into the handle. Cultivate, the moon that would arrive after Gather and before Sustain, all of which would only be in Dyava's future if the labor of Toil moon saw fit to give him a future at all.

He pulled the pan down from the hook carefully, trying not to jangle the others surrounding it.

"Thank you, Rina," Dyava said. "It's perfect."

She waved a hand at him dismissively but got up from her stool and went to a chest at the end of the workbench, kneeling on one knee to open it.

"If you don't mind, I have something for Lyari that she requested. I was going to bring it by her roundhome later, but if you're here—" Rina rummaged in the chest, pulling out a parcel wrapped in rose-colored wool and tied with a black leather thong.

Dyava went to her, reaching her just as she stood and proffered the parcel. It was heavier than it looked, and through the thin wool cloth, he could feel the shape of it. A knife in a sheath.

"I'll give it to her," he said, but his voice cracked on the last word. He cleared his throat. "Thank you."

"Take care, Dyava," Rina said as if she had noticed nothing amiss.

"You as well, Rina." Dyava hurried out of the smithy.

Once, Rina had told him to be careful with Lyari. What did she know? His parents would have told him if she was involved with their plan, he thought. Or perhaps not. Rina was an elder, and with Old Wend gone, Varsu and Ohlry had deferred some of the duties to her. Dyava didn't even really know what duties those were other than meeting with villagers and helping settle disputes. His parents had kept enough from him on the premise of it being for his own good that he could never be sure if they had told him the whole truth.

He forgot even the knife in his hands when he left the smithy and almost ran into someone's cart, laden with people and supplies.

"Oh! Sorry about that," said the hyrsin leading ihstal harnessed to the cart.

"It's okay," Dyava said. "You're from Bemin's Fan, right?"

The hyrsin gave him a good-natured smile. Sy was a little taller than Dyava, which meant sy was quite tall, and hys dark hair was plaited over one shoulder not unlike Lyari's used to be every day. "Yep. We're here for the Reinvocation."

Dyava looked beyond the cart and registered what he'd been too startled to see a moment before. In a small caravan behind this cart was a trail of several others, and walking alongside them with an intricately carved driftwood walking stick was Harag ve Beminohna, soothsayer of Bemin's Fan.

"Welcome to Haveranth," Dyava managed to get out. "I trust you know where you're going?"

The hyrsin nodded with another smile and clucked at the ihstal to pull the cart farther away from the door to the smithy to let Dyava pass.

Surely Lyari wouldn't have invited all these people—which meant it had to be Reynah. Or Merin.

His stomach sickened as he hurried away, refusing to glance over his shoulder to wonder which of those people wouldn't live to see the moon wane.

• • • • •

"I invited them," Lyari said when Dyava asked her later that evening.

They were settled in her roundhome finally, the ceremonial knife still in its innocuous packaging on the polished maha table. Dyava could still see the strands of magic from her warding so they wouldn't be overheard, and it unnerved him. What once had been barely filaments had turned into something that looked almost solid to his eyes. And it moved—where a spiderweb simply gave with the wind or with something tugging on its strands, the strings of magic that formed a spell's webs were in constant motion. He couldn't have described it except as a flow, the way a river was one body of water, always moving, always going somewhere.

She was seated on the opposite side of the table from him, her elbows on the surface of it, looking far more at ease than Dyava felt. Next to her arm was a stack of parchment she had been studying, and she'd gotten some crumbs of bread on it that she noticed and blew away.

Dyava let her words sink in. "You invited Harag."

"Harag was going to come anyway," Lyari said dismissively. "I invited the other villagers, both from Bemin's Fan and from Cantoranth. It is customary."

"Why?" he asked and immediately regretted it.

"Because our ancestors learned that a sacrifice given willingly is more power-ful than one taken, though I must be prepared to volunteer sacrifices if they do not volunteer themselves," she said with a small smile as if she were discussing who was going to clean the ash out of the hearth rather than whose blood she was going to spill on a rock.

"You trust the soothsayers to be here?" he asked finally, at a loss for what else to say.

"I trust them about as far as I could throw you," she said. "But it is better to have one's enemies in sight rather than hiding and ready to spring upon you in an ambush."

"They think the Reinvocation will succeed a cycle early?" Another question to which Dyava wasn't sure he wanted the answer.

"They would not risk supporting me in it if they thought it would fail," Lyari said, satisfaction in the small half smile that lurked on her lips. "They know we have exactly one chance. That they are willing to support me in it now, this sum-mer, says to me they know what is at stake. They must know that something has gone wrong."

Dyava swallowed. Despite the ceramic cup of water he had been sipping all evening, his tongue felt dry and sticky. There was another illness going around the village, but today he didn't think he was getting sick.

"You are troubled," Lyari said.

She rose from where she sat and came around to his side of the table, strad-dling the bench next to him and scooting closer until her outside leg brushed his rear. Her grey-green eyes looked out at him from under her immaculate coronet of plaits that was her usual hairstyle these days.

"If something has happened with the hearthstones up north, how do we know there won't be some sort of backlash?" Dyava asked. This was the biggest question he wasn't sure he wanted an answer for, but it was also one he needed to ask. "Something so powerful could rebound upon the land here, upon you."

He didn't have to fake the hitch in his breath or the way his heart crunched in his chest. He had gotten close to her, fallen in love with her, lied to her, told her the truth, and now he was going to betray her. He had reason enough to be troubled.

"That is a valid concern," she murmured, brushing his hair back from his right cheek.

Dyava didn't know the last time he'd had a haircut. It was getting longer than he liked it.

"I was worried about it too," Lyari continued after a moment. "But the ancestors—they were wise. They knew that every plan needs a contingency. In all this time, it is a wonder nothing happened to upset the balance of the spell before now."

Dyava's mind had stuck on the word *contingency*, like this was the same as bringing an extra bow string with you when you went to hunt.

"What sort of contingency?" he asked in spite of himself.

"Two things, really," Lyari said, as if she were trying to reassure him. Maybe she was. "The first is that all of the stones must break for the spell to break in full, and even if they reach the first four, there is one they cannot."

"The one you have here," Dyava said. He swallowed, trying not to panic. "The one you'll use to perform the Reinvocation."

"Yes," she said. "And no."

Dyava's breath caught again. "What do you mean?"

"The stone I have is only half of the stone needed for the Reinvocation. The other half is hidden on the other side of a bridge that no one will be able to access." A smile ghosted about her mouth. "A bridge like no other bridge, one that people have long forgotten is a bridge at all. The root of all magic."

Her smile widened almost as if she had told a joke.

"You do not need to worry, my love," Lyari said, leaning forward and kissing him on the cheek. "There is no way at all to prevent the Reinvocation from succeeding."

CARIN DIDN'T think she would get used to traveling back the very direction she had come only to see that the land had already become unrecognizable in her wake. It unnerved her. Streams where there had before been only rolling plains, the water flowing over grass that hadn't yet washed away with the current. Saplings everywhere. The forests of Crevasses spread northward from the mountains, reaching for land that had been bare of any vegetation larger than a bush for two and a half thousand cycles of the moons.

And bushes were spreading out, like stretching after a long nap. Carin counted at least three types of berries she didn't recognize, along with redberries and wait-for-me shrubs that would bear small, shiny red fruits that had a light, refreshing flavor when they ripened—which they wouldn't do until near harvest time.

She and Culy had been riding for turns now almost without cease. They rested when the ihstal needed to rest, which was rarely. They ate what they could hunt or fish in those short rest breaks, which was not much. And they carried on to the south, weaving west for a time before turning back toward the ancient halm in its glen, hoping that their meandering trail was enough to keep the army at their backs far away. With the ihstal, they should have been fast enough to get away no matter what, but twice they caught glimpses of Marefi scouts in the distance and only barely managed to evade notice.

Culy did not want to traverse the unseen world while they slept, sensing it was unsafe even without the possibility of Rela haunting their dreams. This left them cut off from Ryd and the others, cut off from knowing what was happening to their home and their people.

"Do you think Lahivar is safe?" Carin asked as they finally spotted the foothills in the distance that said they would reach Alar Marhasan within a day.

The ihstal were both antsy, their pace picking up in waves every so often, and Carin's knees were getting tired from needing to remind Tahin to slow down. Both Tahin and Siuhn gave the occasional low whistle that Carin had come to recognize as a sound of frustration.

"I hope so," said Culy. "I trust Sart to keep our people out of harm's way, though I would feel better if I could speak to her as easily as Valon."

"As would I." Carin cast a look back over her shoulder as if the land itself would somehow tell her how far away the army was. "Or with Jenin."

"I truly hope that Jenin is staying out of the dream world." Atop Siuhn, Culy sat as if sy had been born to ride, back straight and one hand atop the back of the ihstal's neck. "With magic as volatile as it is right now, there are any number of dangers beyond the usual fears. And the usual fears are not scarce."

Carin sensed that the spirit within her had been guarding her as she slept, though she didn't know from what. All she knew was that both she and Culy were feeling a pull to the south again, not fully unlike what had led them to the other stones but just different enough to put them ill at ease.

"You lived a very long time," she said suddenly over Tahin's eager whistle at the sight of a squirrel. "Do you think there could be others like you? In the Hearthland?"

She was thinking of Merin's hawk. Perhaps Lyari controlled it now, but they had no way of knowing. Merin was dead, but that didn't mean there weren't others in Haveranth or the other villages of the Hearthland who could have hidden in plain sight all this time.

"With so many impossible things happening every day, I would be a fool to say no," Culy answered, glancing at the sky, where afternoon clouds were conspiring to send a thunderstorm their way by the look of it.

"There is too much we don't know," said Carin.

"I hope that after we reach the halm again, we will be able to find more answers. Like the location of the final stone, for example." Culy tapped hys fingers on the gleaming, short fur of Siuhn's neck, which didn't seem to help the animal's restlessness.

"Could it be in Crevasses? Or in Alar Marhasan?" There was something they were missing, clearly, but with no one to ask and no safe way to explore while they slept, Carin couldn't shake the feeling time was getting away from them. "It has to be somewhere."

"We may have to risk searching tonight," Culy said. "We cannot allow the army to find the stone, and I doubt we will be able to evade them entirely for the fullness of a cycle before the Reinvocation. Another winter, another spring—there is too much time for them to send reinforcements, and there is too large a chance that they will prevent us from breaking the stone before your former friend casts the spell that will send all we know to ruin."

"I agree," Carin said softly. "If the Reinvocation happens before we can find that stone, no one will be safe from the cataclysm it brings. If the first invocation reduced cities to rubble with the force spread out across five stones, we cannot begin to guess at the destruction that would be unleashed."

As if agitated by Carin's words, Tahin whistled loudly and leapt forward, Siuhn following, much to both Carin's and Culy's alarm.

Tahin ignored Carin's attempts to slow hyr, plunging headlong through the grass and eating up the ground with every long stride.

"Whoa," Carin said, trying to stroke the ihstal's neck while also trying not to completely lose her seat.

"Something has clearly spooked them," Culy called to her, already several spans away, with Siuhn pulling ahead of Tahin.

If Culy could not tell what, that was a bad sign. Carin tried to reach out through the wind, as she had once done when Wyt's rovers kidnapped Culy to try and ascertain whether sy was safe, but her tendrils of thought met what felt like bottled lightning. The air was *alive* with magic. The moment she reached out, it reached back, and it felt like she had licked something that shocked her, like the sparks she sometimes saw at night on dry evenings in Haveranth when her blankets moved together.

Carin recoiled reflexively. She was glad she hadn't tried to do anything more.

They would have to trust the ihstal—it wasn't like they had any other choice. Siuhn and Tahin loped over the plains toward the mountains in the distance, and time slipped by both quickly and with agonizing slowness as her legs and core grew tired from trying to maintain her seat atop an animal that was running at full tilt over uneven ground. She was afraid Tahin would stumble and hurt hyrself, but ihstal, amazing beasts that they were, seemed to be able to rival even goats for their ability to keep themselves upright and to adapt to even minute changes beneath their padded hooves.

Tahin grew lathered, whistles punctuating the bursts of grass-scented air sy blew out hys nose, and Siuhn was in a similar state by the time the animals finally slowed, their flesh quivering.

"What *happened*?" Carin asked as soon as Tahin half stumbled to a stop in a grove of trees near a stream. She immediately slid off the animal's back.

Her legs almost gave out from exhaustion, and she had to catch herself with a hand on Tahin's heaving flank so as not to fall.

Tahin took a few wobbly steps as soon as Carin took her hand back, collapsing to hys knees on the banks of a burn, face in the water to slurp drink after drink from the burbling current.

Sy was joined a moment later by Siuhn, who looked even worse for wear than Tahin.

Culy leaned against the trunk of a sugar tree, perspiration beading on hys bald head. Sy looked as ready to fall over as Carin was.

"I cannot say," Culy answered belatedly. "Ihstal are sensitive to magic, as we saw with the halm the first time. It is likely the shifts in the energies of the breaking spell did something, though I could not say what."

"It felt like we'd ridden into a pocket of lightning," Carin said. "I was trying to see if I could sense anything that could have triggered their agitation, but instead I just got shocked."

"We are on new ground," Culy murmured. With effort, sy pushed hyrself away from the sugar tree and closed the distance to Carin. "Are you all right?"

Carin swallowed, weaving her fingers through the hyrsin's. "Jangled," she said. "They will not be able to run again for a while, and we will be slower now because of it."

She didn't want to think of what could happen if the ihstal simply bolted—they could outride an army of trained marchers, but they were still only two, and if they could be caught up by even a relatively small group, it would not lend itself to an outcome that Carin wanted to entertain for even a moment. Even if she and Culy unleashed their magic in this new world where it was so unpredictable, they could not be sure it wouldn't somehow turn back upon them. More fears. More risks. More danger.

"We should try and search tonight," Carin said suddenly. "I do not think we can afford not to. But together. Surely we will be safer together."

Culy nodded after a moment of hesitation. "We will be safer together, but I do not think we will be safe."

• • • • •

Carin had not entered the unseen world consciously since she had contacted Jenin to tell hyr about the third stone. It felt a lifetime since then.

Just as in the waking world, the world of dreams was at the crossroads of change.

She felt more than saw Culy appear beside her, hys hand seeking hers.

"Where should we begin?" she asked.

As always, here, her voice sounded fuller to her ears, more present. Disconcertingly, though, Carin felt herself relaxing into the unseen world like exhaling a deep breath and letting her muscles soften. There were no muscles here in the world of dreams, and she couldn't shake the feeling—almost a scent, almost the brush of a familiar mind—that this was home.

Carin blinked the feeling away as best she could, looking to Culy, who was watching her.

"Do you feel that?" she asked, realizing Culy had yet to answer her first question.

For a moment, she wasn't sure sy was going to answer this one, but Culy nodded.

"Yes." Culy gave a short, self-deprecating laugh. "It feels like it once did. I had all but forgotten."

Alarmed, Carin held tighter to Culy's hand until the hyrsin paused and smiled, a wry smile.

"The spell changed all things, my love," sy said. "It cut us off from the land, severed almost every connection we had to each other, to our history, to our magic. If it is changing back, I welcome it, though nothing will be just as it once was."

Carin felt a tug within her chest, a yearning so full she thought it might drag her to the ground. The grasses here were blurred, almost like something seen while running, and the trees were the same.

Culy watched her with a strange expression on hys face. "Follow it," sy said.

"Hold on to me," Carin said, and she obeyed.

The grass and the trees vanished.

A moment later, the grass had returned, but there were no trees, only a wide plain and mountains in the distance. To the *north*.

A stone sat in front of them, smaller than the others she had broken. One edge of it had engravings, but she couldn't make sense of them. There were small cup marks on it, five of them.

"Not here," Culy said urgently, and Carin was violently jerked away from it before she could get any closer.

They were in Lahivar.

They hadn't been there a fraction of a heartbeat before Culy yanked them out of the Hearthland so quickly, if Carin had been in her body, she might have thrown up.

"My apologies," Culy murmured, coming to face her. "There was a presence there. I do not think it saw us, but—"

"Do not apologize for keeping us safe," Carin said. She raised a finger to Culy's lips. "That was the Hearthland. It could have been Lyari you sensed."

Culy frowned, shaking hys head. "I do not think it was anyone so young, but I could not say more than that."

Carin tried to puzzle out what she had seen on the stone in the brief glimpse she'd gotten of it.

"If that is the fifth and final hearthstone, we have no hope of reaching it before the Reinvocation unless the ialtag fly us all the way over the mountains," she said. A wave of despair threatened to crash over her. "Even if we made it there, we would be abandoning our people to the Marefi forces, and—"

This time it was Culy who interrupted Carin. "Let us wait until we know as much as we can. Did you see the edge of the stone?"

"Yes," she said. "Though if it was a rune, I couldn't make it out."

"Dyupahsy," Culy said. "But only half of it."

Of course. Carin felt like she had walked out at high day with no clouds in the sky and had to be told the big light was the sun. Five hearthstones, five branches of magic. Dyupahsy was the only one left.

The second bit of what Culy said finally processed.

"Wait," she breathed. "Only half of it."

She and Culy stared at each other for a long moment.

"I know where the other half is," she said.

They had only to blink and they were there, staring down the ancient halm in its glen.

Unlike the maha and sugar trees, the firs and the doubloons, the halm tree was stark and sharp against the backdrop of the craggy stone of the corrie that cut into the Mad Mountains directly southward.

The unseen world would pull you where you wanted to go. And they were where they had expected the stone to be all along.

"It has to be here," Carin said. A flicker of hope lit in her heart. "I can *feel* it now."

Culy gazed at the halm, a perplexed expression on hys face. "It is possible it is inside the tree somehow. If the tree grew around it . . ."

That would be an obstacle indeed.

"Could it have? Could the halm grove have been planted purely to hide this half of the stone?" For the moment, Carin had shoved the other half out of her mind, as it was so out of reach, she couldn't even consider getting to it.

But they were so close to this one.

"Again you ask me of possibilities," Culy said with a small smile. "Again my answer is that it would be foolish to say no."

Carin returned hys smile sheepishly. "You're right."

Culy's eyes held the same wild hope Carin felt. She wanted to kiss hyr, like they had kissed the first time in this unseen world. Carin wanted to feel the rush of this wild new magic rise up to meet them in this place that felt like home.

"Come," Culy said.

Carin felt the ache in hys voice just as she felt the pang at knowing what would happen next.

• • • • •

They woke at the same instant, still clasping hands on their adjacent bedrolls. The ihstal were cushing, asleep under a nearby maha that dappled them in moonlight from the waxing crescent of Toil and her sister high above in the starry sky.

Carin squeezed Culy's hand, wanting more than anything to pull hyr close to her, to claim hys mouth with her own, to press their bodies together and write hope into one another's skin.

But she knew—and she knew Culy knew—they had no time.

Without a word, Culy raised Carin's hand to hys lips and kissed her knuckles, then let her go and went to the ihstal, murmuring gently to them to rouse them.

She heard them wake with plaintive whistles, likely still exhausted without the bright edge of nervous anticipation to goad them into excitement.

Still, as she and Culy hurriedly bundled their bedrolls and sparse belongings back into traveling order, both Tahin and Siuhn seemed to sense the need to go. By the time the two-legged travelers had washed their faces in the burn and refilled their waterskins for the journey, the ihstal were prancing and whistling happily.

"My halm bow for the constitution of an ihstal," Carin said good-naturedly. "If I could be falling over at sundown and dancing before dawn, I could conquer the world."

Culy laughed, a welcome sound that made Carin's belly dip with the unfairness of being unable to touch her lover when she wanted to.

"If this is you without that constitution, then it is more than only one world that would need to beware," sy said. "The moon and her sister would tremble before you."

"Flatterer," Carin said, but her cheeks grew warm as she mounted Tahin's back, stroking the ihstal's neck fondly. "And you, my friend, I'll be cross with you if you run yourself to death."

Tahin let out a whistle that was almost a hoot, and Carin wondered if that was the animal laughing at a joke.

"Let's go," Culy said to Siuhn, and the ihstal bounded forward.

They rode as the sky lightened, watching it paint the eastern horizon a pale green as the moon set, followed by a brightening yellow just as they reached the outskirts of the ruins of Alar Marhasan.

The ihstal, in spite of their hardiness, were tiring, and by the time they reached the gully that would deepen into the ancient halm's glen, Carin knew they would have to dismount. Tahin and Siuhn wouldn't go near the tree anyway, and any time they could give the ihstals without riders would help them recover their stamina.

The sun would not crest the ridge of the glen for some time yet, and they turned the ihstal loose to graze and rest where they felt comfortable.

Culy watched them wander off, hys back straight but hys eyes belying the anxiety of not having the animals close to hand.

"They are intelligent enough to flee the soldiers," Carin said. "And if there are soldiers to flee, we are past helping."

"I would like to think we would not be completely past helping," said Culy. "Though realistically, you are likely correct."

Excitement gathered in Carin's stomach. She wanted to squash it, to push it down where it couldn't disappoint her if this didn't go well, but instead she let it unfurl.

"Let's go," she said.

They left their belongings in a hollow of an old stump from a deadfall that had long since been covered in moss, and they walked deeper into the glen.

The ancient halm had not even come into view yet when Carin's excitement drained from her.

"Why don't I feel it?" she asked, bewildered. "Do you feel it?"

"No," said Culy, frowning.

Already, approaching the halm felt like it had the last time they had been here in the flesh. She could sense the tree itself, but that was all. No sense of the second half of the final hearthstone, no hint of its pull to draw them onward.

"Could it be some kind of trick?" she asked. "Could such a thing have been faked by a mage in the unseen world to make us come back here?"

When Culy opened hys mouth to reply, Carin winced and shook her head.

"Possibilities again," she said. "It is possible this is some kind of trap. Perhaps a better question to ask you is whether it is likely."

Culy paused, stepping around a moss-covered stone. "Possible but not likely," sy answered. "I would say very unlikely. A manipulation that powerful would take a significant amount of magic, and with magic as volatile as it is right now, it would be far too likely to go awry, even for a mage of immense experience."

For some reason, that did not make Carin feel better.

The halm appeared in the distance of the glen, surrounded by morning mist that had yet to be burned off by the rising sun. It was even more imposing than Carin remembered, even more striking in the waking world than when she had seen it in her sleep.

"If the stone is indeed inside the halm somehow, could we reach it?" she asked.

"I wish I knew." If Culy tired of her questions, sy didn't show it.

They continued on in silence until they entered the space between the massive tree's exposed roots. To think of this having been five trees once—Carin could scarcely imagine the amount of time it would take for the trees to grow together so closely they fused. Her mother sometimes worked with softer metals, sometimes twining them together to make designs or puzzles where it became difficult to see where one piece ended and another began. But with the halm, this was alive.

Halm had a will.

Something was dawning on her, like the light of the sun climbing up the arc of the morning sky was slowly revealing something, but like a lost word of Khardish on the tip of her tongue, it eluded her, hovering just outside her grasp.

"No," she whispered. "How would they manage such a thing?"

Culy turned to look at her, one eyebrow raised.

"It's not here," she said, the edges of her mind still grasping at something that didn't want to be made into words. "It's not *here*."

"Carin?" Culy's confusion grew alarmed.

"We could feel it in the unseen world but not here because it's *not here*," Carin said. Hysterical laughter threatened to bubble out of her mouth. "It's inside the halm. But it isn't inside the halm here."

Impossibilities.

It hit Culy just as it had hit her, just as the first rays of the sun crested the ridge to light the bone-white halm with a near blinding aura of palest gold.

And something else.

From the direction they had come, the sound of an ihstal's angry whistle pierced the morning air.

"How have they gotten here so quickly?" She didn't need to ask who had caused that sound; she only hoped Tahin and Siuhn would run.

Culy's eyes went distant as sy placed a hand on the root of the halm. "They have ihstal of their own. They must have taken them from someone."

The thought made Carin recoil in revulsion, and for a moment she simply stared toward the mouth of the glen to the north.

Sudden calm stole over her.

"You need to go," she said to Culy. "Before they see you. I know you can escape here. Take the ihstal. Go to Lahivar if you must, but go. We cannot defeat them, and they will want me alive."

It was a strange feeling, a distance, like some part of her was still dosed with sparkleaf, held prisoner deep within herself.

"Carin," Culy began. Fear crossed hys face, fear Carin had seen once before and had never wanted to see again.

"No, my love," she said. "You are the one Asurashk cannot touch. You are the one they cannot capture. You hold memories and knowledge of this land that go deeper than the roots of this tree. I will not let Rela and Asurashk have you. Once you told me to flee, not so very far from here. You need to flee now."

"My heart," sy said, and hys voice cracked on the words.

Carin opened herself to the spirit inside her and the magic that surrounded her, wild, surging, free. "Go!"

She did the only thing she could think of that would draw the Marefi forces here and distract them enough that they would miss one person who knew how to hide.

Carin released a torrent of light straight up into the morning sky.

BASHA HAPPENED to be looking southward when it happened. Far in the distance, in the foothills of the enormous mountains, a column of pure light shot out of the earth. It reached so high into the sky, for a moment Basha wondered if it reached the vastness of space.

Gasps and alarmed epithets rippled through the marching army. Basha could not pull his eyes away from the phenomenon.

"What could do such a thing?" he murmured.

Magic was the obvious answer, but even the light shows the mages of Sahesh performed were merely sparkles and fanfare. This was stark and harsh, a knife of light cutting across the heavens, like it would rend the very fabric between two sides of an unseen curtain.

They were still two days' march from the mountains, Basha had been told, but the army had come upon travelers in a group some two turns back, and they had had ihsaln with them, the strange beasts the people of this land rode and used to pull their carts. Upon Basha's insistence, they had left the people alive, and that was only because he was the only person of any rank who arrived fast enough to stop the Marefi soldiers from killing them outright. He hadn't been able to stop the robbery or the people's fear, but at least they left with their lives.

The ihsaln (Basha still wasn't certain about their name, and he kept forgetting to ask Valon) were given to the scouts, five of them in total. Part of Basha had hoped the ihsaln would refuse to be ridden, but they seemed docile enough, and it wasn't long before they were off to the south at breakneck speed, leaving the army far behind.

According to Rela, the army had somehow managed to gain on Carin, though for the life of him, Basha could not imagine how unless Carin had been zigzagging all over the place, which he supposed was possible.

He hoped she would escape the scouts.

The imprint of the pillar of light still showed in Basha's vision long after it faded. If that was Carin's doing, he did not think it a good omen. It would draw the mounted scouts right to her. He wouldn't have thought Carin to be so careless.

The rest of the day passed with increasing tension, which was not helped by the sight of an Arelashk, who was almost giddy with anticipation when they made camp that night.

"We grow closer to her with every passing moment," Arelashk said, his eyes gleaming. "She will answer for her escape."

Asurashk sat quietly at the edge of the low table as she so often did for these evening meetings, and Oshu and Basha maintained their distance against the far wall. Sometimes, she would glance their way, and Basha would steel himself, trying for all he was worth to ascertain if there was any hint of recognition in her gaze when her eyes seemed to skip right over Oshu's presence.

Basha may have had little magic of his own, but he did know good mages he trusted, and the necklace he had given to Oshu to make him unremarkable clearly worked. Asurashk had no idea she had spent moons now in the company of her dead lover.

At times, Basha felt guilty for the deception. If he had thought someone he loved was dead only to discover that person had been in the same room with him for the better part of three seasons, he would want to rend the floor with his hands upon finding out. But clearly Oshu was alive, and clearly Asurashk had simply given up on finding him. After all, she had survived the death wave—had she really thought it so impossible that he had done the same?

Most of the time, however, Basha did not feel guilty. He did not feel guilty because he'd had to stop Marefi mercenaries from murdering people on foreign soil. He did not feel guilty because Arelashk was tampering with forces—political, magical, social—that could and would change the course of nations. And he did not feel guilty because Basha still believed in Khardan. He believed in Khardish democracy and the land that had been a beacon for others for ages past. All that would crumble if the corruption in the Da'sash Dan was allowed to spread. And Arelashk, enabled and empowered by the magic of Asurashk and his own greed, sowed that corruption wherever he went.

Asurashk had said something that Basha had missed. He tried to snap back to his normal attentiveness despite the anxieties that threatened to pull him apart limb by limb.

"You are dismissed," Arelashk said with a cursory glance at Basha and Oshu.

The two men rose from their seats and left as ordered.

When they had retreated to their tent and sat stretching out the kinks from holding the same position for far too long, Oshu was quiet.

"This Carin," he said, keeping his voice low as was their custom to avoid being overheard. "Has that one truly done something wrong?"

Basha had not told him much about Carin, only that Asurashk had looked inside her mind and blamed her for the death wave.

"I think it depends on how you define the word," Basha said. "I was not party to the entirety of what Asurashk saw in Carin's mind, but it seems that what that one has done is attempt to break an ancient spell that kept this land isolated for a very long time. Long enough for our world to move on."

Oshu considered that, then shrugged. "Whether the death wave can be laid at Carin's feet or not, I think that is only an excuse. Perhaps for Asurashk it is the end goal. That Asurashk thinks the purpose is to avenge me is something else entirely, but for the Arelashk, it is not about the death wave."

"You are very sanguine for someone who that wave almost killed," Basha said dryly. He leaned forward to stretch his lower back, counting to fifteen breaths before sitting back up.

When he did, Oshu was frowning at him.

"Do you blame a butterfly in Sahesh for a tornado in the Triyan plains?" Oshu asked. "The wave killed many people, but that doesn't mean it was Carin's fault. You have said there have been waves that were far worse, and you have said that they came every five hundred cycles without fail. This one broke that pattern, coming early and not laying waste to every islet on the eastern fringe of Khardan."

"You asked me if Carin had done something wrong, but it seems you have your answer already," Basha said, somewhere between amusement and exhaustion.

"I wanted your opinion. Do you have one?" Oshu's gaze grew more intense, like he was trying to puzzle something out.

"I do not think that one did anything wrong," Basha said softly. "I regret my role in taking Carin captive. I regret more that taking that one captive led, directly or indirectly, to an army invading Carin's homeland."

"Ah, you do blame the butterfly in Sahesh for the tornado in the Triyan plains," Oshu said, but his tone was only gently chiding. "Or perhaps only if you are that butterfly."

Startled, Basha sat back, leaning on his hands. "Perhaps you are correct." He paused for a moment to think. "Perhaps I want only the chance to make it right."

At that, Oshu's eyes flashed, and he smiled a genuine smile, the first Basha had seen on his face in some time.

"Why are you smiling?" Basha asked, nonplussed.

"Because I want to know if you'll take that chance when it comes." Oshu's smile faded, and he pushed himself off the floor of their tent to come and kneel in front of Basha. "I want you to know that when that time comes, I am with you to the end."

Basha sucked in a breath, too shocked to say anything, so he instead took Oshu's face between his hands and pulled the other man to him.

Until the end.

Basha never wanted this to end.

• • • • •

If Arelashk had been giddy when they camped, the mage was positively beaming when the scouts returned word that they had captured someone near a very old ruin in the foothills of the mountains. The Arelashk had insisted on traveling on ahead of the column, though they could not move all that much faster.

As seneschal, Basha went with the advance party, so he was present when they reached the ruin, and his hope dissolved when he saw who it was the scouts had captured.

She looked . . . different than he had last seen her. Taller, somehow. She stood at least half a head taller than the tallest Marefi soldier standing near her with a spear pointed at her chest, but despite being surrounded by armed guards, in their midst, Carin looked as though she merely deigned to let them pretend to hold her.

Her loose dark curls were plaited back from her face and secured with a leather tie. She wore soft leggings tucked into knee-high leather boots that looked well-worn and even better made. Her tunic was a soft grey-blue and travel-worn, and she looked right through him with those unnerving dark blue eyes as if she'd never seen him before.

"Rela," she said as he approached. "Just the one I never wanted to see again. And your tame mage friend. Asu."

Her Khardish had somehow become almost flawless. Her pronunciation was precise, and her ease with speaking it was such a contrast to her halting—if competent—mastery before that Basha blinked.

Not only that, but she would also know the insult she paid both Arelashk and Asurashk by addressing them by their shortened titles. Basha seldom even wanted to do that in his head, and then only with the Arelashk, out of his intense disregard for the man. He would never address an Arelashk or an Asurashk so flippantly.

Her impudence did not go unnoticed by Arelashk or Asurashk, and even the Marefi soldiers tensed, their spear points held a bit steadier as they looked to the mages for instructions.

"Carin," Arelashk said after a brief pause, so smoothly one could be forgiven for mistaking the address for a friendly one. "You left so suddenly in Sahesh. We thought it only right to ensure the hand of justice reached its necessary goal."

"You are quite correct," Carin said. "I intend to see justice done. Perhaps we can begin with the war crimes you have committed against my people under the banner of Maref. I'm sure your Da'sash Dan would be intrigued to hear such a story."

If Arelashk was shocked by her pronouncement, he didn't let it show. Instead, he chuckled.

"Don't worry," he said. "You will whet your appetite for justice in due time. I am pleased to know that we are rowing the same oar."

Asurashk had said nothing, and she did not change that now, only watched Carin with undisguised hatred.

Arelashk tossed a vial of something to the closest guard just before he turned away. "See that she is secured. If there is so much as a whiff of magic, pour that down her throat, and she won't move for a day. I will know if she tries."

The mage produced a small coin that flashed in the sunlight, and he made sure Carin saw it before it vanished again into the pocket of his trousers.

For Carin's bravado, Basha happened to be looking at her when Arelashk said those words, and he did not miss the flash of fear that passed over her face. Nor did Asurashk. She gave Carin an even smile before following Arelashk to the east. Basha hurried to keep up, wishing Oshu was with him.

"Look at this," Arelashk said, motioning at a pile of white rock, overgrown with vegetation. "This was once a city—it must have been."

Basha looked around, not convinced at first, but in the distance, he could see it. The shapes of buildings still held to some degree, more and more the closer they got to the mountains. Basha could hear a river somewhere close by, though he couldn't see it through the trees.

"We will make camp here," Arelashk said. To Basha, he went on. "You will return to meet the forward scouts. Tell them they are to make camp and send runners back to the fleet as quickly as they can. We need our reserve to meet us here, if they are not already on their way."

"Yes, honored Arelashk. Do we intend to make this a more settled encampment?" The reserve. Arelashk must have ordered them to move turns ago, and Basha had had no idea.

"Yes," said the mage. "There is something here that she did not get before us."

His smile was triumphant, and it struck a chord of fear that hummed up Basha's spine.

Basha tried to distract himself as he followed his orders, directing the forward scouts and preparing for the army to occupy the ruins of the city. Try as he might, however, he couldn't stop thinking of the reserve. Where would they march? From what Basha could guess, if they were to come inland from the coast anywhere near where his section of the army had turned east, it would almost certainly take the reserve force right past Lahivar.

He wished he were alone so he could yell the curses he wanted to yell. He wanted to see Arelashk dragged down the abyss in the Unan trench that split the sea floor on the western side of the Khardish archipelago. All of Arelashk's posturing about not wanting to go to Lahivar, and he must have been putting the fleet in place to do exactly that, knowing that if the initial force came at Carin from one side, the reserve could hem her in from the other.

And with Arelashk able to track her wherever she went, it would have been only a matter of time before she was supremely outnumbered.

Basha hoped for her sake that she would keep a handle on her magic, that she wouldn't try anything foolish. Arelashk seemed to have gotten his hands on all sorts of trinkets, though no amulet had reappeared around Valon's neck since Basha had destroyed the first, which made Basha think that wherever these arcane playthings had originated, the mage's supply was finite. But Carin would not know that, nor would she likely consider what Basha was considering: that Arelashk was simply trying to scare her as a control tactic. Basha had seen Carin briefly after her kidnapping from the bhamuoa; she had been terrified. He was certain she wasn't nearly as brave as she looked, and Arelashk's threats were seldom idle, even if he was bluffing.

Carin had not addressed him. It was Basha who had spent the most time with her, teaching her Khardish day after day in the brig. She had always shown him respect and kindness, perhaps because he had always done the same for her.

Perhaps she simply hadn't recognized him, but Basha didn't think that was the case.

He barked an order at a soldier who almost hit him with a tent pole, getting himself out of the way of the now-steady trickle of advance marchers who had quickly closed the distance to the ruin. Soon there would be an army camped out here, and Basha dreaded what would come of it.

• • • • •

First thing the next morning, Basha heard about the tree.

Some of the soldiers had tried to camp in the glen, but the ihsaln they had stolen from the travelers put up such a racket that they actually kicked two unfortunate privates who got too close, and the Marefi captain who intervened was so spooked that he sent a full company to investigate.

Tales spread from there. Basha was never more aware of his station than when it became clear that he was important enough to be present at some decision-making meetings but never important enough to be told vital pieces of news. Such was the tree.

They had seen a few of the strange white trees throughout the march. With no apparent bark and being completely smooth to the touch, they were another enigma in a land of mysteries. Their leaves were blood red and glowed like jewels when the sun hit them. Basha had heard some of the Marefi soldiers muttering about how they must be cursed, but he hadn't thought it was anything more than superstition until he went to see the tree with Arelashk.

There was a constant guard posted in the glen since none of the soldiers would camp there willingly, and while the commanders insisted it was safe, Arelashk insisted just as emphatically that he wanted to bring guards with him. High in a tree up on a ridge, a raven sat, watching the army as if expecting the gathered soldiers to make something into carrion.

Discomfited by the thought, Basha followed Arelashk and the soldiers into the cleft between the hills.

Basha had thought people were exaggerating when they spoke of the tree up until the moment he saw it.

The first thing that crossed his mind when he saw the enormous white roots up close was that it had to be some sort of mineral, not a tree at all. He had never seen anything like it, and even the other white trees they had come across—always in groups of five—seemed like pale shades in comparison to the behemoth that occupied the glen.

Eerier still was the heavy blanket of moss that coated almost every inch of the glen's floor and much of its walls where a deep gouge behind the tree cut directly into what looked like a sheer cliff face or a mountain that had somehow been cloven in two. The gouge in the cliff was hardly visible through the canopy of the tree, which stretched into the air taller than any building in Sahesh that Basha had seen. He wasn't sure he had a word to describe the size of it. With an entire army at their disposal, Basha was tempted to suggest seeing just how many legionnaires it would take link hands around the circumference of the trunk.

Beyond that, though, was Arelashk's reaction to it.

The mage approached the tree with reverence, trailing one hand along one enormous root almost like a lover caressing the leg of his beloved. Asurashk walked behind him, keeping her hands to herself, and a few of the Marefi officers seemed to stay as far away from the tree roots as they could, looking up nervously every so often as if expecting bird droppings to rain down on their heads.

Except there were no birds. No animals made a sound in the glen, in a tree that could house entire colonies of birds, rodents, any number of creatures.

Any hope Basha had fled.

Arelashk had come to these shores in search of power. Basha had no great knowledge of magic, but he didn't have to in order to know the mage had found it.

I T FELT like a long time since Ryd had walked for days on end. Sometimes he thought back to the long moons with Carin and Ras as they made their way north across the mountains through autumn and into the winter, of meeting the ialtag and the first steps they had taken into the Northlands, which Ryd now just thought of as home.

It was so different now. In every way, from the sounds in the air to the feel of the land under his feet, somehow Ryd had walked himself into a new world.

Most days he walked with Jenin, the two of them talking about what they had seen in the Hearthland over and over, backward and forward, trying to see if they could make sense of any of it—mostly in vain. They passed a massive lake forming in what had been Boggers. They followed the trail of the army eastward across the plains with Sart muttering about sand and how it was unnatural for a desert to suddenly burst into bloom, with which Ras seemed to agree. Ryd had never seen Sands when it was a desert, so he didn't really have anything to compare it to. That didn't keep him from seeing the changes all around them, though.

It was impossible to miss how the trees were taller when he woke up than they had been when he went to sleep. They walked through a young forest, now, the path of the army still visible but fading with every handspan the sun crept across the sky. Plants grew that Ryd had never seen before, some that even the Lahivarans who had lived their entire lives crisscrossing the land could not identify.

There were doubloon trees and birches, junipers and willows, and more flowers than Ryd could hope to name. Tiny stardrops and cheery lion flowers. Speckles of white morning mist and blushing pink bashful grace. There were bright purple-pink sprays that seemed to drip from their stems and clusters of blue flowers with folded petals that were almost precisely the color of Carin's eyes. It would have been easy to spend the entire summer wandering this lush and blooming land, but when the trail turned southward, Jenin and Ryd became uneasy.

"If the second half of the army came due east, they will intercept the first half near Alar Marhasan, Sart says." Ryd peered southward, though it was all rolling plains and trees now. He couldn't yet see the mountains in the distance, but he knew they would soon appear.

They hadn't yet decided what they would do. No one wanted to simply continue closing the distance between themselves and what would now be two armies. If Hoyu was right, it would be a fighting force four thousand strong, which was a number Ryd could not even imagine. He didn't know if there were even that many people in the Hearthland, and while he thought there were several times that many in the Northlands, they were all so scattered that the few hundred here with them were the most he'd ever seen in any one place. Even at Ryhnas Lu Sesim there hadn't been more than this with all Wyt's rovers.

Jenin hadn't answered and was instead frowning in a southerly direction.

"I think someone's coming," sy said, and Ryd snapped to attention, following his friend's gaze.

"Sart," Ryd called, but the warning died on his lips when the rider came into view.

Two riders, actually. One was a familiar sight—Kat and Suhnsuoc constantly patrolled the surrounding areas to make sure the Lahivarans could escape at a moment's notice.

The other was Culy, but Ryd didn't see Carin.

A murmur went through the Lahivarans at the sight of Culy atop hys ihstal, leading Tahin beside them. Culy looked healthy enough, and the two ihstal looked tired but still hale. Tahin whistled happily at the sight of Ryd—he thought, anyway—and Culy's eyes found him almost immediately.

Ryd pushed through the crowd to meet hyr, mind whirling. He couldn't assume the worst. Carin had to be okay. He hadn't been prepared for the stab of fear that lodged itself in his heart. He hurried to Culy, preparing to ask a question to which he would dread the answer.

Culy dismounted and came to meet him. "She is safe," sy said without preamble, anticipating what Ryd was about to ask. "But she has been captured by the Marefi force. They have occupied Alar Marhasan."

The murmur in the crowd swelled to sounds of dismay.

"You let her get captured?" Sart said, appearing from the left side of the group where Ryd hadn't even seen her approach.

"'Let' is a bit of a stretch," Culy replied. "She insisted I leave her."

From the sound of it, Ryd didn't think Culy was happy about it, but still sy had done as Carin had wanted. Carin had willingly put herself back in the grasp of Asu—Asurashk.

"Why would she do that?" Ryd blurted out.

"She decided it would not do for Asurashk to have access to my mind and memories, and I could not argue with that point. There are things this Asurashk could take from me that would be disastrous in the hands of a hostile force," Culy said. "Still, I am sorry."

The crowd fell silent, and Jenin stepped closer to Ryd tentatively. "Did you find anything of use? I'm afraid our news is not much better."

Briefly, they tried to catch Culy up on what they had learned, about Merin— the hyrsin's face went stony at that—and about Lahivar. It had been Suhnsuoc who caught Culy's scent as sy traveled northward from Alar Marhasan, allowing Kat to intercept hyr and bring hyr to the Lahivarans purely by chance. Ryd supposed they had been due a stroke of good luck in exchange for the parade of ill luck that had plagued them throughout this cycle. Or longer than that.

When they got to the last bit about the kazytya leading Kat to Culy, Jenin winced as sy admitted, "We tried to seek the final stone in the unseen realm—it is what we were searching for when we encountered the presence we assume to be Merin. We think we found it, but it is . . . out of reach."

"It is," Culy said softly. "Half of the stone is in the Hearthland."

Jenin had been preparing to say something else, but hys mouth dropped open at Culy's words. "Half?"

The crowd had not dissipated, instead gathering close enough that Ryd was starting to feel crowded. Perhaps they should not be discussing this in front of everyone, but at this point, Ryd figured it made little sense to cling to any kind of secrecy. Everyone would be affected by whatever happened next. No one deserved to stumble into it without warning.

Culy glanced around, appearing to do the same logical calculation as Ryd.

Finally, Culy sighed. "Yes. Half of it is in the Hearthland, and the other half is somehow concealed in Crevasses."

"In Alar Marhasan," Sart said flatly. "Where Carin is being held captive by an army that will soon be four thousand strong."

Culy blinked at that, then sighed again. "Yes."

"And we have nowhere to go that is safe, no fighting force to combat an army of any size, let alone that large. Culy, this is starting to look suspiciously close to hopeless, and I don't like hopeless." Sart fixed Culy with a glare that said she was considering holding hyr personally responsible if she couldn't get her hands on someone more worthy of blame. "One of these problems alone was plenty, thank you very much."

Ryd wished he knew what to do. Last time he was stuck, he'd apparently grown a halm grove, but he wasn't entirely sure that would be of use here. Besides, who was to say he could even do it on purpose? His hand rested on the hilt of the halm knife he had made for himself as Ryd listened half-heartedly to people offering suggestions and arguing about their merit, trying to keep Carin in the back of his mind so he wouldn't simply fall to his knees and cry.

She had been so terrified when she was first taken by the Khardish. And at least then Hoyu had been there to mitigate Asurashk. With someone like Rela, who would certainly do the exact opposite of mitigation, Ryd couldn't even allow himself to think of it. *She must be so frightened*, he thought.

He met Clar's eyes between the heads of other Lahivarans, and he almost despaired at the look of defeated hopelessness in her gaze. Ras and Hoyu were here, along with Mari and Dunal and so many of the others Ryd had come to know and care for in his time in Lahivar. Even Talnyt, the halmer who had taught him, was hovering around the edges of the conversation, usually unwilling to stay in the company of many for long. Some of the parents were keeping the children back away from Culy and the discussion, likely so as to not frighten them. Not that they hadn't been frightened enough already, having to flee their homes and trudge across a continent. The sound of a clucker in someone's cart cut through the tension in the air momentarily, but Ryd barely heard it. It did seem hopeless.

Still. Ryd mulled over what Culy had said.

The final stone had two halves.

Maybe that had been the initial problem, the one that had directly or indirectly given birth to all the rest, but Ryd thought the stones were still the key. The hearthstone spell had to break, and they had only one cycle of the moons, fifteen moons altogether, to fix it. This High Lights would be the final one before their world irrevocably changed again, for better or for worse.

Perhaps it was foolish of him to think if they could just solve this problem—*just* was quite a word to use about breaking a powerful ancient spell that had stood for two and a half thousand cycles—the rest would follow. Ryd remembered when his problems consisted of being sat on by children. He had progressed to slightly larger problems.

His thumb found the small rune he had carved into the pommel of the halm knife. Ryh, the rune for indomitable will, from which came his name. It was one of the branches of magic. It had been carved on the second hearthstone, the one at Ryhnas Lu Sesim, which, ironically, also stemmed from the same root.

Roots.

"Why can halmers grow halms without seeds?" Ryd asked suddenly aloud.

The conversation around him broke off, Sart looking exasperated at his interruption. She hadn't known the answer to this question and had previously told Ryd it was something they *just did*, the way the sun *just rose* in the east.

But Culy was looking at him appraisingly. "An interesting question. Is this something you have done?"

They must have left that part out. "Yes," Ryd said. "It's how we were able to find the stone—the half of the stone—in the Hearthland."

"Halm is not a typical tree," Culy said. "As you well know by now. While it does occasionally bear the fruit that gives us its seeds, such a thing is so rare as to be virtually meaningless. In ages past, it was only halmers who grew new halms."

"But why can we do it?" Ryd pressed.

Culy reached back to pull hys staff from where it rested in its sling across hys back, planting the butt of it in the grass and peering at it.

"This staff I made myself—or, more correctly, the halm and I made it together. Like the tree in Alar Marhasan, this staff is made of five halms, but it is also only one halm." Culy looked at Ryd and gave him a wry smile. "I planted seeds to grow those halms, for I am not entirely a halmer. But halm has a will. It is, in some ways, the essence of magic itself. No other wood is harder than bronze. No other wood refuses to be cut. No other wood can do this."

At that, Culy's staff shone bright white, growing more intense before winking out again, leaving afterimages in Ryd's vision when he blinked.

"A halmer can grow halms without seeds because the halmer's will is one with the halm's." Culy's smile grew even more wry, if that was possible. "You chose an appropriate profession for your name, my friend."

"So the grove in Lahivar wanted to grow?" Ryd asked dubiously.

"Very simply, yes." Culy drummed hys fingers on the shaft of hys staff.

"What does this have to do with anything?" Sart said irritably. "Unless the halms of this land want to rise up and fight an army, Ryd could raise groves enough to make a forest out of that rotted new lake in Boggers and it wouldn't make any difference to Carin."

Ryd couldn't really disagree with that, but Kat, who had been sitting atop Suhnsuoc the whole time looking pensive, cleared her throat.

"You said that you sensed the stone in Alar Marhasan in the unseen world but not in the physical world," Kat said.

Ryd started. Had Culy said that? It must have been when he had been lost in thought and people were arguing.

Culy nodded hys assent.

"And a halm of that size would hardly go unnoticed for so long with you around, Culy," Kat went on. "I find it difficult to believe it could escape notice."

"Unless it wanted to," Culy agreed. "Which is, I think, your point."

Kat nodded, and Ryd's eyes widened as he realized where she was going with this.

"You think the other half of the stone is hidden in the unseen world?" Ryd asked incredulously.

Kat nodded again, and Sart and Jenin were staring at him as if they hadn't quite made the leap yet. Even Culy started, hys eyes narrowing. Then sy snorted.

"It would be a feat indeed," Culy said, frowning. "But what we know fits that theory. Just before Carin told me to flee, she came to the same conclusion."

"Halm is different in the unseen world," Jenin said suddenly. "Everything else is almost blurred, like it is in motion. But halm is sharp. Defined. Immutable."

"I like things I can deal with face to face," Sart muttered. "One half of this rot-gut stone is in the Hearthland, which would take moons to reach, if we could even get close to it with the Hearthlanders preparing for the Reinvocation one cycle hence. The other is invisible and probably inside a giant tree that we can't even cut. Why are any of you looking like you think this is somehow a good thing? What good does it do if we know where the blasted thing is if we can't break it?"

"Another good question," said Culy. Sy paused. "When we broke the fourth stone, the spirit warned us that if we didn't break the stone before the Reinvocation, the result would be catastrophic. If we are correct and half of the final hearthstone is concealed somehow, bound to that halm, the force that would be channeled into that spot would be unimaginable. I doubt anything would survive. The first invocation leveled cities."

Involuntarily, Ryd glanced southward, toward the mountains he could not see.

"If they try to reinvoke the spell and that army is still camped out in Alar Marhasan," Ryd said, "it would annihilate them. And Carin too."

"You think they're going to sit still for an entire cycle?" Sart asked.

Hoyu and Ras had been quietly listening this entire time, off to the side with some of the Lahivarans, and Ras opened his mouth to say something just as Hoyu said, "If Rela has found a source of magic, a source of power like this halm you speak of, he will not budge until he has extracted every bit of benefit from it. Not only will they stay, but it is very likely they will bring more people. I would not be surprised if he sent for the Keeper of Mysteries, the arcane seat of the Da'sash Dan, our ruling body."

Seemingly uncomfortable with everyone looking at her, Hoyu shifted her weight and looked at Culy intensely.

"The Keeper of Mysteries is one of the Da'sash Dan you say is allied with Rela already, is sy not?" Culy asked, and Hoyu nodded. "Is it Khardish policy to invade other lands for their magical artifacts?"

Hoyu shook her head vehemently and made a sound of disgust. "No!" She realized she had said it very loudly and took a breath. "No. It is not. Traditionally it would constitute a war crime, but Rela has already engaged in war crimes by hiring Marefi mercenary legions to invade a foreign power. Not to mention what he and Asurashk did to Carin in Sahesh with the full knowledge and supervision of members of the Da'sash Dan. He must be . . . casting his net into the shark's waters and hoping to catch fish."

Ryd figured Hoyu had translated a Khardish idiom literally, but he understood what she meant.

Surprisingly, Kat made a noise of agreement from Suhnsuoc's back. "He gambles all on this journey. If he fails, he is a traitor. If he succeeds—"

"He will upset the balance of power in his homeland and likely claim some of it for his own," Culy finished.

"What do we do?" Ryd asked. "If they bring more people here before the Reinvocation, it will kill thousands."

Culy seemed to consider that, then laughed, causing a few of the Lahivarans to jump.

"Is that funny now?" Sart asked. "I know they're worse than the rotted rovers, but do you really want them to end up magically exploded into the sky because a bunch of *other* rotted fiends did a blood sacrifice?"

"No, it's not funny," Culy said, though hys lip still quirked as if that was only partly true. "I was laughing at the thought that perhaps our best course of action now is to warn them."

WITH EVERY passing day, Carin waited for Asurashk to show up and invade her mind. She didn't know why it hadn't happened yet. Some cynical part of her said that the waiting was part of her punishment. She knew they had Valon somewhere, and she heard people talking about other prisoners in Khardish, so she figured there were others about, but she was kept in a tent separate from everyone else.

She had preferred the brig on Hoyu's ship with its toilet and its sink. Here she had a bucket, a step down from a chamber pot, which at least would have a lid.

From what she could tell, the army was very well organized. No one had mistreated her—yet—but she was wary of the emotionless way her guards looked at her. On the ship, there hadn't been guards, just a locked door.

Rela had told her casually that the guards had a way of detecting magic and would dose her with the sparkleaf infusion if they caught her using it, and so far she hadn't worked up the courage to call his bluff. For all she knew, there was such a thing in Khardan. Rela had made a big deal about her lack of training as a mage, implying that in Khardan there was such a thing as formal mage training, so Carin was, if ignorant, aware of her own ignorance.

The spirit sulked a bit more with every passing day too. Rela still didn't know how exactly Carin had managed to escape Sahesh, but regardless, she wasn't on a boat over the ocean right now. Besides, even if she could travel through the waterways like she had before, where would she go?

She hoped Culy had escaped. She had heard no whispers of anyone else being captured with her, so Carin thought her plan had worked, insofar as it was a plan at all.

Good plan, she thought. *Get captured by the people who want to wriggle around inside your memories without consent.*

Though what she had said to Culy was still true. As awful as it would be to fall under Asurashk's invasive magic again, it would be far worse if she gained access to Culy's memories.

When there was a rustle of the tent flap, Carin didn't look up, assuming it was just a guard, but the quiet "Hello" in Tuan startled her.

She turned from where she sat to see Basha just as he let the flap of the tent fall again.

"Hello," she said cautiously.

This would be an interesting tactic if Basha was working for Rela after helping her. Using someone for whom she had a modicum of trust and more than a modicum of respect could lull her into complacency.

Great bounty, but she'd become paranoid.

Basha surprised her again by sitting cross-legged on the ground in front of her.

"You look well," he said, also in Tuan.

"Thank you," she said. "You look tired."

"Thank you," Basha replied. "If I only look tired, that is a . . . da ba'lar. What is da ba'lar in Tuan?"

Literally it meant "a good enough thing," but Carin knew it was an idiomatic usage in Khardish, applied to any number of situations where it implied a certain amount of wry, unexpected pleasure or relief.

"I don't know," she said after a beat. "Simply a good thing, though that doesn't carry the same meaning."

"Your Khardish is much improved," Basha said.

"As is your Tuan. I have had a very diligent teacher. What's your excuse?"

Basha frowned for a moment before deducing the meaning of her flippant words, then said carefully, "I have had a very diligent prisoner."

"Valon?" Carin asked.

Basha nodded.

Poor Valon. First captured by Wyt and her rovers, now by Rela. If they survived this, Valon would be more paranoid than Carin.

"Is she well? Are they treating her with dignity?" At Basha's look, Carin gave him a tight smile. "Dignity is *saba* in Khardish."

Basha's lips moved as he repeated the word under his breath and nodded. "Not at first, but now yes. I convinced the Arelashk it would be not practical to hurt her."

Trust Basha to have learned the word practical.

"What does Rela want?" Carin asked quietly, her voice dropping on Rela's name.

It was unlikely anyone would really match that name with his official title Arelashk, but Carin had greeted him with it when they first captured her, and people talked.

"Who has been teaching you Khardish?" Basha asked instead of answering.

"Hoyu," she said. "Please answer my question."

Basha frowned in consternation. He seemed to consider for a moment. He had always seemed one to choose his words carefully, and he did so now.

"Who is Hoyu? I will answer your question once you tell me this." Basha peered at her.

The man had changed in some ways. His hair was growing out, in small twists away from his scalp, almost like Hoyu's might have been cycles and cycles before. He indeed looked tired. His face was drawn, and his skin looked like the dry mountain air wasn't agreeing with it.

"You know Hoyu by another name," Carin said softly. "She was with me the last time I saw you."

Basha went utterly still. "She is here. She is *here*? How?"

"I cannot tell you all my secrets," Carin said. "It would spoil Asu's fun."

She wanted to trust that Basha did not mean her harm, but she could not ignore that he had somehow ingratiated himself to Rela, that he was here with an army at his back.

"You promised to answer me," she said then.

It was a test, she supposed, to see if his bargain was true. It could also be a test on his end, to see if offering information would get her to divulge it. Carin didn't know which was more correct.

"He wants the tree now," Basha said, and this time it was he who kept his voice low despite the fact that they were speaking Tuan and likely no one within leagues outside of the prisoners would understand them.

"How does he expect to get that back to Khardan?" Carin asked dryly. "I don't know if you have seen it, but it's rather large."

Basha didn't say anything, and Carin waited while the silence stretched out.

"Oh," she said when she understood.

"Yes," said Basha.

"He is going to bring Khardan to the tree." She ought to have anticipated that possibility, knowing Rela was searching for things of immense power like the hearthstones. "The army will not leave us alone, then."

He shook his head, a minute movement.

"Basha," she said and then stopped.

If they had no intention of leaving, that meant they would likely stay exactly where they were. They would build shelters and settle in for who knew how long. Weakly, she started to laugh. She was very glad she had gotten Culy to leave.

"What is funny?" Basha asked flatly.

"Nothing," Carin said. "And everything."

Could she tell them about the stone? Should she? These people had no idea what they had stumbled into the middle of. From what the ahrclys had communicated to her and Culy, if this army remained in the ruins of Alar Marhasan, they would get to see firsthand precisely what had ruined the city in the first place.

That was one way to defeat an invading army that had you vastly outnumbered, Carin supposed, except for the unfortunate additional fact that she was a prisoner right in the middle of it.

Basha was waiting expectantly, but Carin didn't want to tell him. She didn't know if she could trust him, and she was dubious at best at the prospect of Rela believing that some people on the other side of the mountains would unleash the magical equivalent of a hundred death waves exactly where he was, conveniently where Carin also needed to be but was kept from her purpose. Her mother used to say that sticky situations were like trying to forge a sword made of clay without breaking it.

The Khardish man drummed one dark brown hand on his knee, seeming to decide Carin wasn't about to expound on her laughter.

"Where is . . . Hoyu now?" he asked hesitantly.

"Lahivar," Carin said promptly. "Or she was."

His face went even more wan if that was possible. "That is unfortunate."

"Why?" Carin watched the rhythm of his fingers on his kneecap, sharp, punctuating taps that looked like anxiety felt.

"The other half of the army is marching to join us," he said in Khardish, then switched back to Tuan. "They will go through Lahivar. The fleet is just off the coast where—where we first met you."

Carin could almost feel the blood draining from her face. Lahivar.

She wanted to believe that the people would have fled by now, but they were expecting an invasion from the north, not from the west, and she hadn't considered this enormous army had another half.

"I am sorry," Basha said. "I must go. I will return."

He rose from the floor of the tent, leaving her alone with her fear.

• • • • •

Carin didn't have to wait much longer before Rela deigned to visit her. She was relieved at least that he didn't bring Asurashk with him.

He entered her tent with the same arrogance he'd had entering the chamber of the Da'sash Dan in Sahesh, which Carin would have found impressive perhaps if she hadn't been using every fragment of her self-control to keep her composure.

"Good afternoon," he said in Tuan.

She raised an eyebrow. His pronunciation was still atrocious, but since she thought he had been learning from her hand-written notes in the book of hers he'd stolen—she was certain he still had it—she grudgingly had to admit that was a feat.

"Is it?" she asked in Khardish instead of greeting him back.

He watched her for a moment. He didn't look much like Basha. His skin was much lighter, and his hair was still cropped short with the same designs etched into it that she had seen in Udum Dhu'e. Perhaps the Marefi army brought hair styling instruments with them when they invaded. His nose was smaller than Basha's, and he was lankier, though still short compared to her. Carin was tall even among her people, and in her time with the Khardish and Marefi people, as well as her brief glimpses of others in Sahesh, she had learned that her people were extraordinarily tall in comparison.

"It seems you have no wish for pleasantries," Rela said then in Khardish. "I hope you will cooperate. The Asurashk is eager to see you again, but her methods are indirect, and while useful, they create more work in piecing together her findings into something coherent."

"Imagine that," Carin said. "Simply violating people's minds doesn't create an ideal outcome?"

She was goading him, which was perhaps not the intelligent thing to do when surrounded by an entire army, but unless an ialtag swooped down from the sky and plucked her out of their midst, she didn't see a way out of this.

The thought came with an ache in her chest, and the spirit gave an indignant and unhappy splash, but Carin didn't particularly know what else to think.

When Rela still hadn't said anything else a moment later, Carin sighed. "What do you want?"

She didn't really expect him to tell her, but it was worth a shot.

"What I want is to see Khardan in its rightful place," Rela said. "Unburdened by the strictures they place upon the most promising fields. Maref is far from perfect, but they see the value in pursuing knowledge that is nadasuru."

"Nadasuru," Carin repeated. The word was unfamiliar. Not . . . one of silence? Or not of one silence. Forbidden, maybe? Anathema? "Pursuing knowledge like what you get out of someone's mind by force?"

"Sometimes," Rela said, unfazed by the condemnation in her tone.

"You wish to be unlimited by ethics," Carin summarized. "Khardan has a high standard of ethics, and you think this is a bad thing."

"How dare you?" Rela's voice was deceptively quiet, but Carin knew she had hit a nerve.

"You brought me to the bhamuoa for justice on evidence you obtained from me by coercion. You have invaded my homeland and now occupy the site of a historical disaster, a massacre of an entire city, and you want to use me to facilitate your quest to mine not just me but the very land for your own greed, and you ask me how *I* dare?" Carin was proud of her Khardish in that speech, thankful to Hoyu for their long conversations and the many nights they had stayed up to talk through the winter cold. "The gall of you. Get Asu if you like. You will get no help from me."

For a moment, she was afraid Rela would do just that—or set her on fire, from the look on his face alone.

But instead, he laughed. "Perhaps you will change your mind in a few days."

With that, he turned and left, and Carin had no idea how much worse she had made things for herself.

She didn't know if it was worth the risk or if Rela truly had outfitted the Marefi guards with some sort of magic detection device, but Carin had one possible way of communicating with her people, and the real failure would be refusing to try.

Entering the unseen world did take power, but it wasn't something she did consciously, so Carin hesitated before testing Rela's pronouncement with something small beforehand. Lying down on her pallet—they had let her keep her bedroll, at least, though they'd taken everything else of hers from her halm bow to the pouch of seeds on her belt—she tried to calm her mind enough to fall asleep.

It took her a long time to settle. She wasn't tired, since she had little else to do as a prisoner, and her exercises just made her stink. Trying to sleep in the middle of the afternoon when wide awake was a fool's errand at the best of times, and this was far from the best of times.

In the end, it took the spirit's help. The water spirit was eager to be of use, filling Carin's mind with the sound of waves and rain that washed away the clanking and barks of laughter from the Marefi soldiers all around her.

Eventually, she slept.

When she opened her eyes in the unseen world, she almost turned back. The only thing that kept her rooted there was the knowledge that there was little chance Rela would also be asleep at this time of day. If she had any hope of escape from this disaster, she would have to take whatever chances she could get.

Alar Marhasan was occupied again. A strange sight, the transience of the soldiers' tents flickering in and out of existence around her.

With a thought, Carin was at the tree, trying to figure out how she could sense the hearthstone here but not in the waking world.

The halm itself had to be the key somehow. She sensed no spirit here, not like before. When she laid her hands upon the trunk of the enormous halm, it felt as solid here as it did in the physical world.

"Culy," she murmured.

If she hoped sy would simply appear before her, her hope was dashed. She had once reached through to Culy in the waking world, but that had been in the throes of trauma and desperation. She was desperate now, but Carin knew that wasn't the same. She hoped there would be no repetition of the feelings that had allowed her to perform such a feat before.

She made a noise of frustration. Power poured from the halm, especially here. Halm had a will in itself, and Carin had a feeling that her palms rested on something she could use if she were just clever enough to figure out how. It was like handing a child an apple corer and an apple with no explanation of how they went together.

She couldn't shake the feeling she was missing something vital.

There was a painful irony in literally having her hand on the thing she needed but being unable to do what she needed to do with it. Like being hungry and unable to unseal the lid on a jar of food. The food could be in your hands but out of reach as surely as a fish in the river. Breaking the jar would just fill the food with glass.

And for once, she didn't think even Culy knew the answer to this puzzle. If the stone existed here, where she stood, it was still cut off from her completely. The halm was in the way, and though she hadn't tried, Carin was certain halm would not be any easier to manipulate in the unseen world for someone who was not a halmer.

She had more magic at her fingertips than she could rightly know what to do with in other circumstances.

She just couldn't use it to do the one thing her people desperately needed.

With a surging wave of defeat, Carin woke to her body in the physical world. She was still alone, but now she was mentally exhausted.

Whether it was a problem she could solve or one that she would agonize over until her death, Carin didn't know. The only thing she knew was that she would keep trying until she no longer could. If she spent the final cycle of her short life trying to save her people from the hubris of her ancestors, that was a death worth dying.

At least she could rest in the knowledge that the hubris of the Arelashk would take him with her.

DYAVA PACED in the hidden tunnel, trying his best not to curse Jenin out loud for leaving him in the middle of this mess. His parents were supposed to meet him, but they were late.

With everything so close to the Reinvocation, he needed them to give him something—anything—that could allow him to stop Lyari. And Merin-Reynah. And Harag. And the entire village of Haveranth that was ready to put their necks on a rock and water the ground with their blood.

They had left it far too late, and now it probably was too late. Dyava wondered if there had ever been a moment like this before, if any of his forebears had tried to stop the Reinvocation only to fail so miserably as this.

The problem with being angry about injustice without a plan was that the injustice would continue while you were angry if you didn't cobble together the wherewithal to do anything about it. Though his parents had brought him up to be a two-faced liar, living a clandestine double life in an idyllic village, he had at least trusted that they had some idea of what they were doing. Now all the pain, all the loss, all the misery and frustration and lies was simply to be wasted like the lives of the hapless sacrifices.

Now that it was coming so close to the actual day—High Lights was barely ten days away—it seemed far less real to Dyava. He would have thought it would be the other way around, that the deeper into Toil they got, the closer it would feel. The more he would understand that people were really going to die. The more he would be able to wrap his brain around people *volunteering* to die.

Then again, at least he knew that was an option if things got too dire.

The thought didn't cheer him.

Footsteps finally sounded in the tunnel from his parents' house.

"There you are," he said. "I've been waiting for ages."

It was only his mother, and she gave him a terse smile. "Reynah paid us a visit. She's only just left, and your father went with her."

Dyava went still. "She knows about us, Mamo," he said. "Did she—"

"Didn't mention it, of course," his mother said, waving her hand as if it was of no consequence. "Why would she? Better to let us stew in our anxiety. It is not like any of us are going anywhere now."

"You cannot be as sanguine about this as you are trying to seem," Dyava said.

"Sanguine?" Tarwyn ve Haveranth suddenly looked like she had seen a hundred harvests more than she had. "Hardly. We thought we had an entire cycle. We have two turns."

"Lyari said nothing can prevent the Reinvocation now." Dyava could still hear her words, feel the warmth of her leg against him, the touch of her hand on his cheek as her fingertips brushed his hair away from his face. "If you believe otherwise, you need to tell me a way to do it."

His mother gave him a sad smile. "There is always a way," she said. "Though your father and I hoped it would not necessitate something so extreme."

Dyava's lungs stopped mid-inhale, dread seeping into his chest in place of air.

He couldn't make his mouth form words, and Tarwyn's smile turned pitying.

"Had we known—" she began, then stopped as if rethinking what she had been about to say. "We would never ask you to do it, Dyava. We would never have asked you to so much as befriend her if we had thought it would come to this."

That was it, then. The extent of their plan, the culmination of five hundred cycles of waiting for their chance, and their plan was to kill Lyari. Reynah, too, he would think, especially because of Merin. He supposed someone actually had to perform the Reinvocation for it to succeed, and if neither Lyari nor Merin were alive to do it, Harag wouldn't have what she needed.

In a strange way, Merin herself had confirmed it when she had said Lyari needed her. Dyava had thought she was just being presumptuous and arrogant, but maybe she wasn't. Maybe Lyari really did need help.

With a sinking pit in his stomach, he realized that even Lyari had confirmed it. She had told him personally that she hadn't thought it possible to perform the Reinvocation early and that the breaking of the stones in the Northlands had changed that. Most telling was that she had allowed Reynah to stay in Haveranth and invited Harag. Dyava would have given his roundhome to have overheard the conversation that led to that agreement.

"If this is the end design," he said, "I wonder why you didn't just do it after she murdered Merin. It could have saved us the trouble."

His mother would not like the bitterness in his tone, and even Dyava almost choked on it.

But to his surprise, she shook her head slowly.

"I have always told you there were things beyond your understanding," she said. "Beyond all of us, to tell the truth, but though we did not anticipate Merin stepping in from beyond the veil of flame, our ancestors did not make this spell to be easily foiled. Do you think the near-immortals of the ancients would simply step aside and become farmers, son?"

"Then why did you ruin my life to make me think there was a chance at a better one?" he burst out. "Was all this some sort of sick game to you? You were supposed to have a plan!"

Dyava backed himself into the dirt wall of the underground room, trying to get a handle on his anger. If he slipped and reacted with his magic again like he had once with the fire, he could bring this place down on their heads without meaning to, even without the increased volatility of magic.

"The plan was to get someone close enough to Lyari that she would confide the actual workings of the spell," Tarwyn said quietly after a moment. "It can be very difficult to break a spell or disable it if you don't know how it works. But she didn't know the details before her Journeying, and Jenin volunteered to take your place. We thought we had more time."

"There may yet be time for me to find that out," Dyava said. "She trusts me. If we knew—"

"I understand you don't want her to die," Tarwyn said. "We would never expect you to do it."

Dyava's skin felt like it had grown a layer of ice.

"Give me three days," he managed to get out. "Three days to find out exactly how the spell works so we can prevent it from working. If I have not succeeded in three days, do what you must."

For a moment, he thought his mother was going to refuse, but instead she nodded once. Without another word, she turned and went back down the tunnel, leaving Dyava alone.

• • • • •

When Dyava returned to his roundhome, he felt calm.

It was unnerving to say the least, but a weight had lifted from his shoulders with the knowledge that for the first time in his life, there was a time, a line in the dirt, an end to everything that had consumed him. Three days.

He went to his kitchen and began to slice vegetables. Red onions and garlic, purple cave chilies and bright orange yams. With his cleaver, he cracked open a conu fruit and carved away the meat, reserving the milk. In his cold cellar, he had a haunch of mutton he needed to use today, so he pulled it out and stoked the fire, pulling the arm of the metal rack over the hottest part to heat his griddle.

So many things in his home had been made by Rina's hands. There had been a time when he used any excuse to order a new knife, a new kettle, a new hook or bar or scraper—anything that would give him an excuse to bump into Carin. Even before he admitted to himself that he had feelings for her, he had always liked to see her. They had been friends before they were lovers.

He wondered what she was doing now, if Jenin and Calyria had found her. If "her" was even the correct appellation or if she had indeed declared a new one. He would probably never know the answers to those questions.

Preparing a meal for himself felt somehow cleansing. He had cooked for Carin frequently, especially when she was building the roundhome in which Lyari now dwelled. Meat pies and dumplings, rolled up flatbreads with mutton like Tamat made available every day, all sorts of things that would keep her strong for the work she was doing but were easy to carry around and needed no bowls or spoons or anything else to be eaten.

Halfway through cooking, with the smell of caramelized mutton wafting through his roundhome, Dyava understood what he was doing. Cooking had always been a way of showing love for others, something he could do to show that he appreciated their being alive. It made him feel alive to provide sustenance for someone else. And tonight, making himself a meal that only he would eat, he supposed he was doing so as an act of love for himself.

A fine time to have such an epiphany, but it struck him deeply nonetheless. Perhaps in its way it was an act of mourning, too. Mourning the life with Carin he didn't get to have. Mourning his own life and the choices he hadn't been allowed to make. Mourning the loss of another lover on the horizon. Dyava had few illusions. Even if he succeeded in getting Lyari to tell him of the spell, even if such knowledge was enough to prevent the Reinvocation—he wasn't certain it was—there was no turning back.

He had said he would do what he must.

He wasn't due to meet Lyari until late in the evening, so he took his time. He braised the mutton in the conu milk and stewed it with the yams and onions and cave chillies. He served it to himself in his favorite bowl, one Ryd's mother had made. It was glazed a shining, lustrous green in the middle, but the outside was so dark a green it was almost black. He'd always thought it looked a bit magical, like the inside was glowing. He liked the way the purple oils from the cave chillies beaded in the broth and the way the mutton fell off the bone.

When he was done, he heated water for a bath and soaked as if the fragrant water could leach the poison of a duplicitous life from his skin. Dyava put on clean clothes, sat near the fire to dry his hair. Lyari liked the loose waves. Carin had too.

As he put on his boots to walk to Lyari's roundhome, he let himself appreciate that an evening of his three days was already gone. Such a small amount of time.

The village was quiet at this time of night. So near High Lights, the sky had not fully darkened, even though it was passing late. Smoke drifted in tiny wisps from a few chimneys, but aside from cooking, few would be wanting the heat. The night was still warm, a touch of humidity in the air, and a smattering of clouds obscured some of the stars, though he could see the Path of Petals clearly still as if the clouds purposely parted to make it visible.

He made his way down the path to Lyari's door and went inside.

She was waiting for him, a small smile on her face as she sat perched on the bench at the table in a soft vysa robe of pale pink. Her bare feet bounced on the floor as if she were excited. "I was afraid you weren't coming."

He bent to remove his boots. "Why would you think that?"

"You're late," she said.

"I am not. You're just impatient."

"Well, that's true enough." Lyari met him where he stood and kissed him full on the lips. "I am impatient."

He kicked off his second boot with his lips still pressed against hers, almost tripping over the first. He pulled away but wrapped his arms around her waist.

"I think impatience is one of the traits we share," he said.

"Show me," she said.

Dyava wished his body would refuse. He wished his emotions were simple things he could simply switch on or off depending on the need. But he had known Lyari his entire life. He loved her. He had loved her when she was Jenin's friend and lover, he had loved her when she was his friend, and he loved her now. Lyari had made space for him even though he had lied to her—that was something no one else had ever given him.

So he wished his body would deny him as she pulled him toward her bedroom and let the vysa robe fall away from her shoulders. She was wearing nothing underneath it. She slowly stripped away his tunic, his belt, his breeches. Lyari pinched one toe of his sock between her own and the floor, and he chuckled in spite of himself as he pulled his foot free.

His body did not deny him.

For a time, he lost himself in her, and he thought she was perhaps doing the same. He loved their bodies together, the way she laughed in the midst of pleasure, the way she made him do the same. Lyari had never been shy.

Eventually, though, it came to an end, and he lay beside her on her bed, diagonally across it with the summer blanket dangling from one corner and the sheets pushed all the way to one side.

"What will you do when it's done?" he asked in almost a whisper.

She leaned her head to the side to look at him from where she lay with one leg thrown over one of his, splayed out with her head on the mattress.

"The Reinvocation?" she asked.

"No, the harvest," he said and poked her in the arm. "Of course the Reinvocation."

"That is a very good question," she said. "I haven't really thought about it. It might be nice to go to Bemin's Fan."

"Bemin's Fan?" Dyava asked dubiously. "What's in Bemin's Fan?"

"The sea, squash for brains. The last time I was there, I didn't exactly get to enjoy it. I'd like to see it. Maybe go for a swim." Lyari kicked her feet as if to illustrate how to swim, and Dyava snorted.

"You and the water," he said. "I should have guessed."

"Yes, you should have," she teased. "What about you?"

"Might follow this woman to see the sea," he said. "I hear you can swim in it."

Even in his peripheral vision, he could see her rolling her eyes. She rolled one foot back and forth on the bed.

They were both quiet, and Dyava let time slip by, listening to his heartbeat gradually slow.

"How does it work?" he asked, then added hastily, "Not swimming."

Her foot stilled against the sheet. He heard her breath suck in, pause, and then felt a rush of air as she let it out.

"It is complicated," she said.

Dyava tried to keep his own breathing even as he waited to see if she would go on. He hoped she would; if he had to keep asking about it, there was no way she wouldn't know something was wrong.

But after a moment, she cleared her throat, and she continued.

"I wish I didn't need Reynah and Harag," she said. "They will never let me hear the end of it. And I could wait until the next High Lights, until next summer, when I wouldn't need them."

"Why don't you?" he asked, though the thought of it getting put off now that it was so close filled him with something very close to panic.

"I want it done," she said softly. "It must be done, and I must be the one to do it, and I want it behind me. Once it is finished, no one else will need to worry about it for another five hundred cycles."

"I can understand that," he said. "What do you need them for?"

Lyari rolled onto her side and blew a bit of flyaway hair from her face. He had mussed her plaits so thoroughly that, for a heartbeat or two, he could imagine she was the same wild fisher girl who had no magic except with a spear, not a soothsayer about to end fifteen lives.

"I have told you that the spell requires a great deal of magic. It will make me . . . dangerous," she said. "The sacrifices are only part of it. To even utilize the blood, I have to make a connection to the whole hearthstone."

"Don't you only have half of it?" he asked.

She was really telling him about it. He tried to calm himself so his heart would not speed up so much she would hear the rat-a-tat-tat of his nerves from where she lay.

"Yes—and no," she said. "It is bound to its other half, which is on the other side of a very particular bridge. The bridge itself is the key. Not only does it connect the two stones, but it makes each stone the connection to its other half as well. It is hard to explain."

"I think I understand," Dyava said slowly because he thought he did. "A door connects what is on either side of it. Without it, you just have two spaces separated by a wall. But the door also opens both ways, in and out."

"Yes," Lyari said, sounding pleased. "It is a bit like that."

"So you need to . . . open the door?" he asked.

"Essentially, yes. I have to connect to the half of the hearthstone that we have here at the moment the sun is highest in the sky on High Lights. Through it, I can access the bridge and the other half of the stone. That is when I become dangerous."

As if to punctuate this, she turned her head and nipped at the inside of his arm.

"Very dangerous," Dyava said, and this time it was him rolling his eyes.

"Reynah and Harag will have to—how to put this? They will shield me. Contain me, maybe. I will be in a defined space with the hearthstone, and Reynah and Harag will keep the magic I am taking into myself from spilling outside that space. While they don't have much magic themselves, they will draw on mine to make the shield." Lyari turned to look at him again. "You're sure you want to hear the next part?"

"Yes," he said, swallowing. "I need to know. I'd rather hear it from you than see it firsthand with no warning."

She sighed, looking away. "I was hoping you wouldn't say that."

Dyava wondered if she had hoped he would simply ignore what was meant to happen or not attend the Reinvocation. He wouldn't blame her if she had. It would be difficult for anyone to walk away from such a thing with their feelings unchanged toward whoever had spilled the blood of their fellow villagers.

"It's okay," he said. "You can tell me."

"I know," she whispered. "I'm sorry."

Confusion tickled at him, and he turned his head to look at her—or tried to.

"Lyari?" Dyava hated the tinge of fear in his voice.

He couldn't move.

It was as if something had fused his skeleton into one solid piece of bone.

In that wild moment, he was glad he had not told her about Merin, about Reynah. It was perhaps the one right choice he had made since the day of that fated Journeying on Planting Harmonix two cycles before.

"When I am in that space and connected to the stone and the key, I will be vulnerable. That is the other reason I need Reynah and Harag. They will protect me, or so they say." The bed shifted as Lyari's weight rolled off to the side and disappeared from the mattress. "I have to protect myself. The sacrifices will walk in of their own volition. They will be nude, partly so they can conceal no weapons. And I will kill them with my own hands and my own magic. Their blood will be passed through the stone and into the key, binding it anew to our ancestors' will, and thus will I secure the safety and bounty of the Hearthland for another five hundred cycles."

As she spoke, her voice circled around the bed, along with the pat-pat-pat of her bare feet on the wood floor.

"It's funny," she said. "If the other stones really are broken, then the bridge has been revealed. They really could end it, which is why I need to do this now. If I wait until next summer, they will figure it out."

Dyava could still taste her on his lips.

There was a rustle, and he felt her hand on his foot, followed by . . . fabric. She was dressing him?

"Why can't I move?" he asked. "What are you doing?"

"*Ahsh,*" she said, shushing him.

A drop of water splashed against the bare skin of his shin. Not water. A tear. It went from warm to cool in an instant, and it tickled as gravity pulled it around the curve of his calf. A moment later, his other foot in the second leg of his breeches, the bavel fabric brushed all trace of it away.

When she had his breeches pulled up and laced—she did it so perfunctorily, so neatly—she had to kneel on the bed to pull his tunic over his head. For a heartbeat, she vanished, and he saw her face reappear, wet with tears as she picked up one deadweight arm to put it through the arm hole, then the other.

"Lyari—" His mouth snapped shut.

"You've done enough," she said. "I don't even blame you. But I should have known it would come to this, to that question. You wouldn't have asked if your parents hadn't told you to."

It was such a simple thing, and Dyava couldn't deny the truth of it.

"I'm sorry," Lyari said, and she bent over him to kiss him gently on the cheekbone. "It would have been nice to go to Bemin's Fan with you."

He felt the press of her lips, and just as suddenly, it was gone, and she was leaving the room. The front door unlatched and opened.

"He's in the bed," he heard her say. "Be kind to him. He has been good to me."

When footsteps came back into the room, all Dyava could see were blurred shapes in his periphery.

"Sleep," Lyari said, and he did.

AFTER WHAT felt like an age of being supremely unfortunate, Carin got a stroke of luck.

When she woke in her tent again after her experimental foray into the unseen world, she expected Rela and Asurashk to be watching her the way they used to on the ship, when Rela had somehow deduced that she was capable of navigating the dream world. But either he was so arrogant that he truly believed she wouldn't test his pronouncement that he could detect her magic or there was a gap in its abilities to detect the mind traveling when the body did not—or, and this was perhaps just as likely, he'd been sold a goat and told it was an ihstal.

No matter if it was arrogance, accident, or merely a slippery salesperson, Carin was grateful for it. And she was even more grateful when she finally went to sleep at a proper time and was almost immediately face to face with Culy.

"My love," she said, at hys side in an instant. "You are here."

"You are worth the risk," sy said. "You are not drugged?"

"Not yet," Carin told hyr. "Rela told me if I so much as light a candle, he'll know and they'll pour it down my throat, but I suspect he miscalculated."

"You are able to at least do this," Culy said. "And you are alone—there is no other presence around you."

She nodded, intertwining both her hands with hys.

Her chest had a knot in it, fear born and pressurized by the knowledge that she might never see Culy in the physical world again. She had sent hyr away without thinking, only knowing that she could not allow Asurashk to do to Culy what the woman had done to her.

"Forgive me," she said, almost a whisper.

"There is nothing to forgive." Culy squeezed her hands. "It is Rela and Asurashk who are to blame in this, not you."

Culy paused, eyes searching Carin's. She had a feeling she knew what sy was about to ask, and she answered before sy could.

"Asurashk has not come to me yet. I think Rela is hoping I will cooperate without her, which I suspect is partly because he wants the sole credit for anything I share with them." Carin felt a mirthless smile stretch her lips. "But also he knows how much I fear Asurashk being inside my mind again. He can use that to his advantage. And time is on his side, he thinks. Time and numbers and power."

Culy nodded, and Carin appreciated that despite the subject of conversation, Culy made no attempts to coddle her or to downplay the seriousness of her situation. As always, she loved that about hyr. It was part of what had grown her feelings for hyr during her captivity in Khardan, the knowledge that Culy would simply assess, adapt, and act. No lies, no false promises, only taking account of the situation and allowing her to do the same.

"Have you been to the tree?" Culy asked.

Carin knew sy didn't mean in the physical world.

"Yes. There is something we're missing. I am certain the stone is here in this realm. But the tree is in both. It feels like those rotted puzzles where you have to move different sized disks from one peg to another, but the one on top always has to be smaller than the one on the bottom. There is a trick to it, and this feels like that except instead of three posts, there's five, and if we do the wrong thing, the mountains tear themselves apart." Carin was proud of herself for managing to keep fairly calm as she said it, but she wanted to scream.

"I wish I knew the answer," Culy said. "I was not told about the actual process of the spell at the time. But knowing the Tuanye who cast it, they built this puzzle into it by design. I suspect the only reason you were able to break that first stone where Sart failed is because you were born in the Hearthland. It sounds like the precise type of rubbish the Tuanye would weave into it. All magic that large has to have some sort of weakness, but skilled mages learn tricks to turn even those to their benefit."

"Where are you?" Carin asked suddenly. "I should have asked first thing."

"To the north, with—I ought to have told *you* first thing. I am with Ryd and Sart and the others from Lahivar. Kat and Suhnsuoc found me. They were all on the trail of the army, figuring the safest place for them was following quietly in their path while the second half of the force seeks only to meet the first." Culy smiled, but it was more like a baring of teeth. "Clar, purely by chance, stumbled across the second half of the Marefi force coming ashore a day's march from the waymake and returned in time to get everyone out. It seems the army was marching—"

"Here," Carin finished. "Or rather Alar Marhasan. Rela has taken a fancy to our tree."

"I see," said Culy. "Hoyu expects they intend to settle in for some time. The second half of the army will arrive right around High Lights, perhaps a little after."

"Hoyu," Carin said. "Tell her Basha is here. He was her—he helped her when she rescued me. I do not know how or why he has come to be here in service to Rela and Asurashk, but Hoyu should know."

"You have mentioned this name before," Culy said. "He is the one who gave you the book you think Rela still has."

"He is," Carin confirmed. There was so much to discuss, and they could not risk staying here too long. "The army will arrive around High Lights, you said. Which means any window we have for solving this puzzle closes at their arrival. The current situation is nearly impossible, but if the size of the army doubles, there will be no chance of us reaching the tree, let alone having enough time to poke around for a stone somehow stashed *here*."

Carin made a frustrated sound.

"There is another option," Culy said. "Or two. The first is that we warn them. They could very well decide to send their armies to march upon Haveranth, and since they can't take the halm with them, that could buy us some time."

"I do not see Rela leaving the tree." Carin let one of her hands fall from Culy's, though she mourned the absence of hys touch. "Because their people have never encountered halm before, they would need information about it to do anything at all. Not that Asurashk cannot simply take it from the minds of their captives."

"They have more than just Valon now, it seems," Culy said. "So I think you would be correct to assume Asurashk has people who she can exploit for their knowledge."

Carin's lips pressed together. "If this is hopeless, I am going to be very angry."

"At whom?" A small thread of amusement made its way into Carin's voice.

"Everything." She took Culy's hand again. "Do I try to warn Rela about the spell? It is so far off, even if he heeds it, he will have time enough to sit on Alar Marhasan with his army. What is the second option? You said there were two."

She fell silent, her mind working through the reality of being in a position to simply let her enemies die a sudden and horrible death. Granted, it would be an entire cycle of the moons before that happened, but if Culy could find some way to get her out of there, all her people would have to do would be to flee. To spend the cycle evading the Marefi army and whatever Khardish allies Rela could scrounge up while he camped out around . . . the one thing she needed access to if her people had any chance of thriving after this remaining cycle.

Carin's shoulders slumped, and Culy reached up to touch her cheek, about to answer her question, but Carin spoke again.

"The army is a problem that will solve itself, but if we allow that to happen, we risk the Reinvocation," Carin said. "That is the crux of it." She growled with frustration. "If only we could have some way of knowing the chances the Reinvocation would succeed with four stones broken. It feels like there should be little chance of it succeeding, but I also don't think preventing its success will have been that easy."

She looked at Culy as if she might find the answer in hys face, where the brief amusement had faded into similar frustration.

"Easy," Culy said and snorted.

Carin winced. It had been relatively easy for her to break the stones, but Culy had lost much of hys life after one failure. Sometimes she forgot there was a two-thousand-cycle gap in hys age.

"What do we do?" she asked quietly, looking around at the flickering camp that spread through the ruins of Alar Marhasan.

In the strange unlight of the unseen realm, it seemed almost peaceful. It didn't look like a hostile occupation—not that Carin had a point of reference for any other—only a forest full of tents that could have gathered for any reason.

"I think you should wait to tell Rela about the risk," Culy said after a moment. "It is possible Asurashk will come to you and discover it anyway, which is in itself a risk, but the second option I was going to describe is that we attempt to get you out of there with the help of some old friends."

"Old friends?" Carin asked blankly, and then it dawned on her. "You think they would? It would put them at enormous risk, and they seem hesitant to interfere directly."

"I think they will see the danger in failure to act," Culy said. "I cannot promise I am right, but they helped me when Rela put you to sleep—they may help us now."

Hope surged in Carin's heart, and she pressed her lips to Culy's. "Then it is worth trying."

"We may not be able to speak again," Culy said. "If you hear their wings, do what you did in the glen and signal. Just . . . perhaps not as intensely."

Carin gave a small bark of a chuckle. It wouldn't do to blind the ialtag if they indeed came swooping in to save her, even if they didn't fully rely on their eyes at all.

If the ialtag would agree to help, perhaps there was still a chance that everything they had fought for would not go to waste.

In the distance, Carin could almost feel the presence of the halm whispering to her, formless in its massive form, powerful, waiting.

Aware.

· · · · ·

Carin did not know who to expect next in her tent, whether Basha would return or whether at any moment she would be alone with Asurashk or held down and drugged while Asurashk waited patiently to slip into her memories and her mind.

Culy had not explained how sy planned to contact the ialtag, but Carin was certain sy had hys ways. They had come to her rescue once before when things could have been over for her in the highest reaches of the Mad Mountains in winter. Perhaps, like that time, they would see this as the best chance to finish the work they had started by telling Carin to break the stones.

Despite their aversion to interfering with the affairs of Carin's people, they had been spurred to engage now. She hoped that meant there was reason to be optimistic.

All would suffer if the Reinvocation was allowed to proceed, and if Rela somehow gained knowledge of the halm's power and the spell the ancestral Tuanye had used to devastate the Northlands, that suffering would spread like sickness over the whole of the world. To think of such a thing in the hands of Maref was cause enough to shudder. To consider it at the nexus of a corrupted Khardan allied with Maref—unthinkable.

Carin would place her hope and trust in Culy.

One thing Carin did not expect at all was that her Marefi guards would throw open the flap to her tent just after high day.

Without warning, they flanked her and grabbed her by the upper arms, dragging her from the tent despite her willingness and capability to walk peaceably by herself.

Their hands were not gentle, and one of them had kicked her unemptied latrine bucket in the process. The resulting smell bit at her nose, and she tamped down the rising anger urging her to retaliate. They didn't have to stay in a confined tent with their own excrement.

After dragging her outside, though, they pushed her to her knees, two additional guards aiming spears at her.

Perhaps Rela had not been bluffing after all. Maybe he knew she had entered the unseen realm and communicated with Culy, and the guards were about to dose her with sparkleaf. Alarm pulsed in time with her heartbeat as she waited, trying to keep her expression somewhere between aloofness and defiance, though she did not know if she was succeeding.

It was a bright, sunny day, though here in Crevasses where there had always been forest, the light was diffuse as it filtered through the leaves of hardwoods and the needles of the few varieties of evergreens that dotted the ruins.

The Marefi guards did not look Khardish. Their skin was pale, paler than Carin's people and far paler than some of the Khardish folk Carin had seen in Sahesh, though the Khardish people ranged from lighter skin tones like Asurashk to Rela's slightly darker skin and Hoyu and Basha's dark brown. The Marefi soldiers' hair also had a range of dark brown to almost black and also lighter brown like Culy's and even close to the yellow hair Carin had once seen onboard Hoyu's ship. She couldn't see their ears under the helmets they wore, but Carin expected they would closer resemble Hoyu's rounded ones rather than her people's that came to fine points, which Carin had always simply thought was universal before meeting the westerners and had since discovered it was her people who were the anomaly.

As she waited, her knee indented by a pebble beneath it that she could not shift to dislodge with her guards holding her still, Carin wondered what made these men agree to invade another land. What did they get out of it? Hoyu had told her that in the rest of the world, some people hoarded resources they did not need and traded metal obols for items and services rather than items or services in return. That felt alien to Carin, who had no concept of a hoarding type of wealth. Even in the Hearthland where she supposed the Tuanye ancestors had cast a destructive spell to concentrate the bounty of the land, they didn't live extravagantly by Hoyu's standards.

"What is happening?" she asked in Khardish, finally annoyed by the guards' silence. "Why have you dragged me out here?"

"Quiet," the guard on her left said, and she got a spear butt to the shoulder a moment later.

His accent was distinctly not Khardish despite the Khardish word. Carin had no knowledge whatsoever of the Marefi language.

She waited longer, the impact point of the spear throbbing. She would likely have a bruise for daring to ask a question. The shadows changed on the sun-dappled forest floor, and occasionally, other soldiers walked by, staring with open curiosity at the prisoner. Carin watched them back, wondering what they saw.

After some time, Rela appeared, weaving between the tents to the south as he made his way north to her. Basha and Asurashk were with him, along with a man Carin did not recognize. The new man was a little taller than Basha, but not by much. His skin was almost precisely the same golden brown as Asurashk's, and his hair was a similar brown-black. He was utterly unremarkable to Carin's eyes, though he kept close to Basha and carried a board with parchment attached to it, along with one of the writing sticks—pencils—Basha had taught her to use once.

Both Basha and the newcomer kept a dignified distance from Rela and Asurashk, and Carin had learned enough of Khardish propriety to understand that demonstrated a difference in rank.

Basha had briefly mentioned that the Marefi army had commanders here, but it seemed Carin was not enough of a curiosity—or Rela had taken enough control—that they had decided not to be present. It was strange to Carin that the entire camp seemed to be men. Khardan's societal differences were still close enough to what Carin was used to for her not to have considered that elsewhere might have a radically unfamiliar way of understanding identity, and it unnerved her that when bringing a fighting force to a new land, Maref had apparently sent only one gender. Carin could not think of a single time in her life where any labor had been divided so starkly.

She realized she was fixating on details while Rela talked to Asurashk out of earshot. Carin didn't know if Basha spoke Triyan, and she didn't think so, but Rela and Asurashk had frequently conversed in Asurashk's native language in mixed company to avoid Carin understanding them. Perhaps they were doing that again.

That said, from the maps Hoyu had drawn of the world to the west, Maref bordered Triya, so it would be foolish to think they could speak Triyan freely without some of the nearby soldiers understanding at least to a degree. Carin didn't think Rela would be that foolish.

Her knees were beginning to ache. If Rela wasted any more time building suspense, the pebble beneath Carin's weight was going to work its way through her leggings and into her kneecap.

But finally, Rela and Asurashk moved closer, motioning to the guards to let Carin stand.

She climbed gingerly to her feet, hearing a small pat as the pebble unstuck from her knee and fell to the ground. It was a tiny thing to have adhered itself with her weight, tinier still to cause such discomfort.

Carin found that oddly inspiring. If she had to be here, perhaps she could be that pebble in Rela's knee.

"Come with us," Rela said without greeting.

He immediately turned away with Asurashk and began walking. Carin moved to follow, unsurprised when the guards continued to keep hold of her arms. Their hands were getting sweaty, and she hated the sticky feeling of their palms against her bare skin. Basha and the other man hung back, bringing up the rear, and though Carin didn't turn around, she thought the extra pair of guards had also followed.

It didn't seem Rela wanted to take any chances of her escaping again. She would have been flattered if she wasn't facing the end of the world as she knew it.

At first she thought Rela was going to lead her to the halm, but when the gully appeared ahead of them, he turned left instead, westward along the ridge that separated the glen from the wider open space that the ruins of Alar Marhasan had occupied for so long.

She stumbled to a stop when she saw where he was leading.

Between a trio of maha trees, bound with heavy rope and with blood staining hys white fur red, was an ialtag.

I T ALMOST made sense that things had come down to this. Dyava felt a strange, pervasive relief to be done with it.

He sat in Lyari's cellar, in what he had always thought was a pantry (Carin hadn't divided the cellar into rooms, so it must have been Lyari), but now he thought he understood that it had been intended for precisely this purpose: holding a person against hys will.

He had been down here for two entire days and nights, and he could see the weave of magic that covered the walls and floors and kept all noise in—and kept all noise out. Dyava had tried yelling. He had yelled until he was hoarse, and now he was stuck *and* his throat hurt.

Dyava didn't even know if anyone else was down here with him, but Lyari had said his parents were "taken care of," and since the Reinvocation required sacrifices from all living generations of one bloodline, Dyava had little illusion about what that meant for his family.

Oddly, Clar's parents would be safe, insofar as anyone was safe. Or perhaps Lyari would simply kill them too.

It felt almost banal. Lyari had lost her best friend, her first love, a childhood playmate. She had murdered her village's soothsayer in retaliation for what she believed to be the murders of two of those people, and now she was planning to put fifteen more people to death purely because the ancestors had done it first.

Perhaps Dyava shouldn't have been surprised. He had, after all, gotten involved with Lyari knowing she had killed Merin with her bare hands. Or close enough. He still had no idea what had happened to Old Wend, but since the old codger had been a burr in Lyari's boot since she had become soothsayer, Dyava couldn't discount the possibility that she had killed him too.

He regretted not confronting Rina now. He would probably never know why she had been poking about in Lyari's roundhome. Whether the answer was as simple as suspecting she had lost a child as Nameless or as complex as Rina knowing about Merin and conspiring on her behalf, Dyava supposed it didn't really matter.

He would have another turn and a half to live, and then his lover would kill him in front of the entire Hearthland. Or not entire, but everyone who came to bear witness. It would be interesting to see how many people chose to come observe; Dyava suspected most were content to pretend it was a normal High Lights. Recount their sins, smear people with ash, bathe in the river, prepare to do it all again next summer.

Perhaps they'd even forgive each other for their own atrocities. He could see that happening. Tearful faces telling one another they hadn't personally wielded the ceremonial knife. It hadn't been *their* hands covered in blood. They would forgive each other for the crime of standing idly by, and they would believe themselves absolved.

And besides, even if they felt guilt, they would be sure they couldn't have stopped it. Furthermore, it would protect their children, who would grow up never knowing illness or want of any kind. Seventeen or eighteen cycles from now, there would be an entire troop of Journeyers headed north to the Mistaken Pass where they would anxiously fret about finding their names, learn about the supposed plight of their ancestors, and leave knowing their families were justified in inflicting suffering on multitudes of faceless fools who didn't matter.

Easy.

Dyava doubted the next generation would even know they had been born in the first flush of the Reinvocation, that they would hear of the grief of every lost pregnancy leading to it, that they would be anything but ignorant.

He envied them, in a way. It would be his blood that bought their ignorance. At least he wouldn't be around to see it.

When the door of his cupboard opened, interrupting his self-pity, he looked up, expecting Lyari.

It was Reynah.

She came in and closed the door behind her, the delicate weave of magic still covering her from head to toe.

When Lyari had immobilized Dyava on her bed, he hadn't seen so much as a thread of magic. She had been prepared. Careful. Knowing she'd planned that so meticulously made it worse.

"Can I help you?" he asked tiredly. "Or do you just not have anything better to do?"

"The latter," Reynah said, her voice cool and decidedly Merin-like.

Dyava figured he had nothing else to lose. "What do you want, Merin?"

At that, her laughter pealed out and ricocheted off the close walls of the cupboard.

"I wondered if you would figure it out, though I am curious as to how you did," she said. "The hawk was sloppy, admittedly. I was not yet strong enough to exert more control over it or Reynah, and as she was my tether to it, she had to pay the price for my mistake."

At that, she waggled the once-injured arm. It seemed to have healed quickly, though Dyava figured Merin was capable of helping that along these days.

"The squash too," Dyava said. Why not? "I presume that was your work unless someone else exists who is sneaky enough to evade notice."

"That was a test," Merin said. "More of my strength than anything else. Incidental."

He wondered if she was just here to talk to someone. It was strange to hear Merin's—not *voice*, not really. But something of her essence bled through Reynah's voice, and she held herself like Merin had. Straight back, strong shoulders. In Merin's body, those things had marked her as simply spry for her age. In Reynah's, she looked arrogant.

"What do you want?" Dyava asked again.

"I know about your family, Dyava. Meddling fools that they are. There is nothing new in their attempts at secrecy or their grandiose plans to stop the Reinvocation. I hope you are not so silly as to think they were the first to try." Merin leaned against the doorjamb, tossing her head so that the thick plait of black-and-silver hair landed over her shoulder. "But I wanted to tell you that I am sorry they dragged you into it. I always feel bad for the children who are forced to grow up in those families."

"Always?" Dyava couldn't help but interrupt. "Exactly how many of us are there?"

"Fewer than you would hope, but more than you would expect, over the ages," she said.

"So you're a lot older than you looked even before you died," he said flatly. "Congratulations."

"A benefit of my experience," she said, waving one hand dismissively.

"What are the other benefits?" If she was here talking to him, he might as well ask questions. It wasn't like he had anything better to do aside from fill up his chamber pot. "That's one thing I've always wondered. Is being the soothsayer of a village cut off from the rest of the world really worth it?"

Her eyes flashed at that, which was enough of an answer even before she said "Yes" without further elaboration.

But Dyava wasn't sure she needed to say more. She had control over life and death. She had been the midwife at almost every birth in Haveranth, save those who came too quickly for her to get to them—a rarity. She held the "true" names of every child born in the Hearthland and watched them fret over finding them on their Journeying. She let them grow up in fear that they would find themselves Nameless instead.

She sent Silencers after the Nameless and murdered them. Her hawk meant her eyes were anywhere a bird could fly, stalking villagers on their Journeying, even checking in on the Northlands if she really wanted to. Perhaps that was the real goal: an entire land under her dominion. Anyone who dissented died. She even made people forget their own children. He thought again of Rina, of her empty roundhome and the maha table she had given to Carin that had become Lyari's. He pictured the blacksmith wondering why she had given her table away to a Journeyer, wondering why her body had the hallmarks of having birthed and nursed a child.

"Are there others like you?" Dyava asked instead of pressing. "Even if you were the one who initiated all of this, you cannot have done it alone."

"I wasn't alone," she agreed. "I am now."

She offered nothing beyond that, but even that prickled at the edge of Dyava's consciousness.

"Why are you really here, Merin?" he said. Dread grew in his gut, which was a feat, since he felt he must be made of it by now.

"Despite appearances, Dyava, I respect that you tried. I abhor what your parents did to you, to Jenin, and to Calyria. It was unfair and unkind. You gave them everything they asked for, and they failed you at every turn." Merin stood up straighter, her eyes holding his gaze like she was pleading with him to believe her. "And when you could take no more of it, you gave everything you had left to Lyari. You gave her love and comfort, companionship and care, all knowing that she would go through with the thing you were sworn to stop. That shows no small amount of bravery."

"Foolishness," he muttered. "Or are you in ignorance of what it earned me?"

Merin sighed, raising one of Reynah's long-fingered hands to peer at the nail beds.

"Lyari, in turn, has betrayed you far more thoroughly than you betrayed her. You only did what you had been raised to do—it would have been shocking had you done otherwise." Merin continued without acknowledging what Dyava had said. "So beyond my admiration, I decided you had earned one more kindness from me. Lyari told you about the spell, she said. But she is unaware of my power. She is, for all her bravado, still unschooled in magic. You see my spells; she cannot.

"The broken hearthstones are a complication she thinks she can circumvent. She may be right, but what she does not realize is that there is an easier way, one that I will take when the time is right. The bridge she spoke of is an ancient halm," Merin said. "It is the fusion of a grove that one of our halmers brought forth at the first invocation. It has bent to our will for two and a half thousand cycles, and it has grown to its fullest potential with the help of our spell. It cannot be overstated how much power such a halm is capable of holding."

Dyava was stunned, and the dread grew barbs in his stomach. Lyari had said the second half of the final hearthstone was hidden away on the other side of a bridge. At his confusion, Merin smiled.

"I have skipped over something important, it seems," she said. "Halm grows both in this world and the unseen realm of dreams. It binds us to that other world, and it is the root of all magic. If you were to place a precious stone in a halm box and put it on your table, when you dreamt at night, you would be able to open that box and handle the stone. From there, you could leave it in the unseen world, and when you woke, the box would remain on your table, but the stone would be gone."

"The only way to reach that stone would be through the unseen world," Dyava said. "Which means someone could open that box and break it."

"If they could figure out how to open it, yes," Merin said. "But let's just say the halmers of my time were much, much better box makers than exist today."

"That's why you're helping Lyari do it now," Dyava said, almost to himself. When she gave him a stony look, he knew he was right. He took a shallow breath. "You're afraid."

This time, her smile did not reach her eyes. "I have lived for three thousand cycles, child. What do you think I am afraid of?"

Dyava smiled back at her, a genuine smile.

"Carin," he said.

For one heartbeat, maybe two, he thought she was going to turn around and leave right then. Her lack of surprise at the name told him Merin knew Carin had survived to make it to the Northlands and likely that she knew Carin was responsible for the stones breaking.

But when Merin spoke, any hope or optimism Dyava had felt evaporated like water drops flicked into Rina's forge.

"Why would I fear the person who has ensured my victory?" she said softly. "Until she broke the fourth stone, I could barely make myself known to Reynah. Magic returned to the Northlands far faster than here, but I am now close to my former strength. Lyari surprised me when she killed me. I had little time to prepare, but I have had time now."

Dyava wished he hadn't said anything, and Merin wasn't done.

"Without the other stones, adjustments were necessary. But we knew that when we began. The halm we grew at Alar Marhasan will serve as the new anchor for the spell." Merin's face—Reynah's face—was flat and certain, like Dyava truly was a child and she was scarcely deigning to discipline him. "Once Lyari begins the Reinvocation, it will be a simple matter to bind the spell to the halm itself. Indestructible, grown for this purpose alone."

She plucked at her robe as if it were dirty cheesecloth.

"Lyari has performed her purpose. In some ways, I will regret that she cannot join me. But there is room for only one soothsayer in the Hearthland, and I am she." Merin smiled once more, and chills raced up Dyava's arms to the crown of his head as if she had cast a weave of magic over him, though he knew she had not. "But you may take some comfort in her paying the price for her deeds."

With that, she turned and left, abandoning Dyava to his silent cell, where he bitterly wished for death.

CARIN LOST her breath at the sight of the giant bat tethered to the ground, unable to fly.

"What have you done?" she breathed, not sure if she were speaking Tuan or Khardish.

Was this who Culy had sent for her? She had heard no wings, nothing that would have cued her to signal her location.

"You have a variety of interesting life on this continent, Carin," said Arelashk, coming to stand beside her as if having a casual conversation. "The beasts you ride, the beasts you eat, trees the size of a small village—it's all going to be very interesting to study. But this—"

He indicated the ialtag with one hand. Carin did not look at him.

"This is something truly fantastic. Did you know we have legends about these? We call them da'uraoush."

Da'uraoush, *the sky ones* or *ones of the sky*, literally. Carin did not acknowledge Rela's words, only kept her eyes on the ialtag. It took everything in her power not to look at Asurashk. If Asurashk getting her hands on Culy would have been a disaster, Asurashk with access to the entire communal mind of the ialtag would be a catastrophe so dire, Carin did not think she had a word for it in either Khardish or Tuan.

Rela was going on anyway, not seeming to care that Carin wasn't answering him.

"The universities of Khardan, Maref, Triya, Coret—even the collective in Bohoyu—all agree that they are mythical, despite some scholars claiming there is evidence of their actual existence. This discovery alone merits my work here," Rela said.

His work. He said it like invading her land and displacing her people was the same as tending to a crop or building a roundhome.

"They belong to no one," Carin said, finding her voice at last. "Least of all you."

"An interesting choice of words." Rela moved in front of her, which would have broken her line of sight to the ialtag if she hadn't been so much taller, but as it was, she could see over his head as he went on. "You are clearly unsurprised by their existence, which means you have encountered them before. Asurashk failed to mention this."

"Yes, that one is rather terrible, isn't that right?" Carin said absently.

The ialtag was injured, and Carin tried to figure out how badly. Without touching hyr, she couldn't communicate with hyr, but she knew the bat would recognize her. This was not one she had encountered before—that much she knew.

Rela seemed torn between shock at her impudence and exasperation.

Carin decided on a course of action. She looked back to the Arelashk, ignoring Asurashk completely.

"You only value what you can mine for your own benefit," Carin said matter-of-factly. "That is undeniable. But surely even you must concur that you will get far less out of a creature that is suffering and in pain than you would one that is healthy and comfortable. This is the basis of Khardish law, is it not?"

She could almost feel Asurashk's eyes trying to bore a hole between her shoulder blades, but Rela simply gazed thoughtfully at her.

"What are you proposing? We have attempted to tend to the creature's injuries, but that one will allow no one closer than a few spans."

Rela's voice was neutral, but Carin knew she had him.

"It is of little wonder a captive creature shows no trust for the captors that brought pain with their ropes," Carin said. "Let me tend to the da'uraou."

She hoped she had guessed the singular form correctly, and from Rela's lack of correction, she had.

"Very well," Rela said, nodding to the guards to release her. "No magic, and if you injure the da'uroau, I will ensure you receive whatever injury you inflict."

"That won't be a problem," Carin said. "Though if you intend me to not use magic, I suggest you get someone to bring me a healer's supplies."

Without waiting for permission or to see if Rela would do as she said, she stepped toward the ialtag.

Hys body was lying against the ground, though sy had propped hyrself up on hys wings. The wings seemed uninjured to Carin's eyes, but she would wait to ask the ialtag. The main wound seemed to be near hys head, and knowing that head wounds gushed in people, Carin hoped it was just a shallow gash that looked worse than it was. Mostly, she hoped no bones were broken. Ialtag were massive, with a wingspan as wide as a midsized doubloon tree was tall, and she didn't know what sort of injury it would take to keep hyr from flying.

The ialtag watched her with round black eyes, soft yellow ears twitching and swiveling this way and that. Hys yellow nose also twitched, fluttering the skin at the edges. Carin couldn't tell if this was in pain or simply agitation. She didn't remember the other bats she had met displaying similar behavior.

"*Ahsh,*" she said softly. "I will not harm you."

She raised one hand as she drew close enough to touch the ialtag. When sy lowered hys head, she took that as an assent and gently placed her hand on the side of hys face, trying to look like she was simply examining the ialtag's injuries.

Panicked images flooded her mind as the ialtag showed her hys capture. With the panic came a wave of relief—Culy had not sent hyr, and it seemed Culy had not yet even managed to make contact with any ialtag. That was both concerning and reassuring, mostly the latter because it meant this ialtag had not been harmed for her sake.

Can you fly? she asked.

She got an affirmative, though it seemed there was some doubt. Carin could feel the anxiety of the rest of the ialtag for their captured friend. They also continually soothed this one, absolving hyr of blame. If Carin had thought she had a stroke of luck finding Culy in her dreams, this ialtag had had the countermeasure of misfortune, surprised by a soldier's practice arrow that narrowly missed hys chest. The resulting jerk midair had slammed the ialtag into a towering maha tree, and the impact had left hyr dazed and vulnerable.

Carin almost couldn't believe it, and the ialtag was full of self-recrimination for what sy thought was a foolish mistake. That was something Carin felt all too keenly, and with a gentle press of her hand into an uninjured patch of fur, Carin showed the ialtag her own capture, when she had trusted Asurashk and thought she was simply going to see the Khardish ship, only to be thrown into a prison cell and taken away from her people.

The ialtag's mind quieted at that, perhaps bolstered by the fact that Carin had managed to return, to escape.

She jolted herself back to her task and busied herself actually examining the ialtag's cut, which was a deep scrape, likely from a sharp branch.

Footsteps behind her warned her of Rela's approach.

"You could have simply let this one go," Carin said in Khardish. "Your ropes have not helped matters."

"The da'uraou would have tried to fly and could have been further injured," Rela said as if Carin were foolish for the very thought of it. "Restraints were prudent."

With one hand still upon the bat, Carin nudged with her mind. *Have you spoken to them?*

The answer was an immediate no that came with the force of a reflex, a knee-jerk reaction.

Carin relaxed somewhat with the intensity of the ialtag's response. If Rela knew the ialtag were capable of speech and intelligent conversation, that would only hasten his desire to have Asurashk step in. Carin hoped to the stars above that she would figure out something to prevent that from happening at all.

"Supplies are coming," Rela said, and to Carin's surprise, he moved away again, giving her space.

If I can free you, would you be able to fly away from here? Carin did her best not to look up at the tree canopy above her.

Yes, came the answer. *But whether or not I could carry you is another question.*

Carin disguised her slight jump of surprise by moving to check under the rope they had crossed over the ialtag's back and wing, where it had already rubbed a bit raw. Pink flesh showed under the white fur, and if Rela and his Marefi henchmen kept the bat confined much longer, there would indeed be more injuries to contend with.

She had not even really considered the possibility that the ialtag could carry her out of Alar Marhasan while injured. Carin would never have expected such a thing.

It's okay, she said, holding the rope away from the friction-burned patch as much as she could with the tension on it. *If I can help you get away, that is enough.*

The ialtag said nothing else for a time, and she continued her examination. It wasn't like she knew what she was doing really; the closest she'd gotten with such things were people and goats. Lyari's family had had goats, and occasionally they hurt themselves, so Carin had been present when Jemil—Lyari's mother— and Lyari had tended to their wounds. It was easier when one could explain and soothe the creature one tended. Even small goats tended to have at least little horns and far less patience.

When the guard arrived with the supplies and set them on a small folding table he'd brought with him, Carin thanked him in Khardish and set about trying to at least soothe the scrapes, even if she doubted there was much she could do about the rope burns when the ropes were still in place. It was impossible to save someone from drowning while sy yet lingered beneath the surface of the water.

There were salves Carin didn't recognize, but they were labeled in Khardish along with what she assumed was Marefi and maybe Triyan. She picked the one that said it was for pain and used a clean cloth to wash the wound and then dab it into the scrape.

The ialtag flinched from her touch, and a startled clank and rustle behind Carin told her the guards had reacted to the sudden movement.

"It's okay," she said aloud in Khardish. "Or have none of you ever felt what it's like to get healing salve in a wound?"

A small pair of chuckles answered her.

She was very tempted to try some small bit of magic as a test, but if Rela indeed had a way of detecting it, that would ruin her chances of getting the ialtag free. She would need magic to remove the ropes all at once, and once she did that, Rela wouldn't need a gadget to tell him what she'd done.

It took some time to do a full examination, and beyond the scrapes, Carin also found a few deep splinters with the ialtag's help, cleaning the puncture wounds and discarding the sharp twigs that had pierced hys flesh.

She was almost done when Rela came up to her again.

"I am curious as to why this creature lets you near but no one else," he said. "Most wild animals are not so discerning and will attack anyone, not just some."

"Most wild animals rightly object to being tied up while injured, but skill and gentleness goes further than brute strength," Carin retorted. "And this one is intelligent. I merely showed that I was not going to display more of the latter than the former."

"Intelligent, you say." Rela looked at the giant bat, who watched him right back with unblinking black eyes. "I would be interested to hear how you define intelligence."

That decided it. Carin looked at the ialtag for a moment to compose herself, then returned her gaze to Rela with as put-upon an air as she could possibly manage—which was not difficult—and said, "If you would be so kind as to let me finish my work here, you might be able to convince me to share, but a creature in pain is more important than your idle curiosity about your prisoner."

If the barb hit, Rela didn't show it, merely gave Carin a nod of acquiescence and returned to the others.

Carin raised her hand to the ialtag's face once more. *If I loosen the ropes, can you prepare yourself to fly? If you can carry me, I would be most thankful, but if you cannot, please do not harm yourself on my account. I don't have much time to pretend to be finishing up. Either way, you will be free.*

The ialtag did not reply in words, only sent a series of images of trying to carry Carin and, almost playfully, one of hyr dropping Carin into a river. She supposed that would be preferable to being dropped onto a tree, depending on the depth of the water.

Now that she had made up her mind, she tried to surreptitiously look around for bows. They would keep her halm bow. That thought made Carin angrier. It had been one of the last gifts from her mother, and because of Rela and Asurashk, it was likely she would never see it again.

She busied herself trying to give the ialtag as much slack in the rope as possible while dabbing salve sparingly onto the bat's fur. Carin hoped her new friend would be able to loosen hys muscles enough that sudden flight wouldn't cause more injury, and she forgot that she was still touching the bat when the thought occurred to her. The ialtag tried to reassure her, and it was backed up by others who lent their own optimism.

When I break the ropes, we won't have much time. Carin had no idea if this was going to work. If not, at least she'd probably have a nice set of more bruises to go with the one on her arm from the butt of the guard's spear.

The image the ialtag sent next gave her a small boost of confidence, and she smiled, giving the bat a soft pat of approval.

Rela was in conversation with Asurashk, and the guards were standing around looking bored, as if stuck in the position they seemed to be required to hold with their feet at shoulder width apart and hands resting on the belts that held their scabbards. None of them had bows, but that didn't mean other soldiers nearby didn't.

Her halm bow could shoot two to three hundred paces, but maha and other woods couldn't shoot that far. She hoped the soldiers had unstrung their bows to settle in here, knowing there was no real threat they might have to fight. Anything that would lessen the chances of the ialtag taking an arrow. Carin would prefer not to be riddled with arrows as well, for that matter.

Her pulse began to speed up with anticipation of what she was about to do. She had to be quick. If Rela really could sense her magic, he would respond the moment she began.

At the ialtag's urging, she positioned herself behind hyr, trusting that she could duck out of the way when hys enormous wings started flapping. Even though she'd been carried by an ialtag before, her nerves picked up with her heartbeat, and the hand that held the salve shook ever so slightly.

She kept her hand in contact with the ialtag, trying to slow her breathing enough to focus. Sy would know when to move—a certain benefit of being able to communicate mind to mind.

The spirit within her waited as well, eager without being too restless.

Carin sliced the ropes with her magic and sprang backward, hitting the ground and scrambling into a crouch as she felt the ialtag's massive wings unfold and *pull* a gust of air past her. It sent a cloud of dust and mulch flying toward Rela and Asurashk, and she heard him yelling.

There was time for her to gasp a breath, and that was all—the ialtag caught her by the upper arms, and her feet were yanked off the ground.

Carin couldn't help but gasp at the rapid ascent, and though the ialtag sent her comforting images to reassure her that sy could indeed carry her after all, the jolt left her shoulders aching as they winged upward and northward, away from the shouts below that grew rapidly fainter.

Soon, they were out of reach of even halm bows, and Carin could barely feel her own relief, suspended as she was so high above the new-growth forests of Crevasses.

Though the ialtag could bear her weight, sy couldn't do it forever, and as clouds rolled in, heralding a summer thunderstorm, sy gently told Carin sy needed to put her down.

They landed in a small dip in the rolling plains, and as she had the last time, Carin missed the contact with the ialtag's mind almost immediately. Her shoulders throbbed even from the relatively short flight. Gratitude outweighed the discomfort, however. She would have coped with both shoulders dislocated to get away from that camp.

The ialtag settled onto the grass, visibly as relieved as Carin felt. Rolling her shoulders to loosen some of the tension, Carin made her way over to her new friend and touched her hand to hys face.

"Thank you," she said aloud. "You saved me."

I think this was the other way around, the ialtag said, and with it came a sense of gentle chiding.

There was a ripple from the rest of the ialtag, borne on urgency. Culy's face, through the eyes of one of their fellows, somewhere not so very different from where she stood. They were close, then. Carin let herself collapse onto the grass, and the ialtag did the same beside her.

Sy must have been exhausted, and Carin had no food, no water. The ialtag were herbivores and ate mostly fruit, but Carin didn't know where she would get enough fruit to help her friend regain hys strength.

She put out one hand to the ialtag to ask and got an image of familiar faces coming their way. It would be some time before they arrived, but help was coming.

Help was coming.

BASHA LEANED against a tree, holding a damp compress to the back of his head where it had smacked into Oshu's cheek. When the enormous bat had broken free of the ropes, the wind from its wings had created a gust strong enough to knock everyone backward, as much from the reflex to get out of the way as from the gust itself.

His head stung, but Oshu had a black eye forming, and he kept sniffing from the stinging in his nose, which thankfully wasn't broken.

The Arelashk had twisted his ankle and was sitting angrily on a camp stool while one of the Marefi medics wrapped it for him.

"I thought you could sense her magic," Asurashk said dryly. "But perhaps talking to giant bats doesn't count."

If Asurashk could sense magic, she would probably sense a deep desire to set her on fire, Basha thought, since that was precisely what the mage looked like he wanted to do.

Arelashk didn't dignify Asurashk with an answer. Whether that was because he truly couldn't sense Carin's magic or because he was simply angry about her getting away anyway, Basha didn't know.

Basha tried to look miserable where he was, which wasn't too difficult, since his head hurt, and he was going to have to listen to whatever Arelashk had to say about what had just happened.

When he was a child, Basha's mother had always said that whatever you throw out into the sea returns to you on the morning tide, and he didn't always agree (plenty of people emptied latrines into the ocean but somehow always found pearls in their oysters), but he thought she was right this time. Or perhaps one of the sailors' more colorful expressions that he'd picked up in his many cycles on the sea: if you play for rotted fish guts, don't be surprised when that's what you win.

Watching Carin interact with the bat had been fascinating, even from a distance. Her care, gentleness, attentiveness—such a contrast to the soldiers who had handled the creature with heavy ropes and lashes. Basha thought there were a couple broken arms in the medic's tent because of that. Plenty of birds could break a person's arms when they had wings only a span or so across. That bat could have reached head to toe on a person five or six times over from wingtip to wingtip.

Basha itched to know more of the animals, and he supposed now he never would, since they were supposed to not exist at all outside of stories. And Arelashk had wasted his opportunity *and* lost the prisoner he'd chased across half a continent.

Unlike Arelashk, Basha was having a reasonably good day.

"When we find her again, you will let me do this my way," Asurashk said. "Your way did not work."

"Carin is inconsequential," Arelashk said. "She has always been inconsequential, and now that we know her goal is that white tree, we no longer need her. She led us directly to the thing we need."

Asurashk opened her mouth to protest, but the mage cut her off.

"You forget yourself," he said. "This was not about your vendetta but about the strength of Khardan. When the reserves get here, we will build what we need to settle in this place and study the tree."

"If you will not find her, I will," Asurashk said. "Perhaps not today or even in the coming moons, but I will."

"We will have time enough for that," Arelashk told her dismissively. "In the meantime, perhaps you will pay our other guests a visit. It would be helpful to know if they have any information about these bats."

Basha froze in the middle of dabbing the cloth against the stinging break in his scalp.

"A translator would be helpful, honored Asurashk," Basha said smoothly, his training dovetailing perfectly with his own goals for the moment. "If they are to understand what you plan to do, it is necessary to speak to them and gain their cooperation."

Basha knew the Arelashk would have let Asurashk go ahead and use her magic on their captives without a second thought, but now that Basha had voiced the protocol, he was ready to bet the man would not want to give a direct order to break the law—or if that was giving the man too much credit, Basha thought he would at least like to get petty revenge on Asurashk for her snide comments.

"Yes," said Arelashk, proving Basha correct. "Basha will attend. Oshu can stay with me while we discuss next steps."

Basha gave Oshu the barest hint of a smile before he followed Asurashk away from the now-empty restraints.

"Why do you persist in this charade?" she asked him before they had gone fifty paces.

"Protocol is not a charade, honored Asurashk," Basha said, keeping his voice as neutral as possible. "Consider how you would feel in their place if you were a prisoner in the middle of a foreign army and they sent someone into your mind for information. One of my earliest mentors always told me that we are never to do that which we would consider an atrocity if done to us."

"You believe my magic to be atrocious," Asurashk said, and her accompanying smile curved with danger.

"Your magic in and of itself is not atrocious," Basha said mildly, "any more than a kitchen knife is atrocious. But a kitchen knife can be used to do atrocious things, as can any magic. It is not my place to say more."

"You have said quite enough. You may inform them of what is to happen and nothing more," she said.

Basha nodded tersely, not trusting his tongue.

Could he do this? He didn't know. The thought of aiding the Asurashk as she committed a war crime—knowingly!—turned his stomach.

Though he knew she had gone to some of the prisoners already, he was not informed of this until after the fact. Basha was not an expert on legal defense, but he was not at all certain that claiming to merely observe a war crime was adequate for exoneration. Particularly when he had knowingly remained in the company of this army and a renegade Arelashk for half a cycle already.

Basha squinted as the day suddenly became noticeably dimmer. The sun had passed behind a cloud, and far from the wispy streamers that had covered the sky when he woke that day, these had heft.

Above his head as he trailed behind Asurashk, bloated clouds darkened the sky further, heavy and unmistakably full of rain. From the shape of the clouds, it was likely just a squall this time of year, but Basha knew such squalls could create a torrential downpour, however brief. He had hardly noticed them rolling in from the mountains, which was unsurprising, since summer storms often came and went in great haste.

Where they had camped was relatively flat, but there were dips in the land that ran between rows of soldiers' tents, and they were in the foothills of the mountains, where crevasses and gullies were plentiful.

Asurashk had almost reached the prisoners' tents when the sky burst open, and the rain poured out from the clouds onto the camp.

• • • • •

Never in his life had Basha thought he would be so thankful for a deluge.

As he had expected, when the rain came, it came fast and hard, churning up the mulch and mud where soldiers had been wearing paths in the grass and underbrush, and within moments, Basha and Asurashk were soaked.

"Come quickly," Asurashk called to him, clearly intending to make for the tent, where at least the rain would be impeded in trying to come at them from above, though Basha had yet to meet a tent that could stop water from getting into it from below.

"Honored Asurashk, the water!" Basha yelled back just as Marefi squad leaders began shouting out alarms, drowning him out with bellows of "Flash flood!"

The camp would have erupted into chaos even without the officers barking orders because all of those gullies and crevasses funneling torrents of water down from the hills to the south of the camp. It came pouring through the camp, filling every dip, and from one heartbeat to the next, soldiers were grabbing tent poles to make sure they were secure even as corners came loose on those unfortunate tents that occupied lower ground.

Asurashk swore in Triyan—Basha understood that much—and looked at him irritably, her hair dripping water into her face.

"It will have to wait," she said and stormed back in the direction they'd come, which was made less impressive by the splashing and squelching of her feet on the now-soggy ground.

Basha hurried after her, doing his best to keep the rainwater out of his eyes. He knew he wasn't saved. At best this was a reprieve for however long it took the camp to reorganize after the storm passed. For now, it did not seem to be letting up, but it would.

Almost involuntarily, Basha glanced northward.

He wanted nothing to do with this anymore. He almost laughed at the absurdity of coming to such a conclusion with water streaming around his feet, but with every step he took back toward his own tent, his urgency grew. If he could grab Oshu, if they could leave now, they could go.

He spoke enough Tuan that he could speak to anyone they found if the people didn't kill them on sight.

Basha never did anything spontaneous, not really. But his one spontaneous decision had been to insert himself into this mission, and look where it had gotten him. Hoyu was here. Carin was here. Surely if he could somehow find them, he could find a way to get word to Khardan. If he had to send word by giant bat, he would.

He had very little time. When Asurashk reached her tent with a dismissive wave, he broke into a run for his own.

Oshu was not there. Perhaps he was still with Arelashk. Basha ducked inside his tent, grabbed his knapsack from the small folding bench it sat upon, and threw everything he could reach into it. The floor in the tent was soaked, and he left anything that was on the floor where it lay. He took his notebooks, his pencils, everything that could be of any value. Food would be a problem, but that was a solvable problem. He threw four empty waterskins into his rucksack and threw both his and Oshu's over his shoulder without a thought. If anyone were to ask, he could tell them he simply couldn't leave his things on the flooded floor of the tent. The treated leather of the bags would keep its contents dry enough that such a thing was plausible, particularly for a bureaucrat who depended on written records.

With that done, he made for the direction of the Arelashk's tent, hoping Oshu would be with him and fearing it at the same time. Basha had no idea what he would say if the mage intended to keep Oshu with him longer.

The flap on Arelashk's tent was pinned open still, and Basha ducked inside without asking.

Arelashk and Oshu stood in the center of the tent, each holding maps and parchments off the floor that had clearly been gathered in a hurry, and the air around them seemed to drip like water on glass.

Magic—it had to be.

"Basha," Arelashk said. "Where is Asurashk?"

"There are flash floods, honored Arelashk," Basha said. "Tents are washing away."

He could barely hear himself over the pounding of the rain on the tent, but Rela had apparently understood what he had said, because the mage swore and looked toward the open tent flap as if he wanted to go out there and tell the floods to stop.

Oshu saw the knapsacks and met Basha's gaze with a questioning look. When Arelashk moved toward the opening to see for himself, Basha mouthed *It's time to go*.

Oshu's eyes widened in surprise, but he nodded, then glanced at the mage's back.

Basha felt lighter than he had in moons. He smiled at Oshu, mouthed *Trust me*, and at Oshu's nod, Basha tapped Arelashk on the shoulder.

"Honored Arelashk," said Basha.

The man turned with an indignant reprisal ready on his tongue to unleash at the breach of protocol—never would someone of Basha's rank *touch* a member of Arelashk's!—and Basha relaxed his shoulder and met Rela's face with his fist as hard as he could.

Rela's head snapped back, and he crumpled to the soggy floor of the flooded tent, dropping his parchments into the water. Basha felt more guilty about the parchments than the mage. His knuckles smarted.

Basha may have been a bureaucrat, but he was a sailor too, and every sailor knew how to throw a punch. Though he'd never knocked someone out with only one before now.

"I've wanted to do that since I met that man," Basha muttered. "And now we truly must leave with all possible haste."

Oshu took his own rucksack from Basha and slung it over his back. After a moment's consideration, he pulled the bag back around and shoved the maps and parchments he was still holding into it.

"That bat flew away with your sense," Oshu said.

"To the contrary, my dear, the rain washed away my cowardice. We should have done this a long time ago." Basha took one last look at the Arelashk, who had not moved.

Without another word, they left the tent, prudently unpinning the flap to let it fall on their way out.

The camp was in uproar, and the rain gave no sign of letting up. It fell in sheets, visibly slanting across Basha's vision.

There were so many people running around, no one gave Basha and Oshu so much as a second glance as they raced northward. A hill partly obscured the ruined city from the lowlands that spread out to the north, and they didn't stop running until they had reached the edge of the camp.

"Scouts," Oshu said curtly in Marefi to the one soldier stationed on the northern edge, and the soldier nodded as the two deserting men hurried past him.

They started jogging again when they rounded the hill.

"Where are we even going to go?" Oshu asked Basha.

"We can't go west or we'll run into the reserve marching this way," Basha said. "And from what Valon has told me, there is nothing to the east except plains and eventually another sea."

"North, then. Back the way we came." Oshu's feet squelched with every step.

The rain was finally slowing to a constant rush instead of a torrent, and the realization of what they had done was catching up to Basha.

"I hope I have not gotten us killed," Basha said. "We have no food, no weapons—this was perhaps the most foolish thing I have ever done."

Oshu glanced behind them, but there wasn't a soul in sight. He then came to stand in front of Basha, putting one hand on each of Basha's shoulders. His eye had swollen prodigiously, and Basha winced to see it, raising his own hand between Oshu's arms to brush his wet fingers gently over the edge of the rain-washed wound.

"You saw an opportunity and seized it, and it worked. We are away from the camp, and if I had to guess, the Arelashk will be out for a while. I'm surprised you didn't break his neck." Oshu took Basha's hand in his and held it to his lips. "If you are a fool, then I am twice the fool for following you. They will send people after us as soon as they are able, but I did not make it across a war zone with every scrap of silver I owned without learning how to avoid notice and how to find food. You got us out. I'll get us to safety."

Basha swallowed, trying to chase away the panic that wanted to ignore Oshu's confidence. "North, then," he said. "If we can find the Ada'sarshk—Hoyu—perhaps there is hope."

They hurried on, Oshu leading the way. It wouldn't be long before there were scouts sent after them, but if Oshu could just keep them hidden for a few days, perhaps a turn, Rela might decide it wasn't worth the resources to keep chasing a sailor and a steward when they had no ship or patron.

Basha's boots were soaked, and each step with wet socks inside them chafed a little more. His freshly healed feet would have new blisters.

He couldn't be bothered to care.

The rain slowed to a drizzle, and then it slowed to a sprinkle. The dark, heavy clouds rolled onward to the north, the rain visible over the hills and plains that spread out before them. The clouds above Basha and Oshu broke almost as quickly as they had formed, and almost as soon as Basha had noticed it, the sun burst through.

Basha lost his breath.

The rain-drenched grassy hills shone deep blue and gold, and the flowers that had framed their trek toward the mountains flashed like jewels in all their myriad colors, water droplets magnifying and refracting the sunlight until the mosaic rainbow below rivaled the arc of the rainbow that formed above to the northeast. Two brilliant curves of color against the mist rising in the aftermath of the storm.

Basha looked to Oshu, who was staring around in wonder, and Basha had never in his life seen anything so beautiful.

CLAR HAD not known Culy all that long, but watching the hyrsin spring into action the moment sy met up with the Lahivarans—and how everyone in Lahivar immediately readied themselves to help—struck Clar as akin to seeing the impetus of a force of nature.

She had sometimes worried that she and the others from the Hearthland seemed to have come in and ended up as decision-makers. Clar knew that Ryd and Carin and Ras had earned the respect of their fellows here, but she and Jenin were new to most people even now, and she was uncomfortable being at the center of choices that would affect the lives of the Northlanders. She had held herself back, trying her best to simply help where help was needed, and Jenin's particular experience and talents were of use in ways Clar felt a bit useless.

But watching Culy arrive, any worry sy felt for Carin buttoned neatly up and out of view, filled Clar with unexpected relief. Culy had directed them to a waymake nearby. It had about ten huts, and most of the Lahivarans were left to camp, giving preference to people with young children and those whose mobility had made travel a greater challenge. Clar had moved her bedroll to the outside of the camp with only a few hunters beyond, where they could react more quickly to threats.

All her life in Haveranth, she had felt like she was on the outside looking in. Because, of course, she was. Her family had made sure of that. Every relationship, every decision more momentous than choosing what to break her fast with, every interaction with other villagers, it all funneled through the single, immutable truth that Clar didn't belong.

Now she had made her way here, to this place that felt like home, and she had hoped that feeling would dissipate with time. It hadn't. Not really. She hovered at the edges of the waymake a few days' walking north of Crevasses, helping anyone who needed it but otherwise keeping to herself. Ras and Mari and some of the others she had become acquainted with were often scouting or hunting. Kat and Suhnsuoc barely passed through the waymake before leaving again, the kazytya covering leagues upon leagues every day in a range those on two legs could only dream to match.

And Culy was with them now. While the Northlands had no ruler, Clar thought Culy was the closest to that role.

She couldn't shake the agitation that gathered in her. Earlier in the afternoon, storm clouds had rolled in from the mountains to the south, and they had brought with them booming thunder and torrents of rain that pummeled the waymake. At the first flash of lightning, the waymake had sprung into action. Clar was shocked, as if the bolt had struck her, by the speed and efficiency with which the Northlanders got important items like bedrolls under the roof of the huts and set up jugs to catch rainwater and cleared debris from small tiled troughs that skirted the perimeter of each of the huts. The reason for the latter became immediately clear when the rain hit in earnest, as it poured from the roof of the hut nearest her and into the trough, which in turn funneled the water away from the walls of canvas that surrounded the hut and into a ditch that led into a natural gully on the eastern edge of the waymake.

After the first few moments of steady downpour, the Northlanders also drained the last from their waterskins and began filling them anew at the edge of the huts' roofs. Some of them showed their children how to do it, telling them they wait to ensure that the rain would wash away the dirt and debris from the roof before filling their skins. After a moment of hesitation, Clar followed their example.

Everyone was soaked, and the rain showed no signs of stopping. Clar finished filling her waterskin and pushed a few strands of hair back from her face that the rain had plastered to her skin.

One of the parents nearby, a woman whose name Clar could not remember, gave her a small smile.

"Before, there was not so much water," she said. "Even if it is more plentiful now, we would be wise not to waste it just because we can replace it."

"Wisdom indeed," Clar said. "A lesson all should heed."

The woman cracked a smile at Clar's accidental rhyme and hurried after her child, who was gleefully making to jump into a swiftly growing puddle with both feet.

Most people were still outside, though some had taken shelter in the huts where there was room. Even if someone had invited her into a hut, Clar couldn't bear the idea of being smushed into a confined space with so many others, hot breath and humid rainy air—she'd rather be wet. At least out here she could feel the wind.

To her surprise, Culy appeared around the edge of the hut she was moving away from. The hyrsin glanced upward at the clouds, leaning on hys halm staff, which was spattered with mud from the force of the raindrops hitting the earth.

"I suppose this is one of the benefits of being bald," Culy said, running hys free hand over hys hairless scalp. "No wet hair to deal with in a rainstorm."

Clar smiled at hyr. "That is definitely a benefit. No hair to wash, either. No tangles."

"All salient points." Culy seemed to hesitate. "You look ill at ease. Is something wrong?"

Not expecting the direct question, Clar was thrown into silence for a moment, listening to the steady beat of rain on roofs and against the ground.

"Carin is still captive," she said finally. "And there are many other things wrong."

"Of course." Culy gave her an apologetic look and a thin-lipped smile. "Once this rain stops, I intend to work on that. I managed to speak with her in dreams last night, and I am hoping the ialtag will agree to interfere this once."

"Interfere?" Since first seeing the giant bats herself, Clar had learned from Kat and others that they were shy creatures who usually kept to themselves.

She didn't really blame them, especially since Clar was somewhat of a shy creature who usually kept to herself.

"They dislike acting too directly upon the affairs of our people," said Culy. "Also due to their size and the fact that they eat only plants—mostly fruit—they haven't the energy to swoop in and rescue prisoners, for example. Though they sometimes make an exception when they can. I am hoping they will see Carin as someone for whom it is worth making such an exception once again."

That the ialtag had carried not only Carin but also Ryd and Ras over mountains then became an even greater honor and feat, Clar thought. If the giant bats were not carnivores, it would indeed be difficult for them to find enough fruit to fuel them for flying long distances, especially with the burden of a person-sized weight dangling from them.

"Thank you," Clar said suddenly and with more force than she meant to. "You have been kind to me and to Jenin, and I appreciate it."

Culy gazed at her, an assessing expression on the hyrsin's face. "It takes no small amount of courage to do what the two of you did. Most might say foolhardiness, for crossing the Mad Mountains in the dead of winter is something few could survive, especially without losing some of one's extremities to the cold."

"We were desperate." Clar could hardly hear her own voice over the rain, and a flash of lightning followed by an immediate boom of thunder made her jump.

The hyrsin had heard her anyway, and sy nodded. "Desperation is fuel for some of the most extraordinary acts. Survival is perhaps our most deeply rooted instinct, so when desperation requires we risk our lives, it is telling. It says that we found something else to be the greater risk to such an extent that chancing death by other means became preferable to remaining in an untenable situation."

Clar shifted her weight, uncomfortable with having her choices described so plainly.

Culy seemed to sense her discomfort and raised one hand as if to reassure her, letting it fall a moment later. "I say this out of admiration, not censure. In all the time this spell has stood, until now no one—not a single person in two and a half thousand cycles—managed to cross the mountains on their own. And now there are five of you."

"Five," Clar said. "Five of us."

It hadn't even occurred to her, but Culy was right. Five was a sacred number, though few would say so outright. Five days in a turn. Five turns in a moon. Fifteen moons in the moon cycle. Five hundred cycles between invocations of the spell, and it had lasted for five of those. It was no coincidence the spell had been based around five hearthstones, nor that it required five sacrifices. Five branches of magic. Five halms in a grove.

"Of all of us, I think I have been the least useful," Clar said, softly but forcefully. "Carin has broken stones. Ryd is a halmer. Ras is a hunter and a protector. Jenin a dream walker. I have nothing to add."

"Ah," said Culy. "We have found the root of what is wrong."

When Clar glanced at hyr, shame welling up at feeling so exposed, she expected to see something mocking in Culy's face, but instead she saw only compassion.

The rain had begun to slow, sounding more like raindrops than a downpour, though it still fell with alacrity, and all the troughs around the huts in the waymake overflowed.

Clar didn't answer for a long time, and Culy said nothing else. Whether waiting for Clar to say something or simply prepared to listen, Clar didn't know.

The rain stopped almost as suddenly as it had begun, the sky lightening imperceptibly at first, then noticeably. Clar saw a flash of lightning in the distance. A few heartbeats later, a now-distant rumble of thunder.

Folk began to emerge from where they had huddled in the huts, and good-natured chuckles reached Clar's ears when they saw those who had ridden out the storm in the thick of it, which drew a small smile from Clar's lips. She was sure she looked like a squirrel that had fallen off a branch into a pond. Culy managed somehow to still look dignified. Perhaps it was the bald head, though droplets of water clung to the tips of hys ears, and sy gave hys head a shake to dislodge them as if they tickled. Clar wondered what sy had looked like with hair.

"All I ever wanted was to belong," she said softly. "I never did, not even in my own family."

Of all the people here, Clar hadn't expected to confide in Culy. The hyrsin's eyes softened, and sy came close enough to put one hand on Clar's shoulder, giving it a brief squeeze before removing it again.

"It may surprise you to know that I have often felt that way myself," Culy said. "As for what you bring to the fire in our hearth, however, I think you may yet surprise yourself."

With that, Culy looked beyond Clar, toward the eastern fringe of the waymake.

"Ah," sy said. "There is indeed to be a rainbow after the rain."

Clar followed hys gaze and saw sy meant it literally, but as Culy strode off in the direction of the arc that stretched double-banded colors across the sky, she saw something far more unexpected.

A pair of ialtag had landed on the ground.

• • • • •

The arrival of the ialtag caused an immediate stir in the waymake, especially as most folk were still milling around in the aftermath of the storm since it was far too muddy to replace bedrolls on the ground outside and everyone's prior tasks had been interrupted in a hurry.

Clar followed Culy toward them, keeping what she hoped was a respectful distance, though she desperately wanted to get close enough to interact with the giant bats. They were unnerving and strange—Clar had only ever seen the smaller brown bats that occupied the twilit skies of the Hearthland, eating insects. Once one of those had gotten into her parents' roundhome, and Clar and her mother had had a mess of a time trying to get the poor creature out again. Those bats had smaller, scrunchy faces and barely had eyes to be seen. Clar's mother said they used other senses to hunt, which Clar found rather magical at the time.

The ialtag were enormous, slightly larger than the average person and a good deal larger than Hoyu, who had come over to gawk with the rest of the waymake. Their fur was white instead of brown, and their ears were bright yellow, the color of a potato boiled in saffron-infused broth, as were their noses, which protruded away from their faces almost like a singular flower petal. Their eyes were black and round, and if their smaller fellows didn't have much use for vision, the ialtag clearly had found reason to use their own.

"My friends," Culy said, approaching them. "What is so important that it has brought you to us?"

The nearest ialtag nudged hys face into Culy's hand, and Culy went immediately still.

The silence stretched out as Culy conversed with the giant bat, unease washing over the sodden folk of the waymake like the sheets of rain that had so recently done the same.

When Culy let hys hand drop, Clar could almost feel the waymake collectively hold its breath.

"The Marefi forces captured an ialtag," Culy said. "But Carin managed to set hyr free, and the two of them escaped to the south of us."

Clar's heart, which had plummeted at the first half of Culy's announcement, gave a wild leap with the second.

"Thank you," Culy said to the ialtag. "We are greatly in your debt. I had intended to seek your help, but it seems that is now unnecessary."

Someone pushed to the front of the crowd, a child who had probably seen only six or seven harvests—Clar mentally tripped over the sudden realization she didn't know if Northlanders marked age with harvests when there were no crops.

She pushed the thought from her mind, watching the child move toward the ialtag. In hys hands was a wooden plate, and in hys eyes hovered a question.

Without a word, the people of the waymake dispersed, some returning quickly and others after a brief delay, but one by one, children and parents and other adults alike filled the wooden plate with fruit. It was still early in the summer for some things, but there were redberries to be had, along with brambles and sweet plums that had sprung up in the past moon and now were eagerly bearing fruit.

The child presented the plate to the ialtag with big, round hazel eyes. Both of the massive bats blinked at the offering, dipping their heads.

There was a large stone that someone had evened out with a chisel nearby, and Culy motioned to the stone. "You can place it there, Anu," sy said to the child.

Anu complied, and when the ialtag both gave their wings a flap, everyone stood back to give them enough space to flutter over to the stone. One of the ialtag, the one to whom Culy had been speaking, waved the small hand at the middle joint of hys wing, and Culy came to meet hyr once more.

Culy placed hys hand on the ialtag's cheek again, then smiled. "Anu," sy said. "The ialtag would like to express their thanks to you directly."

If possible, the child's eyes grew even wider, and for a moment, Clar thought sy might be far too frightened to approach. But after staring at the ialtag and bouncing nervously on hys feet, Anu came to Culy's side and looked up at the hyrsin for encouragement.

"You may put your hand here," said Culy, indicating the ialtag's chest.

Anu stretched out hys hand and obeyed, hesitating for the barest moment before hys fingers made contact with the bat's white fur.

The child jumped, and even from Clar's vantage point, she could see hys cheeks flush with pride. When sy withdrew hys hand, hys head turned to seek out hys father's eyes.

"Tato, sy *spoke* to me!" sy blurted out, racing back to hys father with a wonderstruck backward glance at the ialtag that almost caused hyr to run headlong into Hoyu, who prudently sidestepped the collision.

A ripple of laughter moved through the gathered people, and Clar smiled with a small chuckle, though she felt a small pang of envy she immediately tried to squash. Little Anu would remember the day sy met an ialtag for the rest of hys life, she was sure.

Everyone gave the ialtag some space to eat, which they did with surprising delicacy despite being unable to hold their food with their wings.

She was so focused on the ialtag that Clar didn't notice Suhnsuoc's arrival until the kazytya was almost upon her. The ialtag looked up, alerting her to the large feline, and Kat began to dismount.

"Wait, if you will," Culy said and proceeded to tell Kat what the ialtag had said about Carin. When sy was finished, Culy went on. "If you and Suhnsuoc are able, it would be good if you could bring Carin back to us."

"Of course," Kat said, glancing down at Clar. "I will bring Clar with me."

"Is the ialtag who escaped with Carin still with her?" Clar asked. "If so, we should also bring some fruit for hyr. You mentioned that they would be exhausted after carrying people any distance, and if this one was captured, sy might not have eaten in some time."

Culy raised a hand to one of the ialtag, then nodded after a moment. "Sy could still fly if necessary, but it would be a risk."

Clar nodded and hurried to the hut where she had left her rucksack. She had some little fruit with her own things, but she didn't think it would be enough. By the time she returned, though, the waymake had provided. Someone had tied together a tidy bundle of waxed canvas, and Clar looked up gratefully.

"Thank you," she said, unsure who had done it.

"Down, Suhnsuoc," Kat said. "Come, Clar. We must hurry. The last Marefi scouts we saw were far closer to Carin's location than I would like."

Clar hurried to Suhnsuoc as the kazytya lowered hyrself to the ground and climbed on hys back behind Kat.

"Bring her home," Culy said softly. "Please."

Kat only nodded, and Suhnsuoc turned from the crowd and loped off in the direction Kat had come from.

"Will Suhnsuoc be okay carrying all three of us?" Clar asked.

"We hunted earlier today. Sy will be fine." Kat, though, sounded tired.

Clar tightened her arms around the other woman's waist, leaning into her.

For a time, she simply rested in the now-familiar rhythm of Suhnsuoc's gait. The sun returned with the storm now passed, and the world around them came alive with it, birds and insects returning from whatever shelter they had found from the deluge, and Suhnsuoc kept to higher ground to avoid the standing water that had not yet sunk into the earth.

"How far is she?" Clar asked when the sun began to sink toward the western horizon.

"We will stop soon," Kat replied. "She is not much farther, but Suhnsuoc cannot keep running without rest. We will leave again at first light."

True to Kat's word, Suhnsuoc slowed not long after, and both women dismounted in a grove of young saplings. Before the stones had been broken, Clar would have been able to guess the age of such trees, but now, she had no idea. They could have grown in the past day or the past cycle—she had no way of knowing.

Kat had not spoken much at all as they rode, which was unusual. Something seemed to be bothering the other woman, and as Clar sat with a few strips of dried meat that were doing little to settle her hunger, she wondered if she had done something to upset her.

They had yet to talk about their kisses and of the small touches that had grown and flourished much like the saplings that surrounded them. Clar had little experience with such things, so she wouldn't have known if she had erred in some way.

Kat ate in silence, cross-legged with one elbow leaning on her knee.

"Is something wrong?" Clar asked cautiously. Working up the courage to say something had taken an embarrassing amount of time.

Kat looked up, startled, sitting up straighter, then shifted to lean on her hand in the grass.

The other woman laughed helplessly, a short, musical sound. "I think a better question is whether something isn't," she said in reply. "Everything is wrong."

That did not set Clar's nerves at ease, and she shifted her own weight where she sat, unable to find a position that felt comfortable or relaxed. She settled on pulling her knees into her chest and hugging them with her arms.

"Carin escaped at least," she said finally.

"Yes, that is a boon," Kat agreed, though a moment later her face soured. "What little hope we have rests on her, I think."

The way she said *her* seemed to hold some bitterness.

"You don't like that she is from the Hearthland," Clar said after a beat. "I am also from the Hearthland."

Kat froze, and Clar thought she was about to agree. Her heart twisted in her chest, tears pricking at her eyes. Which was silly. She had not known Kat so very long, and besides, any antipathy the other woman felt for the Hearthland was well-earned. Hadn't Clar fled her own supposed homeland in the middle of winter for that very reason?

But Kat sighed and leaned forward again, plucking a few stray blades of grass.

"It is not that. Or it is, but also it's not. I don't like that our hopes seem to rest on someone from the Hearthland, no. Those who created this spell did so in a way that seems to have made it impossible for anyone else to break it—it had to be those on the inside to get out. It had to be Tuanye to rise up against the Tuanye. It feels wrong that this is true." Kat didn't meet Clar's eyes. "But if I am being truthful, it is not only that."

Clar couldn't bring herself to look at Kat's face, so she focused on the patch of grass in front of her bare toes, wondering what Kat would say.

"You will think me a fool," Kat muttered, tearing a blade of grass in half. "Selfish, at the very least."

"I doubt it," Clar said faintly, thinking of how she had, only that day, envied a child for getting to touch an ialtag.

Kat did look up then, giving Clar a look that said *You asked for it.*

"I thought I was going to be the one to save us," Kat said, all in a rush. "I was raised to believe that that was my place in all this. I was supposed to follow the wolves as they retook their homeland, a kazytya rider coming in from the wilds of the north to lead the warmlanders to victory against their enemies. But I got here and there was a Tuanye in my place at A'cu Lystel's side."

Clar stared at her. She'd thought what?

Kat went on, and even in the fading light of the summer gloaming, embarrassment was writ plain on her features. "I know it's ridiculous, but that's what I was taught. I was trained for this, kept apart from everyone else in my village most of my life."

"That is . . . surprisingly close to my own upbringing," Clar said, her voice quiet.

"What?"

She had not told Kat everything, of course. Though they had traveled together for turns on end, shared stories and secrets and soft touches, they had not delved into the particulars of their lives. Clar hadn't thought Kat would want to hear such things about the Hearthland villages, and she simply hadn't expected the other woman to confide in her.

So Clar told her then, about her family, about Jenin and Dyava (Kat did know some of the circumstances around her arrival here, just not the extent of them). It felt good to talk about it with someone who understood. Clar hadn't been raised as a hero, really; to the contrary, her parents had instilled in her a sense of sacrificial martyrdom. Yet despite that, as she talked, Kat nodded, eventually scooting close to her so they sat cross-legged in the grass, their knees touching.

"It's funny," Clar said after a time. "I just told Culy today that I feel useless here. My friends all have some—some tangible talent or gift to share. I am just frightened and trying to not panic."

Kat gave her a rueful smile and lightly chucked Clar's knee with the heel of her hand. "That is hardly true. Sometimes it is the small, simple tasks that fill in gaps that let the water into the boat. You need someone to row, but you can't row a sinking boat very far."

"I don't know boats," Clar admitted, "but I suppose you're right."

She hesitated before going on. She had that *feeling* again, like something was almost within her grasp.

On impulse, she leaned forward and kissed Kat on the lips. If Kat was startled, she didn't show it, only leaned into the kiss and reached up to cup Clar's jaw with her hand.

A breeze ruffled Clar's hair, long since dry from the heavy rain earlier in the day, and the feeling of it lifted her spirits. She deepened the kiss, twining her own fingers in Kat's hair, which had come loose from its plait sometime since they'd stopped to rest.

And something else happened.

Clar felt the strangest sensation, as if the grass were tickling the backs of her legs, the parts that rested flush against the ground. Suddenly Kat made a surprised sound, and they broke apart. Instinctively, Clar reached behind to steady herself, and her hand dipped farther than she thought it should before it hit grass.

With a startled yelp, she dropped a full handspan, hearing a noise of surprise from Kat at the same time.

They stared at each other with wide eyes, and Clar's lips still tingled from the kiss.

"Please tell me I did not imagine that," Clar said.

"What did you *do*?" Kat blurted out.

"Me? It had to have been you." Clar scrambled to her feet, her heart beating out a quick rhythm somewhere in the vicinity of her throat.

Kat was shaking her head even as she got to her feet. "I didn't do anything."

"Neither did I!"

Suhnsuoc stirred from where sy rested, making a grumble of a growl at being woken from hys sleep.

"Yes, I *know*," Kat said irritably, turning to fix the kazytya with a look of annoyance. "Very helpful."

"What did sy say?" Clar asked, biting off the protest that had been about to follow.

"That it must be magic." Kat crossed her arms. "And to be quiet so sy can sleep."

Clar's cheeks warmed. "Sorry, Suhnsuoc."

The kazytya huffed and rolled over, the tip of hys tail flicking.

Kat motioned to Clar, and Clar followed her a short ways away.

The strange feeling had not subsided, and the hairs on Clar's arms stood up straight. Oddly, when she glanced down at Kat's arms, she could clearly see the other woman's doing the same.

"Do you feel that?" Clar asked in a near-whisper. "You must."

Kat rubbed her hands against her arms, looking like she wanted to deny it. She took a breath and opened her mouth, then shut it again.

"Yes," Kat said finally. She laughed.

"Why is that funny?" said Clar.

"Sart and Ryd and Jenin, even Culy—they've all been talking about how things have shifted since the last two stones broke. I seldom use my magic, and I hadn't bothered to try anything. I guess I assumed it wouldn't affect me." Kat laughed again, then took one step forward, closing the distance to Clar. "It's you."

Somehow Clar didn't think Kat meant just what had happened. "What do you mean?"

"I mean it's you. All this time we've been drawn to each other. I know we haven't even talked about it, just floated with it like a lion flower's seed on the wind." Kat reached out and took hold of Clar's waist, pulling her closer. "Magic requires a catalyst to find purchase on a person."

"I don't understand," Clar said.

She did, to a point. But her parents had always taught her the catalyst tended to be trauma, and she hadn't experienced any magic after Jenin's "death" or her Journeying or even the terrible trek over the mountains.

"Kiss me and find out," said Kat.

She pulled Clar up against her, which sent a thrill of heat through Clar's belly. Clar obeyed, finding Kat's lips once more.

Once more the wind rose, the breeze beginning to buffet them, and far in the distance, wolfsong rose into the night in triumph.

FOR THE second time in as many moons, Carin was greeted by Kat and Clar astride Suhnsuoc only a short time into the morning.

Carin and her ialtag friend had passed the day there, with Carin foraging what food she could find for the both of them since the bat was far too exhausted to do so hyrself. She'd ended up refusing to eat anything she found so her rescuer would have more.

It was clear that the ialtag had risked hyrself for Carin after all, and though she was exasperated by that fact, she was far from ungrateful.

When the kazytya came into view, Carin felt a familiar surge of relief.

"Culy sent you," Carin said first thing. "Thank you for coming. They took my bow and everything else I had with me."

Suhnsuoc immediately lowered hyrself to the ground. Both Kat and Clar dismounted, and Clar pulled her rucksack from where it had been strapped to the kazytya's harness.

"We've brought food," Clar said shyly. "For both of you."

The ialtag looked up at that, and Carin watched with some amusement while Clar laid out a small mountain of fruits and cooked yams for hyr to eat.

Kat came to Carin's side. "For you."

Carin took the proffered packet of smoked salmon, her stomach growling loudly enough to betray any attempt at stoicism. She fell upon the salmon as hungrily as the ialtag was devouring hys fruit.

Clar sat back in a comfortable squat, looking over at Carin. "Are you injured?"

"No, thankfully. A few bruises is all. Our friend here has some scrapes, though." Carin tried not to talk around her food, but she was too hungry to care much about politeness. She hadn't eaten in over a day.

Sensing Carin's need to eat, Clar simply nodded, and Kat walked over to settle herself beside her friend.

When Carin was done, she moved over to the ialtag and placed one hand on hys wing.

"Will you be able to fly now?" she asked.

The ialtag sent a few images of hyrself soaring above the plains, which Carin took as a yes. She smiled at the thought. A moment later, the ialtag followed the images with one of Clar with her hand on hys face—as well as an image of the younger woman soaking wet, watching from a crowd in a muddy waymake as a child called Anu greeted one of the other ialtag. Clar's face looked almost childishly wonderstruck, and Carin grinned.

"Sy'd like to meet you," Carin said to Clar, and a blush immediately lit Clar's cheeks.

Clar rose from her spot, looking tentative and a little embarrassed as she came closer to the giant bat and put out a hand. Her face immediately softened, a slight smile tugging at the corners of her mouth.

Carin knew that feeling well. Even after encountering the ialtag many times now, she could not look upon them without a measure of awe. Carin didn't blame them for keeping their distance from people—and after what she had seen with the Marefi army, she never would. The thought of Asurashk gaining access to the entirety of the ialtag's communal mind still froze her spine in fear.

When Clar finally pulled away, it was with reluctance, and she shot a questioning glance back at Kat that Carin did not understand. If Kat did, she didn't look like it.

"Sy's going to leave now," Clar said softly. "I hope we'll see you again."

Carin looked to the ialtag, who shifted on the ground. "Once you have healed, if you can, I would be pleased to see you again as well. You will always be welcome wherever I am."

The ialtag raised a wing and brushed Carin's shoulder with it gently in farewell, and then sy lifted off into the air as Carin and the others stepped back to give hyr room. Sy was immediately gone from sight, camouflaged by whatever strange twist of magic or nature had allowed the bats to blend with their surroundings, though the sound of hys wings remained like a ghost on the wind.

· · · · ·

While Clar and Kat seemed perfectly comfortable on Suhnsuoc's back, Carin was very relieved when they arrived at the waymake where the Lahivarans had apparently settled for now. Sitting at the rear just to the front of Suhnsuoc's hips made Carin afraid she was going to fall off the whole way back; she had been so tense as a result that by the time she got onto her feet again near sunset, she could have cried.

Culy was there to greet her, and hys usual stoic demeanor dissolved when sy saw her, leaning hys staff hastily against a hut to sweep her up in hys arms.

Carin hadn't realized just how terrified she'd been that she would never see hys face again until that moment. She kissed hyr full on the mouth, her arms tightening around hys neck to pull hyr down to her.

She tore herself away after too short a time, only to be quickly embraced all over again by her friends and folk from Lahivar.

Among them, Sart clasped Carin by the back of the neck and pressed her forehead into Carin's before pulling back to mutter, "If you get captured again, I will kill you myself," and then giving her a sharp smack on the rear, causing Carin to make a very embarrassing squeak in surprise.

It seemed to break the tension a bit, though, so Carin couldn't be too put out. She tried to relax into the evening as people quickly realized she didn't want to be coddled—she needed to do something after being cooped up in a tent with nothing but a bucket of her own excrement for company—and side by side with Culy, she helped get everyone's bedrolls organized after they had been rescued from the oncoming storm.

By high dark, the waymake had quieted, and she and Culy were finally alone.

"I'm sorry I couldn't get Valon and the others out too," Carin said as they lay next to each other on their own bedrolls. "I never even found out where they were being kept. Or if they still live. I hope they still live."

"Valon certainly deserves our help if we can find a way," Culy agreed with a sigh. "I have not been able to contact her again, though I am unsure why. It could be only bad luck."

"What are we going to do?" Carin asked after a beat. "With another army descending on Alar Marhasan in a mere few days, if we have any hope of rescuing the prisoners, we will need to move quickly. Though I would be lying if I said I had any idea of how to do such a thing."

"When I first was able to meet up with the people here after leaving your side"—Culy squeezed Carin's hand, sending a pleasant pang through her—"I thought that perhaps we should warn them of the danger. After speaking with you during your captivity, we had decided not to. But now, perhaps it is worth a try."

"We have little time," Carin said. Always, always, always running out of time.

Above them, Toil moon waxed in the sky. It would only be a few days before High Lights, and Ras said the second army was due to arrive in Alar Marhasan on High Lights itself or the day after.

"We should leave tomorrow if we have any hope of warning them before their reinforcements arrive. Though whether they will listen to us or simply try to capture us is anyone's guess," Carin said. "I suppose it doesn't make much difference to a group of five or ten if we are facing a force of two thousand or four thousand." Carin dreaded the answer, but she needed to ask. "Worst-case scenario. What happens in the worst-case scenario?"

Culy was quiet in response. "The Reinvocation succeeds and somehow this army escapes and takes the knowledge of the spell back to their homelands to use it against one another."

Carin had not thought of anything quite that bad. "Even though the Reinvocation is one cycle away, Rela could still learn enough from the halm, maybe even from the hearthstone if he figures out a way to access the unseen world. He is a trained mage, and he is angry that I have now escaped him twice. I think he was genuinely curious about the ialtag."

"Plenty of horrible people can be curious," Culy said dryly.

"You are correct." Carin paused. "I do not think the worst-case scenario is likely. Of the two, the Reinvocation and this army using the ancients' spell as a weapon, which poses the greater danger?"

This time, Culy's silence stretched out a long time, so long Carin half wondered if her lover had fallen asleep. She squeezed hys hand and heard hyr swallow. Not asleep, then.

"The latter," came hys answer. "If the Reinvocation succeeds, it will destroy everything we have worked for. It will return this land to the husk it was when you first arrived. Worse, since you arrived when the spell was already in its waning days. It will mean starvation and disease for another five hundred cycles before we even have a hope of another chance. Neither of us can be certain we will live that long."

Carin's breath hitched at the thought. It was nothing she didn't already know, but she had allowed herself to hope. Her left hand, the one that was not tightly gripping Culy's, dug into the grass on the other side of her bedroll. All this life, all this rich, blooming life that they had watched spread joyfully across their land for moons now—all of it would be sapped away, held jealously for the Hearthland and the Hearthland alone.

Culy went on. "But it will be limited to this continent, this land," sy said, confirming what Carin had known was coming. "It will be trapped by the storm line, isolated from Khardan and Maref and all the other lands Hoyu has told us about. We will suffer greatly, but the rest of the world will be safe. If Rela and his armies are still here when the Reinvocation happens, they will likely be destroyed—or they will be trapped with us for the rest of our days. If he somehow takes knowledge of this spell across the seas, he will doom the world. Perhaps not this cycle or the next, but the Tuanye created a poison, and it will spread."

Carin nodded, blinking away the tears that gathered at the corners of her eyes. She lay on her back, and the action made them spill down her temples into her hair.

Could Rela be convinced to turn the army aside? Carin did not know. What power would it possibly take for him to leave? She didn't think she could stand to be trapped on the same side of the ocean as him for another cycle, let alone the rest of her life. But if that was the price of keeping the rest of the world safe from the spell that had devoured so many lives, so be it.

When the thought came to her, though, she sat straight up with a sharp intake of breath.

"What is it?" Culy asked.

She turned to him, letting the breath out in a shudder of air. "I have a very bad, very desperate idea."

• • • • •

Carin looked southward toward Alar Marhasan with no little amount of trepidation. Part of her couldn't believe she was this rotting foolish to come within a day's ride of the place so soon after escaping it, but at least this time, she wasn't alone.

With her were Culy, Ryd, Hoyu, Kat, Clar, Sart, and Jenin—Ras and everyone else had been told to head northward as far away from the mountains as they could get in a turn. If they had any luck at all, that would keep them far from the path of the army, and they could at least live out the last cycle before the Reinvocation in relative peace.

Ras had objected. Carin thought because he believed the Hearthlanders should bear the brunt of the risk in this, and while Carin couldn't fault his logic, he and his people who had escaped Ryhnas Lu Sesim were capable fighters. If Carin and her group failed, the risk would come back to him before long.

It was a bleak thought, but standing here with High Lights a bare day and a half away, Carin was trying to focus entirely on the task at hand. Otherwise she didn't think she would be on her feet.

She couldn't believe Culy had agreed, but more than that, she couldn't believe the ialtag had agreed.

They stood on a hilltop in clear sight of anyone searching for movement from Alar Marhasan, waiting for the ialtag to join them.

Carin hoped it would be enough to entice Rela to come out to meet them. If he tried anything tricky, the ihstal would flee, and the assembled ialtag would carry the others a safe distance away. There was room for error in this. But in terms of plans, it was the only one they had.

Hoyu had told her that by Khardish and Marefi custom, waving the branch of a tree or a sheaf of grain would signal to an opposing force that one wanted to meet to talk. To ambush someone under those terms was considered an atrocity by both sides, which, while not entirely promising given the army's lack of similar consideration in other things, was at least worth testing.

That is why she stood in front of the group, waving a tree branch back and forth. She had chosen a halm when Ryd offered—there had been a grove not far from their path south—and that was the other piece of bait. Carin was certain they had tried to cut the ancient halm or at least to break off a branch or two by now, so waving a bough from an uncuttable tree ought to be too much to resist along with the ialtag once they arrived.

As if her thought had summoned them, Carin felt a rush of sudden wind at her back, and it was accompanied by the gentle thuds of the ialtag coming to rest upon the ground.

Unhelpfully, she wondered if it was uncomfortable for them to be on the ground since they were accustomed to hanging upside down in caves and from sturdy branches.

When she glanced behind her, she saw that they were all clearly visible, not hiding.

If the sight of Carin—and Hoyu—accompanied by eight ialtag and waving a halm branch wasn't enough to have Rela climbing over soldiers' tents to meet them, she didn't know what would do it.

It wasn't long before scouts appeared on the next hill to the south. Hardly close enough to make out, they lingered for a moment before most turned and vanished again, leaving two on the hill, presumably to keep an eye on the new arrivals.

"Someone will approach us and ask for our terms," Hoyu said softly from behind Carin. "It will not be long."

True to her word, a runner trotted down the hill shortly after, coming to stand at the bottom of Carin's hill.

"You wish to speak?" the Marefi soldier yelled up the hill in Khardish.

"Tell the Arelashk that he will come alone with a retainer. He may bring Basha the seneschal and others, but no more than we have here, and he is not to bring the Asurashk under any circumstances," Carin called back. "And tell him I will take it as a symbol of his goodwill if he returns our people to us. Your army has done murder and taken prisoners from peaceable folk who did neither you nor your country any wrong. The Arelashk and the Asurashk take issue with me alone. Let him come and speak to me on equal ground and undo the wrong he has done to our own."

Hoyu had helped her figure out what to say, and Carin thought it was good— or as good as it was going to get, anyway. Carin was mostly proud of herself for getting through it without sounding too angry.

The runner down below scribbled in a small book not unlike the one Rela had stolen from Carin, and he nodded after a moment. "I will bring your message to the Arelashk and bring their response ahead if it pleases the Arelashk to meet with you."

"Thank you," Carin said, which made the runner hesitate.

He was hardly old enough to have gone on his Journeying if he were from Haveranth, which wasn't saying much since Carin had not seen many more summers than he had, despite having an ancient spirit in her head and memories of thousands of cycles mixed in with her own. She wondered how someone so young had ended up in a Marefi mercenary legion on the other side of an ocean from where he'd been born. His Khardish was immaculate, though markedly not his first language from his accent.

The soldier nodded after another appraising moment and turned to trot back up the far hill.

"Now we wait, I suppose," said Carin, giving the others a wan smile. "If and when they arrive, I will hold this branch in my right hand. If I switch it to my left, that is the signal to be prepared to flee. If I move it back, we go immediately."

She held the halm branch up to show everyone it was in her right hand, and once she was satisfied everyone had heard her, she turned it over to look at it more closely. Usually when a branch was pulled from a tree, it broke like a clucker's wishbone, leaving a jagged bit that didn't snap cleanly from the bough or trunk it had left behind. But halm was different in this, as it was in every other way. The thicker end where it had been attached to its tree was simply rounded and smooth, cool to the touch like polished wood and not stone, but there were no marks to suggest it had ever been broken.

The blood-red leaves had not wilted, and Ryd had said they would not, though when autumn came, they would fall.

"What does a halm leaf do?" Carin wondered aloud. "It's the only part of the tree that behaves like a tree in any way but shape."

The murmur of quiet conversation behind her ceased abruptly, and Carin heard a chuckle from Culy.

She glanced at Ryd. "Any thoughts, halmer?"

He stared at her as if she had asked him the last question he'd expected. Maybe she had.

"I have absolutely no idea," he said, shaking his head. "I don't know how anything works."

For some reason, that struck Carin as funny, and she scrubbed her hand against her face, trying to shake off the urge to laugh. With them were a man who could grow trees with his mind, a two-and-a-half-thousand-cycle-old mage who'd slept most of that time, a ship commander as far from the sea as one could get on this continent, a kazytya rider who'd appeared on her own to fight ancient would-be gods, and a pair of her childhood friends who, of the two of them, one had been dead for two cycles and could walk in dreams, and the other had eyes for the kazytya rider.

And there was herself, the stonebreaker with no appellation, home to an ancient spirit and with a tendency to make very bad decisions.

None of them had a clue what they were doing.

"Great bounty, I'm tired," Carin said, and this time no one seemed to hear her.

As time stretched out, she started to worry that she had misjudged the Arelashk after all. Perhaps he would not come or would attempt some trickery. If he got his hands on her again, Carin was certain he would not hesitate any longer to turn her over to Asurashk's magic.

She glanced worriedly over her shoulder at the ialtag, who radiated an impossible serenity despite the circumstances. This was a lot to ask of them, and Carin would never forgive herself if they bore the consequences.

"He's coming," said Hoyu softly beside her. She spoke in Tuan, and Carin reached out and took her friend's hand and squeezed it.

"If it is possible to find anything out about Basha, we will try," Carin promised her.

Hoyu nodded.

Sure enough, Rela had crested the hill and was on his way down already. While Carin could see the red of his tarke'e, it was the only splash of color against the blue of the grassy ridge. He was flanked by fifteen Marefi soldiers, but there was no sign of Basha.

Hoyu noticed that as well, but she drew herself up, and the mask of the Ada'sarshk appeared despite her Tuan dress and company. An understandable reflex, Carin thought.

Carin and Culy stood at the front of their group with Hoyu between them; the others fanned out behind them, forming a line between the approaching Marefi mercenaries and the ialtag at the rear. It was notable that Rela had brought fifteen fighters against their number though none of her people were armed for battle. She hoped that was not an ill omen.

"An interesting answer to my question" was the first thing Rela said when he made it up the hill looking none too happy with the location.

Carin supposed he was referring to what he had said about her perception of intelligence. She could see why he would take this meeting as evidence, though she wasn't sure how she felt about it. His cheek looked swollen, as if he had had a blow to the face, though he paid it no notice.

"Well, you have an interesting definition of ethics, so I suppose we are at an impasse," Carin said in Khardish.

She could hear Hoyu translating beside her for the others, though Culy could likely follow the conversation by now.

Rela's eyes landed on Hoyu with the kind of weight Carin herself had felt when he looked at her, and she did not envy the woman that stare. Hoyu returned it without blinking.

"Are you going to tell me why you wanted me to come all the way out here?" Rela prompted.

"Where is Basha?" Carin asked.

"A good question," said Arelashk. "One that is an answer in itself to one I had not asked."

If he didn't know where Basha was, that could not be a good sign.

"Did you consider my message?" Carin asked.

"I will not be releasing my prisoners, no," said Rela. "As the disadvantaged party here, it is bold of you to make such a demand."

Carin suppressed the sardonic smile that wanted to answer that. "I thought you might say something like that."

If her reply flummoxed Rela, he didn't show it. "I presume you had some reason for bringing me here."

"Several, actually. The first is what one might call a friendly warning, which I do not expect you to heed, but I am prepared to provide you with ample evidence."

Carin found now, face to face with the man on something closer to equal terms, that her anger swirled inside her, demanding to be unleashed. The spirit encouraged it, remembering the claustrophobia of being trapped inside her own body as it had been trapped for so long in the hearthstone she broke to free it. She focused on Hoyu's translating as a distraction, something to keep her steady.

Rela made an impatient motion with his hand as if telling Carin to get on with it. His manner was so different away from Khardish eyes. In Sahesh at least, he had acted with some degree of restraint, going through the motions of Khardish legality if not adhering to it behind closed doors.

"I assume Asurashk has told you about the spell upon this land," Carin said, and she didn't wait for his agreement. "That spell is to be renewed one cycle from tomorrow. You are an educated mage. You should have at least some idea of the amount of magic it would take to invoke such a spell, and subsequently, you should have some understanding of the consequences were something of that magnitude to go awry."

"Yes, yes, the spell that has sent death waves westward for two millennia," said Rela. "Are you threatening to do the same? Or did you get your fill the first time?"

It took all Carin's self-control not to grit her teeth hard enough to crack them.

"I have spent the past three cycles doing everything within my power to stop such a thing from happening," she said, proud to have kept a handle on her tongue as well as her teeth. "But your army stands between me and the one thing that would ensure my success, and because I do not expect you to move, I think you should know the price of your arrogance."

Rela did not move even now, his eyes dark and stony as he stared her down. But he was not the only one present. He had chosen fifteen Marefi soldiers to come with him, and Carin was certain at least some of them had a modicum of the Khardish language. This was the second part of her idea: that if she could not convince Rela of the danger, perhaps the soldiers would decide that the risk of all dying at once was enough to merit dissent.

"Say what you are going to say so I can leave," Rela said. "I ought to have brought Asurashk despite your demands."

"You have no need of Asurashk for me to provide evidence of this," Carin said softly. "In one cycle, far to the south on the other side of the mountains, a mage will reinvoke the hearthstone spell, and in doing so, she will pour an immense amount of power into that bone-white tree in the glen."

Carin waved the halm branch in her hand, and though Rela pretended not to notice, his gaze flickered to the blood-red leaves and the perfectly rounded end that had no splinter.

On the other side of Hoyu, Culy shifted hys weight, holding hys staff laconically in hys right hand, and Rela did not manage to conceal his interest then.

"An interesting tree," Rela said. "No one seems able to cut it, but its power is formidable. A mage of any talent would be able to sense that."

"Halm is indestructible," Carin said. "But everything around it is not. When the spell was first invoked, it punched a hole through mountains, and that was with its power spread across five hearthstones, not just one. Your army is sitting on top of a death wave that needs no water to kill."

She had gotten his attention now.

"One cycle will be enough time for us to be gone from these shores," he said after a beat, though his voice did not sound quite as confident as it had.

"In which you will do what? Try and learn the secrets of this magic so you can bring the rest of the world to ruin?" Carin asked. "Even you should not be so foolish as that, Arelashk. It is one thing to collect venomous snakes. It is something else altogether to find oneself in a pit of them with no chance of escaping unbitten. There is no way for you to get what you want without endangering yourself and everything you think you're protecting."

This was it. Carin motioned to the ialtag behind her.

"You were curious about them. This now is your chance to learn something new. If you harm them, I will kill you and every soldier you brought with you and leave the lot of those in Alar Marhasan to be annihilated when that spell is reinvoked if they stay. Greet my friends in peace, and you will leave here in one piece. Seven of your soldiers may come too. The rest stay back." Carin gestured to her companions, and they parted to allow a way through.

Rela looked warily at the ialtag, but he nodded curtly at the seven soldiers on his right, and they came forward with Rela as he approached the ialtag.

"Place one bare hand on their shoulders," Carin said. "You will understand when you do."

The soldiers looked as if they would rather be staring down the Reinvocation than giant bats, and they looked to Rela. When he let his hand fall upon the middle ialtag's white fur, the soldiers glanced at one another and did the same.

They all jumped when they did so, likely in surprise, and the remaining soldiers shifted uncomfortably, hands going to the hilts of swords.

"Hold," Carin said. "They will not be harmed."

If waiting for Rela to show up had felt like a long time, waiting for him to turn away from the ialtag took an eternity. It couldn't have been longer than the amount of time they had spent talking, but to Carin it felt as if it would never end.

When he finally pulled his hand back, it was shaking, and the soldiers on either side of him were no more stoic than he. Carin suspected it was only their training that kept their reactions to a few wild-eyed glances in her direction, but they all walked back to their previous positions with straight backs and without a word.

Rela did the same.

"I have underestimated you," he said after a long pause.

No trace of emotion stood out on his face, and he stood with his hands held behind his back, the long tails of his tarke'e rippling in the breeze.

"In what way?" Carin asked, hearing her words and Rela's echoed behind her in Tuan.

"An extravagant trick," he said. "It is convenient that you come with this warning, that this spell just happens to be a threat to my army, but you have a solution, and it is the one thing you have ever wanted. You wish us gone from these shores to keep us from possessing knowledge you jealously guard."

The sound of Hoyu's voice took on a much sharper tone as she translated for the others.

"You think what they showed you was a trick?" Carin asked. "Are you so incapable of integrity that you cannot identify it in others?"

On the other hill opposite them, the runner reappeared by the cluster of scouts who still occupied it, and he jogged back down the slope in Carin's direction.

Carin shifted the halm branch into her left hand.

"That is quite enough," said Rela. "If that is all you have to say, be gone from here. If you do not wish your next visit to be far more trying than your last, I would suggest you put a great deal of distance between yourself and my army, because the moment custom negates this negotiation period, believe we will hunt you down."

For all they knew, Rela was assembling an ambush on the far side of that hill where they could not see it. There were other ialtag in the area, and they would send warning if there was imminent danger, but Carin could not discount the possibility of surprises.

"Very well," Carin said. "If that is your choice, you can bear the consequences."

For their part, the soldiers did not look as certain as Rela, which was one small, good thing to come of this bad idea.

The runner made it up the hill, breathing heavily. "Honored Arelashk," he said. "They've apprehended the seneschal."

Hoyu tripped over her translation, looking sharply at the runner just as Rela waved him away.

Rela gave Hoyu a knowing smile. "Remember what I told you," Rela said smoothly to Carin. "It would behoove all of you to heed me. Either way, I am certain I will see you again soon."

With that, he turned and signaled with a curt hand to the soldiers to follow as he moved back down the hill to the south.

"How much time do we have until the negotiations stop protecting us?" Carin asked Hoyu in Tuan.

Hoyu was staring after Rela, looking like she was about to launch herself down the hill at him.

"Hoyu," Carin said gently, and she switched to Khardish. "How long do we have?"

Hoyu blinked at her, anguish on her face. "Not long," she said in Tuan. "Forgive me. Basha—"

"I know," said Carin. "If there is anything we can do, we will do it. But I think first we should be gone from here."

There was no need for her signal. Everyone was already moving for their ihstal or for Suhnsuoc. Carin mounted Tahin as quickly as she could, nudging the ihstal over to the ialtag so she could lay a hand on one's head.

Thank you for trying, she said.

The answer she got came with an image of a place to the north, a place their fellows said was safe.

Carin nodded. "Show Culy," she said aloud, and she heeled Tahin into a run.

B ASHA'S ENTIRE body hurt.

It had been a very long time since he'd been beaten, let alone this badly, and the one salve he had been given was that Oshu had been thrown in the same tent with him. For what reason, Basha knew not.

Oshu was in similar shape, breathing raggedly through a broken nose that Basha had set for him. That was an experience Basha hoped never to repeat.

He lay on his back on the floor, which was damp. They hadn't been restrained. Basha didn't know what to make of that. He had been trying to figure out what would happen to them since they'd been captured by an entire scouting party (twenty of them—Basha and Oshu hadn't had a chance against such numbers), but so far all he could come up with was "something bad."

Oshu stirred, groaning. He turned his head to look at Basha. "Are you okay?"

"Okay is a relative term," Basha said. "You?"

"I have had better days." Oshu closed his eyes again, swallowing. His throat-mound bobbed with the action. "But I have also had worse days."

"That is impressive." Basha paused. "Though I suppose I can say the same."

"If we live through this, we shall have to have a contest between the two of us." Oshu laughed weakly. "I'll win."

Footsteps sounded outside the tent, differentiated from the usual passersby only by the fact that they stopped, and Basha reached out to squeeze Oshu's hand once before the flap pulled back and Rela walked in.

The Arelashk was dressed in his ceremonial tarke'e, which was a strange choice for interrogating a pair of deserters, but Rela had enough strange proclivities.

Asurashk was with him, and she stepped into the tent a moment after the mage. *That* was remarkable, because unlike Rela, she did not wear her ceremonial tarke'e but the one she had been wearing for travel. Usually both of them would not be without the ceremonial garb when in public, but being so far from any required replacements, it was customary only to put them on for important occasions.

Which meant that Rela had gone to an important occasion without Asurashk.

"It is rare someone surprises me so thoroughly," Rela said. "The uptight seneschal, former first mate to an Ada'sarshk, was not the person I expected to do so, but I must say you did it admirably."

Rela's fingers rose to his swollen cheek, which was already healing faster than it ought to. Likely because Rela had helped it along with his magic. Basha wished he could do the same for Oshu.

"It was overdue," Basha said hoarsely. "The two of you have betrayed Khardan so thoroughly that I could not stomach being in your employ for one moment longer."

Rela's hand fell back to his side, and Asurashk's lips thinned to a straight line.

"The scouts tell me you also stole my maps, which I ought to thank you for. The ones you did not steal were ruined by the rain." Rela peered at Oshu for a long moment. "And the guards also tell me that your friend here has an interesting bauble that they could not take off."

Basha turned his head to meet Oshu's eyes, and the other man simply gave Basha a wan smile, pushing himself to a sitting position with some difficulty.

"Are you sure?" Basha asked him softly, ignoring both Rela and Asurashk, the latter of whom was about to get a terrible shock.

In answer, Oshu reached behind his neck to the clasp of the strangely twisted metal cord Basha had given him in Sahesh. A tricky bit of magic that had cost Basha far more than it ought to have because he had been in so much of a hurry. But it had worked. He found now that the moment had finally come, he could not feel any pity for Asurashk—the woman Oshu had loved was long gone.

Oshu undid the clasp.

Rela merely looked at the man, nonplussed, but all color drained from Asurashk's face as she came face to face with the lover she had presumed dead.

Oshu said nothing at first, but he made no effort to hide the rage on his face, and Basha had only the barest twitch of warning before Oshu spat at her.

Asurashk stood frozen, and Rela, having been focused only on Oshu, finally noticed her reaction.

The Arelashk looked back and forth between the two of them for a moment, then seemed to put something together.

"Ah," he said. "I know the spell now. Clever, Basha, to somehow bring our Asurashk's lover back from the dead."

"I didn't know I had," Basha said and coughed. "Perhaps that one ought not to have simply assumed Tel was dead at all. I assure you, he is very much alive."

"Tel," Asurashk said, and for the first time in Basha's memory, there was something beneath the implacable surface. "What have you done?"

"What have I done?" Telmoryn Sih said. "What I have done is watched the woman I loved turn into a monster before my very eyes. I have watched you use the gift of your magic to poison rather than to heal. Seven moons have waxed and waned while you rewrote everything I knew of you until you became a stranger to me. All I have done is try to ensure that your crimes will not go unpunished. Eya dyu e."

The last words he said was a phrase Tel had taught Basha in Triyan. A curse that meant *may you learn*.

Without another word, Asurashk spun and slapped open the flap on the tent to leave, an ignominious exit that Basha would have pitied had he not agreed with every word Tel had said.

Rela was left on his own, considering. "I should have you both put to death," he said. "But I think I prefer to leave you to the Keeper of Mysteries."

He looked at the two prisoners for a moment longer and then followed behind Asurashk, leaving them alone.

Tel collapsed back onto the floor of the tent, his hand probing at his ribs, which were probably broken. "You should have gotten another one of those things made. Maybe we wouldn't have been caught."

"I'll remember to do that next time," Basha said weakly.

His ears were ringing. He'd had the problem periodically throughout his life, but it hadn't plagued him for some time after he'd last been treated by the mage healer he saw in Sahesh. He raised one hand to his ear, massaging the tender bit just in front of it with his fingertips.

The ringing didn't abate, not that he had expected it to.

"What now?" Tel groaned where he lay. "Is there a mosquito in here?"

"You hear that?" Basha propped himself up on one elbow.

Sure enough, the sound grew stronger, and as it did, it shifted in resonance and pitch, like someone singing with polyphonic overtones or like that strange instrument that he'd heard at the philharmonic orchestra once in Sahesh. A theremin.

Tel sat up as well, though it clearly pained him to move.

"What could be making a sound like that?" Tel asked, and Basha's heartbeat began to echo Tel's alarm.

"I don't know," said Basha.

It sounded like it was coming from everywhere at once. It grew no louder now, but Basha could almost feel the fluctuations in frequency. It made his skin hum with dread.

With no way of looking outside—if he wanted a chance to heal before his next beating—Basha lay there with Tel hand in hand, each moment the sound went on adding layers to their fear.

D YAVA WOKE and immediately wished he hadn't.

Lyari had given him something—sparkleaf mush, he was fairly sure—and he couldn't tell exactly how long he'd been asleep. The sun was up, which meant it had been half a day at the very least. Which meant it was the day before High Lights.

As his head cleared, he tried to sit up and found that he couldn't. Ropes pressed into his wrists and ankles, and his ankles were then secured to his hips. He lay on his side in tall grass, dread seeping through every pore on his body.

They had moved him to the Reinvocation site. He could maneuver enough to see through the grass, far enough to see the stone.

From this vantage point, it looked almost boring.

"Help," Dyava said. His voice was barely a croak, and he didn't really expect anyone to answer.

"They can't hear you," Lyari said from the other side of him.

Dyava couldn't turn his head far enough to see her, which made his predicament somehow worse.

"Why can't they hear me?" he asked.

"Because I told them not to," she said. "I shouldn't even be speaking to you now. It will be over soon."

Dyava tried to shift his shoulders to look in the direction of her voice, but found that he couldn't because of the way he was tied. The weight of his legs kept him in one place more effectively than he would have thought possible.

"I suppose 'soon' is not the best word. Tomorrow is High Lights, but we must get things started today." Lyari's voice sounded a bit farther away now. "You'll see soon enough."

She left him alone to the eerie music of the wind in the grass, swirling around him but bringing no other sounds.

If this had been ten cycles ago, Dyava would have thought it a good prank. But now he couldn't even access his magic. How, he could not say. Lyari seemed to have learned more powerful magic than he and his family even knew existed. Again, his foolishness, to think she could prepare to do a spell such as the Reinvocation without learning all manner of things.

The wind in the grass started to sound strange. All around him, a hum grew, like ringing in his ears that could not be the wind. Sometimes when there was a gale and he was out working in it all day, he would come inside to noise he could not escape, a persistent resonance only he could hear. But this grew beyond that immediately.

In his strange, soundless bubble, Dyava drowned in the growing hum. It pervaded every corner of him, wriggling into nooks and crannies throughout his mind and body until it felt like it had worked its way into his very bones. He almost didn't feel it when his wrists and ankles suddenly broke free, so tense was he in his curled-up ball. The pressure of the ropes vanished suddenly, and before Dyava could register the change on a conscious level, he was flung upward from the earth into the air.

It will be over soon.

That was what Lyari had said before she corrected herself. But she had at least been correct that things would begin.

Dyava was suspended in midair, and he was not alone.

Lyari stood with her back to him at the center of a wide circle with Merin and Harag on either side of her. Dimly, Dyava was aware that he ought to have told Lyari about Merin, that it had been his one last chance to convince her to do something else, but he hadn't, and now he was going to die.

All around the circle beyond the three soothsayers were the fifteen sacrific- es. His parents were across from him, as if Lyari had wanted him to see what his betrayal had wrought. As he had suspected, he did not see Calyria's parents, but he recognized Stil the carpenter and his child, the child who had tormented Ryd so much he'd become Nameless to escape.

Stil's mother still lived, and she was there too, on the other side of the circle from Stil. Three generations of the same family, here to bleed.

There was the hyrsin Dyava had bumped into outside of the smithy only days before, and from Cantoranth, to his left, Dyava could see Ohrya.

Lyari had chosen people who had wronged her or people close to her to fill the gaps where others did not volunteer.

He had no way of knowing if that was true, but Dyava felt it in every inch of his weightless body.

Stil's mouth was open wide, veins bulging in his face as he screamed noiseless- ly into an uncaring void.

All Dyava could hear was that endless, tuneless hum.

It would be the last sound he ever heard.

THE HUM felt like it was lodged in his bones. Ryd bit the inside of his cheek to avoid crying out, aware that he was not the only one in their group who had half-fallen from their ihstal when the sound had begun, faint at first and then increasing in strength and intensity.

"What is that?" Sart yelled.

The ihstal whistled shrilly, their feet stamping in the grass.

Carin and Culy had both turned to the south, their faces ashen, and Clar and Kat were both trying to calm Suhnsuoc, who was stumbling in pain.

Ryd took two staggering steps southward, where he could *feel* something there, something he knew.

"The Reinvocation," he heard himself say. "It's starting."

Both Carin and Culy swiveled immediately to stare at him, then looked at each other, any semblance of stoicism long gone.

"How could they do it an entire cycle early?" Carin breathed, and Culy's eyes closed in defeat or some other emotion Ryd could not identify.

"Breaking the stones has broken enough of the spell that magic is much stronger," said Culy.

Though hys voice was steady enough, hys knuckles were white where sy gripped the shaft of hys halm staff, and Ryd stared at the staff, almost fixated on it.

"Then it is done," said Jenin, walking toward them as if drawn, hys face drained of color.

"No," Culy said. "It will finish at high day tomorrow—of that much, I am certain."

The hum stretched out to fill the silence left by Ryd's companions. He didn't know if he could stand an entire day of this, but . . .

"We are far too close to the halm," Carin said. "If we are here when the spell finishes—I don't know if we can get far enough away to survive this now."

The ialtag had flown on after they left the meeting with Rela, and even if Culy could contact the ialtag in time, Ryd didn't think anyone would abandon the ihstal and Suhnsuoc to their deaths to be flown to safety.

"This is it," Clar said. "What do we do?"

She had moved a little away from Suhnsuoc, who was sitting half-splayed on the ground, paws shaking and pelt quivering. The ihstal had not bolted, not yet, but Ryd was half tempted to send them fleeing to give them a chance.

Ryd stared into the south. He could feel the ghost of the bulb in his gut, like some fragment of it remained, waiting to grow anew and claim him. It was a silly thought; bulber bloat wouldn't have time to kill. The Reinvocation itself would take care of that. There was no way they could escape the blast.

The hum was a resonance, one that felt almost familiar. Like he should know it. It rang through every inch of him from marrow to fingernails. It felt like the delicate glass cups that someone in Haveranth had played with a wet finger, the water level of the cups changing the pitch as she ran her finger around the edges of the glass. But where that had been tuneful, harmonious, this clashed. Only slightly, but enough that it felt like biting into a snowball and the jarring pain it caused in his teeth from the cold. If such a sound had lived inside him, it would be something like this.

"The halm," he said, louder than he meant to because the hum had overtaken his ears.

"You are likely correct," Culy said. "But what exactly do you mean?"

"They are channeling magic into the halm," Ryd said. "That's what's making the noise." He pointed at Culy's staff. "May I hold that?"

It was a hunch, one Ryd couldn't account for. When Culy held the staff out to him, Ryd took it, and immediately he knew it was right.

His gaze flickered to the west, toward Lahivar where his own grove grew and where, to the north, Culy hyrself had planted the grove that had borne this staff.

"Doubloon trees," Ryd said softly. "Halm *behaves*."

Carin turned to him, looking startled, and the others shifted, confused by his nonsensical train of thought.

Except it wasn't nonsense.

Something wild and probably hopeless took root in his core and burst into a bloom of excitement.

"Doubloon trees," he said again, this time with eagerness.

He saw the exact moment Culy understood, the flash of comprehension flickering across the hyrsin's face like lightning.

"Yes," sy said. "Explain for the others."

Carin gave Culy a sharp look before directing her attention to Ryd.

He didn't know if he *could* explain, but since the word had been Carin's, the word that had sparked this strange theory, he would try. For all their sakes.

"Doubloon trees are like . . . hm. One tree is not one tree," Ryd said. "If you see one doubloon tree, there are others around it, connected to it beneath the earth. They are all one tree, all one creature."

"The halm," Carin murmured. "Culy's staff."

Ryd nodded, his excitement growing despite his bones nearly vibrating with the terrible magic of the Reinvocation.

"Culy's staff is one piece formed by five halms, but so is the halm in the glen. It's only one tree. The root of all magic is halm." Ryd wanted to laugh. He turned to Jenin eagerly. "Halm ties it all together. You said that halm is unlike anything else in the unseen realm. It is immutable, sharp where everything else is shadowed, blurred. And you."

Ryd turned to Carin, unable to stop himself from going to her and grabbing her hand.

"You said it yesterday when we met with Rela. Halm doesn't *behave* like other trees. It has behavior because it has *will*." Ryd was vibrating with more than just the discordant resonance of Lyari's magic.

Magic that was in his bones, magic he could pull through the earth with his own will, because his will was the will of the halm. Because he was a halmer.

He could feel it. Halm was like one other tree in one other way.

It was all one being, one grove. One magic.

He reached for it, and it responded to him through the staff he held and the recognition in his own magic. It leaped to his touch, and all around them, five bone-white saplings shot from the earth, reaching skyward like they had been released from captivity. Their trunks stretched, splitting into boughs and branches, spreading against the sky where they reached further fingers into the air that unfurled a spray of deep red buds opening to the sun.

The terrible resonance calmed within that circle, and the ihstal let out whistles of relief, sinking to their elbows in the grass with shaking sides. Suhnsuoc collapsed next to Kat, and a deep rumble filled the air with the kazytya's purr.

"Ryd," Culy said urgently. "You have done something remarkable. But we have little time. Despite this providing some protection, we must decide what to do."

Ryd could feel the new trees around him, rooting him. He smiled at Culy.

"I have an idea."

Not far away, a wolf's howl rose into the air, and moments later, more voices joined.

· · · · ·

He had managed it once with Jenin in a halm grove, and with Culy and Carin there to help, he thought he could do it again.

Carin had given him the idea when she had said halm behaved differently. That halm had a will was important. It tickled the edges of Ryd's consciousness, something he couldn't quite reach but knew he needed. Until then, though, they had something to start with.

Culy's staff was the other piece. Culy had shaped it with the will of the halm—though sy said sy wasn't a halmer in truth, sy had done what a halmer did.

Ryd could look back on the halm he had worked before he knew how he was working it. Every piece shaved from a block, every slice into a bough, every curve of every grain, all of it was simply *allowed* by the halm. Halm could not be cut or sliced or curved; it could, however, decide to change shape.

Carin was a short distance away with the still-jittery ihstal, talking to Kat and Clar about something, and Sart and Hoyu were similarly looking jittery, like they wanted to do something, anything, if it would mean they could get their minds off what was happening.

Ryd turned to Culy, who kept staring balefully into the south with tamped-down rage evident in waves as sy fought with the emotions of losing a cycle of time all at once. Maybe all of time.

He didn't know what it would be like to have been alive as long as Culy had only to lose one's future in the space of a few heartbeats.

Ryd didn't know what the chances of success were, but at the very least, he finally had something he could *try*.

The wolves sounded again in the distance, but closer. Ryd glanced in their general direction, but he could see nothing through the trees.

"Culy," he said, trying to get the hyrsin's attention. Jenin was eating a few pieces of dried meat so sy wouldn't go into Ryd's plan with an empty stomach, but Ryd had a question only Culy might be able to answer.

Culy tore hys gaze away from the mountains. "Yes?"

"Could someone alter the will of halm?" he asked quietly, purposely trying to avoid being overheard. If he was wrong, he didn't want to give anyone false hope.

The hyrsin considered that. "As with many things lately, I would hesitate to say it is impossible, but I would say it would have to be extraordinarily difficult. To get halm to do something it doesn't want to do—that is beyond my knowledge. What is it you are thinking?"

Like Ryd, Culy's voice remained low. Not quite a whisper, but respecting Ryd's desire not to be overheard.

"I know you can't read the intentions of the trees, and neither can I," Ryd said, "but perhaps a better question is whether you can imagine that halm would cooperate with the hearthstone spell to the point of conspiring to hide the other half of the final stone."

Culy blinked at that. "You are suggesting that the reason that tree was unknown to everyone for so long is that it was purposely hiding the stone, in this world and the unseen."

"The halmer asks a good question." Kat had been so quiet coming up behind them that Ryd hadn't heard her footsteps.

Apparently, he hadn't been as unobtrusive as he thought. Though the others didn't seem to have noticed.

Culy nodded to the kazytya rider. "Do you have a thought on the subject?"

"It is worth asking two things that struck me when I first saw the tree myself. First is why it remained hidden for so long—and second is if it revealed itself for the first time now, why?" Kat looked at Ryd with something akin to respect. "And Ryd's question ties in with what is happening today. The Tuanye are reinvoking the spell early because they *can*."

"Which means the tree may have done the same in revealing itself. It implies that until now, something actively prevented it." Culy's posture straightened, hys hands at hys sides unmoving.

"Exactly," said Ryd with a flare of triumph. "Perhaps the same thing that made the spirit of healing in Ryhnas Lu Sesim allow sickness to run rampant in these lands but not in the Hearthland. Perhaps the same thing that changed the course of the watershed. Perhaps the same thing that is happening right now, attempting to undo everything we have fought for."

"Ryd," said Culy, clapping hys hand on the halmer's shoulder with strength like the halm itself, "if you are right, we may yet have a chance."

"If I am right, that chance will not last for long," he said. "We need to hurry."

K AT COULDN'T stop the surge of hope that germinated in her and grew like the halms Ryd had drawn from the earth around them. She was afraid to hope; her body still rang with the terrible resonance from the Reinvocation despite the halms muting it here. She felt it twofold, through her own body and through Suhnsuoc's, and feeling Suhnsuoc in pain was nearly debilitating.

She had seen Suhnsuoc in pain before, but never when it was something Kat couldn't somehow help. A pulled muscle, an infected claw, a gash from a spat with another kazytya—all of those were things Kat had tended over the cycles of their bond, but never had she been faced with something that threatened to simply end . . . everything.

Everyone else was either milling around or preparing for Ryd's plan, which Kat had no part of. Milling around was the last thing Kat wanted to do at the end of everything.

"Give me something to do," she growled at Clar, who was standing nearby looking lost.

Clar blinked at her, her mouth falling open, but she appeared to be at a loss. Sart and Hoyu were close enough to hear, and they both looked like they were ready to vibrate to pieces as much as Kat was.

"Is that noise everywhere?" Hoyu asked with her softly accented Tuan.

"If I had to guess, yes," Sart said. "Not exactly the music I would choose to accompany the death of most of my friends and loved ones, but I suppose the whole point of this is that we don't get to choose."

Sart bared her teeth, and Kat felt a surge of respect and agreement from Suhnsuoc.

Hoyu turned to stare southward. It was hard not to do that, to just look in the direction from which death would come rumbling out of the mountains to overtake them all.

But after only a moment, Hoyu turned back to the group, glancing briefly at Culy and Ryd, who were deep in conversation with Carin.

"They all have something to do, and none of us know if it will work," Hoyu said softly. "If it does, though, perhaps we can also do some useful thing."

Kat was ready to climb a tree if it would mean anything but standing around waiting for the world to end, so Hoyu immediately had her complete attention.

She could hear the wolves again over the now-dimmer resonance from the spell. They were closer again, so close she thought she should be able to see them. Suhnsuoc's ears perked up at the sound, and the kazytya rose from hys prone position for the first time since sy had collapsed.

"What is your idea, Hoyu?" Kat asked.

"We have people in Alar Marhasan," Hoyu said. Her fingers twitched at the hem of her tunic. "Your Valon and others. And one of my friends."

"If we go and fail—" Sart began, but then she laughed. "There's a good chance we'll die anyway, so why not?"

Clar roused herself from her quietude. "We should try."

"I like this idea, but once we step outside of this lovely new grove Ryd made us, the ihstal won't be able to bear it. Suhnsuoc won't hold up any better." Sart's enthusiasm dimmed as quickly as it had flared.

"Ryd," Kat said, interrupting him midsentence. "Why are the halms protecting us from the noise? And could you perhaps extend that protection out of this grove somehow?"

She didn't expect him to know the answer to that, but by the way he and Culy immediately locked eyes, she had accidentally asked something pertinent to their discussion.

"I don't entirely know, but despite that, I think I could," he said. Then to Culy, "It supports the theory they have subverted its will."

But Kat barely heard his answer—she was looking over his shoulder at an entire pack of wolves just on the other side of the halm behind him.

Something tugged at her.

You will know what to do. Her mamo's voice, spoken into her ear just before she and Suhnsuoc moved south.

And another voice—this one from the ialtag she had spoken with some time before. *You need not fight the shark under the sea if you wish to win. You must simply use the tools best suited to the endeavor.*

"Bounty," she said, almost breathless. "The rotted bat was right."

The others had noticed the wolves and some, like Jenin, were stumbling backward. The wolves stood almost as tall as Suhnsuoc. Bigger than the ihstal, who whistled uneasily at their proximity but did not bolt.

She almost laughed, understanding finally something that had long bothered her. The ialtag were shy, yes, but they were also powerful. They could change the course of things if it suited them, yet they seldom meddled. Perhaps they had once, but not since the hearthstone spell.

And suddenly Kat knew why.

If they had made themselves available all this time, if they had intervened where they could, it would look now like they were abandoning everyone precisely at the moment of greatest need.

But outside this circle of halms, extending who knew how far from the mountains, that horrid noise that caused even the ihstal and Suhnsuoc so much pain—how much more debilitating would such a thing be to a bat, a creature that navigated flight by the tiniest changes in sounds people could not hear?

Kat knew what to do.

The wolves approached cautiously, nosing into the circle of halms with obvious relief, and those on two legs hastily retreated to make space for the enormous canines.

Kat moved toward the wolves instead.

She greeted the closest one, unsure if sy would have any way of communicating that she would understand.

"Have you come to help us?" she asked softly.

All her life, Kat had been surrounded by kazytya and wolves. They had formed the rhythm and music of her nights and days, and it had been the wolves that had signaled her that it was time to move south, time to fight.

In answer, the wolf lowered hys head, tail up and alert, and ears forward. Hys coat was dark grey, and hys eyes were almost precisely the color of Culy's—a paler grey that seemed almost silver when the light hit them.

She counted fifteen wolves. There were only four riders, and Kat would be with Suhnsuoc. How she was going to tell Clar and Sart and Hoyu that they were supposed to ride the wolves, she didn't know.

"Ryd," Kat said. "Whatever you can do to help us with that noise, I think you need to do it now."

"What are you doing?" Carin asked. Of all of them except Culy, she seemed the least perturbed by the presence of the wolves.

"You mages have your fight. We have ours," Kat said. "We're going to go try to save our friends."

DYAVA LOST all track of time.

He hung suspended in the circle Lyari had created for the Reinvocation, hovering in a sea of weightlessness. At some point in the days or turns or heartbeats that had passed since Lyari began the spell, Dyava had stopped caring that he was going to die.

Instead, he wondered what it was that had made Merin the way she was. How entitled did someone have to be to think that they could put others in danger simply to appease their own whims? He thought about this for a long time while he hung there, watching as Lyari glowed with power and attempted to mold it into something pliable, something directed. He could see every strand of magic pouring into her and back out, how it flowed through her and was transformed.

In a way, it was a truer answer to the question he had asked her than he ever could have hoped for. Here, as his world came to a bloody end, he would perhaps be the only person to every truly see how the hearthstone spell worked.

For a while, at least.

He knew why Lyari did it. She had told him in a hundred different ways, a hundred different days of watching her try to prove to everyone around her that she was worthy of the soothsayer's cuffs around her wrists.

Dyava finally figured out then, far too late, that those cuffs had become shackles. They had tied her to this path, and now she would likely die with him, once Merin twisted the knife.

He thought about all of that, and he realized it didn't matter. Ultimately, he didn't care why Merin had chosen herself over everyone else in her world. He didn't care why Lyari had killed her or why his parents had spent their lives hurting the people they loved out of some misguided attempt to do what was right. All that mattered was the fruits of their actions and the effects those actions had upon others.

Somewhere in all of that, Dyava realized he wasn't powerless.

He was restrained, yes. And he had no voice to scream where anyone could hear. He could see Hearthlanders gathered around the stone, spending the lead-up to High Lights complicit in the greatest sin anyone could commit on the very day they asked one another for forgiveness.

He couldn't speak to them, but his bonds had been broken. Though he hovered in the air, he could move.

Lyari stood where she could likely see him in her peripheral vision—if she could see anything at all with what she was doing. The other soothsayers, though, they stood slightly ahead of Lyari, like she was the bottom of the rune gaiety, the cup rune. Two diagonal lines that met at a point, opening upward like its namesake. Lyari was the bottom point; Merin-Reynah and Harag formed its sides. And Merin was closest to Dyava.

He doubted it would make any difference, but he had to try. He didn't want the Reinvocation to succeed at all, but if Merin had her way, there would be little hope of anyone ever breaking the spell again. If she bound it to an ancient halm itself, it would literally be unbreakable. No one would have a chance.

But if he could prepare Lyari somehow, if he could get her to focus on Merin, perhaps he could avert that. With the amount of power Lyari was channeling, he knew it would lead to his death. He'd seen firsthand what happened when even the smallest magic went awry—a spell of this magnitude, well . . . there wouldn't be much of a Hearthland to worry about anymore.

It filled him with a strange sense of peace.

He started by testing how much he could move.

It wasn't much; his legs were nearly useless, almost as if they were still bound by rope.

But he could move his head enough to speak or yell, and his arms had more range. Not much—he couldn't lift them farther than about waist level, but it was enough for him to push in Merin's direction.

He didn't know how Lyari had cut him off from his magic, and there was so much magic floating around everywhere that pinpointing it would be both nigh impossible and dangerous. If he tried to unravel it, all he would manage to do is kill everyone faster, which he grimly kept in his mind as a possibility of escape. If he wanted to actually help, he would need to be more careful.

Dyava began to push his arms and his head at the same time in Merin's direction. At first, he did it sporadically, then realized it might be more noticeable as intentional if he found some sort of rhythm. He began to push in tandem with his heart, the main force of movement on the downbeat.

He thought he saw Lyari's eyes flick in his direction.

He was almost equidistant between Lyari and Merin, and he thought—but wasn't sure—Lyari could see him if she even glanced to her left.

Across the circle, he could see Stil's child moving hys mouth with hys eyes closed, saying something Dyava couldn't make out, but probably pleading with Lyari or any power that could possibly hear hyr to save hyr.

Dyava didn't know if Lyari could read his lips, but Merin's name would look distinctive enough.

He began to say her name over and over again with the pulse of his heart. Merin. Merin. Merin. Merin. Merin. Merin. Merin. Merin. Merin.

Something flickered in the circle, quickly righted.

Dyava felt a flash of triumph. Lyari had seen him. He knew it.

He continued what he was doing, but with more urgency. He didn't know if Merin could sense what he was doing—there was no magic involved—but he doubted she would be paying much attention to the people she planned to kill.

The sun was still high in the sky, but it would soon begin its descent toward the horizon for the shortest night of the cycle. He didn't know at what point in the spell Lyari would kill the sacrifices. He didn't know how he would end up naked in that circle with her, bared to the ceremonial blade he himself had delivered into her hands.

But until that moment when the knife plunged into his heart, he would keep trying.

And then Dyava felt something he had thought he would never feel again.

It pulled his attention northward, making both his heart and his movements skip a beat.

Unmistakable for someone who had spent so long tending to this particular magic, and unignorable for reasons that went far beyond blood.

Somewhere in the distant north, a presence appeared.

Jenin.

NOW THAT they were ready, Ryd's stomach was tied in knots. He was both thankful and resentful that he hadn't followed Jenin's example and eaten anything. On one hand, he thought he would run the chance of throwing it right back up again. On the other, as empty as it was, it was naught but sloshing acid.

He had one last thing to do before he, Culy, Jenin, and Carin ventured into the unseen realm. Ryd closed his eyes, concentrating on that sense of connection he felt to the trees he had coaxed from the earth. They responded to him, reaching back.

Once, a lifetime ago, Ryd had sat under a halm on the eve of his Journeying with Carin. Only a few moons ago, he had vowed that he would stop the Reinvocation. He hoped he had not already failed. The halms felt alive in his awareness, waiting. If they yet waited, perhaps it was not too late.

The halms had given the group a haven from the tumult of the Reinvocation's discordant melody. He was certain if they willed it, they could extend that protection. If not totally, at least so that those who needed to leave would be able to function. Perhaps where Rela's army could not.

Ryd left it to the halms to decide what they would provide. He had never done it before, but he held in his mind an image of Suhnsuoc and Kat, of Clar and Sart and Hoyu, of the fifteen wolves that now crowded into the grove with the rest of them.

There was a murmur of surprise around him, but Ryd didn't open his eyes to see what the people were reacting to. He heard movement, heard the sound of the wind changing through moving branches, branches that extended the will of the halm into whatever it was they would share with the travelers.

He felt when it was done, an almost audible sensation of satisfaction, like the way he felt when the dovetails of a joinery project fit perfectly and the seam between two pieces of wood became the artistic evidence of strength and design.

When he opened his eyes, he was met with wide-eyed stares from all but Culy, who hyrself wore only an amused half smile.

Each of the wolves wore a strange sort of open collar, a torc of halm that rested around their necks with the open section at their throats, where each end finished in an array of blood-red halm leaves fanning out away from a rounded cap. The people each had similar torcs, though theirs seemed to twist impossibly like Culy's staff, and while they did not end the way the wolves' did and simply widened to twin knobs of halm, the halm had placed crowns of red leaves upon their heads.

"It's going to fall right off," Sart muttered, poking at it with one hand and looking up through her eyelashes as if seeing it in her periphery was akin to the buzz of a bite-me just out of swatting reach.

"I don't think it will," Ryd said.

The wolves looked unbothered by the additions to their thick ruffs, though one's tongue lolled out of an open mouth when sy looked at Sart, stalking over to her and giving her shoulder a nudge.

"I think that one's yours to ride," Kat said solemnly, and for once Sart didn't seem to have anything to say to that, though Carin cracked a smile.

"I can't say goodbye," said Clar all in a rush. "I know I kind of just did, but—we need to go now."

"Yes," said Carin, the smile gone as quickly as it had come. "May whatever comes come swiftly."

Hoyu, however, went to Carin's side and clasped the back of her neck with her hand. After freezing for a moment, Carin's face crumpled, and she gripped the back of Hoyu's neck, pressing her forehead to the Khardish woman's.

"Tark emmar, tark tur," Hoyu said, and then she pulled away.

Three of the wolves lowered themselves to allow Hoyu, Sart, and Clar to climb onto their backs, and though Clar hesitated with an uncertain glance at Kat and Suhnsuoc, after a moment, she mounted the wolf in front of her as Kat climbed onto the kazytya's back.

"May whatever comes come swiftly," Sart said, and she flashed a smile as bright as the halm was white. "And it shall because it is we who bring it."

Suhnsuoc stamped one enormous paw defiantly and screamed, and the wolves yipped and howled, and for a moment every hair on Ryd's arms stood up straight with that sound, an angry sound, a sound of rage and rebellion, and as one, the wolves and the kazytya broke into a run.

The hills took them out of sight almost immediately, and just like that, they were gone.

The grove felt empty in their absence. It was only the four of them now among the trees, and their work was just beginning.

"What did Hoyu say to you?" Ryd asked in the silence that followed.

Carin looked up, surreptitiously swiping the back of her hand over a flash of wetness on her cheek. "A Khardish blessing. Our strength, your strength. It means we are in this together."

"Let us do our part, then, yes?" said Culy, motioning to Jenin, who was staring down the hill in the direction the others had left.

"Yes," said Jenin. "It's time."

THOUGH CARIN had walked her dreams with Culy and explored the unseen realm with hyr together and alone, she had never done so with Jenin or Ryd, and Ryd had done it only once.

They sat in the center of the grove of halms, all four of them cross-legged and close enough for their knees to touch. Culy's staff sat in the middle, and one by one, they each placed their left hand upon it, forming a sunwise rotation that made Carin think of the wheel at the mill that caught the waters of the Bemin downriver from Haveranth. The water this wheel would catch was magic, and Carin did not know what their power would churn out.

She had never entered the unseen world without sleeping except immediately after her first capture. Certainly never on purpose. That she'd managed it the other way round was marvel enough. But here, now, on the cusp of the Reinvocation and in this circle of halms with Culy's staff at its center, it felt as easy as walking through an open doorway.

The four of them stood in the grove where in the waking world they knelt. The resonance of the spell was both less present here and more. It felt like Carin should be able to reach out and touch it, the way it felt to breathe in heavy fog instead of crisp, clear air.

But even more than that was something else.

The halms, usually so sharp in contrast to the blur of the grass and bushes beyond, seemed to flicker in and out of being. It looked like being drugged had felt, like a body pushed into something against its will, an unwanted force, a battering of the edges of self.

"I can feel it," Ryd said, breathless. He looked at his own hand like he was surprised to see it. "Culy, we need to hurry."

"It will be easier if you all take hold of the staff again," said Culy. "Let myself and Carin guide you. Think of following us, of needing to stay near us."

Culy met Carin's gaze, and despite her lover's cool demeanor, she felt hys urgency, hys fear.

She held the ancient halm in her mind, picturing it like she could lay a reassuring hand upon its roots to say *I'm here. We're coming. We see you.*

When the world flashed around them, Carin immediately knew this wasn't like before.

She cried out and heard the others do the same. This close to the tree, the resonance of the Reinvocation's torrent of magic threatened to tear her apart. The spirit inside her cowered in the face of it, retreated into the deep, beckoned Carin to do the same.

The sound seemed to burrow into her skin, under her skin, wriggling through her like a metal knife on a ceramic plate. The halm itself was aflame with magic, so bright she could not look at it without pain. High Lights was when the longest day revealed all for good or ill, but this light would grow no plants, would warm no backs, would make no rainbows. It burned and devoured and created ugliness where there had been beauty. Rot instead of ripeness. Sickness instead of health. Famine where feast had rested and barren waste where fertile fields had grown.

"Ryd!" Carin yelled.

But if this place hurt her, it tortured him. Carin squinted into the brightness of the halm to find him, and when she did, she took a half step toward him before almost falling. He was on his knees in the blur of moss, both hands clawing into the strangely tumultuous earth.

"Take this!" Culy bellowed, thrusting the halm staff in front of Ryd's face where he latched onto it like it was fresh water after being lost for turns at sea.

Jenin was not in much better shape. Sy had one hand on a giant root of the halm and shuddered with every pulse of the spell's hum.

"Lyari," sy gasped. "She has Dyava."

Carin froze where she stood. "What?"

Dyava.

"I felt it before—before we came here. I thought I was imagining it. The moment those halms grew, it was like—like I was connected to the spell, but I thought . . ." Jenin's body contracted like someone had punched hyr in the gut. "I don't know how long I can bear it. She has my parents. She has my brother."

Carin looked at Culy in desperation. "Can you do anything?"

But Culy was already shaking hys head. "Jenin is not a halmer—the staff would be of little use. This is something else. Jenin is connected to this realm in a way the rest of us are not."

"The only thing that will help is breaking that stone," Jenin said. "And if we can't do that, nothing else matters anyway. Nothing."

Carin couldn't fathom what would have possessed Lyari to take Dyava as one of her sacrifices. Even if he angered her, betrayed her. The Lyah she had shared a pillow with her whole life would have never done such a thing.

But she had.

Which meant that the truth of the matter was that Carin had never truly known Lyah. This was who she was—there had never really been a Lyah. Lyari was who she was. This was the woman she had chosen to become when she left that cave with Carin high in the passes of the Mad Mountains. A murderer and worse.

This was the truth of who Lyari was.

The realization stole over Carin with a surreal sense of calm.

She turned to Ryd, who stood on shaky legs, braced against the staff.

She went to him. "Are you okay?"

"No," he said, and he winced. "But I can do this."

Carin's heart flared with pride in her friend. In all the time she had known him, in all the leagues they had walked side by side, slept side by side, cried side by side, almost *died* side by side, this *was* the Ryd she knew.

He didn't look back as he turned toward the trunk of the ancient halm.

Carin followed him.

Part of her wanted to hold Culy's hand, to take some comfort from hys presence in the face of—everything. But like Clar had been unable to say goodbye, Carin could not face the thought that her last memory of her lover's touch could be in the painfully bright light of the sharpest summer sun as it cut through the mountains to rend the earth from itself.

It seemed to take a lifetime to reach the trunk of the halm. What had already been a considerable distance had grown somehow longer than the Journeying itself, longer than Carin's trek from Haveranth to the Northlands. They bought each step with pain and fear.

Only one thing spurred her onward: with the Reinvocation itself raging through the halm, the hidden half of the ancient hearthstone called to her.

Like a song she had heard before, its melody was faint, overshadowed by the cacophony beyond.

And the closer they came to that age-spread tree, the more she felt something else.

It started as a wisp, a wanting. Tendrils reached from root and branch, filled with aching as they arced overland. Like she had watched Ryd's halms respond to him and dress their friends in torcs and leaves, these trailed above them like a caress. They yearned with every swell of noise, longing to smooth it into song.

This tree was as much a prisoner as the spirit Carin carried within her breast had been in its cell of rock. She had been uncertain of Ryd's theory, unconvinced until now, but she felt it falter under the weight of Lyari's power in the distance.

She felt it falter, but she also felt it *fight*.

For every twig and branch that grasped at her and her friends, a hundred more shuddered and slapped at the power that kept them ensnared.

The halm loomed in front of them, impossible to look at for the force of its sickening, unnatural light. Relentless in its assault, there lingered the aspect of two trees, warring against one another. One raised its ire against Carin and her companions; the other sought only their aid.

As it had in person, here in the unseen realm, up close the halm was a wall of white. Carin's gaze remained fixed to the moss that moved like algae, and the sensation of transience melded with the implacable tree.

"Ryd," she said, unable to look up even to see her friend's face. "Whatever you think you can do, do it quickly."

Behind her she heard Jenin sob, and the sound seemed to suck itself into the halm, echoing through its roots and branches and doubling, tripling like a shout in a cave. Culy's voice rose in a low murmur, but Carin could not understand hyr.

Ryd raised his hands and laid them against the tree so gently, the touch of a caring friend.

The yearning within the tree leapt to him, and in their small pocket between two enormous roots, the light that flayed them retreated. The catastrophic resonance grew dimmer, and Carin almost collapsed in relief. Her eyes flashed purple and orange with the absence of the glaring white, and as she watched, where Ryd's hands lay softly on the smooth, barkless wood, the tree's trunk parted for him and opened.

THE HALM torc she wore did not negate the Reinvocation's horrid dissonance, but Clar was deeply grateful for what it did to mitigate it, nonetheless.

If she had thought ihstal were fast, they were nothing like these wolves. They kept pace with Suhnsuoc, and the giant cat seemed to revel in it. Clar wondered if Kat had run with wolves in her home in the north. She knew she might never have a chance to ask now.

Ryd had been right; the crowns of halm leaves upon their heads did not budge with the frenzied race southward. Clar couldn't have said how she knew, but when the very branches of the halms had reached out to them and woven their wreaths upon their heads, she had felt the intent behind them. They rooted her in peace, in the knowledge that if she were not to see the sun set after the longest day, it would only mean she had given her life for those she loved.

Clar had watched the sun climb as the wolves and Suhnsuoc ran, racing against time itself. The wolves seemed to know exactly where they were going. If she could have asked them how, she would have, but all she knew was that she had heard them everywhere along the army's path, and Clar couldn't help but think that had been no accident.

She had never seen Alar Marhasan. She wished she had come here with Kat moons before when Kat had discovered the halm and seen the ruins for herself. But Clar had arrived in Lahivar with Kat already gone and had not even met her for turns after that.

If she continued to think of all the things that she might have done in her too-short life, Clar would collapse on top of this pale grey wolf and be of no use to anyone.

As it was, she could not fight; she had no weapons. Her magic. Well, there had been no time to explore that with the constant need to move, to flee, to survive. She still wasn't entirely sure what had happened with Kat had been real. Even if the wind had risen around them, in even the most fantastical stories told to her in her childhood, she had never heard that a person could fly.

And, of course, there was Jenin.

Clar allowed herself to think of hyr. The ache of leaving hyr behind was too much to bear. It was Jenin who had been her rock. The only person who understood when even Dyava felt too far away. What Carin had said that first day in Lahivar stuck with Clar. That no one would ever understand the journey she had made except for Jenin. No one would know the secrets born of frost and bone and blood. Of frigid nights and colder days, of wondering if this day would be the one where Jenin's magic proved insufficient against the might of a mountain winter.

Yet it had gotten them through. Jenin had gotten them through. Through frostbite and blizzards, through mountains and madness, through night after shivering night. Together, always together. And now Jenin had gone where Clar could not follow, and her own magic was all she had against the chill of her ancestors' folly.

The wind blew at her back, ruffling her hair without dislodging the coronet of halm upon her brow.

They were close now. The landscape shifted from the easy rolling plains and meadows and new-growth forest to foothills and glades. The sun would set soon.

It slanted upon them from low in the west, casting Crevasses in gold. Once, she had thought she knew beauty. She had thought it lived in the blue-green waters of the swift-flowing Bemin, and later on her Journeying, she had thought it dwelled in the sparkling music of the Hanging Falls in the Hidden Vale where a cave full of liars had whispered to her a false name and insisted she wear it forever.

Here, now, in the waning sunlight of perhaps her final day, Clar rewrote beauty in her mind.

It was Kat's giggle as they lay on their backs in the grass. It was the rumble of Suhnsuoc's purr. Jenin curled up against her. Carin's ancient eyes. It was the touch of the ialtag and knowing her desire to meet them had been noted, not with mocking but with earnest friendship. It was Hoyu's gentle Tuan and Culy's Khardish in response. Sart's jokes. Ryd's caring, careful hands. Wolfsong in the night. A place to call home.

She twined her fingers in her wolf's fur, gently as she could without pulling. If this was all the life she got to live, she had known fortune. She had known bounty.

The wolves and Suhnsuoc bounded up the slope of a hill, and when they reached the top, they howled. Suhnsuoc joined them with hys scream, and before them, the ruins of Alar Marhasan splayed out through the woods, dotted with tents of an army two thousand strong.

They had arrived.

THE SUN crept toward the horizon now.

Dyava's life seemed to fade with the light of day, though he knew not when it would come to an end.

He continued his charade, banging against the walls of his prison while Lyari carried on her path of cruelty, never faltering again after that once.

But even as Dyava despaired—through the ongoing chant of Merin, Merin, Merin, Merin, Merin, Merin in his mind—something changed.

Jenin's presence had grown in his awareness, first faint, then stronger. And then all at once, it was gone. Except in its place was something else. Something alien and wild and frightening.

Something that was fighting Lyari.

He couldn't be certain how he knew this. Only someone who had known her intimately would notice. Far beyond something as base as the lines of her body, he knew the way she stood when confronted. The way her shoulders crept up toward her ears.

He knew that the burden of this much magic was one few could bear, and he knew it took everything she had to continue.

Merin hadn't told him when she would try to wrest control from Lyari, but though she had said "when the Reinvocation begins," Dyava didn't think that meant now. His only guess was that she would do it after the sacrifices, when Lyari herself had said she would be vulnerable—and the dirty work was already done.

Until she began to kill people, Dyava had time left.

Whatever was fighting her could be prolonging things. From his vantage point, he could see sweat pouring off of her. It was likely hot outside his prison; who could tell? Where he was felt like he had been removed from time and weather.

He kept up his movements, knowing it was in vain.

He kept up his movements . . . until something changed.

His mother was watching him. Staring, really. Tarwyn had looked everywhere but at Dyava for some time—he was certain she blamed him for her impending death. But now she was looking, and so was his father.

Across the circle, on the other side of Lyari's sweat-drenched face, his mother mouthed Merin's name.

Relief surged through him. She understood. She had seen him, and she had understood. He nodded frantically, trying to tell her she was right. His heartbeat picked up, and so did his pace, his hands pushing toward Reynah as his mouth said Merin's name over and over.

And his mother joined him.

His father watched them carefully for a long time. The sun began to sink beyond the horizon; before long few would be able to read lips even if they were right in front of them.

But Silan frowned, and Dyava saw his father's eyes widen as he understood.

He glanced at his bondmate, and she looked away from Reynah only long enough to nod at Silan. The two of them met Dyava's eyes only once more, and they took up his silent chant.

What he didn't expect was for Stil the carpenter to stare at the three of them. Stil wasn't alone.

Dyava looked around the circle at strangers and neighbors alike, and others were paying attention.

He had to assume some had volunteered for this—Lyari had been certain people would. But then again, who would volunteer their own children? Who would offer up a parent's blood and a child's? Stil would not have; Dyava knew that much.

It took a long time for understanding to dawn with the setting sun. The sky grew darker for the shortest night, and with the stretching out of the endless summer gloaming, Dyava felt a burst of hope.

Lu dyu, pah, artus lu suo dyosu suon.

From darkness, birth, and light reveals all for good or ill.

From darkness, birth.

Lu dyu, pah.

It was from the endless dark the universe had sprung. From nothing came everything. Light revealed all for good or ill.

And in that moment, Dyava knew.

He had the night, and with the dawn breaking to the east, the sun would reveal the truth of tomorrow, whatever it could be.

A LAR MARHASAN lay spread out before her, and Kat felt dread curl in her gut.

There were so many tents. So many soldiers, all of them armed and trained. She had fifteen wolves, a kazytya, and four women who had no weapons except belt knives and teeth.

Kat did not truly have hope that would be enough, but if teeth was what this required of her, teeth is what these fools would get.

The wolves know the trail, Suhnsuoc said to her. *One allows them to lead where they have the scent and one does not.*

That was something, at least. Through her bond with Suhnsuoc, she understood what the kazytya meant. The wolves had *tracked* the prisoners across the warmlands. They had hounded the army, howled their fury through the night, and they had followed their footsteps, waiting for this day.

Kat had always wondered how the wolves knew to come south. Perhaps the ialtag had taught them, too. She would never know.

Whether they would find Hoyu's friend, Kat could not say. Nor Valon, in truth. Valon had been captured so early into their invasion. Yet Suhnsuoc was confident, and Kat had learned over the cycles of their bond that the kazytya's confidence was not to be discounted.

The wolves slowed on the approach to the camp. Hanging back out of bow range, Kat thought. She was glad for that.

"Do we have a plan?" Sart asked dryly. "Or are we just going to go howling through their camp and hope for the best?"

"The wolves can follow the prisoners' scents," Kat said. "Though I don't know if that includes your friend, Hoyu. I'm sorry. Suhnsuoc can communicate with the wolves after a fashion, but it's not exact. More like feelings."

Hoyu nodded, face pensive. "I will hope."

Clar was watching Hoyu with open admiration, and Kat had to agree.

"Try to avoid fighting, if that's even possible," Kat said. "We may have an advantage because of the halm, but against trained soldiers, I could not say what we will face."

"What is that?" Clar asked suddenly, pointing to the south. "Is that—is that the tree?"

Beyond the far ridge on the southernmost edge of the Alar Marhasan ruins was an unmistakable glow of white light.

"Right, if that's the tree, I'm going to assume it getting brighter is a bad thing, and I'm going to insist we move. Now." Sart nudged her wolf, and sy seemed to agree with hys rider's assessment because sy took off toward the camp.

Suhnsuoc sprang into motion as well. Kat's blood raced in her veins.

A spear will skewer a salmon as readily as a trout, the ialtag had said.

"Well," Kat muttered. "Let's skewer some salmon."

Yelling filtered through the trees ahead, and at first Kat thought it was in response to the sudden appearance of a pack of wolves and a giant cat, but as they ran unimpeded through the first rows of Marefi tents, she changed her opinion.

The soldiers who came into view were stumbling through the camp, hands clapped to their ears. Some screamed, curled up in tight balls on the forest floor, ignoring—or simply unaware of—everything around them.

Some have fled, Suhnsuoc said, and Kat got an image of scores of soldiers staggering westward, some with rucksacks but most without, as if the only thing that mattered was to escape the sound.

Kat shuddered to think of what she would hear without the halm around her neck and brow. The hum was still there, constant but ebbing and flowing, yet it did not dominate her mind.

They started to see more Marefi mercenaries the deeper they got into the camp, and a few tried to mount an attack on the wolves, but the wolves without riders charged on ahead, crashing into soldiers without biting. The few soldiers with the wherewithal to realize the wolves were not attacking, simply set on their goal, quickly got out of the way.

No one seemed to be giving orders, which seemed strange. Hoyu had said the army was based on rigid structure and orders followed without question, which Kat found bizarre. Even in her most zealous moments where she had been overcome with emotion about the task laid before her, Kat had always questioned. Her mamo had been in a constant state of exasperation.

But as they roamed deeper into the ruins, Kat soon found out why things were relatively quiet.

She felt the magic before she saw its effects.

Though Kat was not much of a mage—and she hadn't the ability of some to see the threads of magic's workings—the result of magic was visible to all.

It glimmered ahead of them, a dome of gold that flickered in the dying light of the day.

Immediately, Kat knew it for what it was: a shield.

Around it crowded soldiers scores deep, clamoring at its edges but unable to push through. It would take a skilled mage to hold a shield of that size.

Kat glanced at Hoyu, who had sat up rigidly at the sight of the shield.

"That is where the Arelashk will be," Hoyu said softly. "And my friend, I think. Rela will guard his captives jealously."

Sart let out a long-suffering sigh. "Of course. Valon, you beautiful disaster. You owe me for this if we live."

Clar nudged her wolf up alongside Suhnsuoc. "If we find the prisoners and get them out, what do we do with them?"

Kat hadn't thought that far ahead, and she glanced around, flummoxed.

"They might be injured," said Hoyu. "And they may not be able to ride on their own if that is the case."

"Then we hope there are no more than four injured, and that if there are, there are others who are hale enough to ride with them," said Sart. "That tree is getting brighter. If anyone has any ideas of how to break through that shield, now would be an ideal time to speak up."

"I do," said Clar. "Though I will need Kat's help."

Startled, Kat looked at Clar. "Of course," she said. "Help how?"

A gust of wind blew Clar's hair back from her face, and Kat could almost see the young woman's breath coming faster as the wind picked up, lifting her hair until it almost floated there.

"Do you feel it?" Clar asked, almost inaudibly over the wind.

Kat didn't think she meant the breeze.

There had been little time to question, less time to find answers. But as Clar reached out and took Kat's hand, leaning to bridge the distance between Suhnsuoc and the wolf, the wind encircled them.

Before, Kat could have brushed it off as simply coincidence. Hadn't the wind blown at other moments in her life when she felt fierce joy or fury or grief?

But as it picked up around them, drawing Sart and Hoyu into the circle, something expanded out from Kat and Clar. It encompassed the others, drew from them. Drew them in. The sound of the wind drowned out the remaining hum of the Reinvocation, washed it away.

It wasn't just them.

Kat's eyes went involuntarily to the glow behind the ridge, where a battle would be taking place in the unseen realm.

And Kat understood.

This was what she had been born to do. Not to lead armies against the Tuanye—not even to fall in love with one of them.

She had followed the wolves south to see something breaking free beyond any spell.

Suhnsuoc let out a chuffing yowl, both satisfied and impatient. *We wake*, the kazytya said in Kat's mind.

We wake.

Hoyu and Sart were casting their gaze around wildly.

"Is this you?" Sart shouted over the wind.

"It's all of us!" Clar called out, and Kat saw her eyes meet Hoyu's.

It was Hoyu who started it. "Tark emmar, tark tur!"

The words she had said to Carin before they left.

Kat didn't know what they meant, but she didn't need to.

Hoyu's wolf leapt forward, and the rest followed.

Soldiers were turning their way now, distracted from their goal of fighting to get inside the shield by the rising wind at their backs.

Startled yells turned into epithets, and though Kat had none of the Marefi language, she recognized the tone of men barking orders. Some of the soldiers fell into formation; others turned tail and fled. Still others redoubled their efforts to push through the crowd toward the shield.

This time the wolves did not seek mere passage alone. Their snarls made that clear as they closed the distance between themselves and the Marefi mercenary legionnaires with a swiftness that had the soldiers stumbling backward in fear despite the yells of their commanders.

At the exact moment that distance vanished, Suhnsuoc screamed.

The wind howled at their backs, surrounding them as they crashed into the soldiers.

Even armed, there was little hope for them against creatures so large, so fast. Screams joined the snarls of the wolves. As the glimmering gold of the shield grew closer, the wind tore away from the runners and riders, and a cyclone shrieked through the crowd of mercenaries, sending bodies flying through the air.

The sound of those bodies colliding with tree trunks and tents alike made Kat's skin pebble into gooseflesh as she rode.

The glow beyond the ridge was brighter now, and Kat did not think it was simply the darkening night sky making it look that way.

As her mamo had said when she wandered too far away from her village, every step you took out, you had to take back in. Kat cast a glance over her shoulder to the north.

If Carin and the others did not succeed, it would matter little what happened here. Kat and her companions could rescue the prisoners and race back out the way they'd come only to have death swallow them whole as they fled.

Suhnsuoc dashed ahead with the wolves, though those without riders formed the spearhead, clearing the way for those behind them. The shield grew larger as they advanced, and with some relief, Kat could see it was faltering.

As if reading her mind, Sart yelled over her shoulder, "That will not hold much longer! The soldiers did us a favor!"

Kat doubted that had been their intent, but she wasn't about to count the fish in a parcel given as a gift.

Those we seek are inside the light ball, Suhnsuoc said.

"All of them?" Kat asked incredulously.

Suhnsuoc's affirmative came as the wolves slowed at the edge of the shield, and Kat pulled her spear from her back. The remaining soldiers seemed torn between fighting and covering their ears, and Kat had to admit that though the wolves had certainly struck fear into the hearts of the Marefi men, the advantage was hardly the wolves alone.

We will protect your bellies. Suhnsuoc's words came on an insistent wave that demanded Kat dismount.

The kazytya had never used the bond like that—Kat found herself sliding almost meekly from the giant cat's back without even waiting for hyr to lower hyrself.

The wind still raged around them, whipping her hair into her face, though it was far greater outwith their small circle.

"How do you propose we get through this shield?" Sart asked. "My magic is mostly tricks and fun, and while he cannot hold it forever, we don't have long."

"The only reason it's held this long is the spell breaking down," Kat said. "Without the strengthening of magic here, holding something like this for even a handspan of the sun's journey would be impossible even for Culy—even with hys staff."

At that, Sart looked over the shield appraisingly, and then she turned back to Kat with a grin.

"What are you going to do?" Kat asked warily.

"Tricks and fun," said Sart, winking.

She reached into her belt pouch and pulled out a handful of something, settling back on her wolf like she'd been riding wolves her whole life. There was a glint of purple that wiped the smirk from Sart's face for the barest moment, and she slipped whatever that was back into her pouch. She then tossed something in the air, then something else.

Was she *juggling*?

Hoyu stared at the woman as if she wasn't sure whether to laugh or cry. Clar's face said almost the same, and Kat ruefully thought her own reaction must have equalled the other two women's.

"You should see the three of you," Sart said. "You might want to stand back. I really don't know what this is going to do."

Kat scrambled backward even as Clar and Hoyu did the same, which was complicated by the fact that they had both been in the process of dismounting their wolf companions.

As they watched, the stones whirling between Sart's hands reached higher and higher, seemingly untouched by the wind, and her hands moved faster, her eyes tracking the stones somehow. Kat couldn't even make them out. Just as Kat was certain Sart's plan was to simply juggle at the shield, Sart flung the stones one by one up into the air, but this time they arced out over the shield and hovered there, suspended.

Sart bounced one last stone in the palm of her right hand.

"Duck," she suggested, and she lobbed it at the hovering pebbles like she was skipping rocks on a pond.

Kat hit the ground, covering the back of her neck with her hands, and she saw Hoyu and Clar land near her just as a burst of heat and light sparked across her peripheral vision.

"You can get up now," Sart said, sounding almost disappointed. "It worked."

Inside the shield were about ten people. One of them was Rela, who was standing shocked next to a woman dressed similarly to him who had to be the one Carin and Hoyu called Asurashk. Everyone who had been under the shield cringed away from something they could not see, most of them casting their eyes skyward as if the sound would manifest there.

A Marefi man in uniform began yelling angrily in either Khardish or Marefi—Kat couldn't tell—and without a word, Sart plucked another pebble from her belt pouch, spit on it, and threw it in one smooth action. It struck the Marefi soldier right between the eyes, and he dropped like the pebble that had felled him.

"O'dan ba," Hoyu said, moving to the front of their small group.

Without a moment's hesitation, she closed the distance between herself and Rela, and though he opened his mouth to say something, he was slower than her fist, which hit him in a deft right hook right in an already-swollen part of his cheek.

Asurashk moved quickly as if to retaliate, but a menacing growl sounded from three sides at once, and she blanched and thought better of it.

"Bind them," Hoyu said in Tuan. "We will take them with us. For justice."

The others who were left were in far worse shape. A man with dark skin lay unconscious next to a lighter-skinned man who was half-prodding him, half-trying to cover his ears. Sart almost flew to the side of a woman who was sprawled near them. A few others were not so injured, but whether they could both ride and help keep an unconscious person on the back of a running wolf would be a question they would all need to find the answers to together.

Clar's eyes were fixed on the glow beyond the ridge. "Kat," she said urgently. "It's getting brighter with every heartbeat now."

Even as she said it, for the first time as Kat watched, the glow flared all at once, lighting the ruins of Alar Marhasan brighter than Toil moon and her sister that had risen at some point during their frantic ride.

The ground lurched beneath them.

WHEN SHE stepped through the arch of white wood into the heart of the ancient halm, Carin lost track of time.

Or maybe time stopped. She couldn't be sure.

The brash harshness of the Reinvocation simply ceased to be in the core of the tree. Ryd moved on before her, almost as if in a trance. Behind her, she was aware of Culy and Jenin, Jenin's quivering breaths slowing to near normal again, the sound loud to Carin's ears against the relative silence that followed the excruciating din they had left behind.

Here the light did not burn. It simply . . . was.

The song she had felt tugging at her sang within the walls here, walls that shifted as they walked as if the halm flowed with the wind of their movement like a field of ripe barley in a breeze.

Outside in the unseen realm, there was uncertainty and worse. Inside, for the first time in her life, Carin felt as though she had found something sacred.

She didn't know how long they had walked. The spirit in her quieted, as lulled by the song as she was.

Part of her feared this was some sort of trap laid by the ancestors to ensnare anyone who got too close to the hearthstone, but when she glanced back at Culy, hys face was serene, relieved, as if sy had set down hys burdens at the end of a grueling day.

Ryd moved before them all, running his right hand along the wood as he walked, and Carin could almost hear the song swell where he touched.

No one bothered to ask what came next. Everyone knew that no one knew. Whatever followed, they would find together.

The fear was still present. None of them had forgotten what was at stake. In the back of her mind, Carin could see Hoyu and Clar, Sart and Kat as they rode directly into danger, trusting that if there was a chance for any of them to live, their companions would find it.

Carin had seen the tree from the outside, but walking through it, passing through the heart of it—that was different. She had no concept of how long they had been walking or how far they had gone. Perhaps they were merely going in circles. Perhaps in a moment, the path in front of them would give way to the glen, and they would be lost, along with everything they loved.

On and on, they walked.

Somewhere on that journey, Carin reached out and took Culy's hand. The hyrsin's grip was strong, as strong in this world as in any other, and Carin thought if this were her last moments with hyr, she would be proud. Content. When she had left Haveranth on High Lights a bare few cycles before, she had hardly expected to survive the winter.

She squeezed Culy's hand.

They walked on.

• • • • •

The Reinvocation could have come and gone. Even the next five hundred cycles in the future. So altered was the flow of time in that place this Carin would never be able to account for it.

Nothing changed as they walked . . . until something did.

She couldn't say what or when, but the song shifted, and she reached ahead to Ryd with a sense of urgency she could not explain, only to find that he had stopped with one hand outstretched in front of him.

There, with white roots grown up all around the base, was the other half of the hearthstone.

On its right side was a triangle, one she knew was only half of a larger triangle trisected by three lines that met in the middle. The rune dyupahsy, potential.

It had been cleaved in half by her Tuanye ancestors, its other half far to the south where none of them could reach.

If Jenin was right, that half of the stone lay in the center of a circle of sacrifices, waiting to be wet with their blood.

This one felt different than the others.

"There is no spirit here," Ryd said. No one else had spoken the whole time they had been walking, and his words hung in the air as if they were supported by the song itself. "They bound the halm instead."

As if in confirmation, the song swelled, and the spirit in Carin seemed to drop into the depths where it had lurked for two and a half thousand cycles, tied to a stone. It knew what it was to be bound. Through it, Carin did too.

"You were right," Culy said to Ryd. "I do not know how they managed it."

"I do," Ryd replied softly. "They used halmers as the first sacrifices."

The words struck Culy like a blow. Carin could not recall that she had ever seen her lover truly at a loss for words, but while sy opened hys mouth to speak, no sounds came out.

"That's why we have lost so much," Ryd went on. "In one strike, they brought the halmers to begin the grove that became this tree, and they watered the saplings with the halmers' blood. That one strike robbed the Northlands of ages of knowledge. The ancient halmers knew—"

"Everything the halm knew," Culy finished, finding hys voice at last. "It would be like the loss of every ialtag at once. A collective will and consciousness. I slept so long that when I woke, I could not see how we got here, only that we had."

"It's time," Ryd said. "We can't wait longer."

Carin turned to look at Jenin.

"Will you do this with me?" she asked.

Jenin's dark eyes were fathomless, opaque like river pebbles, but sy nodded.

"Be careful," said Ryd. "Remember that this is only one half of a whole. They may be separated, but they are still one stone."

His words settled into Carin like cold water dripped down the back of her tunic. She nodded, moving around the hearthstone to the far side of it.

"Culy?" she asked. She hated how her voice sounded, small and frightened.

"Ryd and I will be here. We will do what we can to protect you." Culy placed one hand on Ryd's shoulder, and Jenin moved past them to kneel opposite Carin.

It felt right to her that it was Jenin here with her now. Jenin had set her entire path into motion without even knowing it at the time. Sy deserved to be here to put an end to it.

"Together," she said, barely louder than a whisper.

Carin raised her hands in front of the hearthstone, and Jenin mirrored her. As one, they lowered their palms against the surface of the rock.

The inside of the ancient halm vanished.

EVERY SACRIFICE in the circle that surrounded the soothsayers moved as one. Even the children, whether they knew what they were saying or not, they all pointed at Reynah, chanting Merin's name.

They were all old enough to remember Merin, but Dyava didn't think they could possibly know that what they were doing was pointing at the woman herself, in the body of someone else.

Lyari was flagging. Above them, Toil moon and her sister were heavy and full in the sky where they rose, climbing up the firmament ahead of the sun.

Already the sky lightened to the east, though it had never fully darkened. The shortest night was precisely that.

Dyava was tired too. He had been moving throughout the night, in constant back and forth, and whether it had had any effect or not, he almost didn't care.

It was Stil's child who alerted him to the hearthstone.

Hys frightened face stopped in the middle of the Merin's name, and sy squirmed backward as far as hys arcane cage would hold hyr, eyes on the grass at Lyari's feet.

Dyava looked to see white tendrils sprouting from the ground around the base of the stone. They seemed to cradle it like a candlestick holding a candle.

Dyava did a double take. The stone *was* bigger. He wasn't imagining it.

Lyari didn't seem to notice, but the stone had doubled in size, and where dyupahsy had been split down the middle at the left edge of the hearthstone, now it was whole, as if the stone had never been two pieces at all.

Despite himself, his peace deserted him, and fear crept up his legs like the white tendrils around that sacrificial stone.

The night was coming to an end.

Dyava had failed.

Lyari spasmed once, her chest leaping forward as her back bent at a sharp curve, and the brass cuffs of the soothsayer on her wrists flashed in the moonlight.

For the first time all night, Harag and Merin moved.

Dread filled Dyava. He didn't want to see this. He didn't want to see this. He didn't want to see the woman he loved murder innocents before his eyes.

He didn't want her to kill him.

He closed his eyes. It was childish and absurd. There was no escaping from this prison, no running away. But it was one thing in his power, and he was a frightened child little different than Stil's across the circle. Little different than Stil himself. Dyava kept his eyes screwed tightly shut, unable to hear anything, unable to see. He hung suspended like that for as long as he could bear, long enough that even behind closed eyelids, he could see the difference in the light as the dawn crept closer.

With every inch of the coming sun's approach, Dyava could feel his death waiting for him.

When he opened his eyes, the hearthstone was stained red.

He kept his eyes fixed upon it, unable to make himself look around the circle to see who was missing. The sight of it froze him where he hung, and he beat his hands against his legs, the only thing he could do besides cry, and he was crying, too.

Somewhere in the night he had lost the sense of Jenin. His sathren's presence had vanished, winked out like a candle flame.

Dyava stared at the stone in front of Lyari, stared at the blood dripping down its sides, stared at the red droplets clinging to her fingertips. He could not look away.

And then he blinked to rid his eyes of tears that would not fall, and in the space of time it took him to do that one, tiny action, Jenin appeared kneeling in front of the stone.

Not just Jenin.

Kneeling in front of Lyari, her back to the woman who had been her fyahiul, her pillow-friend since earliest childhood, was Carin.

Carin.

C ARIN HAD placed her clean hands upon a bare grey stone. When the halm around them vanished, the stone remained, but it was red, red.

Wet.

Her ears popped, almost painfully.

Across from her, Jenin began to shake, twitching as if sy were about to jerk hys hands away from the stone.

"Don't!" Carin said sharply. "Not yet."

"Carin," Jenin replied, shaking hys head and staring at something above Carin's. "I can't—"

"You can, and you must." Carin's voice came out shockingly calm despite the sticky wetness beneath her hands. "I'm sorry, Jenin."

"It's *her*," Jenin said, and it was only then Carin realized they were not alone.

Carin had thought many times about what it might be like to see Lyari again. In all those times, having that moment come at the precise instant of the ongoing Reinvocation was never a scenario she had imagined. It was never turning around from where she knelt to see Lyari's hands dripping red blood into the lush, deep-blue grasses of the Hearthland. It was never looking past her to see two bodies side by side and recognizing one of them as Dyava's father Silan.

It was never with Jenin seeing Lyari's face in person and not yet realizing that she had just killed hys father.

And it was never with Dyava's face streaming tears as he hovered impossibly, horribly, in the air staring stricken at her.

And beyond all of that, beyond the nightmare Carin had been transported into, when she met Dyava's eyes, all she saw was love.

Love for her, love for Jenin.

His lips moved, but she couldn't hear him. She didn't need to.

I'm sorry.

His body jerked as he moved as much as he could, slamming against an invisible barrier. And then he moved again, his hands pushing outward, his head nodding emphatically as his lips formed another word.

Over and over again.

If Jenin had not told her what sy and Ryd suspected, Carin might have been too slow.

"Merin," she said aloud.

Jenin was still staring vacantly at Lyari's blood-stained hands, but sy looked up when Carin said that word out loud.

"Don't move," she whispered.

Hys whole body quivered, and Carin didn't know if it was fear or grief or both or neither. She was probably doing the same; she didn't know.

The woman who turned then was only vaguely familiar to Carin. She had seen her in Cantoranth, even less frequently when passing through Haveranth, and it wasn't the Merin Carin knew.

But if Dyava was certain . . .

On the verge of his own death, if he was this desperate, Carin had to trust him.

Without removing her hands from the stone, Carin slid them across it until they touched Jenin's. The tips of their fingers were still clean despite the blood; it was not a puddle. It had flowed over the edges of the stone and off the sides.

When she touched Jenin, she felt Ryd beyond hyr, felt Culy. They were still there, still connected to the ancient halm. There, at its heart.

"You always did have terrible timing, child," Merin said in Reynah's voice.

Carin didn't know what Lyari was doing. Perhaps it took all of her energy to contain the magic she was channeling. It didn't even matter.

She found her voice. "That's a fascinating accusation from someone who's supposed to be dead."

Through the stone, Carin could feel the halm. Ryd whispered through it, a quiet voice in her ear.

"I'm not supposed to be dead, child. Though I suppose that's a question of semantics, since your friend there saw to it that what I wanted didn't matter."

Carin felt incredulous laughter bubble up inside of her. "You don't get to pretend you are some kind of victim when there are innocents dead in the grass behind me. They may not be dead by your hand, but I've a list hundreds long that doesn't even come close to accounting for the blood that is."

Merin took a step toward her, but something seemed to stop her.

Her eyes flickered from Carin to Lyari, and then they went distant as if searching for something out of sight for everyone else.

"If you wanted to talk, you should have stayed in Haveranth," Merin said. "You are Nameless. If the blood spilled has to be yours, so be it."

Merin had caught her when she was born.

Hers had been the first hands to touch Carin when she entered the world.

"You're welcome to try," Carin heard herself say.

"Carin," Jenin said, but she met hys eyes and shook her head.

But Merin's eyes flashed and went distant once more, and when she smiled, it was like staring into the sun. "You've brought a halmer into my tree," she said. "I don't know where you found one after all this time, but he'll do quite well."

Merin was at the hearthstone in the blink of an eye, and her hand came down into the blood, and then Ryd was on his back on the stone, his shoulders landing on top of Carin and Jenin's hands.

"Ryd!" Carin's heart gave a frantic, stuttering leap.

He didn't even look at Merin. He just smiled up at Carin and Jenin, the sweetest smile Carin had ever seen.

"Don't worry," he said. "I've borrowed my share of time."

Carin didn't see where the knife came from. It was in Merin's hand when a moment before, it hadn't been. It was an exquisite knife, bronze and silver tooling in the runes down the hilt.

Carin would recognize her mother's work anywhere.

Merin brought the knife down, point straight at Ryd's chest.

It was reflex.

The knife came down, and both Carin and Jenin instinctively recoiled backward from the force of the blow, trying to correct themselves even as their hands jerked away from the stone. Carin felt the bloodied rock scrape her palms even as the heat and solidity of Ryd's body vanished from the backs of her hands, and she was screaming, and Jenin was screaming, and she could see Dyava screaming soundlessly in his cage of air.

It took the space of several heartbeats to realize that Merin had brought the knife down—and she hadn't moved farther than that.

She stood frozen with the tip of that beautifully crafted instrument of murder bent, impossibly bent, against a lattice of halm.

The halm had seemingly grown up from the base of the stone, like roots turned upside down, growing around an obstacle in their path.

But she and Jenin had let go of the stone. It remained unbroken. The Reinvocation was still going on.

Slowly, ever so slowly, though, the lattice of halm across Ryd's chest retreated—or so Carin thought at first.

As she watched, it moved from Ryd, climbing up the bent tip of the knife, the hilt, the hands that held it.

White tendrils, first slowly and then faster, crawled up the length of Merin's arms, reaching around her shoulders and looping across her collarbone to encircle her neck.

By inches, the halm pulled her back. Ryd slowly rose from the stone, his back somehow pristine and free from the blood that marred the place he had been thrown through space.

His eyes showed white all over. No pupil. No pale green Carin knew so well.

"It's over," he said.

Merin could not move; that much, Carin could see. But she could still speak, and she opened her mouth.

Carin's hand grasped for Jenin's across the stone, and together they replaced their hands where they had been. Carin wished she could scrub the blood off her palms until the skin was raw, yet she kept them in place, touching Jenin's.

"You can't kill me, boy," Merin managed to choke out.

"Maybe not," Ryd said. "But we can."

With a sharp report, the hearthstone cracked in half. Not down the middle like it had been divided before, but diagonally, along the triune lines of the dyupahsy rune, shattering the stone into three pieces.

Between the chunks of jagged rock, white tendrils shot upward toward the sky and branched outward.

Carin and Jenin scrambled backward, and Carin collided with knees that had to be Lyari's, sending the soothsayer lurching back into the corpses she had made with her hands.

There was a collective gasp as the remaining sacrifices fell to the ground. Most immediately flopped, unable to stand, and some cried out.

Ryd was still facing down Merin, and Carin shoved against the ground to get to her feet, reaching Ryd's side only an instant before Jenin did the same.

Ryd's hand reached out and took hold of the halm that bound Merin's hands together as she had brought them down to stab him.

"A'cu Lystel sends hys regards," Ryd said, and he gave Merin's hands a push.

It was not a hard push, but Merin almost flew backward, landing on her back in the grass beyond Dyava, at the feet of a crowd of wide-eyed Hearthlanders.

Despite her top half being encased in heavy halm, Merin struggled to her feet, which was a mistake.

The tendrils snaking across her torso shot down into the ground before she could move so much as a toe from the spot, faster than Carin could even make sense of. The tendrils grew from there, finding purchase in the rich soil and searching downward, outward, even as they thickened and grew heavier around Merin's legs, her chest, her arms, her face. Harag, until then standing stark still and stricken in her staring, chose that moment to try and run. A tendril of halm sprang from the earth and caught her ankles, freezing her to the spot—or her legs, anyway. The rest of her, still stuck in her body's committed motion, fell forward with a sharp jerk, and there was a crack of something breaking that was most certainly not halm. Harag's cry was lost as the white wood swallowed her up, reaching ever skyward with branches that immediately burst into blood-red leaves.

Someone started screaming, and others began to panic, stumbling over one another in their hurry to flee.

Carin stared at them in disbelief. Two of them lay dead on the ground, but *this* is what sent them over the edge?

"Carin?"

The voice that said her name cracked in the middle of it, and Carin turned to see what the people were running away from.

Lyari stood behind her, looking like she was about to fall over. Her hair was plaited immaculately—or had been—and dripping sweat that was only just beginning to dry on her face and neck and arms. She wore a pale-yellow shift that was stained red, and her hands were still dripping blood. Where she had fallen on the corpse of Jenin's father, her entire side was soaked through with it.

Carin hated that part of her wanted to comfort Lyari. When Lyari's eyes moved past Carin, though, her gasp ripped through what was left of Carin's heart.

"Jenin," came Lyari's voice. "Jenin—you—"

Carin got one look at Jenin's stricken face as sy finally saw the bodies behind hys former lover.

One look was enough. This was something she could do.

She put herself between Lyari and Jenin, and she wasn't alone.

Ryd moved with her, coming to stand by her side.

When Clar had arrived in Lahivar after trekking across the mountains with Jenin in the dead of winter, Carin had told her that no one would ever understand that journey. No one would know what it was like to make that trek. No one but those who had done it together. No two journeys were ever the same.

Standing with Ryd at her side and staring into the face of someone they had both known since birth, Carin knew it was true that no one would ever understand the journey that she and Ryd had made with Lyari. Their Journeying, that fateful spring that felt so long ago now. When they had left Haveranth believing Jenin was dead, having seen Clar's hands stained with blood like Lyari's were now.

No one would know what it had been like to trek up the Bemin River to Haver's Glen, up through the glen to the Jewel, shining a blue everyone always said was the precise color of Carin's eyes.

From there to the Mistaken Pass and into the Hidden Vale, where the Hanging Falls dropped diamonds onto a land so lush it seemed like nothing could ever be so alive. And then into the cave, where young Hearthlanders were told poisonous lies and given more poison to swallow if they wanted to live. They would live a cursed life—or become Nameless.

No one would know what it was like to take those steps together, the specter of a beloved friend's ghost haunting their every move, appearing to them in their dreams, forever lost to them. Moon after torturous moon.

After all that, Carin and Ryd had chosen to leave rather than be complicit in feeding poison to future generations.

Lyari had chosen to brew that poison herself.

"You don't get to speak to hyr," Carin said softly, the first words she had spoken to Lyari in cycles.

She didn't even remember what the last had been.

Lyari opened her mouth, casting an anguished look over Carin's and Ryd's shoulders.

"No," said Ryd.

Carin had never heard his voice so firm. It felt like the halm felt. Implacable. Permanent.

She looked at him. He took Carin's hand, and with a shock, she *felt* him like she had felt the halm. The spirit with her rose up enthusiastically, eager, like recognizing an old, old friend.

With that touch came the knowledge of what he needed to do, and he wanted her permission to do it.

There was a commotion behind them, but Carin didn't turn. Jenin would alert them if it was anything dire, and she only hoped Dyava had reached hyr.

Carin couldn't think of Dyava right now, as much as she wanted to.

"Lyari," Carin said, and Lyari startled as if Carin had said something shocking, which perhaps she had. When she'd last seen the woman, she hadn't known her name. "What have you done?"

Carin didn't truly want to hear what Lyari had to say. She didn't think anyone did, at least not anyone within earshot. Everyone here had either been planning to murder the rest or had been on the precipice of being murdered.

"What have I done?" Lyari asked. "What have *you* done?"

"Should I tell her?" Carin said to Ryd.

He shrugged.

"I left everything I knew behind because it was the right thing to do," Carin said. "I have devoted my every day since to undoing the horrors our ancestors wrought while you sought only to add to them. I saw firsthand the truth Merin made into lies. I have sailed across the sea for moons as a prisoner and returned in a day by magic. I have watched a land come back to life that was stolen from it to feed your children.

"And Ryd has been with me through all of it, though he thankfully escaped being a prisoner. He has suffered disease that we brought upon strangers, and he was healed by a spirit freed from a stone like that." Carin pointed behind her with her free hand. "Ryd has spent his days making gifts for children, helping anyone who needed it. He is a halmer and a more faithful friend than you have ever been."

Lyari stared at her open-mouthed, still looking over Carin's shoulder as if she expected Jenin to speak up for her.

Or maybe not Jenin.

"You killed our *father*," said Dyava's voice.

It was barely a croak, and it took all of Carin's power not to turn and go to him. She didn't dare move.

"I *had to*," Lyari cried out.

"Shut your mouth, child. You will hear what you have done."

That was a voice that did make Carin turn, her own mouth falling open as she looked to see her mother making her way through the tall grasses from the crowd of faceless Hearthlanders that were huddled at a presumably safe distance.

Rina ve Haveranth was a blacksmith, and she moved like one. She wore a sleeveless tunic Carin had seen countless times in her life, and her hair was pulled back into its usual bun at the nape of her neck where it couldn't get into her face or catch sparks from the forge.

Her muscles were taut, and when she stopped near Carin, she looked ready to use them.

"The knife," Carin said faintly. "You sabotaged the knife."

Stabbing halm or not, Rina's work did not bend.

"I failed," Rina said. She swallowed, looking over Lyari's shoulder at Silan's body in the grass.

Carin didn't recognize the other corpse, but someone would.

At Carin's questioning look, Rina went on. "I thought the spell required stabbing through the breastbone. I was wrong. I searched everything I could find to learn about the spell, but nothing I found told me differently than I had heard. My assumption cost two lives."

"No, Mamo," Carin said. "Lyari took two lives. Three, counting Merin. There's a difference."

"A very great difference," said Ryd. He looked at Rina. "We're going to take her now. But we will be back, with others. You can keep Dyava and Jenin safe?"

Carin whipped her head around to stare at Ryd. Jenin?

But though it ached, she knew Ryd was right. Jenin needed Dyava, and when she allowed herself one pained glance back, she saw that Dyava needed Jenin just as much, if not more.

She took a quavering breath and faced her mother, still clinging to Ryd's hand. She didn't know what to say.

"You will return?" Rina asked softly. "There is much to discuss."

All Carin could do was nod.

Lyari seemed to realize what was happening a moment too late. Ryd didn't even gesture, and halm sprang from the earth so quickly, her hands were bound in front of her before she could so much as twitch.

That was going to take some getting used to.

Ryd dropped Carin's hand, and together they walked to Lyari, taking her by the elbows and walking her toward the stone.

She started to struggle, her eyes widening with panic as she dug her feet into the blood-stained dirt.

Carin stopped pulling her in disgust. "We're not going to kill you like you were going to kill them."

"Then where are you taking me?" Lyari's voice was high and shrill.

"Home," said Ryd, reaching his free hand out toward the halm-cracked hearthstone.

The Hearthland blurred and vanished.

N O ONE had been prepared for the earth to move.

Clar was shaken to the ground, nearly everything forgotten except holding on for her life.

Holding onto what, she didn't know. The earth was supposed to be the thing that stayed still when everything else moved. But she lay there as the tremors came over and over, and the sound of tumbling rock accompanied the fear of the mountain falling on their heads.

But when it subsided—and it did—Clar looked up; the first thing she noticed was that the glow beyond the ridge had faded.

"Kat!" she called out. "The halm!"

She heard the others getting to their feet, and a low growl from several points around her told her they were not yet out of danger.

Kat was up, one hand on Suhnsuoc's flank, murmuring to the kazytya.

Hoyu was already up too, and not only that, but she had Asurashk in a choke hold and was calmly refusing to budge. She said something in Khardish, and the Triyan woman stopped struggling, her limbs going slack.

"What did you say to her?" Clar asked in spite of herself.

"I told her I'd feed her to the wolves if she didn't stop it." Hoyu's grin could most appropriately be described as wolfish herself. The pale grey wolf she'd been riding seemed to have heard, because sy turned to look in Hoyu's direction with hys tongue lolling out as if she'd made a good joke.

"That would most be against Khardish law," said an unfamiliar voice in precise but clearly still-learning Tuan.

The man who had spoken was Hoyu's height and had similarly dark brown skin. He looked . . . bad. His left eye was nearly swollen shut, and he moved painfully as if just being upright hurt.

"Basha," Hoyu said, then rattled off a string of Khardish that Clar most definitely didn't understand, but left Basha looking flustered as he scuffed his foot in the dirt and then gave Hoyu a sheepish grin.

Sart was on her feet and surveying the surrounding army, who were gingerly orienting themselves after the ground-shaking. "If we want to get out of here alive, I think we need to go."

Clar didn't disagree. Sart's friend-or-lover-or-both Valon was in the best shape of the prisoners, though she looked at the wolves like Sart had asked her to fly home by flapping her arms.

The others were in varying states of hunger and exposure, but even the unfamiliar faces were prepared to run. Clar wished she knew some of them, any of them—just to give them the comfort of a familiar face.

The wolves were gentle with their new riders, lying down to allow them to get on and looking around at the soldiers as if daring them to venture near.

Hoyu came up to Clar with Asurashk bound and scowling. "I need to be the one to take Arelashk," Hoyu said. "Will you take this one? If she is trouble, push her off and let the wolf step on her."

"Doesn't she have magic that can—get inside my mind?" Clar asked hesitantly.

"You will feel it if she tries, and I have told her if she tries—" Hoyu looked pointedly at the wolf.

Asurashk said something in Khardish, and Hoyu gave her a stone-faced look in response.

"She told me that kidnapping an Asurashk is against the law," Hoyu said to Clar. Then to Asurashk, "Tark emmar, tark tur."

"What does that mean?" Clar asked, perplexed. Hoyu had said it in different situations like it had weight in all of them.

"It means 'our strength, your strength,' and usually it is a saying to build others up," Hoyu replied, choosing her words carefully. "But other times it is a reminder to someone how far sy has fallen."

With that, Clar's wolf companion lay down for Clar to get on, and she positioned Asurashk in front of her, looping her own arms around Asurashk's waist.

"You are lucky," Clar said, though it was unlikely Asurashk would understand her. "You are lucky we will not do to you what you have done to us."

Kat was astride Suhnsuoc with a lighter-skinned man who had been with Hoyu's friend Basha. His dark hair was matted with blood, and he swayed in front of Kat on the kazytya, barely able to keep upright even with Kat's support.

Asurashk's head turned to look at the man, and Clar did not have to speak Khardish or Triyan to feel the tension when Asurashk's entire body stiffened.

"Let's go, Suhnsuoc," Kat said, her eyes on Clar's as if her passenger and Clar's alike did not exist.

As they rode away through the camp, no one tried to stop them, despite them taking some of the army's commanders. Clar didn't know how armies usually worked, but she had expected them to be less inclined to let a small group of injured people pass, particularly when those people had sustained their injuries at the army's hands.

To the contrary, the soldiers got out of the way, many ignoring them completely where they sat with their heads in their hands. Some, Clar saw, had blood coming out of their ears.

Hoyu edged into the lead, sitting straighter on her wolf. She raised her voice a moment later, calling out loudly, "Em Ada'sarshk. U'urasham tun amura 'mar. Na'usam gael sura'sa're. U'uam tun uasam ba—e uam em u'Da'sash Dan o'osush."

Asurashk, Clar noted, did not relax at those words.

She also couldn't help but see nods among the Marefi mercenaries. Clar knew nothing about Maref except what Hoyu had told her and what she had seen secondhand from the people of Lahivar and Ryhnas Lu Sesim.

None of that was encouraging, but while Clar saw a few soldiers who looked on the verge of belligerence, their fellows held them back.

Clar had forgotten to see what happened to the Marefi commander, and when she turned, instead of Valon on the wolf with Sart, it was he who rode ahead of Sart, looking much smaller than she was and—it was very obvious—none too happy about that.

Perhaps they had simply been unprepared for a magical assault of this magnitude, or perhaps word of Carin's meeting with Arelashk had spread far enough to think their small group capable of incapacitating an army.

The more Clar thought about it, the more she figured that was precisely what had happened. The wariness on the soldier's faces was not just about the wolves, though they were met with more fear than curiosity by a wide margin.

But to the soldiers' eyes, Clar could imagine what the day must have looked like. They would have seen nothing of Carin or Culy, nothing of the halm in the glen unless they were immediately beside it, and then would have fled as soon as the Reinvocation pierced the air.

After half a day of extreme, inescapable noise, they would have seen wolves and a giant cat bearing riders into their midst, riders who cut through their mage's defense and captured their leaders while everyone else suffered—and the strangers were immune.

All of that only to have the earth shake beneath their feet, after which the noise stopped as suddenly as it had begun.

Clar had not allowed herself to hope. That they were alive meant the Reinvocation had somehow failed.

She found herself smiling as they left Alar Marhasan behind with the dawning of the longest day, and the light revealed a new land and the second half of a leaderless army, retreating back to the sea.

Around them, the wind raced along the hilltops, running ahead of them with a promise of home.

THE FIRST thing Carin saw when they stepped out of the ancient halm with Lyari was half a hundred dead bodies, all of them bleeding from their noses and ears.

"Marefi soldiers," Culy said grimly.

By silent agreement, she and Culy and Ryd were speaking the Northlander dialect, and Lyari, whose face had at first gone slack with panic, eventually ignored them completely.

But these deaths were not something Carin could let go by untouched. She switched to the dialect of Haveranth.

"This blood too is on your hands," she said to her oldest friend, and Lyari's head snapped up.

"Who are these people?" Lyari asked.

"People," was all Carin said.

If Ryd knew how they had left the unseen world and entered the waking one without returning to the grove on the hill to the north, he didn't offer an explanation or even a comment, despite Carin and Culy's obvious shock. Ryd seemed to be listening to something Carin could hear only faintly, the song of the halm that stretched out beneath the earth.

To travel instantly over mountains and seas—Carin could not fully believe it even though she had done it twice. The spirit proceeded to show her all the ways it was possible; her first time she had done it the hard way, but that there were other ways now, ways it would show her. The thought was frightening and exhilarating at the same time.

When she said as much out loud, Ryd turned to her and said, "Halm is the root of all magic, and magic is everywhere," as if that explained everything, and in a frustrating, ineffable way, it did.

They left the glen on foot, weaving through the soldiers unseen. Many more of them had the same blood smears at their ears and noses, though they were beginning to clean themselves up. Beyond that, they were pulling up tents.

It may have been Culy's staff of halm or that they had a prisoner bound in the stuff, but the Marefi mercenaries gave their small party a wide berth.

"What happened here?" Carin called in Khardish, and one of the soldiers spat on the ground and shook his head.

"Your people shook the earth and burned the air and called down cyclones. They came riding wolves and giant cats." The soldier looked like he would be happy if he never ventured farther than his own front door for the rest of his life.

"And did they leave alive?" Carin prompted.

The soldier nodded. "Took the soul stealer and her collector with them. And the general," he added as an afterthought. "I wasn't going to try and stop them."

Culy raised an eyebrow at that. "Who is paying you?" sy asked in careful Khardish.

"Someone who takes a bite without looking at it first," came the reply. "And not enough at that, not for wolves and magic earthquake cyclones and songs that kill."

"A fair assessment," said Culy dryly. "Perhaps, if you don't mind the suggestion, it would be good to spread the word that while we are a hospitable people, our wolves and earthquake cyclones and killing songs do not look kindly on abuses of our hospitality."

The soldier peered at Culy, and Carin pressed her lips together to keep from smiling.

After a beat, the Marefi man nodded solemnly. "Don't think you'll have much to worry about when it comes to that. Already sent runners to order the reserves to retreat double time."

"They say a smart person learns from one's own mistakes, but a wise one learns from the mistakes of others," Culy said. "Seek wisdom."

"Saba ku tun," said the soldier.

"E ku tun," Carin replied.

Ryd gave her a questioning look, and she quickly translated as best as she could remember.

"What was the last thing you said?" he asked.

"A figure of speech," said Carin. "May you have dignity, or goodness be with you. I wished him the same."

Lyari's confusion would have been comical if she hadn't been responsible for the murder of who knew how many.

"Are we walking back to the grove?" Carin asked Culy. "I don't know about either of you, but I would prefer to be as far away from this army as possible, whether they are retreating or not."

"Oh," said Ryd, looking abashed. "I could have taken us there. I still can."

Culy blinked at him.

"I can—I can show you how," he added.

• • • • •

"One of these days," Carin said as they watched the midsummer sun dip behind the blood-red leaves of new-grown halms, "we will need to make a point of not learning anything earth-shattering for two moons together."

"I was just thinking how nice it would be to go study magic in Sahesh," said Culy blandly.

Carin was so tired she stared at hyr unblinking until she realized sy was joking.

She laughed weakly, leaning against Culy's shoulder. "We're still alive," she murmured. "And the spell is gone."

Just then, the wind picked up, rustling the leaves above that flickered like pomegranate seeds as they caught the sunlight.

"Clar," said Carin, climbing to her feet despite the protests of her knees.

Culy followed her gaze and her action, using hys staff to push hyrself up.

"I might steal that from you," Carin said.

She glanced behind her at Lyari, who was sitting by herself while Ryd whittled nearby. Not halm this time, just a stick of maha he'd found near the grove. Carin smiled at the sight, then hurried to greet Clar and the others.

They were decidedly not alone. Of the fifteen wolves who had arrived to help, all but two had two riders now, and of *them*, Carin searched their faces.

"Valon!" she cried, hurrying to the woman's side. "Great bounty, you look about to drop."

"Then catch me. Make Sart jealous," said Valon. "I'm serious, I think. I need help."

The black wolf she rode immediately lowered hyrself to the grass, and Carin saw the others all doing the same. Both Culy and Ryd hurried to help, leaving Lyari sitting by herself, still bound in halm.

Carin clasped Valon's arm to help her dismount, smiling tentatively at the person who sat behind her and slid to the grass without assistance, if without much ease either.

"Clar," Carin called out hurriedly. "Jenin is okay."

Clar appeared around the side of the grey wolf she rode, relief warring with concern on her face. "Where is sy?"

Carin swallowed. "Haveranth. With Dyava."

Clar's eyes bulged, and she took an entire step backward. "I—how?"

"We'll tell you. Just know that sy is safe. There is more, but that is most important, aside from one other thing, which is that Lyari is here." Carin almost dreaded this news more, and she wasn't wrong to, she thought.

The rage that that flashed across Clar's face was accompanied by a gust of wind so strong, one of the wolves yelped in surprise, and several of the strangers they'd rescued started shaking. Valon, still holding onto Carin's arm, dug in her nails before realizing she was clawing Carin's skin and released her, lowering herself to the ground next to the wolf.

Kat wove through the crowd and made her way to Clar's side, slipping an arm around her shoulders, and the wind calmed immediately.

Your people . . . called down cyclones, the Marefi soldier had said.

It was Carin's turn to stare. She looked to Culy, whose face was every bit as nonplussed as her own.

"Lyari is confined," Carin said softly. "She will harm no one else."

"Else?" Clar held Kat's hand as if it was the only thing keeping her feet on the ground, and she closed her eyes briefly as her chest rose slowly and then fell just as slowly. When she opened her eyes again, she nodded. "You said Dyava is okay. Who—who is not?"

Carin winced, turning to Valon and clasping her on the shoulder. "I'll be back," she said.

Clar shot Valon an apologetic look, but the older woman simply waved a hand and gave her a tight smile that Carin thought was more physical discomfort than feeling jilted.

Carin took Clar and Kat aside—out of line of sight from Lyari—and told her about Silan. Silan was Clar's uncle, and as Carin spoke, Kat held Clar tightly around the shoulders. Carin held her hand, trying to reassure her that Dyava and her parents and Tarwyn were fine, that Jenin had needed hys brother and the other way around. The lost look in Clar's eyes bit at Carin; she understood that look.

Carin had spent turns and moons among strangers alone, used to sleeping with Ryd curled up against her back. To lose that person even temporarily—especially when not knowing when you would meet again—was a shock.

No sooner had Carin parted with Clar than she looked over the lumps of sleeping people who had dropped where they landed to see a familiar and welcome face—and one that was far less welcome.

Carin decided to ignore the unwelcome one and made her way to the Khardish seneschal with a genuine grin spreading across her face and, to her surprise, a prickle of tears in her eyes.

"Basha-lan," she said. "O'dem ba, da re'?"

His face lit up at the sight of her, and though one eye was painfully swollen, he grinned right back, showing all his teeth, which Carin didn't think she'd ever seen him do.

She stopped caring about Khardish protocol, and though Basha would probably scold her for it later, she threw her arms around him and hugged him tight.

To her surprise, his arms scooped around her right back, and he actually lifted her off the ground, which Carin found impressive, since he was shorter than her and had not been treated as kindly by the past turn as she had. Basha, however, did seem to regret it immediately, because she felt him wince and carefully backed away, though she left her hands on his shoulders. Hoyu came up beside her, also grinning widely, and Carin felt her eyes prickling again.

"It's usually that one who makes you cry," Basha said in Tuan, pointing an elbow at Asurashk, who sat in a surly heap with her back against one of Ryd's halms.

Carin smiled wider at his use of Khardish structure in Tuan.

"I was just saving it for a special occasion," she told him. "I think this counts."

"This is Tel," Basha said, indicating a man Carin had only briefly seen.

He stepped toward her, looking uncertain, but he offered a tentative "Dem ba," to which she responded with a clasp of his shoulder.

Hoyu was watching Asurashk, who seemed to be making a concerted effort not to look at this Tel, and with a jolt, Carin remembered the name. She hadn't spoken enough Khardish at the time to understand, but Carin happened to share her mind with a very helpful, if occasionally overeager spirit, who offered her Asurashk's words verbatim.

Suram tun emmar dan. Suram tun emam Tel.

You killed our people. You killed my Tel.

Carin let out a slow breath, putting several things together at once. When she met Hoyu's eyes, the Khardish woman gave her a grim nod, then gestured with her chin in Lyari's direction, where there was an eddy of empty grass surrounding the former soothsayer of Haveranth.

"Those two have things in common, I think. Yours has the look of someone who has set fire to her own ship on the open sea, just like mine," Hoyu said.

"You are more right than you know, my friend," Carin said. "I suspect you and Basha have a very long story to tell me."

"You are more right than you know, my friend," Hoyu said with a tight smile. "But it can wait until tomorrow."

Carin smiled back.

It could.

Later on, when Carin tried to check on Valon, she found that Sart had already taken over that responsibility and was applying herself with . . . vigor. Carin prudently removed herself, so as not to impede Valon's recovery.

She drifted away for a short time, looking around at the joy and relief on faces both familiar and new, and she also looked at the two miserable women—and the two miserable men—who had wrought so much pain and destruction in such a short time. Arelashk and the Marefi general were now both also bound by halm at Hoyu's request, though Culy had asked to keep Asurashk unbound, and sy took Asurashk aside for some time, speaking to her in Khardish. After a while of that, with the sky at twilight on High Lights, Culy and Asurashk walked down the hill from the grove, and Carin heard the unmistakable sound of large, powerful wings.

When they returned some time later, Asurashk offered her hands to Ryd, and though he shot Culy a questioning look, he did as requested.

Lyari did not miss that interaction, and when Culy returned, she stared at hyr in open fear.

Perhaps it was cruel to walk away from Lyari then. Carin did not know. But the day was too fresh, and there was too much relief and joy to try and comfort the ones who had caused so much pain.

Carin felt Lyari's eyes on her as she took Culy's hand and walked with hyr out of the grove, in the opposite direction from where sy had gone with Asurashk. They walked until the hearthfire was only a flickering orange glow on the hill. The sky had darkened to its deepest blue, and few clouds marred the view of the stars.

Toil moon had passed her fullness, and already she hung near the horizon, heavy and ready to give way to Gather in a pair of turns, her sister drooping already behind a hill.

"What did they show her?" Carin asked quietly. "I will ask nothing more, because I don't think I want to know."

"Asurashk wanted access to the ialtag. They offered it freely. They showed her nothing more than that, nothing more than what her choices have wrought—and yours. She did not like what she saw." Culy's voice, while steady, held a hint of anger that Carin could understand all too well. "It was perhaps selfish of me to facilitate. But her actions have also caused me much pain."

"I know," Carin said. "You will have no blame from me. Let us talk of other things, my love. The harsh light of that endless day is gone. We remain."

"We remain," Culy echoed.

Sy pulled Carin down with hyr into the grass, where they sat flush up against one another, and after a time, Carin lay back and tugged Culy with her. With the moon set and the sky as dark as it would get, she could see the Path of Petals splayed out across it, though dimmer toward the still-glowing horizon than it would be in winter.

"Do you believe the stories that say there are other worlds out there?" Carin asked, her voice hushed in the soft comfort of night.

"There must be," replied Culy. "Though two are quite enough for me."

Carin rolled onto her side, her breath catching as she hooked one leg over Culy's. She could barely see hyr, but it didn't matter.

Ryd had murmured to her, in the brief moments between conversations and finding food for everyone, that he thought he could go anywhere.

Tomorrow they would talk about it. They would decide how to return Arelashk and Asurashk and their Marefi mercenary general to Sahesh, and if Carin perhaps felt a bit of smug anticipation at the idea of depositing them in the middle of the Da'sash Dan's chamber in the bhamuoa, well, who could blame her?

Tomorrow they would send word to Ras and Mari and Dunal and all the others who had scattered to the north. They would send word to Kat's people in the much farther north, and they would find out what exactly that Marefi soldier had meant about their people calling down cyclones.

Tomorrow, they would be A'cu Lystel and Carin Lysiu, and Ryd A'halm. They'd be Valon ve Ryhnas Lu Sesim, washing away Wyt's memory with Valon's story of capture and survival—again—the name forever burned into the minds of the Northlanders as Valon's protection, Valon's sacrifice, Valon's strength that protected her people at the harshest light of the longest day. They'd be Sart Lahivar and a heroic Ada'sarshk who could fill the sails on her ship with the wind at her whim. Clar Avarsylasu and Kat Madahu and Basha-lan Da Dhu'e and Telmoryn Dhasama.

All that could wait till tomorrow. They had a tomorrow.

Tonight, though, Carin was just Carin, and Culy was just Culy, and they needed no ash to wash away the day, only soft kisses and starlight and the promise of life laid out before them.

EPILOGUE

IT'S SO easy to be wrong.

All the things we think we know can change in an instant. We go to sleep in a field and wake in a forest. We thought we were alone, but there was an entire world out there all along.

I wish I had all the answers—or maybe I don't. Either way, I got to see my brother again. Maybe that is all I needed, at the end of all this, at the beginning of something entirely new.

I could tell you how the Lahivarans were greeted and welcomed back into their waymake by Uroda of the Khardish Eduashae, a shapechanger and an ancient mage, who brought word that the Da'sash Dan had been replaced in a new election and Khardish law restored.

I could tell you the shock this brought, not just to Carin and the Northlanders, but also to Hoyu and Basha and Tel—but probably most notably to the disgraced Arelashk. It is said that when Uroda told Hoyu that she had been elected to take the place of the Keeper of Ways, the wind rose around the waymake at Hoyu's inner conflict, then faded to a gentle breeze as she declined, for Hoyu had made peace with the wind, made friends with the wind, and she knew she belonged at sea.

There are so many stories, bright and painful and cozy and flickering, stories of Clar and Kat and their fierce joy running together through lush woodlands and over grasslands, exploring from sea to sea the land they helped to free. Their stories are also borne on the wind that responds to their call. I could tell you of Ryd, gentle Ryd, who forever seemed to be listening to the song of the halm. He would appear sometimes without a moment's notice, smiling, in some waymake or another, there to build, there to carve, there to help. So many children north and south of the mountains now carry baubles made by his hands, of halm or maha or any number of other things. I could tell you how the children love him—oh, how they love him. Sometimes he can even be seen beneath a pile of them, but now they listen when he gently tells them to stop, and more often he welcomes them as they come to play with his hair or marvel over his missing earlobe or ask him to tell them about the ialtag again. I could tell you how he came to Haveranth, how he comforted Stil the carpenter's child, that child who almost died at Lyari's hands.

There are stories I could tell that would hurt.

Some of them hurt good—I will forever see Carin cradling a sobbing Dyava in her arms in Haveranth, hear her whisper into his ear that he is family and that he is free. I will see her tears drip from her jaw into his hair, healing tears. Necessary tears.

I could tell you how the Khardish came in peace to Lahivar in the Eduashae's wake, bringing gifts and assurances, how they came to learn our languages and stood in humble delight as they heard Khardish on the lips of our people. I could tell you what it felt like to see the delegation from the Da'sash Dan leave with Arelashk, with General Ludo, with Asurashk, with Lyari. Lyari will return one day. The Khardish do not have prisons, not permanent ones. I see Carin's face that day when she asks what will become of those sent for justice. I see her relief knowing that whatever faces them, it will be guided by teaching, by healing, for the sake of those who were wronged and of those who did the wrongs themselves.

It is a quiet day, a lull in the joy and excitement and curiosity, but I know one day Lyari will return if she desires, that she will be given a chance to make amends.

There comes a day where a Marefi delegation arrives, escorted by the watchful eye of the Eduashae themselves, the Marefi bringing gifts and the closest thing to apology Maref is capable of giving: a shipment of good red sunset stone for the rebuilding of Ryhnas Lu Sesim under their emperor's snow leopard banner.

I could tell you of Hoyu's ship, her crew that arrived with the Khardish, of the joy upon her face when she got to show Carin her world without fear, as friends. I could tell you of Carin and Culy's visit to the Da'sash Dan in Sahesh. Hoyu took them to an ancient hall where the philharmonic played, and they sat in the place of honored guests, and for the first time in her life, Carin heard a symphony. Ryd joined them the next day, where he gifted the Da'sash Dan with an intricate arch of halm that would stand in the park where Carin had been taken. The arch has a twin in Lahivar, and it is said that if you sit by them, you will hear the soft song of halm in your ears, and the voices of people a half a world away. Perhaps those who yearn for it will even see the distant faces of another land.

I could tell you of the tales that spread from Tuan into the west, tales of bravery and legends and grief. Tales of the trickster who leaped from beast to beast at the edge of a cliff, the trickster who brought down an Arelashk's magic with a few pebbles and a smirk. The trickster who is never without a rounded marble of purple Khardish sea glass that she carries with her. Sometimes she is seen in the islands of Khardan with her love, where they bring mischief and laughter, and the sea winds calm with their presence.

There are so many worlds that meet and pass one another every day. So many who move between them. I have seen hope falter into nothingness, into a pit where nothing escapes, but in the darkness, there is birth, and from those moments, the future is born.

There is halm now in Khardan in that park, a grove of five trees that sprang up around Ryd's arch, and strange and wondrous things happen around those trees. Any attempts to enclose them fail; sometimes someone will come to them and leave with a tool, a flute, a carving, a crown.

I could tell you of Carin and Culy, how they raised up a hill in the center of that new inland lake where a bog once swallowed the land and how with Ryd's help, the halm reached through the earth and became a temple with soaring ceilings that cradle all sound. I could tell you how people travel from all over the continent and the world to hear the music of the Tuan choirs. The clarity of voices melding in that place is one of our world's new wonders.

There are rumors that even more ancient things stir and wake, but there is grief too, at the loss of so much time.

I could tell you how Basha and Tel stayed in Lahivar, how they learned the language and shared their own. Their love grows with every passing moon, and their roots grow deep into the land of their new home, and whenever Basha hears laughter on the wind, he rides Saba to the sea and meets Hoyu as she sails. She brings news from afar, ignoring the legends she leaves in her wake of the seafarer who was an Ada'sarshk and how the wind follows her wherever she leads. I could tell you of the way she and Carin always seem to know what the other needs, how frequently their messages arrive in each other's hands on the same day.

I could tell you of the tundra folk who visit Lahivar, of their surprise at Kat's story and their rueful laughter at discovering just how their expectations came to be. There is so much to tell you, so much bound up with cheerful firelight tunes and a people finding their way out of a nightmare and into a world awake and singing.

The ialtag too—they come forth these days and share their stories with all.

There is so much of those first few moons, so much that I feel and witness and watch from afar, one foot, as always, in each world.

And I could tell you all of it, but I am tired now, and your imagination is well suited for the task of knowing what becomes of these folk. None of us expected that we would all live to see a new world born from the chaos of the old. But sometimes that is the truest lesson: that despite pain, despite sweat and tears and blood, it is never too late to try to make things better. Sometimes we even succeed. This is the worthiest work.

· · · · ·

Haveranth is different even from how I left it at midwinter with Clar. Dyava is different. Angrier, sadder. I hope one day his jokes and playful nature will re-emerge. For now, I sit with him in his grief. I hold him when Carin leaves again after one of her visits when he again refuses to come north, but I know deep down that one day he will be ready.

We both grieve Lyari.

Though she is not dead, there will be consequences for her actions. For her, for all who enabled her, and Merin. Reynah has already paid her own price, as has Harag. The halm that grew up through them will remain forever in that meadow, watered by my father's blood.

As I walk through Haveranth, the air is hushed. Few people speak to me since the Reinvocation, and even when I venture close to people deep in conversation, their voices halt, stutter, and go silent. I sometimes feel more like a ghost than I did when I was dead to them.

Everyone seems to be waiting for something to break.

It's Rina who breaks the silence at last.

She finds me at the hearth-home, where the fire has gone out.

"It is good to see you, Jenin," she says quietly.

"It was you," I say just as quietly. "Old Wend."

No one is here to hear me—even Tamat is not tending a spit by the cold fire that has not been reduced to ash for two and a half thousand cycles. But Rina flinches anyway, glancing around.

"Yes," she says finally.

"I couldn't even tell how he died," I say to her.

Both Lyari and I had looked, but there seemed to be no sign of magic, nothing.

"He was as old as Merin, you know," Rina says, looking at the ground beneath her feet instead of at me. "I am amazed it even worked."

"What worked?"

"A simple poison. One I learned of almost twenty cycles back, when Merin used it to kill Carin's father." Rina recites the words so softly that they hang in the air like there is not enough gravity to pull them down to earth and not enough wind in this stillness to carry them away.

I haven't bothered to wonder about Carin's father in some time. I remember there being no real questions about it whatsoever. Rina was just the blacksmith, raising her child alone, or as alone as anyone raises a child in a village. It is not so very uncommon.

"Why did Merin kill him?" It is the obvious question.

"There were Nameless two cycles in a row," Rina says. "Talam discovered what Merin did to them by chance. He was incensed. I already knew, of course, as an elder, but it was he who taught me my own folly. Merin didn't even hide that she killed him. She poisoned him at dinner, at my maha table. He made that table for me, for us. When he dropped dead—the poison stops the heart and leaves no other sign—in my grief she told me it was necessary, and she told me one day I would learn."

Rina's words sink into me, and without thinking, I reach out for her hand and take it.

Startled, she raises her eyes to mine.

"I think you learned the right lessons," I say.

Rina smiles, but it doesn't reach her eyes. Hers are a lighter blue than Carin's, and I wonder about Talam. Who he was and what he looked like.

"Why does no one remember him?" I ask suddenly.

The smile drops from Rina's face. "Merin made sure no one would."

That fills me with a sick feeling. Rina would have been pregnant with Carin already. And Merin made sure to isolate her further by not only taking her bond-mate but also stripping from her the ability to even grieve publicly. Making her lover's murderer her only source of comfort.

After another moment, Rina takes her hand back.

"What will you do?" I ask.

"I think . . ." Rina meets my gaze. "I'd like to see my child."

It hangs in the air for a time because I do not know what to say to that.

For a long time, we simply sit.

In the morning, Rina is gone, her forge silent. She will take her time in her journey north, and because of her, we will discover something even Culy and Carin missed.

• • • • •

It takes some time for us to notice—with no Journeyers going north, no one has reason to travel to the Hidden Glen. And with the Khardish taking responsibility for the Marefi army at Alar Marhasan and what they left behind, both bodies and equipment, no one dares venture beyond the ancient halm to that deep gouge of a crack in the mountain.

Because of that, it is a cycle before we realize what has happened.

We knew that the Reinvocation would break the world, but none of us knew what might happen if we broke the spell before it could.

In the end, Rina emerges from that crack in the rock behind the ancient halm, having followed the fissure all the way north after wintering alone in the Hidden Vale. There is now a pathway with a carpet of moss that joins the Hearthland to the Northlands, and some time later, people move both ways on that path. Curiosity, anger, eagerness, exploration—so many things bring people to seek each other out. It is strange to think of a massive rift as something that can heal a fractured people, but as we have all learned, stranger things are always possible.

When I died and lived, I spent moons upon moons walking between two worlds, but the secret is that they have always been one. The borders between them are only as powerful as our own making—it is we who choose what pieces of the past to continue to carry upon our shoulders.

After all this time, we can choose to build something new instead.

After all this time, I am alive, and I hope.

ACKNOWLEDGMENTS

Finishing a series is always difficult. This is officially the third concluding book I've written in my career, and you'd think after blowing past twenty novels penned, it might get easier.

But this series has been with me for almost a decade. I started *Hearthfire* in autumn of 2014, on a whim inspired by a single throwaway line from Pat Rothfuss's *The Name of the Wind*. From that sprang the entire Stonebreaker world. I was writing *Hearthfire* when I lost all my 2013 and 2014 book deals. I was writing *Hearthfire* when my first agent needed to leave the business. And it was *Hearthfire* that got me seven new offers of representation—including one from my agent Sara Megibow, who loved it so much from moment one that she set up a call before she even finished reading. We were ecstatic to get the book on submission . . . only for it to get to acquisitions heaps of times and not sell until 2017, when BHC Press offered. I'll always be grateful to them for giving this trilogy a home.

I wrote *Tidewater* in the wake of deep personal betrayal. And I wrote *Windtaker* in the midst of a global pandemic.

This story became even more meaningful as time went on—it's a story of hope, of doing the work even when it's hard, and of making space in fantastical worlds for all peoples.

I couldn't have done this without my online communities across Slack and Discord for global sprints, gnashing of teeth, and triumphant The Ends. When I was isolated in my flat by myself for two years, I was never fully alone because of them.

To all the readers who have picked up this trilogy, thank you.

Just like Carin and her found family, we can make the changes we need to make for Earth to remain our home without destroying it for others. It's up to all of us, whether we have magic or not.

Here's to building a better world and to imagining something entirely new.

ABOUT THE AUTHOR

Emmie Mears is a Scottish-American fantasy author based in Glasgow, where they write and edit the gamut of speculative fiction and collect names like the fae. A fluent Gaelic speaker and an award-winning Gaelic singer and songwriter, Emmie writes and publishes bilingually in both English and Gaelic.

With over twenty novels published, Emmie has been long-listed for a Hugo award for their short fiction as M. Evan MacGriogair, and as Emmie Mears has been a Rone award finalist for *Look to the Sun*. Their debut YA novel as Maya Mac-Gregor, *The Many Half-Lived Lives of Sam Sylvester*, is a 2023 Andre Norton Nebula Award finalist and earned starred reviews from *Publishers Weekly* and *Kirkus Reviews*.

They live in historically Gaelic Partick with their two purrfect cats.